Praise for Dalton Fury's Delta Force series

"Packed with speed, surprise, and overwhelming violence of action . . . Want to know what Spec Ops really look like? Read Dalton Fury. Simply put—nobody does it better."

—Brad Thor, #1 *New York Times* bestselling author

"Feverishly paced . . . Fury isn't afraid to portray a flawed hero." —*Library Journal* on *One Killer Force*

"Crackles with gut-wrenching action and authenticity."
—*Publishers Weekly* (starred review)
on *Full Assault Mode*

"Fury is retired Delta Force, giving the action a rapid-fire, realistic air . . . Racer is locked and loaded for a series of adventures." —*Kirkus Reviews*

"Step aside, Jack Ryan—Kolt Raynor is the true hero of the new millennium . . . I kept having to remind myself this was fiction."

—James Rollins, *New York Times* bestselling author

"Dalton Fury and I came up in the Unit together, flip-flopping troops and missions from Afghanistan to Iraq. What makes his writing unique is not just the tactical accuracy . . . but his unique understanding of the geopolitical events that propel the plot[s]. He is the real deal. If you want to know what it's like on the front lines of the shadow war, pick up his book[s]."

Praise for
KILL BIN LADEN

were there. *Kill Bin Laden* is a proud, riveting, warts-and-all account of that battle, one of the most important special operations missions of all time."

—Michael Smith, author of *Killer Elite: The Inside Story of America's Most Secret Special Operations Team*

"An important, must-read book about real warriors. A story that so positively reflects what on-the-ground decision making, professional acceptance of risk and maximizing interagency cooperation can do. Dalton Fury shows us with amazing detail and insight what highly trained and motivated special operators can accomplish successfully in combat, out of all proportion to their numbers."

—Cofer Black, former chief of the Central Intelligence Agency's Counter Terrorist Center

"The most compelling and comprehensive account of the Battle of Tora Bora that I have read, heard, or seen in any format."

—COL(R) John T. Carney, author of *No Room For Error* and President/ CEO of the Special Operations Warrior Foundation

ALSO BY DALTON FURY

EXECUTE AUTHORITY

A DELTA FORCE NOVEL

DALTON FURY

St. Martin's Paperbacks

This is a work of fiction. All of the characters, organizations, and events portrayed in this novel are either products of the author's imagination or are used fictitiously.

EXECUTE AUTHORITY

Copyright © 2017 by Dalton Fury.

For information, address St. Martin's Press, 175 Fifth Avenue, New York, NY 10010.

ISBN 978-1-250-19071-0

Our books may be purchased in bulk for promotional, educational, or business use. Please contact your local bookseller or the Macmillan Corporate and Premium Sales Department at 1-800-221-7945, ext. 5442, or by e-mail at MacmillanSpecialMarkets@macmillan.com.

Printed in the United States of America

St. Martin's Press hardcover edition / September 2017
St. Martin's Paperbacks edition / October 2018

St. Martin's Paperbacks are published by St. Martin's Press, 175 Fifth Avenue, New York, NY 10010.

10 9 8 7 6 5 4 3 2 1

In loving memory of Dalton Fury

A NOTE FROM THE EDITOR

I am lucky enough to have known and worked with Dalton Fury for nearly a decade, beginning with the publication of his memoir, *Kill Bin Laden,* the story of his time as the senior ranking military officer at the Battle of Tora Bora. As a Delta Force commander, he helped create, along with some of Delta's most talented sergeants, the tactical concept of the operation to hunt and kill bin Laden. *Kill Bin Laden* was tremendously successful, a national bestseller and the first book to detail just how close Delta Force came to capturing bin Laden, how close U.S. bombers and fighter aircraft came to killing him, and exactly why he slipped through our fingers—though he couldn't hide forever, of course.

Dalton was an extremely private man (thus the pseudonym) but also a man of principle. He wanted people to know what happened, why the world's most wanted man got away when we had him in our sights. The book's success was a mixed blessing for Dalton. His story reached a wide audience and his somewhat reluctant appearance on *60 Minutes,* in full disguise, helped bring attention to the book. Unfortunately, it also brought attention to him personally. He was conflicted: He wanted to help promote the book, but he didn't want the attention to be on him. He decided after the *60 Minutes* interview that he wouldn't appear on television and was unlikely to even do radio interviews again. He was in the office one day and I told him, "You don't have to do anything you don't want to." He stopped what he was doing and gave me a look and smiled. With that one look, he reminded me that few people can tell a Delta Force operator, a member of one of the most fearsome military units ever assembled, what to do.

We had a wonderful working relationship. He was professional and funny, warm and personable. He loved book publishing, and when I said to him, "With a pseudonym like Dalton Fury, you should be writing thrillers," he admitted he always wanted to write fiction. Thus, the Kolt "Racer" Raynor series of Delta Force novels was born. They, too, became bestsellers, and with their mix of action and detailed accuracy, they attracted fans that include authors James Rollins and Brad Thor, members of America's special operations community, and many thousands of others. Most important, he had a blast with the novels. He didn't have to give interviews, he could go back to doing what he loved, which, when he wasn't working or writing, involved spending quiet time with his family.

In September of 2016, while hard at work on the fifth book of the series, *Execute Authority,* which you now hold in your hands, he e-mailed me with terrible news:

Just the day before, he was diagnosed with stage 4 pancreatic cancer. In typical Dalton Fury form, he wrote, "I just wanted you guys to know that I am committed to doing my part to at least meet my writing obligation." He told me he knew he wouldn't live to see it published, but he hoped it would hit the bookstore shelves regardless—"if you guys are OK with it." OK with it? I assured him that nothing would keep me from seeing this book to publication. I told him that he's the toughest guy I know, and that if anyone can beat this, it's him. True to his word, he turned in the finished manuscript two weeks later. Unfortunately, two months after his diagnosis, he passed away.

It is my tremendous honor to present to you the final Kolt Raynor novel. I hope you enjoy it as much as Dalton enjoyed writing it. I will never forget him, and with these books, a part of him will live on forever.

Marc Resnick
St. Martin's Press, January 2017

PROLOGUE

Athens, Greece

The view was impressive, spectacular even, but the man lying prone on the hillside was interested only in what was happening in a very small slice of that panorama—the six-degree arc captured and magnified in the objective of the PSO-1M2 optical scope paired to his SVD-63 Dragunov sniper rifle.

His specific focus was an area almost exactly one kilometer to the south, and a hundred meters below his present elevation. At that distance, the scope encompassed an area roughly eighty meters across. The right side of the aiming reticle was an unbroken mass of green: the treetops and vegetation of the sprawling National Garden. To the left, a few trees were visible, but much of the foreground was dominated by tall buildings. The four chevrons lined up vertically at the center of the scope spanned the gray-black ribbon of asphalt between these contrasting environments. That area was the only thing in the world that mattered to him.

The sidewalk on the park side was crowded with

people, held back by wooden barricades and caution tape, but there was no vehicle traffic on the street, which had been closed the night before and cleared of parked cars.

The sniper let his gaze drift to the stadiametric range-finding pattern in the lower left of the objective, an upward-curving broken line marked with distances in hundred-meter increments—from one thousand meters at the far left of the curve, the low point, to two hundred meters at the high right.

Using his right shoulder—neither of his hands were anywhere near the trigger guard—he shifted the rifle on its bipod, making an almost imperceptible adjustment, and placed the rangefinding pattern on a policeman standing to the left of the barricade, so that the man's feet just touched the bottom line and the top of his peaked cap met the curve, ever so slightly to the right of the unmarked tick that indicated nine hundred meters. That estimate disagreed with the far more precise GPS plot he had run, and he was inclined to believe the latter.

The rangefinder was calibrated to the average height of a man—1.7 meters or five feet, seven inches—which was slightly taller than the sniper's 166 centimeters, but shorter than average in the Western world. He had been told that his height, or lack thereof, was the result of early childhood malnutrition, but it was a matter of no consequence to him. Many men were vain when it came to their height, wearing shoe lifts and thick heels to compensate for their perceived lack of stature, but the sniper knew all too well that standing out in a crowd got you noticed, and getting noticed could get you killed, especially in his profession. The policeman was probably taller, closer to six feet, which would account for the discrepancy. There were ways of double-checking those measurements, of course. Heights were variable, but weapons less so. If the policeman had been carrying a rifle, the sniper could have compared the length of his forearms to the weapon, and thus determined the man's height to a reasonable degree of certainty, but at this distance, well beyond what was considered to be the effective range of the Dragunov, it was almost impossible to make that kind of determination. He only knew that the man was a police officer because of the light blue uniform shirt and the dark cap, and of course, the fact that he was standing on the other side of the barricade. In any case, beyond about eight hundred meters the rangefinder was merely a tool for estimation. He was using it now just to stave off boredom.

He had been here for several hours now, motionless on the hillside, just five meters from one of the trails that meandered across the slope. Dozens of hikers and tourists had passed his location during that time, but none had noticed him beneath the camouflage screen covering him, the scoped rifle, and the sandbags that kept the weapon almost completely immobilized. Patience and discipline were the only things keeping him motionless, but they were enough.

He closed his eye and the world vanished, but the details remained in his mind's eye like an afterimage. The forested slope around him. The city sprawled out below. The street. The crowd.

Nine hundred and eighty-three meters. That was the

actual distance—as measured by the GPS, which was reliable to within a meter—to the spot at the tip of the uppermost chevron, the spot where, if he pulled the trigger, the 7.62×54-millimeter bullet would go, provided his elevation adjustment was correct and the wind did not change. Of course, when the time came to pull the trigger, it would almost certainly not go to that precise spot. The target would be somewhere else, a few meters from that reference point, maybe a few meters farther away or closer, and those minor differences would translate into increasing degrees of uncertainty. He would have to make rapid adjustments to the orientation of the rifle, and to the scope.

Without opening his eye, he slowly moved his right hand to the cheap transistor radio in his breast pocket and thumbed the wheel to turn it on. The radio was tuned to a local news-talk station, broadcasting in Greek, a language that he spoke, though not fluently. He had left the radio off until now, partly because it would have been an unnecessary distraction, but mostly because, despite the low-profile earbuds that piped the broadcast directly into his ear canal, there was always a chance that a keen-eared passerby might hear and then investigate. Now, however, he needed to know what was going on in the world beyond that narrow slice he had been observing through the scope.

He listened for almost a full minute, struggling to piece together the mosaic of familiar words in an unfamiliar context, until something clicked in his head and a clear picture began to emerge.

He opened his eye, returning to that singular point

in space, nine hundred-odd meters away, but kept listening until the weather report was given.

Clear skies. The temperature was thirty degrees Celsius, humidity 40 percent, with no chance of rain and an occasional five-mile-per-hour wind from the north.

The sniper peered through the scope again, noting the slight movement of tree branches in the park to the right, and made the determination to leave the scope as it was. If the trees were still moving when the moment of truth arrived, he would make the correction by aiming ever so slightly to the right to compensate, a technique, he had once been told, called "Kentucky windage."

An American military officer had used that term, and in the same breath, called him "a natural." The sniper spoke fluent English, even then, but the term had confused him, prompting the American to expand on the definition. "It means you've got a gift," the officer had explained. "A natural talent for distance shooting."

He would never forget those words, or the man who had uttered them.

It was true, though. He had received only basic instruction in the fundamentals of shooting, but had intuitively grasped the interplay of spatial and ballistic factors that determined whether a round would strike its target. With time and experience, he had refined his abilities to the point where he could, with near-perfect reliability, make a bullet go exactly where he wanted it to, every single time he pulled the trigger.

Today would be no different.

When the weather report concluded, he thumbed the wheel and turned off the radio. He could see in the faces and gestures of the spectators that the moment of arrival was imminent. And then, right on cue, a line of police cars and motorcycles moved through the field of view, escorting four nearly identical black Cadillac Escalades with blacked-out windows.

The imposing luxury sport utility vehicles rolled to a stop. Three of them were visible in the scope, the aiming chevron just touching the one in the middle.

The sniper waited.

At exactly the same moment, the side doors of the black SUVs opened, swinging out over the macadam, and then, in perfect synchronization, men in black suits emerged.

The sniper's eye drifted to the edge of the scope, checking the treetops for movement. All was still. The wind had died.

The men in suits were now standing a few steps away from the vehicles, their heads moving back and forth as they scanned their surroundings, looking for threats. The sniper knew these men were only the public face of the protection detail; there would surely be many more agents in the area, some blending in with the crowd, others occupying the surrounding buildings, watching the arrival through sniper scopes, just as he was, only their rifles were not trained on the street, but roving the park tree line and the rooftops, looking for potential threats.

Looking in the wrong place.

The sniper did not allow himself even a faint smile of satisfaction. Not yet.

Another figure, wearing a light gray suit, emerged

from the vehicle at the top of the sniper's field of view. He smoothly adjusted his aim, repositioning the reticle onto this new target.

The scope was not powerful enough to reveal recognizable facial features, but the sniper had no doubt about the man's identity.

The President of the United States.

He checked the trees again. A light breeze had come up in the twenty seconds since his last check. He watched the foliage moving, instantly judging the strength of the wind, and shifted the weapon just enough to move the target to the left of the aimpoint.

He reviewed the distance to the target, calculating and verifying his bullet-drop adjustment. At this distance, the bullet would fall almost ten meters from a perfectly straight line, five times the height of the distant target.

He tilted the barrel up by an infinitesimal degree.

Once he pulled the trigger, it would take about two seconds for the 7.62 round to reach the target, two seconds in which the man could move out of the path of the bullet.

He shifted the aiming reticle a few more ticks to the left and brought his finger to the trigger, confident that when he broke the trigger, the round would go exactly where he wanted it to. He visualized the eruption of pink mist that would signal the success of his shot and the end of a man's life.

This, he knew, was what it meant to be "a natural."

"Soon," he whispered, and then shifted the scope again.

PART ONE
NATURAL

ONE

A faint breeze rustled the branches at the edge of the National Garden, and as the air moved across the back of his naked neck, U.S. Army Delta Force Lieutenant Colonel Kolt Raynor—code name "Racer"—unconsciously shrugged his shoulders and adjusted the blank navy blue ball cap perched atop his head.

After more than fifteen years of "modified grooming standards"—an exception made for elite military commando units, who were often required to blend in to the local populations of hot spots around the globe—he was having trouble getting used to the idea of more frequent haircuts, but that was one of the consequences of pinning on the silver oak leaves and taking charge of a Delta sabre squadron. As a squadron commander, he now spent a lot less time in the shoot house and the sniper condo, and a lot more time in meetings with people who wore either tailored suits or stars on the shoulders of their Class A uniforms, men who were not at all comfortable meeting with a shaggy-haired, bearded operator in combat-tested Multicam. Raynor's current hairstyle, while still nowhere within the regs, and considerably longer than the high and tight he had sported in his younger days as an Airborne Ranger captain, still managed to accentuate the fact that his hairline was in full retreat, which, perhaps more than anything else, made him self-conscious about his appearance.

It was by no means the biggest sacrifice he had made to stay in the Unit, and, trade-offs notwithstanding, he wouldn't have had it any other way.

Aside from what was mostly a reflex response, Raynor barely noticed the breeze. The reason for his latest haircut, and in fact the reason he was standing on a Greek sidewalk, had just arrived, and Kolt's senses were now fully occupied with what was happening around him. He turned his head slowly, eyes sweeping back and forth, not focusing on any one detail but rather taking in the entire tableau as it unfolded around him.

From the corner of one eye, he saw the Secret Service agents emerging from the identical vehicles comprising the motorcade. They alone knew which vehicle actually carried POTUS—the forty-fifth president of the United States of America—and which were decoys. Raynor did not look directly at the vehicles or the men fanning out in front of him. That was the one place he knew he would not find an emerging threat. He was watching the crowd, and the trees behind them, and the buildings to the north and south of the Maximos Megaron, the official seat of the prime minister of Greece. Mostly, though, he was watching the faces of the Delta operators—his men . . . and women—who were dispersed throughout the crowd, and in the trees and nearby buildings. He could only see so much, but collectively, the Delta squadron saw nearly everything.

It was the "nearly" that kept Raynor on his toes.

His eyes briefly lit upon a face in the crowd, a big man with shaggy brown hair and a thick reddish brown beard. The man's arms were crossed over his broad chest as he gazed serenely out over the assemblage, but then his gaze swung toward Raynor, and his lips puckered into a kiss.

"Right back at you, Slap," Raynor murmured, and resumed his scan.

Slap was "Slapshot," the code name of Jason Holcomb, Kolt's friend and the sergeant major of Noble Squadron, two roles that were not always readily compatible. Despite his senior leadership position, Slapshot could be counted on to inject his own unique irreverent—and to Kolt's way of thinking, not particularly funny—brand of humor into any stressful situations, which pretty much described all the situations Delta operators found themselves in.

Kolt next spotted Major Brett Barnes, one of his subordinate troop commanders. The twenty-nine-year-old West Point graduate was a recent addition to the squadron, and so far hadn't screwed up majorly enough to earn a nickname from the sergeants. Barnes was still adjusting to Raynor's style of leadership, which bore no resemblance whatsoever to what he had learned as a cadet or in any subsequent mandatory military schooling. To his credit, the young Delta troop commander had quickly grasped the most critical lesson of being an officer in the army's premier counterterrorism unit, and that was to always trust his NCOs. Barnes's team leaders were, without exception, the most capable operators Raynor had ever had the privilege of working with.

Barnes, like Raynor and a handful of the other operators, was wearing a loose-fitting blue windbreaker, blue ball cap, khaki chinos, and dark aviator-style sunglasses. The ad hoc—and highly visible—uniform served a broad range of purposes. The loose-fitting jackets concealed lightweight body armor and tactical rigs with chest-holstered semiautomatic pistols, or short-barreled and suppressed MP5SDs with folding stocks under their strong side armpit. The easily recognizable ensemble marked them as part of the presidential protection detail for the benefit of both the American Secret Service agents and the HP—Hellenic Police, the national law enforcement service of Greece—who were providing an additional layer of security. If the shit hit the fan and they had to draw the weapons hidden under those windbreakers, being readily identifiable would be of paramount importance. For similar reasons, the conspicuous attire would serve as a passive crowd control measure, while at the same time refocusing the attention of spectators away from the Delta operators' facial features. Last but not least, the "work uniforms" would also distract attention from Slapshot and the rest of the operators in civilian attire, making it easier for them to mingle with the crowd and spot potential threats up close.

Not five steps away from Slapshot stood "Shaft," otherwise known as Master Sergeant Ken Knight. The

Boston-born African-American operator was one of the team leaders in Barnes's troop, but you wouldn't have guessed it from looking at him. Shaft's hair was braided in cornrows, and he wore baggy denim jeans and a cast-off T-shirt with a faded silkscreen image of Captain Jack Sparrow from the *Pirates of the Caribbean* movies. A large bag crocheted in Rastafarian red, green, and yellow hung over his shoulder. Slapshot had taken to calling the bag Shaft's "murse."

Although he was an assault team leader, Shaft was also the most experienced medic in the entire Unit—he was working his way through med school in between deployments, which was no mean feat—and so pulled double duty as lead medic. The bag contained a full combat lifesaver medical kit—bandages, tourniquets, several rolls of Kerlix gauze, packets of QuikClot, and three bags of saline solution—but no weapons. That did not mean Shaft was unarmed, however. His loose-fitting jeans concealed a Glock 23 in a Thunderwear holster right above his crotch. However, like the other under-cover operators, his primary role was to identify threats so that others—ideally the HP, so as to avoid a diplomatic incident—could intercept and deal with them.

Right behind Shaft was Sarah Bell. Sarah was one of a handful of females assigned to Delta's augmentation cell—often shortened to simply aug cell—whose job it was to provide advance target reconnaissance and gather site intel. Sarah wasn't an operator, meaning she had not gone through Delta selection and the Operator Training Course. To date, only one woman had that distinction: Sergeant First Class Cindy "Hawk" Bird.

Kolt resumed searching the crowd. He didn't see Hawk, but he knew she was there, somewhere.

A voice sounded from the earbud in Raynor's left ear. "Champ is in the open."

The voice belonged to Secret Service Special Agent Jess Simmons, the SAIC—special agent in charge—of the presidential protection detail. "Champ" was the Secret Service code name for the current POTUS—Gerald Noonan, who was now six months into his term—and the update signaled that Champ had emerged from his up-armored Cadillac and was now standing out in the open.

Simmons was a typical by-the-book leader, which meant he and Raynor—who had little use for "the book"—had butted heads at first. Simmons kept trying to tell Kolt's people what to do, and Kolt had to keep patiently explaining to him why that wasn't going to work.

Well, maybe not that patiently.

Once they had cleared the air between them—more or less—things had gone a little more smoothly. The Secret Service agents, who were all a little high strung, seemed genuinely grateful to have some help, and Kolt's people were as good at making friends as they were at getting rid of enemies. Digger—Master Sergeant Pete Chambliss—was bromancing an eager young special agent, a former soldier who had "almost tried out for Delta," and Hawk practically had her own fan club.

Days of preparation and coordination with Simmons and his people had all been leading up to this: forty-five seconds—the amount of time it would take for Champ to shake hands with the Greek prime minister, pose for a photo or two, and move inside the Maximos Megaron—when the leader of the free world would be at his most vulnerable.

A change in the pitch and volume of crowd noise confirmed Simmons's statement—as if such confirmation was needed. The boisterous reception was not by any stretch of the imagination warm and welcoming. President Noonan was, it seemed, as unpopular in Athens as he was back home, though for vastly different reasons.

Over the course of his time in service, first as an enlisted infantryman, then as a commissioned officer, and now as the leader of a Delta sabre squadron, Kolt Raynor had served under four different presidential administrations. Some were better than others, none had been perfect, but not once had Raynor been tempted to resign his commission in order to avoid serving under a commander in chief with whom he was at odds, politically speaking. It was the duty of every soldier to follow orders, orders that originated with elected officials, regardless of whether the soldier personally agreed with the orders or supported the people who issued them. Raynor took this commitment seriously, steering clear of policy debates and keeping vocal criticism of the POTUS and other elected leaders to a bare minimum in the squadron. A little bitching and moaning was to be expected, but anything more than that could be a career-ender.

Raynor had no particular issue with President Noonan, a career politician and former speaker of the House of

Representatives. The man had the experience and potential to be a capable if not exactly outstanding chief executive—by no means the worst in Raynor's personal experience. But Noonan had the misfortune of taking office at a moment in history when decades of festering political, social, and economic unrest had erupted in a gigantic shit volcano.

Things had reached a head during the primary season. Frustrated by years of gridlock and political "business as usual," voters from both parties had gravitated to revolutionary candidates who, while at opposite ends of the political spectrum, had enormous populist appeal. One of those political outsiders had narrowly lost the nomination after a divisive primary season that had left his party irreparably fractured. His opponent in the contest, a deeply flawed career politician who had waged a scorched-earth campaign through political proxies, was not only loathed by the opposition party but mired in scandal, and deeply in the pocket of wealthy elites and multinational corporations.

The turmoil on the other side of the fence was even more alarming.

Their populist candidate had driven his outspoken, outrageous personality like a stake through the heart of the party machine, knocking off more than a dozen rivals, many of whom had been considered a lock for the nomination. Against all odds, and to the utter dismay of party power brokers and news pundits alike, he had won.

And that was when things had taken a truly bizarre turn.

Faced with two deeply unpopular and controversial candidates, the congressional leadership had conspired to place a spoiler candidate on the ballot in all fifty states—former speaker Gerald Noonan. As expected, Noonan had siphoned off votes from both major party candidates. Not nearly enough to win outright, but just enough to prevent either of his opponents from reaching a majority of electoral votes, which was exactly what the architect of the conspiracy—the current speaker of the house—had been counting on.

As outlined in the Twelfth Amendment to the Constitution, when no candidate receives a clear majority of electoral votes, it falls to the House of Representatives to select a president from the top three candidates in the general election. The clause had been invoked only once in American history, following the election of 1824, when Congress had chosen John Quincy Adams to be president despite his second-place finish in the general election. Now, for a second time, the United States Congress had used a Constitutional technicality to set aside the will of the electorate in order to place their own man in the White House, and, in so doing, touched off a powder keg.

One unexpected outcome was that the fractured electorate now found something upon which they could agree: Congress had hijacked the election. Millions of voters who already felt disenfranchised by a rigged system weren't interested in being lectured about the Constitution or the inner workings of a republic. They were ready for bloody revolution.

Raynor had known it was bad, but hadn't realized

how bad until Jess Simmons revealed that there had been a four-fold increase in actionable threats against President Noonan, the face of this alleged corrupt bargain. Simmons had confided that his agency, already weakened by several very high-profile scandals during the closing years of the previous administration, was now stressed to the breaking point.

As bad as the domestic situation was, things were even worse overseas. A growing national sovereignty movement, which called for, among other things, an end to the European Union and the dissolution of NATO, was spreading like wildfire across Europe. President Noonan's European tour, designed to shore up support for NATO, seemed to be having the opposite effect, fanning the flames of anti-American sentiment in countries that had once been staunch allies.

Providing personal protection details for diplomats abroad was a normal part of the Delta mission, and this wasn't the first time Raynor had been called on to backstop the Secret Service, but it was the first time he could recall where the threat felt so *real*.

Ironically, it was also the first time he felt like he had a personal stake in the outcome of the PPD assignment. Despite Raynor's staunchly apolitical work ethic, the man who was presently a heartbeat away from the presidency—retired Admiral William Mason—was the one man whose ascension to the office of president would prompt Raynor's immediate resignation.

It wasn't merely that Raynor couldn't stand Mason, or that the feeling was mutual. In truth, if given the chance, Raynor wasn't entirely certain he would be able to resist the temptation to kill Mason himself.

His first collision with Admiral Mason had occurred only a few years earlier, when Mason—then the commanding general of JSOC—had ordered him to abort an operation to extract Shaft following an undercover singleton mission. Raynor had flatly ignored the order to turn back. His decisiveness had saved Shaft, bagged the HVT, and retrieved some critical intel about terrorist operations on American soil in the process. Technically, the abort order was invalid, since they had already passed the point of no return and Raynor already had execute authority—permission to carry out the mission as he saw fit without interference from higher—but technicalities rarely won arguments with men who wore stars, and as a way of saying thank you, Mason had tried to have Raynor court-martialed.

Back then, Bill Mason had been merely an incompetent asshole, but a more recent incident had upgraded the former JSOC commander to top-tier threat. Although he couldn't prove it—not yet, at least—Raynor was 99.97 percent certain that Mason was guilty of treason—specifically, revealing highly sensitive information about Unit personnel and operations to a known enemy of the United States, and helping that enemy set an ambush intended to kill Raynor and his squadron.

As living proof that shit floats to the top, after leaving the navy, Mason had received a series of political appointments, culminating in his being tapped to run the State Department. From there, it had been a short hop to the number-two slot on the dark-horse independent presidential ticket headed by Gerald Noonan.

Admiral Mason was now Vice President Mason, and if something happened to Noonan, Mason would become president of the United States.

There was no fucking way Kolt Raynor was going to let that happen on his watch.

Raynor resisted the urge to look where everyone else was looking. This was the critical moment. If there was an assassin in the crowd, he would reveal himself now.

Kolt scanned the faces, some hopeful and eager, awed at the chance to catch a historic glimpse of a famous world leader, some twisted with snarls of righteous indignation as they shouted taunts and accusations. He didn't linger on the latter. He was looking for quiet, subdued faces, someone who might be silently working up the courage to act. People who appeared jittery or hyperfocused, or, alternately, completely serene, as if the violence they were contemplating was the ultimate narcotic.

There were hundreds of faces and Raynor knew he would never be able to check every single one, but none of those in the foreground, those close enough to pose a real threat, exhibited any of the signs he was looking for.

Champ had been in the open for almost ten seconds now, though still mostly concealed from the crowd behind the bulk of the armored Caddy.

Simmons called out another update. "Midas is moving."

Raynor risked a quick glance at the street, spotting Noonan at the center of a small knot of ever-vigilant Secret Service agents. "Midas"—the code name for the Greek prime minister—was surrounded by his own security detail, moving out to greet his American counterpart. As he drew close, the bodyguards from both contingents repositioned, like two small drops of water touching and combining into one larger mass around both men, while still allowing enough space for the television cameras to capture a permanent record of the meeting at the center.

Champ and Midas extended their hands toward each other simultaneously, as if they had rehearsed the moment, and then in unison turned and smiled at the cameras . . .

Just as a halo of red mist appeared behind Midas's head.

TWO

Kolt and his mates had learned long ago that no amount of training could overcome certain physical realities. When you see death up close, or feel your death is imminent, it takes time for the brain to process stimuli from the eyes and ears, select the appropriate response, and then send the signal to the body. Not long in practical terms—no more than two-tenths of a second—but Kolt Raynor knew that was one-tenth of a second too long.

Being able to assess a threat in the blink of an eye could mean the difference between icing an armed terrorist or accidentally killing an unarmed civilian or a hostage you were trying to rescue. Or getting yourself killed by the guy you missed.

In the fraction of a second between the flash of red mist and the eruption of activity around POTUS—before the body of the Greek leader could hit the ground—Kolt Raynor saw a lot. The way Midas's head had snapped back and the cloud of atomized blood that hung in the air behind him indicated a high-velocity, medium-caliber round, fired from a distance—from somewhere to the north and at an elevation of less than forty degrees.

"SNIPER!" he shouted, repeating the warning. "SNIPER! SNIPER!"

Adrenaline dumped into his bloodstream and he began turning in the direction from which the shot had come, his right hand seeking out the grip of his holstered Glock 23. It was a reflexive action—turn toward the threat, neutralize the threat before he can get off another shot. His rational mind knew better. The sniper was probably at least four or five hundred yards away. There wasn't a damn thing Raynor could do to "neutralize" a threat like that, not with a handgun from where he was standing. There was only one correct response, and the Secret Service agents were already doing it, collapsing on Champ, forming a human shield around him, hustling him into the open and waiting Escalade. The HP protective detail had done the same for Midas, closing on him and removing him from Raynor's line of sight, though Kolt knew it was already too late for the man.

He had not seen the actual exit wound, only the resulting blood spatter, but he had caught a glimpse of the entrance wound.

The bullet had entered through the Greek prime minister's left eye.

It took another hundredth of a second for the full significance of this to hit home.

No. No fucking way.

He looked north, in the direction from which he

knew the shot had come, searching for the shooter's location. Warning bells were ringing in his subconscious. The sniper was still out there and all of them were standing in the open, vulnerable. But if the man was the pro Raynor knew him to be, then he would not be foolish enough to risk betraying his location with a second shot. The shooter had already accomplished his primary mission; all that remained was the exfil.

Raynor raised his eyes slightly, trying to visualize the path of the bullet. It could not have come from a nearby rooftop. The angle had been far too shallow for that, and besides, his own Noble Squadron snipers occupied every one of those rooftops.

No broken windows, no open windows.

Farther out, the shooter's field of fire would have been obstructed by other buildings and vegetation.

So where the hell is—

His eyes settled on the lightly forested slope of a hillside peeking out from behind the rows of buildings. Mount Lycabettus, the three-hundred-meter-tall mountain that looked out across the city.

During his earlier recon, Raynor had taken note of the possible exposure from the west slope of Mount Lycabettus. Simmons had initially been dismissive, pointing out that the mountain was more than half a mile away, to which Kolt had replied that Delta snipers routinely broke plates from the sniper condo at that distance. Simmons had passed the concern along to the locals, who had promised to patrol the hillside, but the SAIC was clearly more concerned with threats of the up close and personal variety. Kolt had not pressed the is-

sue beyond that. Simmons was right about the unlikeli-
hood of a threat originating from the distant hillside.
Outside of JSOC, there were only a handful of men with
the skill to make a shot like that.

He took a step forward, then another, and then before he knew it, he was running. Behind him, the crowd
erupted in pandemonium, only now realizing that something terrible had just happened. Raynor knew there
would be a stampede, with frightened spectators tram-
pling one another to escape the nameless danger that
had triggered the panic. His earpieces—he wore two,
the one on the left monitoring the Secret Service net,
while the right was reserved for Unit comms—crackled
to life with crisscrossing traffic, protocols momentarily
forgotten in the chaos.

"Hold the line. Keep them back."

"Champ is secure!"

"Status. What's happening? Where did the shot come
from?"

Raynor ignored the questions even though he knew
the answer.

Over the tumult, he heard a throaty roar of engines
as the presidential motorcade sped away from the scene,
continuing south to the designated rally point.

Raynor kept going north.

Directly ahead were six police motorcycles—Honda
TransAlp 650s, white with the word POLICE printed in
regular Roman letters on the side fairing—sitting idle
and riderless, facing south and blocking the street. A
dozen officers wearing full tactical kit and motorcycle
helmets stood nearby, staring back at the mayhem in

collective disbelief. Standard operating procedure for DIAS—the controversial Greek police motorcycle squad—was two men to each bike: one to drive and one to shoot. As Raynor drew near he reached inside his windbreaker and secured his cover credentials and badge. The closest officer tensed, one hand drifting toward his weapon.

Raynor held up his hands, flashing his bright silver badge with one and waving as if to get the man's attention with the other. "Don't shoot! I'm one of the good guys."

He didn't even know enough Greek to find a restroom, but he figured the gestures were universal. Without slowing, he pointed his left hand back down the street and shook it emphatically. "They need you back there."

The policeman's gaze flicked away from Raynor and he took a halting step in the indicated direction, giving Raynor the room he needed. Without slowing, Kolt veered in the direction of the last motorcycle in the row. He grasped the handlebars and squeezed the clutch lever on the left. As he threw his full weight behind his outstretched arms, he hauled the bike around in a tight 180, facing north. The vehicle grudgingly began rolling, the spring-loaded kickstand snapping up against the underside of the frame as the bike started picking up momentum.

He got about twenty meters before he heard the policeman's frantic shout. It might have been a threat or warning; Raynor couldn't tell the difference and he didn't look back. When the bike was moving as fast as he could run, Kolt threw himself onto the saddle, giving it one last boost forward. He got his feet on the foot pedals and then, in one smooth motion, let out the clutch and hit the starter. With a lurch of compression, the 647 cc engine turned over and roared to life, and then the machine shot forward under its own power. Raynor gave the throttle a twist, revving the engine up before shifting into the next gear.

He was halfway to the base of Mount Lycabettus before it occurred to him that he should probably let someone know what he was doing.

He had no difficulty hearing the radio traffic over the earpieces screwed deep into each ear canal, but transmitting while riding, with the four-stroke V-twin engine buzzing underneath him, was another matter. He let go of one handlebar and groped for the push-to-talk button.

"This is Racer," he shouted into the collar mic. "I'm going after the shooter. He's on the mountain. About a klick to the north."

He must have keyed the wrong mic, because instead of Slapshot or one of his troop commanders, the first voice he heard was Simmons. "Negative, Raynor. Hercules's people can handle that. I need you and your people at the airport."

Hercules was the code name the Secret Service had given to Police Colonel Kostas Drougas, a senior commander of EKAM—the elite Greek Special Anti-Terrorist Unit—and the man Raynor and Simmons had been liaising with. As Simmons had suggested, EKAM was in a much better position to run the sniper down. It was their city, after all. Raynor's priority was protecting POTUS.

The contingency for an incident like this was to get the president back aboard Air Force One and out of the country as fast as possible. The drawback to that, of course, was that an enemy might easily anticipate such a move, and be waiting in the woods outside the airport with a man-portable surface-to-air missile, ready to shoot down the plane on takeoff. The modified Boeing VC-25 aircraft was equipped with countermeasures, but like any other aircraft, it was particularly vulnerable during takeoff, which was why the contingency plan called for Noble Squadron to establish a two-mile perimeter around the airfield.

Kolt knew that overseeing the efforts to protect Champ's escape route was the correct thing for him, as squadron commander, to be doing under the circumstances. There was every reason to believe that the assassination attempt might have been intended to herd the president into exactly such an ambush, but Raynor didn't think that was the case. He was certain that the sniper was acting alone, and that the single bullet had found its intended target.

Slapshot answered on the Secret Service freq before Raynor could formulate his response. "Way ahead of you," he said. "Our recce teams are reporting the route is clean. Champ is good to go."

There was a brief pause and then Slapshot's voice sounded in Raynor's other ear, and his tone was considerably less diplomatic. "Racer! Champ is the priority. What the hell are you doing, boss?"

Raynor knew the answer he was ready to give Simmons wouldn't clear Slapshot's bullshit detector. He found the push-to-talk for the Unit radio and answered with the truth. "It's Shiner."

Raynor did not disagree that protecting Champ was the first—the only—priority, but he also knew that the American president had never been the sniper's intended victim. There was no immediate threat to POTUS—at least, not one related to the incident that had just occurred—but the sniper, the man designated as "Shiner"—and Kolt had no doubt about the killer's identity—was a threat of a different order; one that the Unit, and Kolt Raynor in particular, were obligated to eradicate. He hadn't been gunning for POTUS today, but tomorrow that could change, so as far as Raynor was concerned, there was no conflict between his current assignment to protect the president and his pursuit of the man who had just killed Midas.

He let go of the push-to-talk and focused on the ride. With the streets cleared in anticipation of the president's motorcade, he was able to accelerate down the empty urban canyon, hitting sixty miles per hour in a matter of seconds, but a few hundred meters ahead, the street split in a Y-junction around a wooded plaza known as Kolonaki Square. Above the treetops and framed by the buildings to either side, Kolt could just make out a small sliver of Lycabettus, still more than a quarter of a mile away.

Kolt had no idea how much time had passed since the sniper's bullet had ended the life of the Greek leader, but he knew it was measured in seconds, not minutes.

Barely enough time for the shooter to move from his location, which meant the sniper—Shiner—was still there, on the mountain.

"Where'd that bullshit assessment come from, Racer?" Slapshot said. "Your gut instinct again?"

Kolt squeezed the Transmit button. "The long-range shot, the eye-orbit point of impact. That's signature Shiner, Slap."

"Fuck, Racer, that's a helluva leap in logic," Slapshot replied. "Ever heard the word 'coincidence'? Maybe it was just a lucky shot."

"Nobody is that lucky. Just get here," Raynor barked, then let go of the push-to-talk so he could gear down, shedding speed as he neared the junction.

He did not turn but instead pushed straight ahead, bouncing the front wheel up and over the curb, and then accelerated into the plaza, slaloming around trees, to reach the broad paved walk that bisected the square. The pavement undulated up and down through a series of terraces and ramps—thankfully the square was only sparsely occupied—ultimately culminating in a short flight of steps that rose to the street on the far side. The TransAlp was a dual-sport motorcycle, built for riding on- or off-road, a necessity in the rugged environs of the Greek Isles, and the front shocks absorbed most of the bone-jarring impact of navigating the plaza, but not quite well enough to keep the business end of his concealed Glock from busting his balls with each bump. As he approached the final set of steps, Raynor leaned forward and twisted the throttle hard forward. He felt the bike shift under him, the front end suddenly almost too light to stay on the ground, and then in a series of a tooth-loosening jolts, the motorcycle began climbing the steps.

Despite the extra boost of gas at the start, the Honda was barely moving at a crawl when it reached the street on the far side of the square, but another twist of the handgrip remedied that. With a shriek of burned rubber, the motorcycle shot out into the street, which, unlike the streets on the other side of the park square, had not been closed off. Over the screech of hastily applied brakes and angry honks, Raynor heard police sirens. A lot of them. He didn't know if they were coming to back him up or arrest him, and he wasn't about to stop to find out. One way or another, they would all be there when he ran Shiner to ground.

The angular profile of the mountain disappeared behind a row of apartment buildings on the far side of the street. The tallest of them stood seven stories high and lay directly in the path of the sniper's bullet. Raynor did a quick calculation in his head: the shooter's position would have to be a lot higher upslope in order for him to shoot past them.

He steered into traffic and headed east, skirting the residential buildings and searching for a route that would take him north to the mountain, but even though he was essentially already on its slope, with so many apartments and trees in the way, he couldn't see the summit. Growling a curse, he took the first available left and headed north.

How long had it been now? Two minutes, maybe? Not much more than that.

Radio traffic continued to buzz in his ears, as distracting as a swarm of mosquitos. Simmons was busy checking and rechecking the route to the airport, urging his people to stay alert. Kolt did his best to ignore it. The noise from his right ear—the squadron freq—was a lot more professional. Every member of the squadron and the aug cell knew the SOP for such a situation: Stay the hell off the net unless you have something important to say.

Kolt knew his plainclothes operators had melted away with the crowd and were en route to their linkup point. Sticking around after the damage had been done was a waste. No need to keep an eye out for suspicious actors, or forward observers for the sniper, or even a shitbag with a GoPro filming the assassination for a propaganda video. No, experience told them all those assholes would be long gone by now. Which reinforced the fact that Kolt was the single main effort of the half-baked mission he was on.

Raynor tuned out the radio chatter and focused on navigating the streets to reach the foot of Lycabettus. He located the trail leading up the mountain, mostly by following the stream of tourists moving along the sidewalks.

Slapshot broke in. "Racer, what's your location?"

"Heading up the southernmost Lycabettus summit," Kolt said.

"Don't do anything stupid. The street cops might mistake you for a terrorist, especially with your Grand Theft Auto performance."

"Got it."

There were several routes leading up to the twin summits of Mount Lycabettus: meandering footpaths, uneven stairs, a paved road, and even a funicular railway. Most were farther east or situated on the north slope, well away from where the sniper's hide was probably located, but there was a narrow footpath leading up from the southwest corner of the hill.

Throughout his entire military career, Kolt Raynor had always trusted his gut. His critics called that proof that he didn't always have his shit together, and once or twice, his gut had gotten him into serious trouble—life-and-death trouble—but when faced with a critical choice, following his instincts was always a better option than mental masturbation or paralysis by analysis.

He could almost visualize Shiner, up on the hillside right above him, shedding his camouflage and abandoning his rifle and then hiking down to the trail where he might blend in with the crowd, strolling out nonchalantly with all the other visitors, who were completely unaware of what had just happened half a mile away.

He would walk, not run.

Kolt slowed and guided the motorcycle up a short flight of steps to the trail. The handful of pedestrians he encountered pushed to the side, getting out of his way, the police markings evidently sufficient to explain the motorized vehicle on the footpath. He checked every adult face—male or female—looking for some hint of the face etched into his memory . . . a memory from sixteen years earlier.

Will I even recognize him? Raynor wondered. *What if he recognizes me first?*

That seemed unlikely. Not only had Kolt been a lot younger back then, but he'd also sported a beard and a thick mane of hair. This was one situation where a shave and a haircut was the better disguise.

The sound of sirens at his back reminded him of an only slightly less immediate problem. He pressed the push-to-talk. "Slap, status. Are the police on our side yet?"

Slapshot came back almost immediately, but he spoke in abrupt bursts, breathing heavy. Raynor realized the other man was probably running to catch up with him. "They're running your shit through Interpol right now, man, but yeah. I convinced Hercules that you've pegged the shooter. You have, right?"

"He's here somewhere." Raynor said it without hesitation or uncertainty. He glanced back, saw the apartment buildings still blocking his view of the National Garden. The shot had come from a more elevated position, but at a normal walking pace, the sniper could have made it this far. Or taken another path.

"Vector us in, Racer," Slap said.

"Tell Hercules to get his people to Mount Lycabettus. They need to block every route off this mountain, ASAP. Nobody leaves. And get Stitch up there, too. He'll know exactly where to look."

Kolt trusted Clay "Stitch" Vickery as much as he did Slapshot and Digger. He had rolled with Kolt in the Mike Squadron assault troop for years, and Webber recently yanked him over to Noble Squadron to be Major Barnes's troop sergeant major. Although he was arguably the top Unit sniper, Stitch considered himself an "advanced assaulter"—a sniper who preferred to kick in doors with an assault team even though he didn't have to. With his hunter's instincts, Stitch was the perfect guy to home in on Shiner's exact position.

"Roger," Slapshot said. There was a pause. "This ain't news yet, but Midas bought it. One through the eye. You were spot on with that."

"That's Shiner's MO."

"If he's that shit hot with the long shot, why would he pass up a chance to take out POTUS? Think he hit the wrong guy?"

Raynor shook his head absently. Anything was possible, but he doubted it. "Not likely" was all he said.

The target file on Shiner was spotty at best. Some of the old guard operators, men who knew the whole story, were convinced that Shiner was Raynor's white whale. Or maybe a windmill he'd mistaken for a monster. But if Shiner did exist, and if he was the man Raynor believed him to be, then he was someone with a deep and abiding hatred of the United States of America. It was hard to imagine that Shiner, or whomever he was presently fighting for, would have regarded the Greek prime minister as a worthier target for assassination than the leader of the free world. It might have been an error. At almost a thousand meters, with no spotter—Shiner reputedly always worked alone—it was entirely possible that he had mistaken one milquetoast Caucasian politician in a suit for another.

Raynor didn't believe that for a second.

He kept going, scooting up the trail with little nudges to the throttle, giving each hiker a perfunctory look, even those that bore absolutely no resemblance to the man he remembered. There was a general lack of ethnic diversity among the faces he passed. Most were white—probably EU citizens or Americans. Shiner would blend right in.

He passed a young couple holding hands, and a shirtless old man with white hair and skin almost the same shade of pale. He passed a huffing, puffing family—the parents dangerously overweight, the two preadolescent kids already headed in the same direction.

Then Raynor saw him.

THREE

Sixteen years earlier

The report of the Barrett M107 antimateriel rifle boomed across the valley like a shout from the god of thunder. It was especially loud where Captain Kolt Raynor was crouching, just a few feet behind the weapon and the young man—a boy, really—who had just pulled the trigger. Raynor felt the rush of air and the blast of hot gasses from the Barrett's arrow-shaped muzzle brake, but kept his eye pressed to the spotting scope. Eight hundred meters and a second or so later, he saw a large puff of dust rise up from the ground, just a few feet away from the metal plate on which a rough approximation of an E-type silhouette had been painted.

"Told you."

"Beginner's luck, Musket," Raynor said, though he wasn't convinced of that.

"It's not," insisted Sergeant First Class Michael "Musket" Overstreet. "He's like a savant."

"Seeing is believing," Raynor said. "Maybe he's hot

shit with his AK at three hundred meters. I'll believe it if he can dial it in with three shots."

"It's a bet."

"Holdover, four point four." Raynor raised his voice, enunciating the words for the kid's benefit. Nineteen-year-old Rasim Miric spoke English pretty well—that was how he'd gotten the job as interpreter for the Delta troop—but it would be just like Musket to blame Miric's poor shooting on Raynor's unclear communication.

"Ready," Miric said without hesitation, the vowels betraying his Slavic heritage.

In the objective of his spotter scope, Raynor noted a faint breeze stirring the tall grass around the target. "Left point three."

The kid adjusted the rifle, fitting the buttstock securely in the bend of his crooked nose, and then there was another thunderous report. A moment later, the .50 caliber round punched a hole through the target, just left of center on the head of the silhouette.

"Shit," Raynor muttered, impressed.

"Looks like you're buying tonight," Musket crowed. "He always goes for the eyes. That's why we call him 'Shiner.' Black eye, every time."

"You're teaching him bad habits. I saw that Kentucky windage."

"Wasn't me," Musket protested.

The young man raised his head, fixing Raynor with his blue-gray eyes. "I know Kentucky. Racing horses, yes? What is Kentucky windage?"

"Compensating for the wind by moving your aim-point off the target, rather than using the windage knob on your scope," Raynor explained. "You've got precision tools, you should use them." He paused a beat. "Someone showed you how to do that, right?"

Miric shook his head. "This is how I have always done it."

"I guess you're a natural."

"Natural?" Miric looked back at him sheepishly. "I know this word also, but . . ."

"It means you've got a gift. A natural talent for distance shooting." Raynor wondered if the kid's proclivity for aiming at the eyes of his targets had also come naturally.

Probably not.

Unlike the language contractors that worked with most regular army units, Delta terps carried weapons and were expected to know how to use them. That didn't mean that they were used tactically to storm target objectives or provide cover and support for assault teams, but if the shit hit the fan, the terp would be in as much danger as any of the rest of them. Being able to shout insults at the enemy in their shared dialect wouldn't do any of them any good. Combat experience was always a plus in the hiring process.

Getting to play with some of the toys in the Delta toy box, like the Barrett, was just a perk of the job.

Shiner had been a shooter long before hiring himself out as an interpreter for NATO forces in his Balkan homeland.

In February of 1992, when Kolt Raynor had been a young platoon leader in the 75th Ranger Regiment and Rasim Miric had probably been ten or eleven years old, the Socialist Republic of Bosnia and Herzegovina passed a referendum for independence from the disintegrating remnants of the Socialist Federal Republic of Yugoslavia. The minority Bosnian Serbs—Orthodox Christians—boycotted the referendum, which would have put most of the power in the hands of the Bosnian Muslim majority. Supported by their cousins in neighboring Serbia, the Bosnian Serbs launched a violent bid to establish their own republic.

The resulting war had introduced a new phrase into the common vernacular: ethnic cleansing.

Serbian forces, in a concerted effort to wipe out their hated ancestral enemy, waged indiscriminate war on Bosnians and Croats, using mass murder and systematic rape to erase the Bosnian people from existence. The beleaguered Bosnians had fought back, sometimes using equally brutal tactics, eventually gaining the upper hand in the conflict with assistance from UN peacekeeping forces.

Raynor guessed that at some point during those three bloody years someone had put a rifle in the hands of a young Bosniak named Rasim Miric, and introduced him to the art of long-distance death dealing.

The formal end of the Bosnian conflict in 1995 with the signing of the Dayton Accords had not meant an end to violence in the region. Serbia, under the leadership of Slobodan Milosevic, shifted their nationalist ambitions to other territories from the former Yugoslavia—Croatia, Kosovo—and the atrocities on both sides continued racking up.

Now, after nearly a decade of conflict, Milosevic was

out of power and in a jail cell, awaiting extradition to the Hague, where he would be tried for crimes against humanity, and Captain Kolt Raynor, fresh out of Delta OTC, was in-country hunting down other war criminals.

As the new kid, Raynor was doing his best to catch up, fit in, and mostly keep his head down. Delta operators— he was still getting used to the idea that he was one of them—were truly the best of the best, which made Raynor feel even more like an average Joe. But his friend—and immediate superior—Major Josh "TJ" Timble assured him that he would catch his stride eventually.

Raynor had spent his first week shadowing Musket and the other operators as they drove around, conducting route reconnaissance, servicing safe houses throughout the region, and mostly just killing time while they waited for Karadzik or one of the other assholes on the list to come up for air. Busting plates on the range was as good a way to blow off steam as any. Raynor was just about to take his turn behind the Barrett when TJ came over to let him know that they'd gotten a source hit.

"Source 3263 swears the Rat is crossing into Bosnia tonight and heading to his sister's house in Bijeljina."

"How many vehicles?" Kolt asked, already formulating a plan in his head.

"Unknown as yet, and I'm not requesting execute authority without better intel."

"C'mon, TJ, how actionable does it have to be?" Kolt asked as he motioned TJ away from the firing line and out of hearing range of the others. "How long have we been after this douche bag?"

"I hear ya, Kolt," TJ said resignedly. "Work some concepts of ops with your troop and we'll see what shakes out."

"Good enough, TJ, we're on it," Kolt said.

Ratko Mladic, former commander of the 9th Corps of the Yugoslav People's Army and code-named "The Rat" by the Joint Special Operations Command, was the architect of the four-year-long siege of Sarajevo and the subsequent massacre of more than eight thousand young men and boys in the UN-designated "safe area" of Srebrenica in 1995. He was also number one with a bullet on the hit list for the CIA-led Balkan Task Force.

The agency had been tracking his movements, mostly with aircraft—RC-135 "Rivet Joint" and U2 spy planes, and MQ-1 Predator unmanned aerial vehicles—occasionally supplemented by human intelligence assets on the ground. Despite changing his location every few days, intel analysts poring over the data usually knew Mladic's approximate location to within a twenty-mile radius. When they were able to pinpoint an exact location, which had happened several times over the four years they had been tracking him, forward-deployed operators from Delta or SEAL Team Six—whoever was up to bat that week—headed out, ready to pounce.

There had been no shortage of opportunities to roll up Mladic and the other war criminals. TJ had told Raynor that he had stopped counting how many times they'd gotten kitted up only to be told to stand down at the last moment.

It wasn't a failure on the ground that was holding

them back, but a lack of political will. Exposing Serb complicity in hiding the war criminals would complicate enforcement of the Dayton Accords, and strain relations with Russia. It was all political bullshit, but that was the nature of the job. Odds were this would be another dry hump, but like a gambler feeding nickels into a slot machine, Raynor clung to the hope that this time they would hit the jackpot.

HUMINT had fingered Mladic's sister's house as a possible target location years earlier, and on at least two occasions, the actionable intel wasn't received until after the Rat had come and gone. The intel on Mladic's location may have been spotty over the years, but in those same years the details on that house had filled the target folder.

A team of CIA officers and sources had picked up Mladic crossing over the Drina river from Serbia. They confirmed two dark four-door sedans separated by roughly thirty seconds passing each checkpoint until they reached the outskirts of Bijeljina. After conferring with the agency spook who was waiting a mile up the road, Raynor and his team of assaulters headed into the woods, accompanied by Miric—the terp—and Rascal—the squadron communicator.

It was just after 2200 and although the assaulters relied on their ANVS-9 night-vision devices to get them to within sight of the objective, the lights were still on inside. The house was lit up like a beacon.

Not ideal conditions for a raid, Raynor knew, but the mission was to capture the Rat, not to kill him, and waiting until the lights went out and the family reunion celebration had ended was the smart assault option. He grabbed the mic to the satellite radio from Rascal. "Wrangler Zero-Two, this is Hunter One-One. We're set. Request execute authority. Over."

There was a brief lag before the reply came back from the safe house in Tuzla where TJ was monitoring the mission. "Hunter Zero-One, sitrep on the target environmentals. Over."

"Inside lights on, two sedans, two SUVs in driveway, over."

There was a momentary pause, then TJ came back with, "Two sedans *and* two SUVs? Over."

Raynor looked again, even though there was no need. He lowered the handset. "Hey, Musket, you see four vehicles down there, right?"

"Roger that."

Raynor hit the push-to-talk. "Affirmative, over."

"Stand by, over," TJ said.

"Stand by, over," Raynor echoed, without keying the mic. Thirty miles away, TJ was waiting for someone at Langley or Foggy Bottom or the Pentagon or maybe even the White House to take his call and give them the green light.

"This is bullshit, man." Musket shook his head in disgust. "I'm getting blue balls, here."

He squatted down, letting his suppressed HK MP5 hang from its sling, and dug a can of Skoal from the cargo pocket of his woodland-camo-pattern BDU. After stuffing a pinch of the wintergreen-flavored chewing tobacco in his lower lip, he held the can up, offering it to any takers. Kolt debated it for a moment, having left his pouch of Red Man in Tuzla, and almost took Musket up on his offer, but passed, knowing he'd likely barf his guts out.

He looked around the tight perimeter, sort of making eye contact with all of them in the darkness before admitting, "Could be a long night. Might as well get comfortable."

"I do not understand," Miric said, his voice loud enough to earn an immediate shushing from several of the assaulters. He pointed at the house. "He is in there. Mladic, the butcher, is in that house. Why do we just sit here?"

Raynor glanced over at him. "Settle down."

"It's politics, kid," Musket supplied.

"Do you know what he did? At Srebrenica? He . . . he . . ." Miric's jaw worked, raw emotion temporarily robbing him of words.

"We'll get him," Raynor said, trying to sound reassuring, evidently with little success. The terp scowled and sank down into a squat on the ground, fidgeting with his Kalashnikov. Raynor leaned closer to Musket. "Is he going to be a problem?"

"Nah, he's a good kid. Besides, we'll all be heading back in a few minutes."

Raynor wasn't so sure on either count, but let it go, hoping that the other man would be proven definitively wrong about the latter point. He glanced over at Rascal, hopeful, but the communicator just shook his head.

Half an hour ticked by. An hour. Two. The word from the JOC remained the same. Stand by. Kolt's instincts told him the report of the SUVs on target was probably giving the powers that be fits, and elevating some pencil head's risk matrix sky high.

"Shit or get off the pot," Musket said with a scowl. "Face it, boss, they're not going to give us the go. We should just—"

"Hey," whispered another of the assaulters. "Somebody is stirring."

Raynor craned his head around to get a look at the house. The front door had opened and a man had stepped outside. He wore an overcoat and held what Raynor guessed was a Skorpion vz. 61 machine pistol in both hands. The man looked around, and then glanced skyward.

"Little cocksucker must think we have eyes in the sky," Musket muttered.

The man in the overcoat looked over his shoulder and shouted something into the house. As the first man moved to an SUV parked nearby, more figures emerged from the house. More men with guns.

Except for one.

Mladic looked a lot older and a little thinner than in his file photos, but the Rat's expression remained as smug and contemptuous as ever.

"They're leaving," Raynor said, then grabbed the mic from Rascal. "Wrangler Zero-Two. Target is on the move. We need execute authority. Now. Over."

The delay was interminable. The answer was exactly what Raynor knew it would be. "Negative, Racer. You do not have execute authority. I'm sorry, brother, but your orders are to stand down."

Raynor lowered the handset, squeezing it in his fist

as if to pulverize it. He could still hear TJ's voice, sounding tinny as it issued from the speaker. "Racer, did you copy my last?"

Seventy-five meters away, Ratko Mladic and his entourage were about to enter the waiting vehicle.

I could do this, Raynor thought. *We could take him. I'll say we lost the satellite. That I have situational awareness and made the call. Easier to ask forgiveness than permission. I'll take the heat. What are they gonna do? Fire me for catching an international war criminal?*

He sucked in a deep breath, then let it out.

He wasn't going to do any of those things, if only because TJ would have his ass.

This was the job he'd signed up for. Not just the Unit, but the army. He was a soldier, had never wanted to be anything else. And soldiers followed orders.

He raised the mic. "Ack—"

"You are letting him go?" Miric hissed.

Raynor turned to Musket, raised a finger to his lips—*shut him up!*—but before the operator could move to silence the terp, Miric spun around, leveled his AK at the mass of men near the SUV, and pulled the trigger.

For a bloated instant, Raynor felt like he was watching a movie—a scene from someone else's life. Musket was still moving, reaching for the terp.

He wasn't close enough.

There was a single report, deafening in the still woods, and one of Mladic's bodyguards went down.

Musket made a grab for Miric, but the interpreter must have glimpsed his approach in the peripheral vision of his nonshooting eye. He sidestepped, and

Musket's arms closed on nothing as he careened past. Miric shifted his rifle again, intent on taking another shot.

Raynor jolted into action, swinging his fist—handset and all—at the terp's head. He connected solidly and Miric staggered forward, flailing, the rifle still in his hands. Raynor threw his arms wide, letting the sat radio handset fall from his fingers, and tackled Miric to the ground, careful to keep the muzzle of the AK pointed away from the rest of the assaulters, but the damage had already been done.

Mladic's men had surrounded their boss and were hustling him behind the vehicle for cover, while two of their number sprayed the woods with 7.65mm rounds from their Skorpions. The bullets raked the trees overhead, close enough that Raynor's men had to duck and cover before returning fire.

But they did return fire.

Raynor might not have been given execute authority, but the rules of engagement permitted lethal force if fired upon. The initiating incident would almost certainly be investigated and dissected in days to come, and Raynor would probably get his ass chewed for not maintaining positive control of the situation, but no one would find fault with his operators for their subsequent actions.

Another of Mladic's bodyguards dropped, slumping to the ground behind the SUV. There were more sounds, like hammers striking metal, as suppressed fire from the Delta weapons pounded into the exterior of the vehicle and struck the house behind it. The other shooter drew back, but extended his weapon into the open, triggering another burst. Even as he did so, the SUV began moving.

Raynor only caught a glimpse of what was happening. His attention was consumed by Miric. Kolt was straddling the younger man's back, pinning him to the ground. The terp was thrashing like someone possessed, shrieking—almost certainly drawing fire their way—but shutting him up now was a secondary priority to restraining him. Raynor caught Miric's right hand and twisted the arm around behind his back, pulling it up hard enough that the pain should have left the young man completely immobilized. It didn't. Miric kept squirming and bucking.

"I got him, boss!" Musket shouted, kneeling beside Raynor. He slapped a zip-tie around Miric's wrist—the one Raynor was holding.

"I got this," Raynor managed to say. He was panting, out of breath. "Get on line, on line."

"Easy, boss, they're gone. Bugged out."

Raynor realized that it had been a few seconds since he'd heard any shooting. He rolled off Miric, letting Musket finish the job of binding the hysterical terp. He reached out to Rascal, who intuitively knew to hand him the radio mic. Miric was still shrieking.

"Shut him the fuck up," Raynor snarled. He took a deep breath, held it, let it out, paused a few seconds, and then did it again, trying to use the discipline of square breathing to damp down the lingering shakiness of adrenaline.

How was he going to explain this clusterfuck?

The terp's cries were abruptly stifled, but in the

relative calm that followed, he heard Musket gasp. "Shit. Somebody get a bandage on that."

Raynor glanced over and saw Miric, now facing up, with Musket's brawny arms wrapped around him from behind. A strip of tape covered his mouth, muting his cries, but his mouth was open under the adhesive, shouting into it. And now, Raynor could see why. The left side of Miric's face was covered in blood, all of which seemed to originate from his eye, which was swollen shut, the skin around it puffed up to the size of a grapefruit. Miric's screams weren't cries of rage, but of pain.

In typical Delta fashion, Raynor was his own harshest critic. TJ was quick to shift blame onto himself, since, as senior officer, he bore the ultimate responsibility for Miric's actions. That was only partially true. Rasim Miric had rolled with the Unit on several occasions with no indicators that he would freak out on target. Safely back at the safe house, both Racer and TJ took an earful from the Unit commander, of which the key takeaway was: "Shit happens. Don't let shit happen again."

After leaving the injured interpreter at a local hospital, Raynor did not see him again, nor did he expect to— Miric was blacklisted—but rumor had it that the young man had lost his left eye as a result of the scuffle in the woods.

An eye-for-an-eye misfire.

A few weeks later, Arab terrorists crashed hijacked passenger jets into the World Trade Center and the Pentagon, and what little interest the administration had in rolling up the architects of genocide in the Balkans evaporated completely. Ten more years would pass before Ratko Mladic's arrest, culminating in a lengthy trial before the war crimes tribunal, which was still ongoing.

In the short term, Raynor found himself in the rugged mountains of Afghanistan, for a very different but equally frustrating manhunt, and he would spend much of the next fifteen years hunting Islamic extremists and fighting in both declared and undeclared wars in the Middle East and Africa. From time to time he would hear rumors of an unusually skillful enemy sniper working those battlefields, moving from one conflict to the next. A lone-wolf mercenary who showed up in Afghanistan, Iraq, Yemen, Chechnya, and then moved on. A killer who signed his work with a unique and grisly signature: a bullet through his target's left eye.

There was no conclusive evidence to support the theory that all the killings were the work of some quasi-mythic assassin—a Carlos the Jackal–type figure. The eye shots could have been a coincidence after all, but Raynor didn't believe that.

Shiner—Rasim Miric—was real, and now Raynor knew it for certain.

FOUR

The plain face with a slightly crooked nose and dark hair were mostly as Kolt remembered. His cheeks looked a little fuller. Better fed. His skin was creased and weathered, giving him the appearance of someone much older. He definitely wasn't a teenager anymore, but Raynor recalled that even in his youth, Miric had looked old beyond his years.

It was the eyes that really caught Raynor's attention and clinched the positive ID; they didn't quite match each other, and when his right eye glanced over in Raynor's direction, the left one didn't follow.

Glass eye. It's Shiner. No doubt about it.

He was just fifty feet away, walking by himself on the edge of the trail, looking at the man on the police motorcycle with innocent curiosity and reasonable apprehension, just like everyone else. Raynor put on his best poker face as he calmly squeezed the clutch and tapped the shift pedal to neutral. He reached down with his feet, letting them drag as the motorcycle used up the last of its momentum. He needed to get closer, close enough to take the other man down without endangering any innocent bystanders.

Something must have given him away.

There was no warning, no change of expression or look of alarm on the bland face. Without any provocation, the sniper dashed forward, plowing into the family that had been walking just ahead of him, only a few yards from Raynor.

Kolt's immediate response was to plant his feet on the ground, stopping the bike completely, and draw the Glock from his appendix holster, but as he twisted around in the saddle to acquire the target, he saw that Shiner had picked up a human shield. When he had bulldozed through the midst of the tourist family, the sniper had seized hold of one of the kids, and now he had one arm wrapped around the child, half carrying, half dragging him down the path. Shiner was shorter than average, making the boy seem even bigger than he really was.

Kolt lined the fleeing sniper's head up with the business end of the Glock and started to exert pressure on the trigger.

Reflex shooting with zero hesitation on paper targets, where at close range there was little chance of accidentally hitting the two-dimensional hostage, was one thing. But in the real world, with every step the sniper took away from Kolt the pucker factor increased and the odds of actually scoring a hit diminished. Yes, Raynor had the shot and he was going to take it, but even though he was confident in his ability, he wasn't cavalier about the potential risk.

Then a shrieking woman stepped in front of him, chasing after the man who had just taken her son.

Raynor jerked the pistol up, letting go of the trigger before it broke. "Shit," he rasped.

Shiner was now twenty yards down the trail, and the woman was still in the way. After a couple more steps, the sniper let go of his hostage, thrusting him into the woman's path, and then plunged to the left, heading off-trail, into the woods.

Raynor jammed the Glock back into its holster and grabbed the handlebars again, trying to clutch, shift, and accelerate all at the same time. The bike lurched, almost stalling, then shot forward up the trail. Kolt hauled the front end around, leaning the opposite way to avoid laying the bike on its side, and headed into the woods in pursuit.

As he steered diagonally across the slope, weaving through the trees, he caught glimpses of his quarry through the screen of pine boughs. In this terrain, the bike's horsepower afforded little advantage, but once the sniper emerged, it would make all the difference.

Kolt groped for the push-to-talk. "Got him. On the southwest footpath."

Even as he said it, the woods abruptly ended and Raynor found himself looking down from a waist-high retaining wall onto the street beyond. The fleeing sniper had just leapt from the abutment, and was stumbling forward across the pavement right into the path of a car—a little silver Volkswagen Polo. The car screeched to a halt, but there wasn't enough stopping distance, and Shiner slammed onto the hood.

Raynor faced a similar problem, except he didn't have time to stop short of the drop-off. He twisted the throttle hard, propelling the motorcycle forward, and as it shot out over the edge, he planted his feet on the side pegs and pulled up on the handlebars with all his might, lifting the front wheel higher.

The landing sucked just about as much as he expected it to. The back wheel slammed down onto the pavement with a screech, the impact jolting up through his legs, slamming his ass down onto the saddle and driving the Glock into his nuts. A stab of pain shot through his lower back. Then the front wheel came down. The shocks absorbed most of the energy, but the bike immediately started to wobble, and for a fleeting instant Raynor was sure he was going to spill it, but resisting the urge to fight with the steering, he gave it some more throttle.

To his complete amazement, it worked.

As the bike righted itself, he turned up the paved street, away from the stalled VW, but only long enough to get the machine back under control. He carved a tight 180 and came around just as Shiner hauled the driver—a middle-aged woman—out of the car and took her place behind the wheel.

Raynor opened the throttle, but Shiner had too much of a head start. The VW pulled away before he could cross half the distance, heading along the road that skirted the base of the mountain.

Raynor backed off, pacing the other vehicle. Trying

to shoot while driving the motorcycle wasn't feasible—
there was a reason the Greek cops rode double—and
trying to run Shiner off the road wouldn't work either.
Kolt simply wasn't in a position to do much to stop
Shiner by himself, but fortunately, he didn't have to.

He shouted a description of the vehicle into the clip
mic, along with his best guess at a direction of travel.
He couldn't make heads or tails of the little blue plac-
ards on each street corner, so "heading north, parallel
to the mountain" and "turning west" and "I can hear sirens to the south" was the best he could do. A few of
the storefronts had legible names, so he dutifully reported these as well.

Shiner drove like someone being chased, blowing
through intersections without stopping, blaring a warning with the VW's horn and passing slower vehicles,
sometimes nudging them out of the way, sometimes
veering onto the sidewalk to get around a jam. Yet, for
all the chaos he was causing, he seemed to be moving
with a purpose other than simply getting away from the
pursuing motorcycle.

After about a minute of this, both the sirens and
Slapshot caught up to Raynor.

"Racer, they need you to back off. Their jurisdiction,
brother. Hold what you have."

"Negative," Raynor fired back. "I have PID. It's
Shiner." As far as Kolt Raynor was concerned, no further explanation was necessary.

"Understood," Slapshot replied. "But you don't need
to be the one to bag him, boss. He just iced their PM.
It's their ass wound."

Kolt could tell from the other man's tone that he was struggling to keep his anger in check, anger almost certainly directed at Raynor for taking off on his own. One of Slapshot's primary duties as squadron sergeant major was to keep Raynor out of trouble, and he was probably regretting that he hadn't been able to tackle and zip-tie Racer when the craziness started.

Raynor let the admonition slide without comment, but he did not back off. Instead, he started flipping switches on the console until the siren started shrieking and the revolving blue emergency light mounted behind him began flashing.

In his other ear, Raynor heard Simmons with an update on POTUS's ETA at the airport, and realized that barely five minutes had passed since the assassination.

The silver VW turned northeast onto a major thoroughfare. Shiner floored it, driving down the center line. The symphony of police sirens grew louder behind Raynor, with additional patrol cars and motorcycles joining the pursuit, some pulling in ahead of him. A pair of police cars appeared ahead and cut the road, but Shiner simply made a sharp left and headed down a narrow side street. Raynor was right behind him.

Shiner took a couple more turns, found another main boulevard, but then after just half a mile, turned into a run-down neighborhood with block after block of seedy apartment flats liberally adorned with spray-painted graffiti. The streets were lined with parked cars, leaving only enough room for one-way traffic.

Without warning, the VW's brake lights flashed and the car came to an abrupt halt in the middle of the street.

Raynor hit the brakes, gearing down, but didn't come to a full stop until the car door was thrown open and Shiner burst from the interior. The sniper dashed toward the entrance to one of the apartment buildings, never once glancing in Raynor's direction.

Raynor braked hard, laid the bike on its side, and leapt free, palming his holstered Glock to be sure he didn't lose it. He sprinted after the fleeing killer, but in the instant Shiner disappeared through the entrance, two men stepped out to cover his retreat. Raynor's eyes fixed on their weapons—from his down-the-barrel vantage, he couldn't tell make or model—and he drew his own on the run.

They hesitated. Kolt didn't.

A controlled pair dropped the guy on the left. Kolt shifted, still running toward the remaining crow, knowing that if he didn't kill the guy *right fucking now,* his survival would depend on luck and body armor. But instead of returning fire, the crow did something completely bat-shit crazy: He dropped his weapon and charged.

The guy was probably in full panic mode, defaulting to his primary threat response setting, which in his case was purely physical. He probably hadn't received any kind of combat training, so when faced with a life-or-death situation, his reptile brain took over. The reasons for it didn't matter. He was a crow—an enemy combatant—and armed or not, Raynor had no compunction about wasting him.

But he didn't.

In the split second it took him to put his sights center

mass, it occurred to him that the crow might be more useful alive than dead. Shiner was a mercenary, a lone-wolf shooter for hire, but this loser was probably with the group that had hired him, and might have some valuable operational intel.

And since he wasn't about to shoot back, taking him alive was actually doable.

Raynor lowered his stance to meet the charge, and a moment later, when they collided, he immediately regretted his decision.

The guy might have been shit with firearms, but he evidently knew a thing or two about hand-to-hand. Raynor could almost hear Slapshot chiding him. *"They call it Greco-Roman wrestling for a reason."*

Only this hit felt more like something from an NFL game. Despite bracing himself, and cleverly trying for a throw, Raynor was put on his ass by the impact, momentarily stunned, the wind knocked out of him. The crow staggered back a little, shaking his head, but recovered quickly and moved in, trying to circle around to Kolt's left side.

Despite the fresh waves of pain radiating up from his sacrum, and the fact that he couldn't seem to draw a breath, Raynor's body remembered what to do. He bent one knee, planted his foot on the ground, and used it to pivot on his butt so that he was still facing his opponent. He got the other leg up, ready to kick at the man if he tried to move in.

Which he did.

As the crow made a grab for him, Kolt used his bent leg to propel himself back, and then hooked his elevated foot behind the man's right knee, sweeping his leg out from under him and putting him flat on his back.

Raynor's breath returned with a gasp as he erupted out of his seated guard position and pounced, throwing himself across the other man's body. Kolt rolled him over, wrapped his legs around the crow's waist, immobilizing him, and then went for the chokehold.

As his opponent fought a futile battle to stay conscious, Raynor heard footsteps coming from behind him. He looked over his shoulder and saw Greek policemen stampeding toward the apartment entrance.

For the first time since initiating pursuit, Raynor's instincts were telling him it was time for some tactical patience.

Shiner had not chosen this place at random. It was probably his base of operations, which meant he would have weapons and probably more confederates waiting inside. The two crows at the entrance had bought Shiner plenty of time to set up an ambush. Or he might have an escape route out the back. Shiner wasn't stupid enough to let himself be cornered. He had led the pursuit here intentionally.

This was a trap.

Raynor's sixth sense was positively on fire.

"Wait!" he shouted, shaking his head. "You need to spread out. Cordon off the area."

The crow in Raynor's arms had stopped struggling, so he let go and waved the cops back, but his sign language seemed to be no more comprehensible to them than his words. The nearest officer made a cutting gesture and growled something in Greek, probably telling Raynor to get out of the way or maybe to fuck off.

"Damn it," Kolt snarled. "Pull back. It's an ambush."

The cop pushed past him into the courtyard with several more of his buddies in tow.

Raynor hastily stuffed the unconscious crow's wrists into a pair of flex-cuffs, then keyed his mic. "Slap, we've got him pinned down in an apartment block, but something stinks here. You've got to convince the cops to pull back, go into siege mode, or a lot of people are going—"

The firecracker pop of semiautomatic pistol fire reverberated in the courtyard, intruding on the transmission. Raynor ducked reflexively, then looked up, searching the landings overhead to locate the site of the battle.

That was when the world exploded.

FIVE

Raynor dragged himself through the haze of smoke and dust, getting out of the way of the police and emergency workers who were heading into the blast zone. From a safer distance, he could see smoke billowing from the second-story windows of the flat.

It was not the first time he'd gotten his bell rung, nor was it the worst. Not even close. The blast had stunned him, knocked him flat, and pelted him with concrete fragments, some as large as both his fists put together, but he was back on his feet in a matter of seconds, or at least it seemed that way. He might have lost consciousness for a minute or two. It was hard to say, really. He ached all over, and knew that he would probably feel a lot worse in the hours and days to come, but didn't think he had sustained anything worse than scrapes and bruises. He was doing better than the police officers who had pushed past him at the entrance. They had been standing at ground zero when the bomb inside detonated.

Raynor reached for the push-to-talk, discovering only then that his radios weren't working. His phone, however, shielded inside an impact-resistant Otter Box, had survived intact. He went to his contacts and initiated a call. His ears were still ringing, masking the signaling tone, then he heard Slapshot's voice. Barely.

"Boss! We heard the shooter blew himself up. You okay?"

Raynor wasn't sure where to start. "Just get here."

"Hey, we're en route, Racer, hang on."

Raynor ended the call and turned back toward the blast site. Something about the scene didn't sit right with him.

Shiner wasn't some newly radicalized jihadist, itching for a chance to die a martyr's death and go out in a literal blaze of glory. He was a sniper, someone who preferred killing from a distance, concealment over confrontation. He certainly hadn't survived as long as he had by making stupid decisions.

Had this been the exception? Had the unexpectedly swift pursuit caused him to panic? Or had he used the bomb to cover his tracks, slipping out a back window after rigging the front door to blow?

Yeah, Raynor thought, nodding. *That's what he did. It's what I would have done.*

Raynor waited until they were back at the airport, in the repurposed hangar building they had been using as a combination bunk room and tactical operations center, to place a call to Colonel Webber at Fort Bragg. Kolt did not doubt that his commanding officer already knew about the incident, and he was a little surprised that Webber hadn't tried to call him first.

One reason for Raynor's delay in making contact was that he wanted to allow some time for things to settle down. In the aftermath of an international incident like this, there would be a tornado of conflicting reports and wild rumors, and truth be told, he didn't have enough information yet to answer the questions he knew the Delta Force commander would ask. Mostly, though, he was stalling because he knew Webber would probably chew his ass out for going Lone Ranger after Shiner.

Slapshot had given him an earful already. The sergeant major, accompanied by the squadron's master breacher, Digger, had found him outside the bombed-out apartment flat, and after a quick medical assessment to ensure that Raynor hadn't suffered anything more than a minor concussion, Slapshot had proceeded to tear him a new asshole. Raynor took the criticism without protest, recognizing the spirit in which it was being given. Slapshot was technically correct about Raynor's operational status—he was a squadron commander now, a coach, not a quarterback—but what Slap was really pissed off about was the fact that Raynor had gone after Shiner with zero backup. He was right, of course, but Raynor wasn't sure what he could have done differently in the moment. No doubt that would be a topic of discussion in the post-mission hotwash once they were back home at Bragg.

Interspersed with the colorfully worded inquiries about Raynor's sanity, Slapshot let slip that Stitch had located the sniper's shooting position on the mountain and recovered the weapon—a Russian-made Dragunov sniper rifle. The weapon was now in the hands of the Greek police, but hopefully it would yield some solid evidence to support Kolt's visual identification of Miric as the killer.

Not that it would matter much in the long run. The primary mission was over. POTUS was safe aboard Air Force One, probably halfway to Germany or some other contingency destination. Now all that remained was for the squadron to turn into pumpkins—Delta-speak for the end-of-mission transition. Raynor's operators were all accounted for, either at the hangar or at the international airport, preparing to fly out commercial once Greek authorities reopened the airspace. It wasn't Raynor's job as squadron CO to oversee the travel arrangements—the folks in the Unit cover shop handled that, which meant he pretty much had no more excuses not to phone Webber at Bragg.

"Racer," Webber growled over the line. "About damn time."

To call Raynor's relationship with Colonel Jeremy Webber unconventional was a monumental understatement. Webber had been his CO for a long time, which was unusual to begin with. By all rights, one or both of them should have been promoted out of the Unit—but Webber had risen about as far as time and politics would allow him to, and Raynor . . . well, Raynor's career trajectory had been about as predictable as a ricochet.

Eight years earlier, following a disastrous mission in Pakistan—a disaster for which Raynor was solely responsible—Webber had pulled the plug on Kolt's career, declaring him persona non grata to the Unit. Then, just three years later, while Kolt was drowning his sorrows in a bottle of Old Grandad, Webber had come to him with an offer of redemption: an off-the-books mission to locate a small group of MIA Delta operators being held captive by a Pashtun warlord in Pakistan.

Initially, Raynor had assumed that Webber was using him, playing on his guilt to get him to do something that no one with official status could do, and maybe even secretly hoping that Kolt would meet his end on that unsanctioned operation, thus balancing the cosmic scales for the lives that had been lost because of Raynor's earlier screwup. Maybe all of that had actually been true at the time, but after completing that mission, and thwarting a terrorist plot to take over a CIA-run black site, Raynor had been given an unprecedented second chance, regaining his rank and operational status.

It had not been easy. Returning to the Unit meant going through the Unit's unique Relook process, essentially a repeat of Delta selection, and a rite of passage to prove you were still physically and mentally fit to return to Delta's ranks. He'd barely skated through tryouts the first time as a young, fit Ranger officer. Relook was, without question, the most grueling experience, physically and emotionally, that he had ever endured, but even more challenging was the naked antipathy of his former mates, who believed the PNG was a life sentence.

But he had not failed. He had made his own luck.

Kolt realized now that Webber must have seen something in him, some unrealized potential, and even though he wasn't really sure what it was, Raynor had made it his personal mission in life to justify Webber's faith in him.

Raynor braced for impact while fumbling with the thought of leading with some bullshit excuse. But before he could launch into an explanation, the colonel added, "Outstanding job, by the way."

Kolt wondered if it had been meant sarcastically. That wasn't Webber's style, but this was an unusual situation. "Sir?"

"You singlehandedly ran down the man who assassinated the Greek prime minister," Webber went on. "From POTUS on down, I'm told you're the man of the hour."

Raynor still couldn't tell if Webber was being disingenuous. "It was Shiner. Rasim Miric."

"Shiner," Webber echoed. "Your bogeyman? The one-eyed sniper, from the Rat abortion in Bosnia? You're sure?"

"PID. My front sight was on his forehead. He grabbed an innocent kid before I could break the shot, but I saw his face. It was him."

"Small world, Kolt. Langley and JSOC are scrubbing the intel traffic to see how we missed the pre-mission threat. We'll add that to the parameters."

"I had the shot, sir," Kolt said. "I hesitated."

"No doubt there will be some international fallout over this. Greeks lost several men in the blast, with a few more on the bubble."

"Damn, sir," Kolt said. "That sucks."

"You've been around long enough to know how it

works, Kolt. Can't control all the variables." He paused, then added, "Regardless, we can close that target folder."

Raynor took a deep breath before answering. "I'm not so sure about that."

"He blew himself up, Racer," Webber said. "CNN is already running the Greek authorities' statement, so it must be true."

Now that was definitely sarcasm, Raynor thought with a faint grin. "Desperation and suicide aren't Shiner's style. Neither is martyrdom."

"Faked his death. You give him a lot of credit, Kolt."

It wasn't really a question, but Raynor felt compelled to present his argument. "He led me straight back to that apartment and thirty seconds later, everything inside was vaporized. That was either a contingency or a rookie mistake. Shiner isn't a rookie, and he hasn't stayed alive and off the radar this long by making mistakes like one."

Webber hummed thoughtfully. "Well, either he's dead or he isn't. Find out."

"He is dead." Kostas Drougas waved a hand dismissively, the unfiltered cigarette in his hand leaving trails of smoke in the air. "We have his body. Thanks to you."

Raynor thought he detected a faintly accusatory tone, but decided to chalk it up to cultural differences—Drougas spoke English well, if not fluently—and the fact that the EKAM commander was clearly redlining in the stress department. Although it was just midafternoon—only about four hours had passed since the assassination of the prime minister—the counterterrorism officer looked exhausted. Like the legendary figure who had inspired his Secret Service code name—Hercules— Drougas, a broadly built man with salt-and-pepper hair, looked like he was holding the weight of the world on his shoulders. The inevitable relentless demand from politicians and reporters alike for answers—answers that could not be simply pulled out of thin air—had already begun. Raynor knew from personal experience that this shit sandwich, and ultimately most of the blame for failing to prevent the tragedy in the first place, would land squarely on Drougas and the counterterror operators who, despite being underfunded and constricted by senseless political decisions, managed to get it right ninety-nine times out of a hundred. None of those earlier successes would matter, though.

The irony of it was that Drougas would blame himself, too.

Raynor glanced past the police colonel to the bombed-out remains of the apartment building. The site was crawling with investigators in hazmat suits. An area of several square blocks had been cordoned off, the residents of neighboring structures presumably removed from their homes, and probably relocated to a police facility for questioning. There wasn't really anything for Drougas, in his capacity as commander of the antiterrorism unit, to do on site. Actionable intel following something like this came out of forensic laboratories and interrogation rooms. Kolt guessed he was there because it was where his superiors expected him to be.

"I'd like to see the body," Raynor said, returning his attention to the police official. He had supplied Drougas with the identity of the sniper, though he had not gone into detail about his personal history with Miric or explicitly told Drougas—or anyone else aside from Webber—of his suspicions that Shiner had faked his death, but the Greek policeman was canny enough to see where Kolt was going with his request.

Drougas sighed. "The remains were taken to hospital. I will arrange for you to see them, but there is not much to see. The blast . . ." He simulated a miniature explosion with his fingertips. "But it is your one-eyed man. I do not doubt this."

"Why not?"

Drougas put the cigarette between his teeth and then tapped his cheek under his right eye. "The eye. It is made of glass."

"Right or left eye?"

Drougas gave an irritated snort and moved his finger to the opposite cheek. "Left. Right. I don't remember. How many one-eyed men did you see going into the flat?"

Raynor let the question slide. If Shiner had gone to the trouble of staging the death scene with a body double, he would not have screwed up a major detail like the placement of the prosthetic eye. "The eye survived intact?"

Drougas waggled a hand. "More or less."

"Find anything else interesting in there?"

"Aside from what remains of three police officers who won't be going home to their wives and children tonight?" Drougas shook his head. "The flat was rented a week ago by someone calling himself Nikos Roupa.

That name appears to be an alias. He listed his previous residence as Komotini. It is a city in the north. Many immigrants there. Turks. Slavs. Many Muslims. The owner of the building said that he spoke with an accent. Bulgarian, she thinks. She also confirmed that this so-called Roupa appeared to have a false eye."

"That's Miric," Raynor said. "He's Bosnian."

"As you say." Drougas gave his cigarette a disdainful flick. "The man you captured. He is with Epanastatikos Agonas."

Raynor was familiar with EA—the name translated to "Revolutionary Struggle"—currently the most active of Greece's many far-left terrorist organizations. Formed in 2002 from the remnants of a similar group called November 17, they were an anarchist paramilitary group opposed to capitalism, globalization, and American influence in Greek politics. They were your garden-variety rabble-rousers dabbling in bank heists and attacks on government-owned buildings using IEDs. More recently they'd added assassination attempts to their portfolio.

Drougas took another drag from the cigarette before tossing it over his shoulder. "We are running down his known associates. We may also be able to link the explosives to other EA bombings."

"Miric isn't a Marxist."

"A hired gun, then."

"Doesn't it strike you as odd that EA would pass up a shot at POTUS?" Raynor asked.

"America is not the center of the world, my friend, no matter what you Americans believe. A dead American president changes nothing in Greece. A dead prime minister not only leaves a vacancy at the top, but it creates fear among those who would seek to fill it. And among the public. Our country has been on the edge for so long. This may be the push that sends us into oblivion." Drougas shook his head again, then straightened as if trying to shed his exhaustion. "From a kilometer away, it is a wonder this one-eyed sniper was able to hit anyone at all."

"Not this sniper," Raynor replied. "Shiner doesn't miss."

Drougas's eyes narrowed in a scrutinizing stare. "You don't believe it was really him in there, do you?"

Raynor still wasn't ready to commit to that position. "I'll know when I see the body."

On the way back to his car, Raynor took out his phone and scrolled down his contact list. Hawk's number leapt out at him and he almost called her directly, but then thought better of it. Instead, he sent a text message to Slapshot, instructing him to have Hawk and Shaft meet him at Laiko General Hospital.

Prior to joining Delta, Cindy "Hawk" Bird had been a 74D—army-speak for Chemical, Biological, Radiological, and Nuclear Specialist—searching for WMDs in Iraq and Libya, a job that required both technical expertise and critical thinking. Kolt wanted her and Shaft to help him make sense of the physical evidence the police investigators had collected, starting with the human remains. It was a perfectly reasonable request, and because Delta operators did not rigidly hew to the regular army chain-of-command procedures, there was nothing inappropriate about contacting either of them directly. But there were other reasons why Raynor tried to avoid casual interactions with Cindy Bird.

Hawk was an operator and one of Kolt's mates, the same as Digger and Slapshot. Just one of the guys. He believed that, and scrupulously treated her that way. His expectations for her were no different than for anyone else in the squadron. She had earned the right to be treated that way, both through her performance in the Delta pilot program to train female operators, and in her subsequent actions in combat situations. She and Raynor had fought together, bled together, and saved each other's asses more times than he could count. But none of that changed the fact that Kolt was both physically and emotionally attracted to her and, unless he was reading the signs wrong, she to him as well.

They were both professional enough to resist the impulse to act on those feelings. In their line of work that kind of relationship could end more than just a career. But Raynor knew the sparks of sexual tension between them had not gone unnoticed by others in the Unit, and possibly some outside it as well. So, to ensure that no one drew any wrong conclusions about the nature of their relationship, Raynor made a point of adding an extra layer of insulation between himself and Cindy Bird.

The hospital was only about a mile from the blasted apartment, but Raynor waited for Hawk and Shaft to arrive before going in. The Delta operators had changed into the generic work uniform. Hawk's black hair was pulled back in a ponytail that protruded from the opening at the back of her cap, and swished back and forth behind her as she walked toward him. She had vaguely Asian features, which were mostly hidden from view by the cap's visor, and her loose-fitting windbreaker concealed a lithe, athletic body that was—pound for pound—as strong and tough as most of her fellow operators.

Raynor realized he was staring at her and forced himself to look away.

"Hey, boss," Shaft called out. "You good?"

It occurred to Kolt that he had not explained his reasons for requesting Hawk and Shaft to join him, and that the location of the meeting must have caused the medically trained operator to assume the worst.

"It's not me," he explained. "They've got—" He stopped himself. No sense in creating bias. "A body was recovered from the apartment that blew up. It's probably the shooter, but I want to get a second opinion." The two assaulters exchanged a glance, then Shaft nodded. "Lead the way."

Raynor did so, and was directed by the receptionist to the hospital morgue, where a medical examiner from the Forensic Science Division was waiting with the remains of the man tentatively identified as Nikos Roupa.

Drougas had not been exaggerating the extent of damage caused by the blast. The pieces of the body lay on a stainless tray table like a partially assembled jigsaw puzzle, a puzzle with a lot of pieces missing. The blast had stripped away a considerable amount of muscle tissue and pulverized the bones, particularly in the torso, which, to Raynor's untrained eye, suggested that the man—he couldn't bring himself to believe that it was actually Miric—had either been holding the bomb when the detonation occurred, or wearing it.

Raynor had seen his share of carnage over the years. It was worse, a lot worse, when the body on the slab belonged to a mate, but even when the victim was a complete stranger—or an asshole terrorist suicide bomber—there was an indefinable wrongness about it. It didn't look like Miric on the table, but then again, it didn't look like anyone anymore. He saw Hawk flinch a little as she got a look at the pieces and knew he wasn't the only one who felt it.

He stood back and let Shaft and Hawk take the lead. They listened patiently as the medical examiner, in his best broken English, inventoried the pieces and explained their significance.

Based on bone measurements, the body was male and approximately 170 centimeters—five feet, six inches—in height. There was nothing left of the hands, so fingerprint identification was impossible. The lower jaw had been pulverized but the medical examiner was confident that a positive identification from dental records would be possible, provided of course that those records existed in the first place. There were no dental or medical records for Rasim Miric, at least none that Raynor had been able to locate, but if the body wasn't Shiner—if it was, for instance, a random homeless person that Shiner had grabbed off the street—such a record might exist. The same was true for DNA identification, but it might be hours or days before a search of those records yielded a result.

Then the medical examiner showed them the one

piece of evidence that he believed might expedite the process: Shiner's glass eye.

Despite the commonly used nomenclature, ocular prosthetics are not typically made of glass, but rather from a shatter-resistant acrylic compound called polymethyl methacrylate, better known by the trade name Plexiglas. The blast had driven the convex shell deep into the skull cavity, which had kept it mostly intact; enough so, the medical examiner assured them, that they would be able to determine the point of manufacture and, quite probably, the identity of the recipient.

Of course, Raynor thought, even if the eye had belonged to Shiner, that wasn't proof positive that the rest of the body did, too.

"Can you pinpoint the time and cause of death?" Raynor asked.

Shaft and Hawk looked back at him with raised eyebrows, but the medical examiner seemed unperturbed by the question. "He was alive when the explosion occurred, if that is what you are asking. I think we can infer the rest."

Raynor nodded, but in his head he was already working out how Miric might have kept his body double alive: sedated perhaps, or maybe just tied up, wearing a bomb vest.

Shaft held his gaze. "Seems cut and dry, boss."

Kolt wondered if he was losing perspective, obsessing on one remote possibility and ignoring the obvious evidence to the contrary. But if Miric was still alive, every second spent trying to prove it was letting him slip farther and farther away.

He shook his head. "Let's get out of here."

As they headed for the exit, his phone buzzed in his pocket. It was Webber. Raynor took a second to order his thoughts, composing his argument for continuing the hunt for Shiner, but Webber didn't give him the chance.

"New orders," the colonel said without preamble. "The state funeral for the prime minister will be happening in four days. The current threat condition won't allow POTUS to attend, so he's sending VPOTUS in his place. In the interest of maintaining regional stability and assisting our NATO partners, you are to coordinate with EKAM and assist in eradicating the terrorist group responsible for the assassination of the Greek prime minister. ASAP. Revolutionary Struggle is now Noble Squadron's gig."

Raynor's nostrils flared at the mention of the vice president, but he kept his ire out of his voice. "Understood, sir. We're all over it."

"And, Colonel Raynor, just in case you missed my last inference," Webber said, "I'm serious. This is your squadron's mission, not Kolt Raynor's personal mission."

"Roger that, sir."

"Take care of the vice, get through the funeral, and get back to Bragg. No international incidents!"

"Yes, sir," Kolt said. "Clean op on our end."

SIX

The close call, coming as it did on the heels of the perfectly executed assassination, had left Rasim Miric rattled.

He had, of course, prepared for the possibility . . . no, the inevitability of discovery. The police were not stupid. He had known they would realize where the killing shot had come from. They would find his rifle, and the fingerprints on it would lead them to the apartment of Nikos Roupa, and a body double with thirty kilos of ANFO on his lap. Ammonium nitrate fuel oil, an improvised explosive compound favored by terrorist organizations worldwide, including his partners of the moment, Epanastatikos Agonas—Revolutionary Struggle. Everything that had actually transpired was according to his plan, but it had all happened much more quickly than he had anticipated.

It had been a close thing. From the moment when he had connected the trigger wire to the door of his flat until the subsequent blast, there had been only about fifteen seconds. He had barely cleared the window, dropping to the ground a fraction of a second before the shock wave knocked him flat. In the immediate aftermath of the explosion, he was just one more victim staggering away from the scene, seeking medical attention.

Now, in the relative safety of another apartment flat, a safe house established by his handler, an officer of the Millî İstihbarat Teşkilatı—the Turkish national intelligence service—he was able to give thought to the man who had almost caught him on the slopes of Mount Lycabettus, appearing out of nowhere as if magnetically drawn to him, and then relentlessly pursued him across half the city.

How did he know?

It did not matter now.

The man who had killed the prime minister was dead—at least that was what the news reports were saying. Miric had no idea how long that fiction would endure; hopefully long enough for him to get out of the country.

His phone began vibrating on the tabletop. He took a breath, then opened his eye and answered the call. "Yes?"

"You called for a ride?"

"I'll be right out."

He rose from the table and headed outside to where a black Toyota Prius was waiting. He opened the door and settled into the passenger's seat. The driver, his MIT handler, who went by the name Mehmet, waited until they were moving to speak. "Well done, my friend."

Miric did not think of Mehmet as a friend, but they had known each other for a few years and spilled the blood of their enemies together, which was probably as close to friendship as Miric would ever get. He also knew he would never be anything more than an asset to the Turkish intelligence officer. "Save your congratulations until we are across the border."

"We have already won," Mehmet said, and even though Miric couldn't see him, he knew the Turk was grinning. "The Golden Dawn nationalists will sweep into power, just as we predicted. They will reject the EU and NATO, reject all Western influence. No matter what else happens, that much is a certainty."

Miric was not as sanguine about this perceived victory, but then he was not an ideologue like Mehmet. It was a game of chess to the Turk, and Miric was his knight, able to leap across the board in order to strike a blow deep in enemy territory.

Ideologies aside, Miric was proud of what he had accomplished. Mehmet was correct in his assessment of the geopolitical fallout.

The death of the Greek prime minister would not merely create a vacancy at the top. It would enrage the already polarized populace. The assassination would be seen as the ultimate failure of the moderate government to protect its citizens from Marxist terrorists and Muslim extremists. Pro-nationalists—men like the radio personality Miric had listened to earlier in the day from his hide—would demand a new government, a strong government, no longer beholden to the European Union or NATO.

Nor was there anything those Western governments could do to stop it from happening. A wildfire of right-wing nationalism was sweeping across Europe. The United Kingdom had already voted to leave the EU. America was a house divided, on the verge of internal collapse, weaker than at any time in modern history, a superpower in name only.

The immediate effect of a Greek exit from the EU and NATO would be an end to opposition to Turkey's bid to join the European Union. The long-standing rivalry between Greece and Turkey would end with a whimper rather than a bang as the former, unable to pay its debts and completely isolated from the international community, slipped further into irrelevancy.

Yet that was only the first move in a far more ambitious endgame. The Turkish government, under the leadership of the charismatic and openly pro-Islamist prime minister Recep Tayyip Erdoğan, would step forward as the economic and political savior of the EU, and the undisputed regional military leader of NATO. After enduring a century of exile, the Ottoman Empire would rise from the ashes.

It was an ambitious game, and the Turks were playing to win. They would not hesitate to sacrifice their knight if it suited their needs, particularly since Miric was both a foreigner and a mercenary. He understood his place in their schemes, but he was a survivor. He wanted . . . no, he needed to live long enough to see America brought to her knees.

Mehmet laughed again. "Don't worry, my friend. We will not be discovered. Nobody is looking for you now."

Miric thought again about the man on the motorcycle. If anyone was looking for him, it would be that man. Had he been one of the three police officers the news reports said had been killed in the bomb blast?

The Turkish intelligence officer said nothing more as he navigated out of the city, but a few minutes later, as they joined the flow of traffic heading north on Motorway 1, he reached over the center console and pointed to the glove box. "Your new identity is in there."

Miric thumbed open the compartment and took out a yellow envelope. He tore it open and shook out the contents: a burgundy-colored EU passport, issued by the government of Croatia; a folded sheet of paper with the biographical details of his legend; and a wallet with credit cards in the name of Dusan Juric and snapshots of people Miric had never seen before.

He flipped open the passport and examined the picture. His picture, taken several months earlier. It showed him with his prosthetic eye instead of the eye patch he now sported, and he self-consciously touched his face, wondering how much the vacancy in his eye socket would alter his appearance. He could certainly feel the difference. Not the absence of his sight—that was something he had mostly come to terms with—but the emptiness.

He wondered when, if ever, he would get a chance to replace the lost prosthetic.

He pocketed the passport and wallet, then skimmed the legend. Dusan Juric was a Bosnian Croat who had relocated to Zagreb following the Balkan conflicts. His mother and sister—presumably the faces in the photographs—still lived in Sarajevo. He would have plenty of time to memorize the details before they reached the border with Macedonia, though it was unlikely that he would need to call upon that knowledge. Dusan Juric would soon be discarded, just as Nikos Roupa before him, albeit in a less dramatic fashion.

He would have many more identities in the days ahead as he made his way to the homeland of his enemies, where he would have his final revenge.

SEVEN

As he reviewed the police files for Revolutionary Struggle and its suspected members, two things became apparent to Raynor.

First, like so many other left-wing groups that popped up across Europe like mushrooms in a cow pasture, EA was a bush-league terrorist outfit. Even that description was overly generous. They were more like an after-school club for home-grown revolutionaries. They had big dreams but only enough in the way of resources to be a nuisance, particularly since 2010, when the police had raided the homes of several suspected members—six were in prison, including the man believed to be the leader of the organization, and one was in the ground. The 2010 raids had also turned up a small arsenal of guns, grenades, rockets, and more than a hundred thousand euros, which indicated they were getting limited financial support from somewhere, enough at least to hire the services of someone like Rasim Miric if he was feeling charitable, but nothing major league. Since then, there had been only a single attack attributed to the group—a car bomb detonated outside the headquarters of the national bank. Raynor was having difficulty accepting Drougas's narrative that EA had masterminded the assassination plot.

The second realization was that it didn't matter what he thought. Drougas was going to move on the group regardless of whether they were actually involved, and Delta was going to have to help him do it.

The EKAM colonel wasn't any happier about the partnership than Raynor. The joint operation felt like an affront to him and his operators, especially in the wake of the assassination they had failed to prevent. For his part, Raynor knew that EKAM had the capability to get the job done without outside assistance, but had concerns about their temperament. Nevertheless, he understood the political motivation behind the partnership, and figured Drougas did as well. Both POTUS and the interim prime minster wanted to give the Greek people a demonstration of international cooperation, proof that the NATO alliance still meant something.

In other words, it was fucked up as a football bat.

"You feeling it on this one, Racer?" Slapshot asked.

Kolt looked away from the eight-by-ten color mug shots of a dozen Revolutionary Struggle dirtbags pinned to the wall, gave a long spit of Red Man into an empty water bottle, and licked his lips. "I'll feel better about it once Kilo gets eyes on."

"No, boss, I'm talking about this joint-op crap JSOC

shit us," Slapshot shot back. "These guys seem to have their act together. We seem to be the ugly sister at the party."

"At least we have separate targets and don't have to worry about their CQB skills," Kolt said.

"This is their show, Racer, not ours. Why are we even on deck?"

"That's not what you were saying after the Paris attacks or the Brussels attacks," Kolt reminded his mate. "You were bitching up and down the Spine about not getting deployment orders to help out."

"Touché, Racer, touché," Slapshot said with a smile. "But these Revolutionary Struggle yo-yos are amateurs."

Raynor couldn't argue that, but regardless, Revolutionary Struggle did pose some kind of real threat, so Kolt had no objection to taking them out. Political opposition to capitalism or globalization was one thing, but acts of violence that endangered innocent civilians automatically voided all philosophical or moral arguments, and as far as Raynor was concerned, the revolutionaries' right to keep sucking oxygen. The only real concern was what Slapshot elected not to mention: that Drougas, in his eagerness, might put the lives of Kolt's operators in unnecessary jeopardy.

From the EA member Kolt had taken down outside Shiner's last known position, Drougas's investigators had produced two targets. EKAM would be going after Dmitris Xiros, a known anarchist and suspected senior leader of Revolutionary Struggle. Delta's target for the night was the home of Angelos Souri, another EA suspect and a known associate of Xiros.

EKAM would be taking point on the operation, calling the shots strategically, but tactical decisions were the jurisdiction of the assaulters on the scene, which also left Raynor out of the process. He was the squadron leader now, overseeing the big-picture stuff, which Hercules had already pretty much laid out. Major Barnes would be designing and leading the assault while Raynor would have to settle for listening to it all live on comms in the JOC with Slapshot and Digger.

"Residential neighborhood," Barnes reported in. "No good spots for Kilo team to set up, so we made a couple of drive-bys. The target building is quiet. Maybe vacant. Looks like a bust to me."

The memory of the explosive device that had been waiting behind Shiner's apartment door was still foremost in Raynor's mind. "The suspect in custody might have been intentionally steering us into trouble. Could be a trap."

"Or just a dry hole." Barnes made no attempt to hide his disdain for Kolt's gut feeling. "We'll be careful going in, but that doesn't change the fact that there's really only one way to know for sure."

Raynor had to fight the impulse to offer any more unsolicited advice. He had already provided his commander's intent and directed some courses of action to consider, but it was Barnes's show now.

Even though the troop commander was slavishly devoted to the sync matrix, Raynor knew that the plan for the hit had been developed with significant input from Stitch, Shaft, and other more experienced operators. They would evacuate and occupy the neighboring

apartment, insert fiberoptic cameras through the walls
to get a look inside, and then, at 0230—H-hour, when
Drougas's people initiated their assault plan at the residence of Dmitris Xiros—Barnes's crew would utilize
multiple entry points to take control of Souri's apartment in one fell swoop. The neighbors wouldn't be happy
about the disruption, but it was nothing some plaster and
a coat of paint couldn't fix, which was more than could
be said for the mess Shiner had left behind.

It was an unconventional plan, well thought out, and
required the skill sets Raynor knew his operators possessed. The only thing wrong with it was that he would
be watching from the sidelines.

Cindy "Hawk" Bird rapped her knuckles gently but in-
sistently on the door. She resisted the urge to look over
her shoulder at the door to the apartment on the opposite side of the landing, the home of Angelos Souri, the
actual target for the impending hit. After a few seconds,
she knocked again, a little more forcefully, stopping
only when a mumbled voice was audible from inside.

She threw a questioning glance at the Greek police
officer dressed in dark blue coveralls complete with a
name tag on one side of his chest and the logo of a local
carpet company on the other. The officer stood just a
few steps to her right, on the second-to-last tread of the
descending stairwell and just out of view of the peep-
holes inset in the doors. He returned a nod to indicate
that she was doing fine.

Outside, holed up in a gray panel van adorned with
the same logo, Shaft, two other assaulters, and the

squadron communicator were in blue coveralls under full kit, with weapons cocked and locked, ready for a hasty assault if things went pear-shaped.

Hawk was in street clothes, unarmed. Her gear and weapons were in the van, stashed in a large black hockey bag.

The apartment door opened to reveal a heavy middle-aged man in a stained undershirt and boxer shorts. The smell of stale tobacco and garlic assaulted her nostrils, but she managed a warm smile and threw her arms wide invitingly. The tenant's mouth was open, ready with a question, but when he got a look at her, his questioning expression became a welcoming smile. But as he stepped out onto the landing, ready to accept her embrace, she drew back and touched a finger to her lips, urging him to silence. The man's smile slipped as he realized that she was not alone, but the ruse had already achieved its intended purpose. Without uttering a word and at minimal risk of exposure, she had gained access to the apartment from which the assault would be launched.

That, Hawk thought, was why the Unit needed more female operators.

She didn't like thinking of herself that way—as a female operator. She had earned her status with Delta, survived selection and OTC the same as every one of the men standing on the steps below. If anything, she had been held to a higher standard by men who were convinced that a woman was physically and emotionally incapable of performing the tasks of a Delta assaulter. She was a better shot than most, and excelled in language acquisition and other critical skills. Ironically,

she had seen a lot more action during her time as a candidate in the training program than she had as an operator. But no amount of hard work or valorous sacrifice
would ever remove the qualifier. Just like Neil Arm-
strong would always be "the first man on the moon,"
she would always be the first female operator in Delta
Force. She just hoped she would not be the last.

The police officer flashed his credentials, spoke
sternly to the man in Greek, and gestured for the man
to follow him. After another quick exchange in Greek,
the officer handed the man a rolled-up wad of euro
banknotes before ushering him back to the front door.
The officer turned to Hawk, whispered in English, "He
lives alone. You can go in."

As the policeman ushered the still-shocked tenant
down the stairs, Hawk took another step back, masking
the peephole in the door behind her with her back while
she thumbed her cell to call up her teammates. A few
minutes later, she heard a light rap on the door and
peered through the peephole. She could see Shaft, oddly
distorted by the peephole lens, with a ten-foot piece of
rolled-up carpet over one shoulder. Several others were
just off the edge of her viewport, but she could make
out two more large rolled pieces of carpet. It was past
the close of business but not so late that anyone in the
neighborhood would be suspicious of a carpet delivery. H-hour was still a ways off. Hawk opened the
door and stood back as her mates silently filed into the
apartment.

Once they were inside she turned and peered through

the peephole for a full two minutes, watching the opposite apartment to see if anyone would come out to investigate her visit. No one did.

She pulled away from the door and went to join the others. While she dug out her tactical light-armor vest, she watched the others unroll the carpets, exposing the gear and weapons they'd need for the hit that night. One of her mates—Venti, so named for his Starbucks addiction—had climbed onto a desktop and was boring a hole in the wall, about an inch below the ceiling. The ACUSTEK low-noise drilling system equipped with a diamond-tipped Teflon-coated drill bit made almost no sound at all, but there was still a risk of discovery, which was why the other assaulter, Joker, was standing by with his HK MP5K-PDW at the ready while Shaft readied the snake camera.

Venti looked down and nodded, then reversed the drill motor, backing the bit out to reveal a hole barely larger than the diameter of a cigarette. He moved the drill rig aside and took the camera from Shaft, inserting it into the hole. The camera, which was connected via Bluetooth to Shaft's laptop computer, showed only darkness for a moment, but then a tiny spot of light appeared on the screen, increasing in size as the camera moved closer to the exit hole on the far side. Hawk held her breath in anticipation of her first glimpse inside the objective.

The two apartments had the same basic floor plan, but reversed, and shared a long wall in the front room and one bedroom. Heavy blankets covered the windows,

which explained why the recce team had been unable
to detect any activity inside. The room was dark except
for the light issuing from a television screen on the opposite wall, but the camera was in FLIR mode and the
interior was fully revealed. The volume on the TV set
was turned down, but Hawk could see that it was tuned
to a news broadcast, with Greek captions running across
the screen. Venti slowly rotated the camera, revealing
more of the room, including the six human figures that
occupied it.

Shaft raised a hand, giving the signal to freeze, and
the camera stopped moving.

There were four men and two women. All were
quietly—almost pensively—watching the television.
Two of them looked like they might be on the verge of
nodding off, but the others appeared alert, almost man-
ically so. No one spoke, and whenever someone moved
to sip from a water bottle or take a drag from a cigarette, it was with a deliberate slowness, as if they knew
that someone might be watching. Hawk studied the
faces and recognized four of them from the list of suspected Revolutionary Struggle members Drougas had
supplied. Souri was there, but so was someone else they
had not expected to see. She reached out a finger and
tapped the screen. "That's Dmitris Xiros," she whispered.

Shaft nodded and keyed the mic of his MBITR radio.
"Noble Two-One, this is Noble Alpha-One."

He spoke quietly, but Hawk heard him clearly in the
earpiece of her own comms unit. She also heard the reply from Barnes, who was on the roof with Stitch and a

second assault team, preparing to rappel down and go in through the windows. "Send it, Alpha."

"Looks like the party's here tonight. We've got six crows in the front room watching the boob tube. Xiros is here."

"Xiros? Hercules won't be happy about that," Barnes said after a moment. "All right, stand by."

Hawk surmised that Barnes was relaying the news to Raynor, who was following the op from the JOC. While they waited, Hawk continued to scrutinize the feed, and saw something she had missed before.

"Subguns," she whispered. "On the coffee table. I make four of them. Might be MP5s."

Shaft looked, then nodded. "Venti, get another camera in the bedroom. Let's make sure there aren't any other surprises in there."

The other assaulter nodded and headed into the adjoining room with his silent drill rig. A moment later, Barnes's voice returned over the comms. "Alpha-One, we have execute authority from Racer. We've got our targets contained, so we're going to move now. What's it look like in there?"

Shaft quickly described the layout of the room and the location of the suspected terrorists, assigning each of them a number. He did not fail to mention the small arsenal sitting on the coffee table.

"Shit," Barnes said. "Hercules wants these guys alive, if possible."

"That ain't really up to us," Shaft pointed out.

Before Barnes could respond, Venti broke in. "Putting the camera in now."

Shaft hit a couple of keys and the screen split to show the feed. The pane on the right revealed the room in glorious monochrome.

"Uuuuuhh . . . don't think I want to sleep in that bedroom," Shaft muttered.

Although there was a mattress, tilted up against the wall, the room appeared to have been repurposed for storage, specifically the storage of at least three dozen twenty-liter plastic buckets, the kind restaurants used for food prep. Hawk was pretty sure the containers weren't full of sliced pickles. The buckets were all lidded, with thin tubes—possibly wires—sprouting from holes drilled in the top of each.

"Okay," Shaft said. "That's not good." He looked up at Hawk. "I'm thinking ANFO."

Hawk did some quick mental math. "About half a ton, I'd say. Enough for a couple of small car bombs. What do you want to bet they're planning to hit the state funeral?"

"Who the hell knows?" Shaft said.

"That stuff's pretty stable, right?" Hawk asked.

Shaft nodded. "You need a small high-explosive booster charge—say a couple sticks of dynamite—to achieve detonation. Explosive breach is out. Nine-bangers are good."

Hawk saw what he was driving at. Their plan was to blast their way into the residence with shaped charges, and then deploy flash-bang grenades to stun the crows inside. By the numbers, it would take a lot more concussive force than that to detonate the ammonium nitrate and fuel oil mixture in the buckets, but she also knew they would all be staking their lives on that calculation. "What if they've already got them rigged with HE triggers?"

"That would change things, yes," Shaft said.

Shaft keyed the comms again and updated Barnes with this latest wrinkle.

The young troop commander considered his reply for several seconds. "Okay, we'll have to scrub the wall breach. Take your element in through the front door."

Shaft switched back to the feed from the first camera. No one in the front room had moved. Two men were seated in chairs to either end of the sofa. Xiros was one of them.

"We'll stay with the window charge. No change to our breach point," Barnes went on. "Alive is the preferred option, but I'm not telling you to ignore the combat ROE. This is a designated hostile target."

"Roger. Give us two mikes to get set." Shaft turned to Joker. "Take point. Venti, number two. I'm pushing the stick."

Cindy Bird listened to Shaft give the lineup, saying a silent prayer that she wouldn't be sidelined again.

"Hawk, you're our eyes."

She bit back an angry protest, and instead simply said, "Roger."

Shaft was the boss, and he probably had his reasons for leaving her behind. Venti and Joker were both seasoned door-kickers, and it just made sense to put them at the tip of the spear. But how was she ever going to get to their level if she was always warming the bench?

She turned to the computer, staring at the screen with

laserlike focus in an unsuccessful attempt to hide her disappointment. As her teammates headed for the front door, Hawk picked up the laptop and moved into the apartment's kitchen, where she hoped the appliances would give her an additional layer of cover in the event that a stray round came through the walls.

Shaft's voice came over the comms. "This is Alpha-One, we're set. Ready to execute."

Barnes spoke next. "Golf-Two, cut building power on 'two.' I say again, on 'two.' How copy, over?"

The recce team operator with the call sign Noble Golf-Two, who was standing by at the electrical main for the building, signaled his readiness. "Cutting power on two, roger."

"Alpha-Four, give final target update. Over."

Hawk started a little when she heard her call sign. In fact, it kind of pissed her off.

How the hell did Barnes know I was going to be stuck with the cameras?

Hawk looked back at the dual screen. No change to the room with the containers. The other camera showed the six crows in the neighboring apartment, still watching the television news, completely unaware of what was about to happen in their world.

She keyed her mic. "This is Alpha-Four. No change; six crows unaware and chilling in the living room. Over."

"All elements, this is Noble Two-One, I have control. Stand by . . . Five . . . four . . ."

As Barnes started the countdown, Hawk realized she was squeezing the pistol grip of her suppressed PDW.

"Three . . . two . . ."

The television screen in the apartment went dark, which only slightly changed the image from the camera feed. The six crows barely reacted, as if a sudden power outage was an everyday event.

"One . . . execute. Execute. Execute."

The blankets over the windows erupted inward and then crumpled to the floor, revealing a pair of Delta assaulters climbing through each, trailing tactical ropes, their faces hidden by NODs and black balaclavas. Something flashed into view briefly in the corner of the display, right about where the front door would have been.

Hawk watched as the seated figures reacted now, but their movements were jerky and uncoordinated. One of them reached for the coffee table, then just as quickly slumped back onto the sofa, stopped cold by a controlled pair from one of the assaulters.

Hawk kept a keen eye on the screen while holding her push-to-talk only centimeters from her mouth, ready to send Shaft or Barnes a message if needed. One of the men seated in a chair threw his hands up, then appeared to have a change of heart and also made a move toward the arsenal on the table. He too went down.

But not before getting his finger on the trigger of a subgun.

Hawk let out a gasp as she saw one of the assaulters near the window take a burst from the dying crow's MP5. She couldn't make out the man's call sign patch, but judging by his broad shoulders and compact build, she knew it had to be "Stitch" Vickery. The burst knocked Stitch back, through the blown-out second-story window, erasing him from the fight.

Hawk knew that Stitch's armor had probably taken the brunt of the attack, and since he was still clipped in to his rappelling line, the fall wasn't likely to be a problem, but even so, a wounded eagle on the objective was every operator's worst nightmare. It was a brutal reminder that any one of them could buy it, anytime. And seeing your buddy go down could be a fatal distraction, no matter how prepared for it you thought you were.

Which was probably why the rest of the assaulting force didn't see one of the female crows making a dash for the edge of the room.

"Shit," Hawk whispered to herself. "Squirter."

Even as she said it, she realized that the squirter was not heading for an exit. She was running for the bedroom.

Hawk jumped in over the assault net. "This is Alpha-Four. Female entered bedroom with containers."

There was no immediate answer from the assaulters.

Hawk watched the female close the bedroom door behind her and jam something under the doorknob, some type of locking device that angled down to the bedroom floor. With the door secure, the woman immediately started dragging the heavy containers in front of the door, creating a secondary barricade. Her actions seemed a little too rehearsed to Hawk.

That bitch isn't panicking. She knows what she's doing!

"Alpha-Four, bedroom door is barricaded with the

containers," Hawk said, trying to remain calm. She watched the woman intently, expecting her to do something crazy.

Shaft came up next. "Roger, we're on it."

"No explosives," Hawk added. "I say again, no explosives."

"Alpha Four, this is Two-One, we're working a mechanical breach now." It was Major Barnes. "Is the woman armed?"

Barnes's transmission from inside the target apartment directly to Hawk barely registered. She had been watching woman dig around a few desk drawers, obviously looking for something. When she stood back up Hawk would swear she saw something in the woman's right hand: a metal capsule about the size of a tennis ball.

Holy shit!

At that instant, Hawk knew that she had the only eyes on the problem, a problem that might potentially drop the entire building, and certainly kill her and her mates next door. There was only one correct response.

"All elements, this is Noble Alpha-Four. FIRE DRILL! FIRE DRILL! FIRE DRILL!"

As soon as the warning was given, Hawk jumped from her position on the floor in the kitchen, left the laptop behind, and triggered the SureFire tactical light attached to the rails of her PDW. She launched into motion, sprinting across the front room and into the door of the bedroom.

The room smelled of tobacco, stale sweat, and body odor. A mattress lay on the floor a few steps away, the linens strewn haphazardly across it. Beyond that was the wall that separated Hawk from the bedroom filled with a thousand pounds of improvised explosives and the female terrorist with a complete case of the ass against the world.

Her earpiece was filled with subsequent calls from her mates, repeating the code word "fire drill," the signal for every operator to unass the target building without question or delay.

There was no way to know for sure what the woman intended, but Hawk was certain that the only chance of stopping her was to take the blind shot. At least give the woman something else to think about and give her mates time to clear the building. She pointed the muzzle of her suppressed subgun straight ahead at chest level, toward where she last knew the woman to be standing, flipped the selector to full auto, and squeezed the trigger.

The copper-jacketed rounds punched through the plaster, throwing up a cloud of dust and wood smoke that swirled in the beam of her tactical flashlight. Hawk kept firing at the same spot as she moved forward, stepping directly onto the mattress, and then past it. The tightly grouped shots formed a hole in the wall big enough for her to shove a fist through, but Hawk put more than her hand into the hole.

Without breaking stride, she raised her right boot and shoved it with all her power into the small hole her bullets had created. She recovered her balance, took several steps back, then lowered her right shoulder and crashed into the wall like an All-Pro outside linebacker, smashing through the drywall to make the hole even larger. She frantically raked the insulation from the space between the walls before kicking out the target apartment's drywall side, and kept pushing, finally forcing her head and shoulders through into the room of the neighboring apartment.

"Alpha-Four, where the hell are you?" Shaft said. "Get the hell out of there, over."

Hawk ignored the call. She raised her weapon to let the SureFire light up the room, revealing the tightly packed rows of plastic buckets. Just past them, between the barricaded doorway and the desk, was the female crow.

The cyclic barrage had done more than just tear a hole through the walls. At least some of the rounds had gone clear through and struck the intended target.

The woman was kneeling, her T-shirt crimson with blood. She stared, unblinking, into the high-intensity tac-light, her face a blank slate, showing neither pain nor emotion. She made no effort to clutch at her wounds, but after a moment, raised both her hands and brought them together in front of her.

There was something in her right hand, the same familiar baseball-sized metal capsule Hawk had seen on the screen.

"Grenade!" Hawk shouted, even as she took aim and squeezed the trigger of her PDW.

Nothing. She had emptied the entire magazine into the wall.

The mortally wounded terrorist fumbled for the ring attached to the safety pin.

Frantic, Hawk let go of her primary weapon, allowing

it to fall the length of its sling. She immediately drew her backup, realizing too late that in doing so, she had lost control of the SureFire. The light beam now shone down at the floor, but there was just enough ambient illumination for her to make out the silhouette of the woman with the grenade.

Hawk extended the Glock fully, picked up the front Trijicon night sight, made a minor adjustment to place it on the woman's nose bridge, then aimed and fired in one smooth, practiced motion.

The woman's head snapped back hard against the wall, her body slumped in an awkward position, gravity slowly pulling her toward the floor. As Hawk settled the sight picture on the terrorist a second time, she heard the distinctive thump of something hard hitting the floor.

The grenade.

Shit!

If the female crow had succeeded in yanking out the safety pin, then Hawk had five seconds . . . maybe five seconds . . . to get through the wall and kick the grenade away from the buckets of ANFO.

One Mississippi.

Hawk braced her elbows against the edges of the hole and heaved herself forward, squeezing her lithe body between the wall's vertical two-by-four studs. The plaster crumbled under her weight and she spilled into the room, crashing onto the buckets.

Two Mississippi.

Each bucket weighed a good forty pounds, heavy enough that they didn't scatter like tenpins, but they nevertheless shifted and tottered as she blundered on hands and knees across the room.

Three Mississippi.

The SureFire's beam danced crazily as she moved, throwing light in random directions like a disco ball. It flashed on the dead woman, creating the illusion of motion, then showed the dull gray-green of the frag grenade wobbling on the floor. Hawk leapt for it as the light shifted again . . .

Four Mississippi.

She landed atop the grenade, the hard metal lump pressing against her armored vest, and curled up around it like a hedgehog. It was too late to attempt kicking the antipersonnel device away, and there was nowhere to kick it anyway. No, Hawk knew full well she was going to eat it. The most she could hope for now was to contain the blast with her body and redirect some of the concussive force away from the buckets; enough, she hoped, to prevent a secondary explosion that would bring down the entire building. Her vest might stop some of the frag. Maybe there would even be enough left of her to ship home.

Five Mississippi.

Six.

Amped on adrenaline, there was no way to know if she could trust her internal clock. She didn't dare let go. Not yet.

Seven.

She was dimly aware of voices coming over the radio, her fellow assaulters calling in their status. It was all a jumble of noise until one word reached through the din.

"Hawk!"

Eight.

She opened her eyes and looked up to see someone peering through the hole in the wall. "Hawk. You okay? Are you hit?"

She couldn't make out his face behind the protective kit, but the voice belonged to Shaft.

"Ummm . . ."

Nine.

She unclenched her arms, revealing the grenade, cradled like an egg against her chest. The spoon was still snugged tight against the spherical casing, the ring attached to the safety pin dangling harmlessly from it.

Ten.

She swallowed, her mouth almost too dry to form words. "I'm good."

EIGHT

Kolt Raynor felt numb as he made the phone call to Colonel Webber, reporting a lost eagle—his mate, his friend, Sergeant Major Clay "Stitch" Vickery.

Every operator—every soldier—knew that getting killed in action was a possibility, and every commander of combat troops knew that losing men was an inevitability. Raynor had attended more than his share of funeral services in Section 60 of the Arlington National Cemetery, and knew that the odds were good that one day he would join his fallen mates there, but that didn't make dealing with the reality of loss any easier. He was still in denial now, but he knew later, he would feel angry.

It had been a fluke, really. Stitch's armor had stopped three rounds from the terrorist's MP5, but the fourth had sliced through Stitch's brachial artery. In the madness of the fire-drill evac, it had taken a few minutes for the rest of the assault team to get the wounded operator down from his rope, only realizing then that he had sustained a mortal injury.

"That's rough," Webber said. Raynor knew the Delta commander felt the loss as acutely as he did. "Did Stitch have any family I don't know about?"

"The Unit was his family," Raynor said. It sounded cliché, but for Stitch, it was the truth. After two failed marriages, Clay Vickery had given up trying to build a life for himself outside the Delta compound. "He went out like he lived," Raynor added. "A warrior."

Webber grunted, signaling that no further discussion on the topic was required. "Three dead crows. And three in a cage. You leave anything for EKAM to take credit for?"

"We've back-briefed them, sir," Raynor said. "They're all over the taking credit thing."

A pat on the back from Webber was about all the praise Kolt could hope for. Police Colonel Drougas and EKAM were taking credit for stopping the attack, and that was fine with Raynor. The Greek commander was still a little butt-hurt over picking the wrong target for his team, which wasn't really Raynor's problem, but the plan was always to let the Greeks have the spotlight on their home turf. None of the Delta operators had signed up looking for glory anyway; they knew the protocol, and Raynor needed to stay on Drougas's good side in order to get a look at the intel recovered from the suspect's apartment.

"Standard stuff, Kolt," Webber said, "and kudos on stopping the plot to blow up the state funeral."

"I'm not sure we really stopped anything," Raynor replied. "Their plan was pretty half-assed."

Raynor wasn't being self-deprecating. Although the three surviving Revolutionary Struggle members weren't talking, the evidence recovered from the apartment suggested the sort of plan that might be concocted by bored college kids whose body of operational knowledge was derived entirely from watching videos on the Internet. "I doubt they could have gotten those explosives within a mile of the funeral."

"A lot of innocent people might have gotten hurt if they had gotten the chance to try. It's a win." He paused a beat, then added, "And despite losing Stitch, it could have been a lot worse."

"Thank Hawk for that."

"I heard what she did, and I intend to," Webber said. "That Tier One wild stunt seemed vaguely familiar. I hope you're not having a bad influence on the next generation of assaulters."

Raynor sensed a subtle dig in the comment, a reminder of his current administrative role within the Delta organization.

"We're pushing the video of her one-man wrecking crew to you now, sir," Kolt said. The cameras had captured every second of the action. Kolt knew Hawk's performance would give the old man a hard-on, since the female pilot program was his baby from the start. "You should probably watch it before it hits YouTube."

"We'll look for it, Raynor," Webber said with a slight laugh. "I'm also looking forward to sharing it with the rest of the building. Pass along my compliments and condolences to Major Barnes and his troop, as well. And then bring Stitch home."

"There are a couple things I'd like to wrap up before I leave, sir," Kolt said.

"It should already be a wrap, Kolt. What 'things' are unsettled?"

Raynor hesitated to answer. He still didn't have definitive proof that Rasim Miric was still alive, only a gut feeling that they had not seen the last of the sniper. "I think this whole thing with Revolutionary Struggle was a feint. Something to distract us from the real threat."

"The real threat," Webber echoed.

"They're working with someone else."

"Who?"

"That's what I'm trying to figure out. ISIS maybe. Revolutionary Struggle has spoken out against Western involvement in the Middle East. Maybe they've partnered up. I'm hoping that when the locals finish processing all the evidence we've recovered, we'll have a thread to tug on. We've still got a couple more days until the funeral."

"No, you don't. I know this will come as a shock, but you're off PPD. In case you're wondering, that comes directly from VPOTUS himself." This time there was no mistaking the sarcasm in the colonel's tone. If anyone had a full read on the extent of the hostility between Kolt Raynor and Vice President Mason, Webber did.

Raynor worked his jaw. He had not been looking forward to the prospect of safeguarding Mason either, but he resented the implication that he would be anything but professional in carrying out his duties. "Are you serious, sir?"

"Damn serious," Webber snapped. "The JSOC commanding general doesn't want you or anybody else in the command to be within a thousand miles of that funeral. Get your ass back here, pronto."

"Shiner's still alive," Raynor blurted. "He's going to hit again."

There was a long silence at the other end of the line. Finally, Webber spoke. "Noble isn't alert squadron. Not for another forty-three days. Your people need to get back to their training and family time. If your mythical one-eyed sniper pops up again before that, he's somebody else's problem. Are you receiving me?"

Kolt took a deep breath before answering. "Loud and clear."

Switching gears gave Raynor some much-needed perspective. As he focused on the logistical challenges of demobilizing an entire squadron of operators, along with headquarters and support personnel, he allowed his subconscious to work over the problem of how to run Shiner to ground. By the time he was wheels-down at Pope Field, he was certain that the state funeral in Athens was the least-probable target for Shiner or any other terrorist.

With more than a dozen world leaders attending, each one bringing along their own protective detail, security would be several layers thick, and with the recent attack still fresh in the memory of both the police and the proud citizens of Athens, paranoia would be at an all-time high. International news agencies were already reporting a spike in hate crimes, particularly against Muslim immigrants, this despite the fact that there was no explicit connection between Revolutionary Struggle and radical Islam. Trying to attack the funeral would be an act of utter futility. Amateurs like the would-be terrorists of Revolutionary Struggle might have been willing to make a mistake like that, but not an experienced killer like Miric.

Raynor also knew that one of the basic rules of survival for a sniper was to never stay in one place for long, especially once your presence was revealed with a kill shot. Shiner was long gone, on his way to his next target, but now that Raynor knew for certain that he was real—that he wasn't just an invention of Kolt's own overactive imagination—finding him was actually within the realm of possibility.

Kolt dropped his kit bag in the Noble Squadron bay, grabbed a beer from the fridge, then headed over to the squadron memorial wall, adorned with color eight-by-tens of Noble's lost warriors. Stitch's photo would be added by tomorrow. Kolt raised the beer to the memory of his fallen brother and took a long pull. He dropped the can in the trash, made good on his bar tab, and then headed to the SCIF.

The sensitive compartmented intelligence facility was the nerve center of Delta, where a team of analysts pored over data, everything from drone footage to wire service reports to documents recovered from raids on terrorist safe houses, looking for triggers and indicators, setting targets for the operators, and providing detailed information critical to mission success. Most were seasoned active duty intel analysts, and Kolt thought the world of them. A few were civilian contractors with prior military service, but even they had undergone intensive security vetting.

Throughout his career, Raynor had made a point of cultivating good relations with the support staff, and in particular, the analysts who worked in the SCIF. Their job was to digest and process data, but Raynor knew from experience that they also had hunches and gut feelings that they weren't always willing to include in their briefs. Raynor was a big believer in listening to gut feelings. Some operators fell victim to the common us-versus-them mentality, treating anyone who couldn't break a plate at four hundred meters or bench press their body weight as beneath contempt, but Raynor knew that reliable intel could mean the difference between bagging a high-value target or coming home in a body bag. A little validation went a long way, which was why he spent a lot of his down time hanging out in the SCIF, listening and asking questions, and generally treating the intel specialists like human beings.

Sometimes the effort paid off in spades. When he had made his return to the Unit after three years in exile, Raynor's partnership with Kenny Farmer, a young former USAF intelligence officer now working as an imagery analyst under contract with Booz Allen Hamilton, had been pivotal in tracking down a Yemeni terrorist training camp, which in turn alerted Raynor to a plot to blow Marine One out of the sky. Kenny Farmer, however, had moved on—where exactly he was working now, Kolt couldn't say for certain, but he still got a Christmas card from him every year—and Raynor wasn't having much success finding anyone as willing to help.

The man Raynor wanted to speak with today, a targeting/counterterror analyst named Brian Kelly, had proven to be an especially tough nut to crack.

Kelly was rail thin, which Raynor guessed owed more to a genetic predisposition than his diet and exercise habits. Like many of his peers, he seemed to subsist on energy drinks and snack foods, and barely moved at all. Kelly was balding but kept what little hair he had cropped short, except for his beard, which was thick and full, and evidently a source of great pride to him. Hawk, who generally shared Raynor's positive attitude toward the support staff, had disdained Kelly as a hipster— which evidently didn't mean what Kolt thought it did. Kelly's work was adequate but uninspired, and he rarely yielded the kind of insights that Raynor had come to expect from people like Kenny Farmer.

But Raynor also believed that you had to make the best of what you were given.

He brought Starbucks coffee down from the Unit chow hall—black, which Hawk assured him was probably Kelly's drink of choice—and set it down in front of the other man.

The analyst looked up and regarded Kolt with all the enthusiasm of a Novocain shot. "Lieutenant Colonel Raynor. Welcome back."

Kolt had given up trying to convince the young man to use his code name. "Thanks, Brian. So . . ." He nodded at the oversized flat-screen monitor on Kelly's desk. "Anything interesting happening out there?"

Kelly blinked. "I guess it depends on your definition of interesting."

Raynor managed a grin. "Try me."

The other man gave a succinct, by-the-numbers rundown of global hotspots and recent intel scoops, none of which seemed particularly newsworthy to Raynor. He wondered if Kelly was being purposefully obtuse.

"Great," he said after enduring several minutes of this. "Hey, I need a favor. Do you know if there are any photos of the guy who capped the Greek PM?"

"Nikos Roupa? Sure. They've been showing his picture on the news."

That was news to Raynor. Sixteen years of hunting Shiner had not yielded a single photograph of Rasim Miric. "Can you show me?"

Kelly affected a put-out expression, but turned to his computer and launched a browser window that opened with the MSNBC Web page. A few mouse clicks brought up what appeared to be a still image from the security camera at some kind of retail store. The image was low-res, but Raynor instantly recognized Shiner.

"That's the only picture of him?"

Kelly cocked his head sideways as if the question confused him. "It's the only one I've seen. My guess is that it's the best they've got."

"No driver's license or passport photos on file?"

"JSOC is working on it. CIA is still a little slow."

"See if you can get that." Raynor doubted the search

would yield any results. If Miric had possessed any sort of identifying documents, they would almost certainly have been forgeries. The real Nikos Roupa was probably a victim of identity theft, and might even have been Miric's unwilling body double. "And get as many pics of him as you can find. Whatever it takes to build a facial recognition profile."

"Why? He's dead."

"Humor me," Kolt said as he slid the Starbucks a little closer to Kelly's keyboard.

Kelly's lips twitched up in a humorless *fuck you* smile. "I'll get right on that."

After the frustration of dealing with Kelly, the post-mission hotwash seemed less of a chore. It was, in typical Delta fashion, a brutally honest self-assessment, but one of the many changes that came with acquisition of a Zero-One call sign was that Raynor now found himself in the role of facilitator and referee, rather than participant. He sat next to Webber, arms folded across his chest, and listened as Slapshot had each operator own up to what they could have done better. It seemed to Kolt like they had to dig deep to find something worthy of criticism.

Despite what amounted to a catastrophic breakdown of security, nothing the squadron had done or failed to do would have prevented the assassination of the Greek prime minister. Raynor himself took responsibility for not insisting that Drougas's men shut down and sweep Mount Lycabettus, but he doubted that would have made a difference either, not with a determined killer like Shiner stalking his prey.

Raynor did not mention Shiner specifically, or provide background on his prior association with Rasim Miric. As he looked around the room, he realized that nearly everyone who had been with him back then was gone. Of those present, only Webber and Slapshot had been in the Unit that long, and neither of them had been directly involved. Everyone else who had been there was retired, promoted out, or dead.

The discussion next turned to the raid on the Revolutionary Struggle hideout. The mood darkened as the assaulters had to revisit the memory of Stitch's death, but all agreed that nothing could have been done to mitigate the risk. It was just one of those things that happened sometimes.

Raynor withheld comment when Barnes mentioned how glad he was that he left Hawk out of the initial assault, because her quick reaction and novel solution to the crisis had probably saved them all. The statement seemed a little disingenuous; Barnes seemed to think of Cindy Bird only as a female who needed to be protected, not a fellow assaulter.

Kolt looked for Hawk's response. She simply nodded and said, "Good to be a part of it all."

The particulars of the assault were picked apart. Digger, who had been back at the JOC with Raynor, thought that Barnes had been too quick to rule out an explosive breach or the use of flash-bangs, but he admitted that he was Monday-morning quarterbacking.

After a couple hours, Slapshot concluded the debrief and gave the troop sergeant majors their marching orders. A date was set for Stitch's service, after which Barnes's troop would head back to Key West to finish their cycle of civilian boat training. The other troops were headed for Wyoming and Nevada, respectively.

The PPD deployment had seriously cut into the readiness plan, and everyone was going to have to double-time in order to meet the expectations, but Raynor saw that as a blessing in disguise. Although the overseas mission had been a net success, Noble Squadron morale had taken a serious hit. After six weeks of hard-core training, alert status would seem like a vacation.

Six weeks.

He wondered if Shiner would wait that long to reveal himself again.

NINE

Ten hours after leaving Athens, the man calling himself Dusan Juric arrived at Alexander the Great Airport in Skopje, Macedonia, where he boarded a Croatian Airlines flight bound for Zagreb. Upon arrival, he went to a dead drop established by an MIT officer working out of the Turkish embassy, and exchanged the documents for Dusan Juric with a new set of papers identifying him as Admir Osmani, an Albanian currently residing in Canada, and on his way home after visiting family in his homeland. Thirty hours after that, he deplaned in Toronto, and Osmani became Vladimir Zdorovetskiy, a Russian émigré living in Detroit, Michigan.

During the train ride from Toronto, Miric memorized the details of his new legend. The border crossing into the United States would be the moment of greatest risk, particularly since there was a good chance that he would be singled out for special scrutiny because of his ethnicity. The Canadian government did not check passports of visitors crossing into Ontario, but the Americans did for everyone returning by the same route, even for U.S. citizens. His American passport was an excellent forgery, but a forgery nonetheless, and the only way to ensure that the Homeland Security agents at the border crossing would not give it too close a look was to absolutely nail his performance as Zdorovetskiy the Russian. He would need to be able to field seemingly insignificant questions without hesitation, and more importantly, without any tells—microexpressions that might betray his answers as fabrications or outright deception.

His physical appearance would bring unwanted attention as well, but there was only so much he could do about that.

His empty left eye socket was now covered with a flesh-colored adhesive eye patch, which in turn was hidden behind dark sunglasses. He would have to remove those glasses at the border crossing, at which point his deformity would be revealed. One deviation from the norm—his pseudo-Russian background—might not stick in the memory of the DHS agents, but a second—his missing eye—would. It would probably not be enough for them to flag him, all other things being equal, but if the investigation into his apparent death in Athens revealed the truth, if international law enforcement agencies were told to be on the lookout for a one-eyed man with a Slavic accent, the memory of his passage would bubble to the surface and the hunters would know where to start looking next.

Still, there was nothing he could do about it, and

soon—within a couple weeks at most—it wouldn't matter anymore.

When his turn came, he handed the customs agent his passport. The man glanced up at him. "What's your citizenship?"

"I am American citizen," Miric replied, trying to inject a note of patriotic pride into his tone while exaggerating his accent. "I pass test two years ago."

"Where are you coming from?"

"Toronto." He nodded his head in the direction from which he had come.

The agent flipped the passport open, made a cursory visual inspection, and then passed it under a UV light, checking the seals. Miric made a conscious effort to keep breathing. *There will be no problem,* he told himself, willing it to be so.

"You're returning home?"

"Yes."

"What was the purpose of your visit?"

"Was visiting old friend."

The agent stared back impassively, and Miric wondered if the man expected more information from him. Needlessly embellishing a cover story was the mark of an amateur, but sometimes ordinary people also volunteered too much information. "Sergei. That is the name of my friend. He lives in Toronto."

"Take off the glasses."

Miric did so, and noticed the subtle change in the man's expression. Surprise, but also disgust. He had seen it many times before, the automatic response of most people to someone who was no longer whole.

The agent looked down quickly, as if embarrassed by his reaction, passed the barcode under a laser scanner, and then handed the passport back. "Next, please."

After the incident that had cost him his left eye, Rasim Miric had spent several months subsisting on the kindness of strangers. He had no family left. The Serbs had seen to that, but his hatred for men like Milosevic and Ratko was nearly exhausted. Theirs was an honest evil. Not like the Americans, who played at being cowboy heroes, pretending to rush in to save the downtrodden, all the while cynically preserving the status quo if it served their political agenda.

His self-pity quickly became an abiding hatred for the Americans, both the government—who had stalled and dissembled in the face of the Bosnian genocide—and the people, men like the army officer who had left him maimed. He had quietly cheered when the television showed images of the Twin Towers burning, collapsing in a cloud of smoke and rubble, but beyond the mere satisfaction of that event, he had come to a profound realization.

America was not invincible.

Nineteen men, armed with box cutters and just a little bit of knowledge, had struck a blow that still resonated throughout the world sixteen years after the fact. The 9/11 attacks had upended the global economy, and goaded the Americans into a state of endless war—an asymmetrical war in which, despite having superiority of numbers and equipment, they would never achieve true victory, and therefore were already defeated.

The wars had shown Miric a way out of his depression. The loss of his nondominant eye had not affected his ability to shoot at all. If anything, the techniques he used to cope with the loss of binocular vision had resulted in a net improvement. He was still a shooter—a natural—and now there were people who would pay him to hunt Americans and their allies.

In Iraq, his deadly prowess played into the urban legend of Qanas Baghdad—the Baghdad Sniper. In Afghanistan, he notched several more kills over a four-year period, feeding the rumors of Chechen mercenary sniper teams working for the Taliban. From there, he had gone back to Iraq to fight with the emerging insurgency known as the Islamic State; not because he subscribed to their apocalyptic vision of Islam, but because he shared their hatred of the West. That was where he encountered Mehmet, who was working secretly on behalf of the Turkish government in support of the Islamic State.

Mehmet had also taught him how to play chess.

He had learned the fundamentals of the game as a child, but the Turk had shown him the importance of strategy and patience—playing the long game. The point was not to remove as many pieces from the board as possible, but rather to maneuver an opponent into destroying himself.

That was what the Turkish government was doing in Iraq and Syria. While paying lip service to the fight against the Islamic State and the effort to unseat Syrian leader Bashar al-Assad, thus satisfying their duties as a NATO member nation, Turkish intelligence agents were actively working with ISIS to defeat one of their key enemies, the Peshmerga of the autonomous region of Kurdistan in Iraq.

Throughout the twentieth century, the Kurdish people had been a stateless nation, an oppressed minority in every land in which they dwelt in exile, including post-Ottoman Turkey. As was their custom, the Americans were willing to overlook the brutal oppression of the Kurds in Turkey because of the nation's strategic importance during the Cold War, but the end of the long conflict with the Soviet Union had drawn attention to the plight of the Kurdish people, particularly in northern Iraq, where they hoped to establish a Kurdish homeland. The Turkish government, under then prime minister and now president Recep Erdogan, strongly opposed the formation of a sovereign Kurdistan following the ouster of Saddam Hussein, as that would be the first step toward legitimizing past claims of human rights violations, as well as fomenting unrest among the large Kurdish population still living in Turkey. Because the United States needed to keep Turkey as a strategic partner in its new long war—the poorly defined War on Terror—early plans to divide Iraq along ethnic lines—much as had been done in the Balkans following the breakup of the Communist Bloc—and creating a Kurdish homeland were scrapped. Iraq remained a single but divided nation, fertile ground for the rise of the new Islamist insurgency, and perversely, offered yet another chance for the Kurds to gain the respect of the West, something the Turkish government could not allow.

Miric was initially appalled at the endemic cynicism on all sides of the political equation. To him, the Turks were no better than the Americans, but Mehmet had assured him that there was no other way to win the long game. Sacrifices had to be made in order to keep the Western nations in a state of perpetual war.

"America has never been weaker," the Turkish intelligence officer had told him. "They are divided. Most of their people cannot be bothered to participate in their great democracy, and those who do are actively working to undermine their own government. They would rather burn their house down than compromise with each other. And we will let them do it."

Fear, Mehmet had gone on to say, was now the dominant spirit in America: fear of another terrorist attack, fear of Muslims and immigrants, fear even of the government itself.

In the three years since that conversation took place, the situation in the United States had grown even more unstable. The fear was now a living thing, a monster poised to consume what had briefly been the most powerful nation on earth.

In chess terms, this was the endgame. With just a few more moves, the Americans would be maneuvered into a fatal position.

Checkmate.

It was generally believed that the term derived from a Persian phrase—*shah'mat*.

The king is dead.

And who better to kill a king than a knight.

Before leaving the train station, Miric located the last of the dead drops set up in advance by his handlers in

Turkish intelligence. From this point forward, at least until the successful execution of the second phase of the plan, he would be working completely on his own, which did not bother him in the least. He knew he could count on himself. Relying on others was dangerous. He did not want to be undone by somebody else's mistake.

The drop yielded a new set of documents—U.S. passport, Michigan driver's license, credit cards, even a gym membership and public library card—all in the name of Konstantin Khavin, along with a prepaid cellular phone, still in its plastic clamshell package. Unlike the other identities he had briefly assumed in the course of his journey halfway around the globe, Khavin was as familiar and comfortable as an old sweater.

He booked a room at a budget motel near the station. He was exhausted, but although it had been more than forty-eight hours since he had slept in a bed, his day was not yet done.

After a quick shower and a change of clothes, he activated his phone and placed a call to a number he had committed to memory.

The voice on the other end was tentative, hesitant. "Hello?"

"Colonel Jeffries," Miric said. "It is Konstantin Khavin."

"Ah, Mr. Khavin. Of course. I didn't recognize the number."

"I change phones many times. You understand." Miric laid his accent on thick, confident that the man on the other end would not be able to distinguish one

Slavic speech pattern from another. "I am calling to make sure that you are still expecting me tomorrow."

"Absolutely. We're all very excited. It's not every day we get a former Russian Spetsnaz sniper as a guest instructor for drill weekend."

"You should not say such things over the telephone," Miric said sharply. Despite the reproof, he was smiling. Under any other circumstances, Jeffries's indiscreet comment would have been a potentially fatal slipup— fatal for Jeffries at least—but this was one time where loose lips were essential to the success of the mission. It was one of the reasons, he suspected, why Mehmet had suggested Jeffries and his New American Revolution Lightfoot Militia for the next phase of his mission.

The arrangements had been made through a cutout—an intermediary whose involvement could not be traced to the Turkish intelligence service—but Miric had been fully briefed nonetheless.

Konstantin Khavin, a former sniper for the elite Russian Spetsnaz, and émigré to the United States, where he was currently working as a private security contractor, would be joining Jeffries's militia group for their weekend training at a commercial shooting range in eastern Michigan. The cover identity was one that Miric himself had established many years earlier—somewhat ironically, since his only experience with Russian military special forces troops had been in Chechnya, where he had put bullets through the eyes of no less than six Spetsnaz operators—but MIT had padded the legend out and smoothed some of the inconsistencies.

"Oh." Jeffries was clearly mortified by his mistake. "I'm sorry. I didn't think—"

"I will need transportation."

"I'll have one of my men collect you."

"No. You come. I will call you in the morning with my location." He hung up before the other man could reply, and removed the battery from the phone.

Miric spent the next two days doing what he loved most. Shooting.

His vagabond lifestyle did not often afford him the opportunity to shoot recreationally, much less on a dedicated thousand-meter range with steel targets. When he was not behind the trigger, he acted as both spotter and shooting coach for the NAR militiamen, and when he was not doing that, he kept them entertained with stories of his exploits abroad.

The stories were true, at least with respect to the technical details—the rifles, ammunition and equipment used, distance to target, and of course, the description of the kill itself—and that was all that mattered to his audience. They had seemed particularly enamored with his nationality, confiding in him that they admired Russian president Vladimir Putin for his strength and decisiveness. Miric had merely nodded, playing along.

Political differences notwithstanding, he felt a measure of admiration for these Americans. Three months earlier, when they had worked out the details of the operation, Mehmet had disparaged the militiamen as "pretend warriors," but Miric saw something different. They reminded him of the men he had fought with in his youth. Eager. Fearless. Naïve. The only difference was that the war they were prepared to fight had not yet materialized.

"This is what I do not understand," he said as they gathered around picnic tables for a meal at the close of the first day's activity. "You say that your country has been hijacked. That the government is illegal and that soon they will begin taking away your weapons and arresting you."

There were nods and murmurs of agreement.

"What are you waiting for?"

Colonel Jeffries, a slightly built man with graying hair and the false charm of a used car salesman, gave him a long-suffering smile but shook his head. "Don't you see? That's exactly what they want. If we make the first move, they'll have an excuse to declare martial law. No, there's gonna be a fight, all right, but it's gonna be self-defense."

This was a variation on the monologue Jeffries had given during the long drive to eastern Michigan earlier in the day. The militia leader had gone on at great length about the many crimes of the current administration and the looming threats from foreign agitators.

The position made no sense at all to Miric. If the government had, as Jeffries and his men believed, been seized by antidemocratic forces, the "first move" had already been made. And if the current regime was as authoritarian as Jeffries claimed, they would have no need of a pretext to begin carrying out their diabolical schemes.

He did not probe deeper into the question. Fomenting

revolution was not his mission, at least not in this way. No, he was here for something else.

As Jeffries expounded on the patriotic nature of their opposition to the federal government, Miric watched the faces of the other men gathered around the tables. The NAR Lightfoot Militia boasted a membership of more than two hundred, but less than fifty had shown up for the weekend training event. Many were too old to suit Miric's needs. Many more were in poor physical shape. The remaining pool of candidates was small— just half a dozen—but he needed only one. He had watched them carefully throughout the day, and paid special attention to their reactions to his question.

What are you waiting for?

Not surprisingly, those six young men were part of a select group within the militia organization. Collectively, they comprised a SWORD team. The impressive acronym stood for "select weapons, ordnance, and reconnaissance detachment," and in practical terms it meant that they had been singled out for additional training in combat skills.

The next day, while most of the militiamen continued burning ammunition, plinking away with rifles at two-hundred-meter targets and shooting on the pistol range, Miric took the SWORD team out to a remote corner of the facility to practice movement to target, and escape-and-evasion techniques.

As they fashioned field-expedient camouflage, Miric outlined his plan for a live-fire training exercise. Each man would, in turn, be given thirty minutes to move out from their assembly area and establish a hidden shooting position. At the end of that interval, Miric would begin hunting them with an airsoft pistol. If they reached the sixty-minute mark undetected, they were to take a shot at the eight-hundred-meter target and then, if possible, make their way back to the assembly area without being caught.

During those thirty-minute waiting periods, Miric continued building rapport with the young men awaiting their turn. He praised them as the embodiment of the true warrior spirit. He drew them out, invited them to express their fears and ambitions. He was a sympathetic listening ear, and he was also, without their knowledge, interviewing them. Testing them.

When the time to hunt arrived, he left the group and headed into the landscape, unfailingly locating each of the would-be snipers with plenty of time to spare. Their mistake, the last mistake many snipers made, was that they did not take into account the fact that, regardless of the conditions, there were only a limited number of places from which a shot could be taken. It was a liability that could be partially overcome with superior camouflage and movement techniques, but the young militiamen, lacking any formal training in those proficiencies, were easy to spot.

The last man to go, who not coincidentally was Miric's leading candidate, proved hardest to find. By that point, Miric was intimately familiar with the terrain, moving quickly and stealthily from one likely hide to the next, his senses fully attuned to any disruption in the environment. His one good eye was for shooting, but when it came to hunting another man in the woods, his ears and nose were far more useful. Men had a smell, Americans especially, with their soaps and shampoos and perfumed deodorant body sprays. The things they ate and drank were full of toxins that oozed from their pores. Their breathing, too, was a dead giveaway. He needed only a few seconds at each potential shooting position to determine whether his prey was there. The last candidate, however, almost eluded him.

It took him just ten minutes to visit all the places from which a shot would have been possible, but there was no sign of the young SWORD soldier at any of them. Miric retraced his steps, spending a little more time at each location, but with no better results. He checked his wristwatch and saw that only a few minutes remained to him.

Had the young man found a way to completely lose himself in the landscape? Or had he chosen an unconventional shooting position?

Rasim Miric considered these two possibilities for no more than thirty seconds before deciding it did not matter. The young man had performed better than any of his peers, but to win the competition, he would have to score a kill shot and return to the assembly area.

Miric hastened back to the spot he would have chosen first and settled in to observe the target through his spotter's scope. As he lay there, listening to the last few seconds tick away, he heard a faint rustling sound. He looked up from the scope and saw movement in the ground cover just a few meters away. It was the young militiaman, and he was on the move, low-crawling toward a spot that would put him almost exactly parallel to Miric.

Miric smiled to himself. The boy had not made the same mistake as the others, finding his shooting position and staying put. Instead, he had hidden himself somewhere else and waited, literally until the last minute.

Miric watched as the young man deployed his rifle, positioning its bipod. The one drawback to waiting so long was that the militia sniper would have only a few seconds to find his target in the scope, determine range, and adjust for variables like wind and bullet drop.

Miric eased closer to the man, careful not to betray his presence. The boy was breathing fast and making too much noise now, which allowed Miric to move up beside him.

The boy took a deep breath, let it out. Took another. Miric raised the scope to his eye and found the distant target. He knew from his earlier visit that the steel target was about 820 meters away, at the outer edge of the reliable range for the boy's Remington 700 SPS .308 rifle.

There was a familiar metallic rasp as the bolt was slid back, and a faint click as the round seated. The boy took another breath. Held it.

The report resonated through Miric's body but he kept his attention unflinchingly focused downrange.

The steel target dropped with the impact.

The boy let out his breath in an audible sigh of satisfaction and immediately started breaking down the rifle.

"Good shot," Miric said aloud.

The boy froze for a moment, then looked back and saw the man who had been stalking him. "Ah, shit."

Miric chuckled. "Don't be so hard on yourself. You did better than all of your friends. And you made the shot."

The young militiaman grinned. "Easy-peasy. I could make that shot in my sleep."

"Is that so? Tell me, Easy-peasy. What is your name?"

"Lyle . . . uh, I mean Sergeant Dooley." He paused a beat, then added, "My friends call me Lizard."

"Lizard." Miric nodded approvingly. "How old are you, Lizard?"

"Twenty."

"Twenty. When I was your age, I had already killed ten men." He let that sink in a moment, then lowered his voice. "I have a confession to make. This is not just training exercise."

"No?"

"No. Is test. I am looking for someone to help me with special assignment."

Lizard's eyes went wide with awe and anticipation, just as Miric knew they would, but there was a note of suspicion in his reply. "What kind of assignment? I ain't gonna do nothing illegal."

"Who decides what is legal? Your government itself is illegal. The colonel knows it. It is time to act. Now."

"Colonel J?"

"Yes. Why do you think he brought me here? You want to take back your country, no?"

"No." Dooley blinked, then shook his head. "I mean, yes. I do."

Miric scooted closer so he could speak in a low whisper. "This must remain between us. Secret, you understand?"

The young man nodded, but then repeated his question. "What kind of assignment?"

"I think you know, Lizard."

The young man swallowed nervously. "I . . . um . . . Do you . . . Why me?"

Miric smiled again. "You are a natural."

PART TWO

FIRST
TARGET

TEN

The call from Brian Kelly a week later caught Raynor off guard, partly because he had expected the analyst to slow-ball his request, but mostly because he didn't think he'd find any leads worth a shit.

He immediately headed to the SCIF, where he found Kelly tucked in at his cubicle, shaking the last few drops of Java Monster Mean Bean energy drink from a can. Kolt made a mental note of the product; if Kelly's lead proved actionable, he would have to hook him up on his next visit.

He clapped a hand down on Kelly's shoulder, giving him what he thought was an encouraging squeeze.

"What's up, brother?" Kolt said with a smile. "Something new?"

Kelly winced—probably jumpy from all the caffeine, Raynor thought, since he hadn't really squeezed that hard. "Colonel Raynor. That was fast."

"It was either you or the long O course with the boys, and I'm not getting any younger. And dude, it's Racer.

Calling me 'colonel' makes me think the JSOC commander is standing behind me."

"Umm, right. So, I collected all the images available of the guy the Greek police are identifying as the assassin. I also pinged the agency for any images that hadn't been released to the public yet. They didn't have anything useful. The Greeks released all the best captures in hopes that someone might recognize him. So, basically, I don't have a whole lot to work with here. The images we've got are low res. It's like trying to find a match of a specific car when all you know is the color and only one or two numbers from the license plate."

"You know we've done that before," Kolt reassured him. "You'll get it."

"Maybe the vehicle analogy isn't the best," Kelly said. "We'll only be able to find matches from people who are actually in the databases that we have access to, and that's only a very small percentage of the population."

Raynor nodded patiently. He was well accustomed to Unit intel analysts underpromising and always overdelivering, but it seemed to be part of the process. "But you did find something?"

"This." Kelly clicked his mouse and brought up an image on his monitor. It was a still frame taken from a surveillance camera, and showed a dark-haired man standing at a counter in what looked like a customs checkpoint, perhaps in an airport. One of the man's eyes was covered with a flesh-colored adhesive patch.

Raynor's pulse quickened. "Fuckin' A, brother. You're the shit!"

"It's only a thirty-two percent match with—"

"It's him," Kolt insisted. "Where was this picture taken?"

"Walk-up customs border station in Detroit."

"Detroit? As in Michigan? He's here? In the States?" Without realizing it, Raynor had let his voice rise to nearly a shout, which caused Kelly to flinch again.

"It looks that way, I mean, if it is him. The passport belongs to Vladimir Zdorovetskiy. Russian. Been living in the U.S. for five years. Naturalized in 2013. The passport photo is a little bit different because it shows him with both eyes, but evidently the border patrol guy thought it was the same guy."

"Where is he now?"

"Excuse me?"

Kolt pointed at the screen. "This asshole is in the United States. We need to find him before he . . ." He faltered. *Before he what? Who is he hunting now?* "Where did he go next?"

Kelly looked up in consternation. "I might be the shit, sir, but I can't shit intel."

Raynor stared at the image. The adrenaline pumping through his veins had left him feeling cold all over. "What about the network of surveillance cameras Homeland Security has in every city in America? We can track him."

"That's technically true, but . . ." Kelly shrugged. "It's not as Jason Bourne simple as they make it look on TV. You need NSA-level computing power, and even with that, it's still easy to fool the system if you know what you're doing. But even if I could do it . . . I can't.

We don't have the authority to conduct an investigation on American soil. We'd need a directive from way above JSOC for that."

Raynor knew the analyst was right on all counts, just as he knew that no one in any U.S. law enforcement agency would take him seriously, not if all he had to give them was a couple pictures and a gut feeling. "Then backtrack him."

The analyst stared at him dumbly.

"If you can't look for him here," Raynor said, speaking slowly as if to a child, "then let's figure out how he got here. Connect his movements. I know he was in Athens a few days ago. How did he get from there to here? Give us something I can take to Webber and the CG."

Kolt could see Brian Kelly's lips pursed together behind his luxurious beard as if he was fighting to hold back a sarcastic retort. After a few seconds, his lips parted just enough for him to utter a single word. "Fine." Then, as if considering, he added, "but I'm swamped with a dozen other pressing target folders as it is."

"I know, man, you guys bust your asses around here," Kolt said. "I tell you what. I'll trade your personal time to run this stuff down for a tandem jump with Digger and a day of pistol shooting with Hawk."

Kelly snapped his head toward Kolt. "Seriously?"

"Yeah, man," Kolt said. He wondered which of the two incentives had been more attractive to the analyst. "You're doing me a huge favor. Deal?"

"Hell yeah, it's a deal."

Raynor knew he was asking a lot of the man, and knew that he should probably be more grateful for what the analyst had already accomplished, but he didn't have time to coddle. Shiner had moved a lot faster than he would have believed possible. He had already chosen his next target, and if he was in the United States, it meant the target was too.

Nobody in the world could convince Kolt otherwise.

"Let me get this straight," said Special Agent in Charge Jess Simmons with a weary sarcasm that was audible over the telephone line. "The guy who didn't take out Champ when he had the chance in Athens, and who blew himself to smithereens, is now back from the dead and ready to take another crack at it. Am I tracking?"

It wasn't the reaction Racer had hoped for, but it wasn't completely unexpected either. Simmons was an arrogant rule-bound jackass, but he was also the only person Racer could think of with the authority to do something about the threat Shiner represented on short notice and without going through the byzantine bureaucracy that came with major threats to the homeland.

"Look, Jess, I can't tell you why he didn't take the shot in Athens. Maybe Champ wasn't his target. But he *is* here now. I've got a picture of him at the border crossing in Michigan."

"So he didn't really blow himself up? He was just pretending?"

"Come on, Jess. Remember who you're talking to. I've got better things to do too. The shooter staged his death and the forensics will prove it." He said this with more confidence than he actually possessed. He did not doubt that Miric was alive, but it was doubtful the Greek authorities would reach that conclusion before Shiner made his move.

Simmons considered this for a moment. "Let's say, for argument's sake, that I believe you, Raynor. What do you want me to do about it? I mean, beyond what I already do every day to keep Champ safe from the hundreds of crazies who also want him dead?"

Racer fought to keep his temper in check. He gazed out through his office window across the Unit parking lot, heavy with Harley-Davidsons and pickups, making sure to keep his composure. Slipping into full hothead mode would definitely not get him closer to his objective. "Shiner isn't just a crazy radical with an axe to grind. You saw what he did in Athens. You were standing right there."

"We have protocols to deal with potential sniper threats."

"Tell that to Midas," Racer shot back, and instantly regretted it. That had been his own failure as much as anyone's. "Look, Jess. I'm telling you that my best unofficial assessment is that Shiner is in the U.S. He's traveling under an alias. Vladimir Zdorovetskiy. That's something you can investigate. That's all I'm asking you to do. Pull that thread and see where it leads."

"It's not enough, Raynor." Simmons's tone was now several degrees cooler. "Someone way above your pay grade needs to show me an explicit threat to the president's safety."

"When it becomes explicit, it will be too late for you to do anything about it," Racer said through clenched teeth. "Are you tracking that?" He slammed the phone back in its cradle.

"Looks like those people skills are working for you," Slapshot remarked.

Racer glanced up to find his sergeant major leaning against the door of the office, arms folded over his broad chest. "Speaking of people skills, it's rude to eavesdrop."

"Yeah? It's also rude to compartmentalize shit that affects me and the boys, too." Then, without waiting for an actual invitation, he strode in and collapsed into the chair opposite Raynor's desk. "So let me guess. Nobody believes you when you say that Harvey the Rabbit is real."

Raynor blinked at him. He had not updated Slapshot with Kelly's latest discovery, but the harsh truth was that it was no more convincing than anything else he had to offer as proof. "Do you believe me?"

"You asking for a no-shitter, boss?"

"From you, I expect nothing less."

Slapshot blew out his cheeks in a long sigh. "Well, Racer, I haven't been zipped up in a body bag following you yet."

"He's here, Slap. We've got a picture of him at the Detroit border crossing. My gut tells me he's going after POTUS."

"That was Simmons you were talking to?"

"Yeah. He's got protocols."

"So go to someone else's boss," Slapshot said, "like starting with Wrangler Zero-One."

Kolt knew he would have to do exactly that. He had

been skating around barging into Colonel Webber's office to lay it all out for him.

"And tell him what? That I've got a gut feeling?" Raynor sagged back in his chair.

"How long have you been looking for this guy?"

Raynor eyed his friend, trying to figure out if there was any subtext to the question. "You think I've lost perspective?"

"How long?"

Kolt searched his memory. "I think the first time it occurred to me that Miric might be freelancing was in . . . oh-five, I guess. Back when everyone was talking about Juba."

"The Baghdad Sniper?" Slapshot nodded. "That was just a myth. Enemy psy-ops."

"Right. But we still lost a lot of guys to AQ snipers, and not just rumors, but some of the classified intel reports matched Shiner's MO. It got my attention. I poked around a little, pinged some folks who had been part of the Balkan Task Force, trying to figure out what happened to him. I wasn't obsessed with him or anything."

"I knew you'd been keeping an ear out, but I didn't realize he's been on your radar this whole time."

"Sorry, brother," Kolt said, "I wasn't intentionally trying to keep you out of the loop."

"And until last week, you didn't even know for sure that he was real."

Raynor straightened in his chair and fixed Slapshot with a hard stare. "Your point?"

"He's a phantom, Kolt. Full stealth mode. Even if

Simmons gets on board, finding this guy before he takes another shot is going to be next to impossible."

"That's *my* point."

Slapshot shook his head. "You aren't going to find him by looking for him. If he is in the States, he's probably gone to ground somewhere. He can wait. Months, if he has to."

Raynor shook his head. "I don't think so. He made it from Greece to Detroit in record time. Must be supported by someone that knows what they are doing. The second hit must be happening soon. Otherwise why the risk of hurrying across so many borders?"

"You really think he's going after POTUS now? Even though he didn't take the shot in Athens when he had the chance?"

Raynor nodded. "I'm banking he was fucking with us. Like you said, it's a psy-op. That was just his opening move. More of a diversion, but a warning just the same."

"So you and I have to sign up for making sure he doesn't get a chance to notch another national leader?"

"I need you on board, Slap," Kolt said. "I'm not sure we have the authority to do much, though. We don't operate on American soil."

There was a gleam in Slapshot's eye as he replied. "How exactly would you define the term 'operate'?"

ELEVEN

Like everyone else in the Unit, Cindy Bird was a slave to her dedicated Unit-issued phone.

She had been looking forward to a couple weeks of being out on the water under the tropical sun, even if it wasn't a vacation, but when a call or text came in, the only correct response was to drop everything and check it, which was exactly what Hawk and the rest of her assault team did when their phones buzzed simultaneously not five minutes after they strolled into the hotel bar after their first day of boat training.

Shaft glanced at the bartender, who did not seem to have noticed the conspicuous timing of the alert signals, then turned to Cindy. "Hawk, make the call."

Cindy popped up from her bar stool and moved away from the small crowd of happy hour patrons, and took a seat at an empty corner table. The text message contained a call-in number, which she knew would provide further information, but the fact that they had all received the alert was troubling.

An emergency recall of all sabre squadrons typically happened only when the shit hit the fan in several different places all at once, exceeding the capabilities of the alert squadron. Or when something really, really bad happened—like 9/11 bad. But when she called the contact number and listened to the recorded message—Slapshot's voice, uncharacteristically flat and humorless—she knew this was something else.

"All personnel are to proceed directly to the following location. Prepare to copy."

Really? An alert for a damn training exercise?

There was a brief pause, just long enough for her to dig out her weatherproof notebook and her pen. She listened intently to Slapshot as he gave an address in Arlington, Virginia.

The message went on. Travel alone under cover creds. Report within forty-eight hours. But then it got strange. Do not return to Bragg. There would be a per diem for general expenses, and reimbursements for purchases in excess of that amount would be made subject to review. Personal weapons and ammunition would not be sanctioned.

No weapons or equipment would be issued. Not sanctioned? What the hell did that mean?

But she knew what it meant. The language was intentionally vague, the message implicit. Bring your personal weapons along, but don't get caught with them.

It was an off-the-books op.

This is training, right?

Cindy returned to the bar, grabbed her go bag off the

back of the bar stool, and nodded to Shaft and the others. "I'm out, fellas, thanks for the drink, have a good one."

Knowing her teammates would call in as soon as they were away from the bar, she headed for her room, grabbed the rest of her gear, and rang the desk clerk to call her a cab.

Forty-eight hours was more than enough time for a quick stopover at her apartment in Fayetteville to pick up some firepower—a Caspian M1911 .45 semiautomatic pistol, which she had inherited from her father. Although she had not learned of it until long after his death, Mike Leland Bird had been a Delta Force squadron commander. Her recruitment into the Unit as part of the aug cell, and her eventual selection to participate in the pilot program to train female operators, had not been a coincidence. The program was the brainchild of Mike Bird and Jeremy Webber years ago, but only Webber had lived to see it come to fruition. It was only fitting that Mike "MLB" Bird's only daughter should be the first to blaze that particular trail. Delta was in her blood.

Although she still had a full day to burn before the deadline, she didn't linger at home. The last thing she needed right now was a chance encounter with Troy, her Green Beret boyfriend, although truth be told, she wasn't sure that's what he was anymore. Their relationship had always been complicated. She had been attracted to Troy in the first place because he was part of that same elite Special Forces world her father had run in, and yet he was nothing like her father. Troy was a snake-eater, brash and hyperconfident, an alpha male. He was possessive, even jealous, and initially, that had made her feel special. Protected. But now it just felt confining. She didn't need to be protected. She was a Delta Force operator.

And that was the real problem.

Hawk was pretty sure that Troy didn't know that she was in the Unit. She hoped he believed her cover story, that she was a CBRN specialist with the 43rd Support Battalion. She didn't want him to know the truth; not because of OPSEC, but because Troy had washed out of Delta selection on "Bloody Thursday," and if he ever learned that his girlfriend had succeeded where he had failed, he would probably blow a gasket. That she had to keep her greatest personal accomplishment a secret just to protect his ego pretty much epitomized why their relationship was doomed.

She knew what she was going to have to do; she had already put it off way too long. But now was definitely not the time for that conversation, or any other conversation, with Troy.

After grabbing her .45 and a couple boxes of ACP hardball, she got in her car and hit the road. D.C. was only a five-hour drive, and she passed the time listening to the audiobook of the latest Brad Taylor novel. She had initially thought the rally point might be a satellite DOD facility or some other federal or military site, but a quick check on Google Earth showed the address to be an ordinary business park in the D.C. suburbs.

It was just after dark when she arrived at the nondescript commercial building, one of about a dozen identical structures in the complex. She parked and walked the rest of the way, noticing only a single black Grand Marquis nearby, before arriving at the door to one of the business suites. There were no signs to identify the occupant, but through the window in the door she could see that there were lights on inside. As she stood there, wondering what to do next, she saw movement behind the glass, and then the door swung open to reveal the grinning face of Pete "Digger" Chambliss.

Digger was one of the good guys. A few years earlier, Hawk had worked closely with him, and Raynor and Slapshot, as part of an AFO cell looking for Libyan surface-to-air missiles in Cairo. That had been her first taste of what life would be like if she survived the training program to become a Delta operator.

Digger was in super-casual mode, wearing an O'Neill logo T-shirt and blue and white Hawaiian-pattern board shorts that revealed the DTOMMF sticker on the shin of the titanium prosthetic where his lower right leg had once been.

Hawk knew Digger had lost the limb *before* going through Delta selection, but it had not slowed him down one bit. Working with Digger was a humbling experience and a constant reminder that the best Delta operators weren't those without limitations, but rather those who overcame them.

"Guess I'm in the right place," Hawk remarked.

"I'm not sure I'd go that far," Digger replied. "But come on in anyway. I'll get you checked in and then you can go find a hotel or Airbnb or whatever."

As she stepped inside she saw a large and mostly empty room, with bare concrete walls and a sealed epoxy floor. The only furnishings were half a dozen folding tables arrayed in a horseshoe pattern, and enough folding chairs to seat forty or fifty people. The tables were all empty except for one, which sported a large pizza box, a half-emptied bottle of Naked Juice, and an open laptop computer plugged into a wall socket. As she rounded the corner, she saw that the computer screen was displaying video of an MMA fight.

Digger gestured to the pizza box. "You hungry?"

Hawk shook her head.

"The boss and Slapshot are still back at the house working out the details, so I'm ADVON-slash-CQ." He pulled a chair out for her and then sat down in front of the computer, minimizing the video player and bringing up a spreadsheet with the squadron roster. Digger was the squadron master breacher and part of the headquarters element, which was probably why he was here, minding the store. "Almost everyone else is still in transit. You're only the fourth person to check in."

"So what's going on?"

"Dunno. Some kind of urban training exercise. That's all I really know. The boss says he'll brief us up when everyone gets here."

"Everyone? The whole squadron?" Hawk shook her head doubtfully. "He pulled us all out of training that we absolutely need to get checked off on to do more training we don't need? Not buying it."

"C'mon, Hawk, did you really need to get certified to captain a forty-foot yacht?" Digger said. "Besides, it's just your troop, everyone else is still at their team training."

After what was clearly a long pause for dramatic effect, he leaned close and lowered his voice to a conspiratorial whisper. "So this is just between you, me, and the fencepost, but it sounds like the boss thinks that the guy who sniped the Greek PM is going to come after POTUS."

Hawk recalled the human jigsaw puzzle she had seen at the hospital in Athens. "The dead guy? Shaft and I went with Racer to PID the body."

"Not dead after all, at least not according to Racer. You know how he can get."

"Yeah. He's usually right," Hawk said. "That sixth sense nobody can ever explain."

Digger conceded this point with a tilt of his head. "I think he's afraid the Secret Service won't be able to stop this guy, so we're going to be providing an additional layer of security. Unofficially, of course. Because it would be illegal for us to go hunting for this guy on U.S. soil."

"So we call it a training exercise, and if we happen to get lucky . . . 'Aw, shucks,' right? Is Colonel Webber in on this?"

"That's between him and Racer, but I would guess so. Wrangler did something like this a few years back. He scheduled a training exercise in Panama, but had the squadron deploy with live ammo, so they'd be in position if the powers that be decided to send them into the jungle to hunt narcos. It was a real cluster. One of the helos had a hard landing and there were some injuries. I don't think Racer's expecting anything that extreme, but he's smart enough to cover his ass with the colonel."

Hawk nodded. Racer's plan embodied the sort of outside-the-box "how to think, not what to think" mentality that had long been a defining characteristic of Delta Force. "How long are we going to be doing this?"

"I guess as long as it takes. Or until we go on alert. Whichever happens first."

Six weeks, Hawk thought. She wasn't in any hurry to get back home, but that was a long time to spend living out of a ruck. "Wait. So we aren't coordinating with the Secret Service this time?"

"That's the impression I get. Strictly a shadow op. If nothing else, it will be a chance to dust off our urban tradecraft."

"How do we fill in the gaps in their coverage if we don't even know what they've got covered?"

Digger shrugged. "I'm sure the boss will think of something."

"Yeah, right. He'll say that's our job. A training objective." Even as she was saying it, the solution came to her. She took out her phone and brought up the contact list. Without a word of explanation to Digger, she scrolled down to a listing that had only a first name—Matt— and a phone number with a Maryland area code. She expected the call to go to voice mail and was mentally composing the message she would leave, but to her surprise the call connected on the second ring.

"Ah, hello?"

Hawk recognized the voice, but not the hesitant tone.

U.S. Secret Service Special Agent Matt "don't call me Matthew" Murphy had not struck her as the type of person to approach anything cautiously. He certainly had not held anything back in Athens when he had almost relentlessly tried to persuade her to "Netflix and chill."

"Oh, hey, Matt. It's Cindy Bird."

"I know. What's up?"

What's up? Hawk felt her ire start to rise. *What's up? You chased me for three days, and now all you can say is "What's up?"* She noticed Digger grinning at her and half turned to avoid his gaze before answering. "Well, I just found out that I'm TDY'd to the Pentagon for the next month or so, and I thought maybe you could . . . I don't know . . . show me the best place in this town to get a dirty martini?"

"Yeah. Look, that's not really gonna work for me. Sorry."

"Well, maybe—" There was a distinctive beep-beep as the connection was severed. Hawk held the phone at arm's length, staring at it in disbelief. "What the actual fuck?"

"Matthew Murphy just blew you off?" Digger asked, still grinning. "I guess his wife won't let him out to play."

She swiveled back to him. "No. Seriously?"

"Yup. What happens on deployment, stays on deployment."

"What an asshole." It occurred to Hawk that her indignation was misplaced. It wasn't as if she had been serious about returning his attention, after all. "Okay . . . delete. Lots of other names here."

"Who?"

She scrolled down her contact list. Not counting Murphy, there were three names from the presidential protective detail—the guys whose job it was to take a bullet for POTUS—and two from the CAT—the special reaction unit that hid in the shadows but was always ready to lay down a mad minute of cover fire in the event of a large-scale attack on the commander in chief. These were only the guys who had insisted on sending her their contact info during the brief partnership between Delta and the Secret Service. She had been very popular, and even though hooking up had been the last thing on her mind, she had enjoyed the attention.

"Jim?"

"Vaught? Married," Digger answered. "But he says they're only staying together for the kids."

"He's got kids?" She rolled her eyes. "Well, he still might be willing to go out for a drink."

"I wouldn't bet on it. These guys are under a lot more scrutiny at home."

"Curt Johnson?"

Digger shook his head. "Not sure about him."

Hawk made the call, got voice mail. She considered leaving a flirty, even suggestive message, but thought better of it and simply rang off without saying anything. "It seemed like a good idea."

"It *is* a good idea," Digger said, looking serious for the first time. He drew out his cell phone, and after a second or two of scrolling through the contacts, held the phone to his ear. "Hey, Todd? It's Pete . . ." He laughed. "Yeah, that's me."

Hawk remembered Todd Kearney, an earnest young special agent—the youngest in the PPD—mostly because he had *not* tried to flirt with her. He had actually seemed a little bit afraid of her.

"So, yeah. I'm working in D.C. for a few weeks and I was wondering if you wanted to grab some beers one night . . . Uh-huh. That's perfect. Cool, bro. Text me the address. Right. Later."

He ended the call and flashed a triumphant grin at Hawk. "I'm in."

"Bastard," she muttered.

"Hey, it was your idea. I'll make sure the boss knows. You deserve the credit." He stood and pushed the computer toward her.

"Where the hell are you going?"

"Didn't you hear? I got a date."

"Tonight?"

"Yep. It's his night off. I should be back in two or three hours. Thanks for covering CQ for me. Make sure everyone grabs their pocket litter and cover business cards from that box, and help yourself to the pizza."

So much for being one of the good guys, she thought. But then she realized that there were worse ways to spend the evening. Like enduring the company of Matt "don't call me Matthew" Murphy.

She pulled the computer to her and clicked on the video player, wondering if the MMA fight Digger had been watching was one she had already seen.

Kolt Raynor did a quick head count to verify that everyone was really there. He had only alerted a single troop for the mission, the one whose teams were closest to the East Coast, in order to recall them quickly. Kolt would bust the squadron budget for any more than a troop, which would bring Webber into the picture, something Raynor wasn't ready to do just yet.

The room looked empty, but Noble Squadron's assault troop two was fully present. The real problem wasn't empty chairs in the room, but empty slots in the roster. Stitch's absence was conspicuous, but it was only the most recent loss.

At full strength, there would be upward of twenty-four operators in the troop, along with a half dozen or so in the headquarters element. They were down to twenty-three total, and Colonel Webber had told him not to expect replacements anytime soon. The squadron—the whole Unit, really—was dangerously understrength, and had been for a while. Combat losses, career-ending injuries, burnout—there were a lot of ways to leave Delta. Selection and training simply couldn't keep pace with attrition, not after a decade and a half of constant war and high-stress operations. The problem had gotten so bad that the previous administration had floated the idea of rolling Delta and SEAL Team Six into a single joint special counterterrorism unit, a typical bullshit bureaucratic solution that would have done nothing to address the real problem.

Raynor cleared his throat. "Okay, first, I owe you all for cutting your team training short, and on short notice.

"In light of recent events, which to some extent we were all involved in, Slapshot and I decided to shake out our urban training and personal protection standard operating procedures. We're on the bubble for the next POTUS protective detail, and other VIPs, so your sergeant major and I have designed a training scenario that will challenge us all and sharpen our threat assessment and reaction skills.

"Big picture, our cover for status is employees of FTP Security Consulting Services. Cover for action is your unit creds." He made a sweeping gesture. "Welcome to FTP HQ."

"For those that don't habla," Slapshot broke in. "For. Training. Purposes."

"Task and purpose," Raynor continued. "We're going to be discreetly shadowing the Secret Service presidential protection detail, looking for gaps in their coverage that a terrorist or assassin might be able to exploit."

"Are we penetration testing the Secret Service?" asked Barnes.

"No." Raynor shook his head. "We aren't going to be probing or testing. In fact, we won't be interacting with them at all." He threw a knowing glance at Digger. "Not officially, anyway. We're just going to observe and collect."

Kolt picked up on the shift in Slapshot's body language. "In fact, if we are burned by the SS, consider that mission failure.

"POTUS's public itinerary, including scheduled public appearances outside the White House, is available online to anyone with an Internet connection. He's in D.C. for the rest of this week, but that could change at a moment's notice. We have to be ready to go wherever he goes.

"We've also got"—another nod to Digger—"a semi-reliable source inside the Presidential Protective Division who can supply additional information about Secret Service coverage. The areas of greatest vulnerability will be at those scheduled public appearances, or during movement to them, so that's where we're going to focus our attention. Recon the routes and locations. Find the weaknesses. Look for places where someone . . . say an expert sniper, like the guy who made the hit in Greece, might set up. If in the course of this training exercise you become aware of an actual immediate threat . . . well, use your best judgment."

Barnes stood up. "Uh, sir, you do realize that we are prohibited by federal law from acting in a law enforcement capacity."

"Is this even legal, boss?" another operator said.

Slapshot leaned close to Raynor and spoke in a stage whisper. "I could have sworn you just talked about this."

Hawk, who was sitting a couple seats away from her troop leader, now stood up as well. "We all know the law. And we all get that you're tiptoeing around it, but if you want us to get the job done, cut out the bullshit and just tell us what we're supposed to do."

There were cheers, but Raynor noticed that the reaction was not unanimous. Barnes sat back down, his cheeks going red under his five-o'clock shadow. Some of the others scowled. Their apprehension was understandable. Raynor was asking them to walk a fine line, to potentially jeopardize their careers by joining in what was essentially a vigilante action thinly disguised as a training exercise.

He had anticipated something like this. The Posse Comitatus Act did prohibit the army from conducting law enforcement activities on U.S. soil, but there were exclusions that allowed JSOC to operate in certain specific roles, which could include VIP protection. However, without official support from higher, Raynor knew he couldn't spin things that way, and he wasn't going to lie to his operators.

"Sit down, Hawk." He waited a moment for the din to die down. "Let me make this clear again. This is a training exercise. You will conduct yourselves accordingly. That said, there is a specific potential real-world threat to POTUS. The Secret Service has been made aware of this threat. They may or may not call upon us for additional manpower, but if they do, I want to be able to hit the ground running."

"And if they don't, sir?" Barnes asked.

"Let me worry about that."

TWELVE

Patience was the greatest asset of both the chess master and the sniper. Patience was essential to winning the long game, and the greatest test of patience came when the end was finally in sight, when the temptation to rush toward the finish became almost overwhelming. For the sniper, patience often meant waiting motionless for many hours, as Rasim Miric had done on Mount Lycabettus and dozens of times before that on battlefields around the world, and the time for that kind of patient waiting was drawing close. He knew when and where the target would appear. But there was still much to do first. Preparations to make. Pieces that needed to be moved, and moves that could not be rushed.

He found lodging at an extended-stay hotel within walking distance of the target zone, and then spent the rest of the week reconnoitering the area: verifying lines of sight and confirming his range estimates, studying traffic flow and potential escape routes. He scouted several possible shooting positions, settling on the rooftop of a twenty-three-story brick condominium property almost three-quarters of a mile away.

He also worked on establishing his cover. People were quick to notice even small changes in their environment, such as the appearance of someone unfamiliar, but after a few days the novelty wore off and they stopped noticing. The former stranger became just one more unremarkable face in the background. Each day, he bought coffee and a newspaper from the same corner store, then proceeded to a public park near the target area. Following that, he would don a polyester jacket and ball cap emblazoned with the logo of the courier service he ostensibly worked for, and with a few packages tucked under his arm, head for the apartment building. His disguise got him past the front desk, and while his initial appearance garnered a few curious looks from tenants, by the third day, he had free run of the building.

When the weekend came, he rented a car and drove back to Michigan for a prearranged meeting with Lyle "Lizard" Dooley. Developing an asset was another part of the game that could not be rushed. Young men like Dooley, and the Revolutionary Struggle cell he had similarly recruited in Athens, were often eager to be part of a heroic struggle, but by the same token were wary to the point of paranoia. Miric made the eight-hour drive without certain knowledge that Dooley would show for their scheduled rendezvous, but the young man was there, waiting for him at a truck stop along the interstate, and they headed into the backcountry to practice movement techniques and shooting. Miric had brought the young man a gift, a Leupold Mark 4 3.5–10×40mm

LR/T illuminated-reticle scope, along with enough ammunition for both of them to zero the weapon.

Throughout the day, Dooley urged him to reveal more
about the special mission for which he had been se-
lected, but Miric demurred. "Not yet. It is safer for
both of us if you do not have that information."

"I can keep a secret, Mr. Khavin."

"I'm sure that you can," Miric lied. "But you must
trust me. Compartmentalization of information is essential to the success of our mission."

"Yeah," Dooley muttered. "I know."

"All I can tell you is that our mission will be very
dangerous. We may not survive."

The warning—a bit of simple reverse psychology—
had the intended effect. "I'd rather die fighting," Dooley
replied solemnly, "than live under tyranny."

"No matter what happens," Miric said with equal
gravity, "history will remember you."

"Damn straight. When are we gonna do it?"

"Soon."

He spent the second week much as the first, moving
through his daily routine, alert to the possibility that he
might have unknowingly attracted unwanted attention,
although there was no sign of any surveillance. His visits to the rooftop where he was setting up his shooting
blind went completely unnoticed by the building's tenants, even though the parcels he carried were now larger
and heavier, and the interval between his arrival and departure increased a little more each day.

The blind, constructed of aluminum sheets brought

up in three separate trips and held together with a strong adhesive, resembled a large rectangular industrial exhaust fan housing. While not identical to the units already installed on the rooftop, the facsimile was close enough to withstand a cursory examination, and certainly good enough to fool the city's aerial surveillance cameras.

At midweek, he began to see increased activity at the target site. Uniformed policemen and official-looking men in suits, possibly police detectives but more likely government agents, walked the site conducting their own reconnaissance, assessing potential danger areas.

Right on schedule.

He watched them work as he ate his lunch in the park, and then from the rooftop blind through his spotter's scope. He took note of the surveillance airplanes that were now circling overhead with greater frequency. They were looking for him even though they did not realize it, but they were looking in the wrong place.

On Wednesday evening, he called Lyle Dooley. "It's time," he said.

"Mr. Khavin?"

"No names," Miric hissed angrily, as if the young man had committed a deadly breach of protocol. "It is time," he repeated, and gave Dooley brief directions to a truck stop off the Pennsylvania Turnpike near New Stanton—roughly the halfway point. "I will meet you there tonight. Leave immediately. Tell no one. Bring your equipment. You know what I am talking about."

"Wait, I can't just drop everything and take off. I got a shift tomorrow."

Miric sucked in his breath sharply. This time, his displeasure was genuine. "I thought that you were dedicated to the cause of freedom. A true warrior. Did I misjudge you?"

"No. I am. It's just . . . I mean, I've got a life here. Responsibilities."

"A life under tyranny?" Miric countered, throwing Dooley's earlier declaration back at him. "How will history remember you?"

There was a long silence on the line. Finally, Dooley said, "This is really it? It's happening?"

There was a nervous quaver in the young man's voice, but Miric knew he was already hooked. "It is," he said. "I will see you in a few hours."

Dooley's last-minute hesitancy was probably a good sign, Miric decided. If he had been turned and was now cooperating with some law enforcement agency, he would have been eager to comply, not the least bit tentative.

That did not mean, of course, that the authorities weren't watching Dooley and his fellow militiamen.

He removed the battery and SIM card from his phone and then headed out. It was a four-hour drive to the truck stop and he needed to get there ahead of Dooley to make sure that the location was safe. If Dooley was compromised in any way, Miric would simply cut him loose. The young man's part in the game was important, but not critically so.

His caution, while warranted, proved unnecessary. There was no indication of surveillance in place at the truck stop, and no sign that Dooley was being followed.

Miric observed the young man waiting pensively in his pickup for a full thirty minutes before making his move, pulling his rental car up behind the truck. He honked the horn to get the other man's attention.

Dooley climbed out and started toward him. "I tried to call you—"

"No more calls," Miric said, cutting him off. "Give me your phone."

The young militiaman frowned, but complied, handing over his mobile device.

Miric took it from him and popped out the battery and SIM card. He would dispose of the pieces later, but for the moment he didn't need any more questions from Dooley. "You brought your gun?"

"Dude, I brought all my guns."

Miric managed to hide his elation at this bit of news. "Bring them. And then lock up your truck. You'll ride with me from here."

The young man frowned but did not protest. He retrieved a large duffel bag and a long Pelican case from the bed of the truck and stowed both in the back-seat of the rental car before climbing into the passenger seat.

"We have a long drive ahead of us," Miric told him. "And long days to come. You should sleep now if you are able."

Dooley shook his head, visibly jittery. "No way. I'm too wired to sleep."

"I understand." Miric let off the brakes and began steering toward the exit. "I know you must have many questions. I will answer them now if I can."

"Where are we going?"

"Baltimore."

Miric's next "delivery" to the residential building consisted of several large parcels, which would have explained the presence of a second employee from the courier service, had anyone in the building cared enough to inquire. No one did.

He led Dooley up to the roof and, working quickly, they transferred the contents of the cardboard boxes, which consisted of heavy sandbags and flats of bottled water, into the camouflaged shooting blind. With that task complete, Miric invited the young militiaman to climb inside and have a look.

There was just barely enough room for the two men inside, and when Miric closed the panel shutting them in, the dark interior quickly became hot and stifling.

"Damn," Dooley whispered. "It's like a coffin in here."

"We will have to spend many hours here in order to complete our mission," Miric said. "Can you do that?"

Dooley's reply was an unenthusiastic "Yeah."

Miric tilted open a hinged port on a side panel, allowing a narrow band of daylight into the cramped blind, and then set up his spotter's scope on a mini-tripod, focusing it on the distant target zone. "Here. Have a look."

With some difficulty they exchanged places within the blind, and then Dooley peered through the eyepiece. He let out a whistle of disbelief. "That's . . . How far is that?"

"Approximately one thousand two hundred thirty meters. They will not think to look for us this far away."

"That's impossible. No way. Not with .308. Maybe with .50 cal or a custom load, but not with the shit I bought at Walmart."

"It is possible. An American soldier in Iraq recorded a kill at over twelve hundred and fifty meters using NATO 7.62×51 millimeter round."

"Yeah, I know about that. Staff Sergeant Jim Gilliland, USMC. He said it was a fluke. A one-in-a-million shot."

"Then you will make it two in a million," Miric assured him.

"Me?"

"Of course. Why else do you think you are here? This blow must be struck by a true American patriot."

"What if I miss?"

Miric smiled in the darkness. "Trust me, Lizard. You will not fail."

They returned the following day, Friday, with a final delivery that included a long box containing Dooley's Remington Model 700 with the attached Leupold scope. At Miric's urging, Dooley also carried one of the pistols from the small arsenal he'd brought along—a Taurus 24/7 G2 .40 caliber. They made their way discreetly to the roof, climbed into the ersatz vent housing, and settled in for a long wait. Dooley set up the rifle, bracing it with sandbags, and Miric positioned his spotter scope right beside him, but beyond that, they spoke little and moved less.

The interior of the blind was like a sauna. To stave
off heat exhaustion they drank copious amounts of water, urinating the excess into the empty bottles. There
were resealable plastic bags to use in the event that it
was necessary to defecate, but Miric knew from experience that they would probably not need them. At night
the outside air temperature dropped to a tolerable level,
but Miric had lined the thin aluminum panels with
insulating blankets in order to avoid giving off a distinctive heat signature, which might have been visible to the
aerial surveillance planes that he knew were watching,
so darkness brought only a little relief. Miric had endured far worse, but convincing Dooley to remain still
was a challenge that only got harder as the Saturday sun
rose into the sky.

"Keep watching the target area," he urged. "Practice
aiming your weapon at different targets. Try to predict
how the bullet will drop or be affected by the wind."

Miric followed his own advice, keeping watch on the
increased security presence at the target zone. He could
not distinguish faces, but he recognized familiar arti-
cles of clothing worn by people who seemed to be
spending a great deal of time in the area captured by
his scope. On Sunday, with just over twenty-four hours
before the target's scheduled arrival, there was a further
uptick in the security presence. Miric spotted men surreptitiously patrolling the streets, and agents in black
tactical gear establishing lookout positions on rooftops
and balconies closer to the objective. They would not set
up a position here, nearly three-quarters of a mile away.

As the last few hours ticked away, Miric closed his

one good eye and began mentally rehearsing the final stages of the plan. Several different things would have to be done in a very short period of time, and in a very specific sequence, if he was to both succeed and survive. He visualized the steps, flexing his muscles to ensure that, when the time came, he would be able to move with the necessary quickness.

"Are you sure they won't look here?" Dooley whispered.

Miric frowned at the interruption. "Not until it's too late." Then, curious despite himself, he opened his eye. "Why do you ask, now?"

"It's just . . . That chick down there. It's like she's looking right at me."

THIRTEEN

Cindy Bird didn't just trust Kolt Raynor, she believed in him. Which was why that nagging voice in her head, telling her what a waste of time the so-called training exercise was, felt like such a betrayal.

It wasn't that she doubted Raynor's identification of the sniper who had killed the Greek prime minister—a Bosnian named Rasim Miric, though Racer called him "Shiner"—or even the somewhat wilder claim that the man was still alive and presently stalking POTUS. She could take all that on faith. The problem was that protecting the president, and attempting to do so in a discreet manner, without official sanction, was damn near impossible.

In the two weeks since being recalled from their various training activities, the operators of Noble Squadron had mostly cooled their heels at the rented building in the Arlington business park, waiting for some last-minute announcement about an unscheduled presidential appearance. POTUS seemed to be conducting the affairs of state entirely from within the walls of the White House, or in locations accessible via the network of secure underground tunnels that connected the executive residence to the Capitol and other official locations. He met with lawmakers and advisers, and gave press conferences in the White House briefing room, but nothing he did would have exposed him as a target for Raynor's mythical undead sniper. The only item on the public schedule was a visit to Baltimore to talk about a new community policing initiative, kicking off with a very public meeting with the mayor on the front steps of city hall.

The prolonged inactivity was taking a toll on morale. Everyone knew that the training exercise was just a cover story—a pretty thin one at that—for Raynor's search for Shiner, and discontent was growing even among Racer's most ardent supporters. His detractors were walking the fine line between mere disrespect and insubordination, and it seemed only a matter of time before Barnes or one of the boys went over the boss's head and spilled the beans to Colonel Webber.

Maybe that had already happened. Maybe Webber was giving Raynor a little more rope to hang himself with.

Hawk had a feeling that if something didn't happen—if Shiner was a no-show—Raynor would have to admit defeat and try to salvage what was left of their training cycle. But they were here now, on the ground in Baltimore, and she was going to do as instructed and give it her all.

POTUS wasn't expected for another two hours, but

the lawn of War Memorial Plaza, just to the east of city hall, was already crowded with people hoping to catch a glimpse of the president, or, more likely, hurl insults at him. Many of them were carrying hand-painted signs with angry accusatory messages directed at both the president and the Baltimore PD. Tensions between the city government and the mostly black, economically disadvantaged population had been hovering near critical mass for years, and the outcome of the recent election had evidently left residents feeling even more disenfranchised.

Between the crowds and the towering baroque building that housed the municipal government stood a phalanx of BPD officers in riot gear, and a smaller contingent of Secret Service special agents, some of whom Hawk recognized from Athens. She wasn't too worried about being recognized by the latter. They were too busy doing their job, looking for threats instead of looking for familiar faces. But if Racer was right, the real threat was a lot farther away.

Standing in front of city hall, Hawk scanned the horizon in every direction, looking for places from which a sniper of exceptional skill might—hypothetically speaking—try to take a shot at POTUS. City hall itself blocked the view to the west. There were several tall buildings to the south, but those had already been checked and cleared by the police. So had all the structures in direct line of sight to the west, which included one of Baltimore's most notable landmarks, the Phoenix Shot Tower. The 234-foot-tall redbrick tower would have been a perfect spot for the sniper to set up if not for two things. First, it was too close, barely two hundred meters from city hall. Second, it was already occupied by a Secret Service counterassault team.

The high-rise buildings of downtown blocked the line of sight in nearly every other direction except almost due north, along the Jones Falls Expressway corridor. Hawk stared in that direction, wishing she possessed the visual acuity her code name suggested. If Shiner really was the shit-hot marksman that Raynor believed he was, then that was the only direction from which he might be able to strike.

"Shaft," she said, pointing north. "How 'bout we go that way?"

As they made their way north, through the downtown business district, Hawk kept checking behind her to verify a direct line of sight with city hall. The buildings to either side of the street averaged about six to eight stories high, and as they continued north into the Mt. Vernon neighborhood, the buildings were even shorter, but there were high-rise buildings visible in the distance at the far limit of her vision. She tagged them using the RaptorX Mobile app on her phone—an open-source version of the satellite mapping system used by the Unit and other military agencies—checking the distance of each to city hall. One likely candidate, a twenty-three-story redbrick condo building, was just over 1,200 meters out. Another, twenty stories high, was almost 1,350 meters.

"Clear lines of sight on both of those," she muttered.

Shaft remained skeptical. "It's a longshot."

"No kidding."

* * *

Miric brought his eye to the spotter scope. He had no difficulty locating the woman to whom Dooley was referring. She stood almost directly at the center of the field of view. He couldn't make out her facial features, but her slight build and distinctive figure were readily apparent, especially in contrast to the men standing around her. And, as Dooley had suggested, she appeared to be looking directly at them.

"It is coincidence," Miric said. "With the naked eye, she cannot even see building."

"Yeah, I guess so. But it's still kind of freaky."

The woman kept staring for a few more seconds, but eventually turned to one of the men with her. Miric saw a flicker of movement behind her, dark hair pulled back in a ponytail. Then, just as quickly, she returned her gaze to whatever it was that had captured her attention, this time raising an arm and pointing a finger that seemed to perfectly align with the scope's central aiming reticle.

"Dude," Dooley whispered. "She sees us."

Miric did not know what to say.

The woman lowered her arm and began moving, walking in the direction she had just indicated. The three men who had been standing beside her followed.

"They're coming!" Dooley said, his voice now rising to a dangerous volume. "What do we do?"

Miric's jaw clenched tight. As impossible as it seemed, they had been discovered. "There is only one thing we can do," he whispered.

*   *   *

"How far out did the SS guy say they checked the perimeter buildings?" Hawk asked.

"One klick, typically," Shaft said. "Rarely more than that, for numerous reasons."

"Shiner used a Dragunov in Greece," Hawk said. "That's within the max effective range for that rifle, right?"

"We'll check them out," Shaft said, though his tone was skeptical.

"Shit!" Hawk said. "Did you see those two light flashes?"

"No. Reflections?"

"I'd swear on it," Hawk said.

They set a brisk pace and reached the closest of the two five minutes later. Shaft flashed his ersatz Secret Service creds to the young African-American woman at the sales desk. "Hi . . ." He checked the plastic nameplate on the desktop. "Grace? We're doing a routine security assessment. I guess you heard the president's in town?"

"Ugh," Grace complained. "Don't remind me. Everyone's talking about it. I wish they would get a clue."

Shaft nodded patiently. "We need to have a look at the rooftop, Grace."

"The rooftop isn't one of our public areas."

Shaft gave her a disarming smile. "That's why we need you to show us up."

As they rode the elevator to the top, the four Delta operators planned their next move, communicating with nothing more than eye movements and head nods. Hawk would run interference with Grace, while the other three assaulters checked every corner of the rooftop. Even though the odds of finding Shiner there were slim, they were going to execute the search with the same level of professionalism as in any other operation—live or simulated. That was the only way to get the job done and, more importantly, ensure that you made it back to the squadron bar for a cold one at the end of the day.

Hawk kept Grace occupied with small talk on the elevator ride up, and then, as soon as the woman unlocked the door to the stairwell leading up to the roof, deftly maneuvered her out of the way so that Venti and Joker could go through first. Grace didn't even seem to notice. Once outside, Hawk let the other woman take the lead again, moving toward the edge of the roof. From the corner of her eye, she could see Joker cautiously peeking around the corner of a concrete structure— probably the mechanical room—before disappearing around it.

There was no sign of anyone else on the roof, but Hawk remained vigilant, surreptitiously slicing the pie as she moved past a large metal vent cover near the southwest corner. When she and Grace reached the edge of the roof facing south, she surveyed the urban mosaic below. It took her a moment to find the distant green rectangle of War Memorial Plaza and City Hall beside it, but when she did, she immediately recognized that the roof was a viable shooting position. With the right weapon, a skilled sniper would absolutely have a shot.

But there was no sniper.

She turned to see her mates approaching from different corners of the roof. Shaft gave an almost imperceptible head shake.

Nothing here.

Feeling slightly deflated, Hawk turned to Grace. "How often is the roof accessed for maintenance and things?"

"Oh, I don't know, maybe twice, three times a week?" Grace said.

"Any services yesterday or today?" Hawk said as she trailed off, realizing that something wasn't right. She glanced to her right, checking the southeast corner, which was wide open and empty, then raised a hand, signaling her mates to close on her. Only then did she turn back to Grace.

"That vent in the corner," she whispered. "How long has it been here?"

Grace glanced back, shrugged. "I don't know. I don't come up here."

Hawk raised a finger to her lips as she drew the M1911 from her shoulder bag. Grace's eyes went wide in alarm, but she said nothing. Hawk waved the others closer, keeping the weapon aimed at the vent cover. Now that she was actually looking at it more closely, it was obvious that the structure was fake. A prop. There were no rivets or seams, just overlapping sheets of metal forming a slightly oblong cube, about one meter high and wide, and almost two meters long. But the real giveaway was the placement. There was no reason to put a large exhaust fan directly above a residential unit, but it was the perfect spot for a shooting blind.

Shaft and the others approached, their weapons drawn and likewise aimed at the metal structure. Shaft nodded to Venti, who crept closer, and then signaled that he would go on three.

Hawk squared her shoulders and found her trigger as Venti started counting silently with raised fingers.

One.

Two.

Three.

He ripped away one of the panels, and then rolled to the side, coming up in a crouch with his pistol aimed into the camouflaged blind.

"Clear!" Shaft called out.

Hawk relaxed her finger. The blind was empty.

No, that wasn't quite right. There wasn't a person inside, but there were objects. Dozens of water bottles—some empty, some obviously filled with piss—were strewn haphazardly around the interior. Several corrugated boxes had been flattened and stacked to form a raised platform, and several sandbags had been arranged on top of it to form a stable firing position.

Venti's face twisted in disgust. "That hide reeks, man."

Shaft leaned in for a closer look. "Someone's been living in here. A few days, at least."

Behind them, Grace let out a squeak of dismay.

"He was here," Hawk said, realizing for the first time that Raynor had been right. Shiner was real.

"Good call, Hawk," Venti said. "You definitely were picking up optics or spotter's glass."

"Hard to believe that spooked them from this far away," Shaft said.

"He saw us coming up the street," Hawk said, thinking aloud. She turned to Grace. "Did someone leave right before we got here? Someone you didn't recognize?"

Grace stared at her, goggle-eyed and mute, so Hawk gripped the woman's shoulders and gave her a shake. "Grace. Stay with me. Did anyone leave right before we showed up?"

"No." A pause. "I mean, I recognized everyone who left. They all live here. Except the couriers."

"Couriers? As in more than one? When did they leave?"

"Maybe five minutes ago," Grace said, clearly rattled by the flurry of questions. "They were early today. I didn't actually see them come in. Someone else must have let them in."

"Describe them," Hawk said. "Do you have security video cameras?"

Grace shrugged helplessly. "The cameras are just decoys, they don't really do anything. They're just the package guys, though."

"Black? White? Tall? Heavy?"

"White. I think the shorter one is Russian. I don't know about the new guy. I really don't talk to them much. Oh, he wears an eye patch. The Russian, not the new guy."

"Eye patch?" Hawk looked over at Shaft, but he was already dialing his phone.

FOURTEEN

Rasim Miric was angry. Angry at whoever it was that had interfered, outmaneuvered him. Angry at himself for having let it happen. It was not the first time he had been forced to abandon a position, but it was the first time he could remember being caught without a backup plan.

He had miscalculated the vast security checks before a POTUS speech, much more thorough than those carried out by officials in Greece. He also realized he should have never let Lizard view the objective area with a spotting scope during the daylight, due to the sun reflection. Yes, he knew better.

In any endgame, it was necessary to commit completely to a course of action, but there was always the possibility of the opponent doing the unexpected, making a move that defied logic. A skillful player weighed the risk, accepted it, but also established contingency plans. He had failed to do that. He had invested himself completely in a successful outcome. Now he had to figure out how to regain the advantage.

With only a few slight changes, he was able to utilize his original egress plan to escape both the high-rise and the city. The first thing he had done was order Dooley to break down and pack up the rifle. He had originally planned to leave it behind, but since it had not yet accomplished its purpose, there was no sense in simply abandoning it. He might still have need of it. Everything else had to be left behind, which was unfortunate, since it would confirm to the American authorities that an attempt had very nearly been made on the life of their president, but there was nothing to be done about that.

After departing the building, they discarded their courier uniforms, and Miric took the further step of donning dark glasses and deploying a white guide cane. If the authorities questioned the tenants of the building, they would be on the lookout for a man with an eye patch, not one evidently blind in both eyes. The ruse got the two of them to Miric's escape car, parked a few blocks away.

That part had gone off mostly as planned, even with last-second modifications, but once in the car and on the move, Dooley had started melting down.

"What do we do now, man? They're gonna know."

"Shut up," Miric hissed. "I need to think. Just drive."

This was much worse than the close call in Greece; not because he had nearly been discovered, but because he had failed to carry out the hit. All the pieces were still in place, the preparations made, and now it was all use-less.

"They'll get our fingerprints," Dooley said, ignoring the admonition. "Our DNA. We're so screwed."

Miric turned to look at him. He was not particularly worried about the physical evidence that had been left behind. Knowing his identity would not help the authorities track him down.

Dooley, however, was another matter. Maintaining the young man's anonymity had never been part of the plan, but then neither had this failure. Miric had been planning to kill him at the first convenient opportunity, when they were well away from Baltimore, but now it occurred to him that perhaps Lizard had not completely outlived his usefulness.

Maybe there was a way to salvage this mess.

"Have you ever been arrested?" Miric asked.

Dooley shook his head.

"You were not in the military?" Miric already knew the answer to that question. Dooley had opted for the militia as an alternative to serving in the army of what he considered to be an illegitimate government. "They do not have your DNA or fingerprints in their data-base. Besides, what crime have you actually commit-ted? Trespassing? No one will know what we intended to do unless you tell them. Are you going to tell them?"

"Of course not."

"Then drive. For now, you will go back to your life as if none of this happened."

Dooley contemplated this for a moment, then nodded.

"Yeah. I'll just . . . Shit. I've missed too much work. No call, no show. My ass is so fired. How am I going to explain where I've been?"

Miric sighed. "I'm sure you will think of something to explain your absence. As for your employment, you need not worry about that. You have other work now. Unfinished business."

Dooley looked over in alarm. "What? No way, man. I can't go through all that again. I'm out."

"You are warrior, now!" Miric said sharply. "While warrior lives, he fights. Quitting is not a choice for you."

The young man looked back at him, eyes wide. "When are we going to . . . ?"

"I do not know," Miric admitted truthfully. "But soon."

FIFTEEN

Kolt Raynor was already en route to the compound when he got the call from Webber's secretary. The message relayed was short and one-sided. "Colonel Webber needs you to report to his office, ASAP," Joyce had said, and then hung up without elaborating further.

Raynor took the terse message as a bad sign. Hawk's discovery of the shooting blind on the rooftop in Baltimore had pulled back the curtain on the squadron's pseudo-unauthorized training activity, and even though they had almost certainly stopped the assassination attempt before it happened, not to mention handing the police and Secret Service a substantial amount of physical evidence—DNA, fingerprints, some fuzzy outdoor surveillance camera footage of Shiner and his as-yet-unidentified accomplice—Raynor got the distinct impression that Webber was not calling him back to the Unit to congratulate him.

He decided to make one quick stop before entering the lion's den. When he reached the Delta Force compound, hidden away in a remote section of Fort Bragg, he went straight to the squadron bay, shaved, and dumped his civvies for his best set of sterile Multicams.

Webber's secretary wore a concerned expression, which Raynor took as another bad sign. "Hello, Kolt, go right in. He's expecting you."

"Thanks, Joyce," he told her, managing a wan smile.

Kolt noticed Joyce lean forward, closer to him. "Just a heads up, Kolt, but Major Taylor and Colonel Johnson are in there too."

Kolt's eyebrows raised and he frowned slightly at hearing both the Unit JAG lawyer and psych were there too. "Coincidence?"

"I'm afraid not."

"Well, the more the merrier. Thanks, Joyce."

He took one final breath and then opened the door and strode in.

Webber sat at his desk, statue-still, but Raynor knew the man well enough to see the barely contained anger under the surface. Kolt advanced to within two steps of the desk—the prescribed distance for reporting to a superior officer—and stood at attention. He could make out the other two in his peripheral vision, but figured he needed to be a little more formal. Kolt thought about saluting and offering the bullshit conventional greeting, but such protocols were never observed in the building, and judging by his mood, Webber would probably assume Raynor was being a smart-ass anyway.

"Damn it, Racer," Webber growled. "What the hell were you thinking?"

Immediately Kolt knew why Doc Johnson was present.

My decision-making process is being questioned?

The tone wasn't quite as harsh as Raynor had expected, but before he could reply, Webber added, "And don't give me some sorry story about a training exercise."

Since Webber had not told him to sit down, Raynor stayed at the position of attention and kept staring straight ahead. "Sir, it *was* a training exercise. I crossed every i and dotted every t. Standard urban recce troop training. That said, I'm damn proud the boys just happened to inadvertently discover and disrupt a threat to POTUS. Right place, right time. It's as simple as that."

"Bullshit. You broke the law."

Kolt realized now why the Unit lawyer was present. "We weren't acting in an official law-enforcement capacity. Posse comitatus doesn't apply."

Kolt noticed Webber look over at Major Taylor. "Well, partially true," Taylor said, "not that simple though."

"And did you authorize your people to carry weapons? Are you aware of the laws concerning concealed weapons in the state of Maryland?"

Ignoring Webber's rapid-fire questions, Kolt said, "Sir, we deployed with cover creds. If rolled up, no official backstop was activated to cover their ass."

"Now that could be a problem," Taylor said.

"My God, Kolt," Webber barked, "this command can't keep turning a blind eye to your personal whims and repeated blowing off of established protocol."

Raynor clenched his teeth, but he wasn't going to

whimper. He had covered his ass on paper by stipulating that personal weapons would not be sanctioned, but he wasn't going to throw his operators under the bus just to dodge that HEAT round. "Sir, we saved POTUS's life. I'll take responsibility—"

"Your accepting responsibility doesn't mean shit, Kolt," Webber said, cutting him off.

"Look, sir, with all due respect, I'm not going to downplay the significance of what we did in Baltimore. I took a chance and we got lucky," Kolt said.

A long moment of silence from Webber as he sat down behind his desk. Kolt tensed, sensing he was about to take it through the chest and be escorted off the compound.

"Raynor, at this point I'm ready to have Doc give you a piss test and tell Taylor to pull your clearance."

Here it comes.

"Unfortunately, the people that really matter are way above my pay grade. Those folks are so grateful that you stopped this threat that they have conveniently chosen to ignore a bunch of gunned-up mavericks roaming the streets of Baltimore. Which is the only reason you're here and not in the slammer. Whether there's still a place for you in our ranks remains to be seen."

Kolt felt a chill at the ominous statement. Webber didn't make such threats lightly. "We didn't," he said.

"Didn't what?"

"Stop the threat. Shiner got away." Raynor paused a beat to let that sink in. "Respectfully, sir, no one else was even tracking this threat. I tried to do this the right way and it didn't work, so I did what I could with what was left. If I hadn't, POTUS would be dead. But Shiner is still out there and he's going to try again. Shitcanning me isn't going to change that."

Webber glowered at him and Kolt immediately felt as if he'd said way too much.

"Shiner." He spat the word out like a curse. "Where's the intel confirming it was Shiner?"

"Sir, it's sketchy, but he is confirmed in the U.S. The key nuggets are that the building in Baltimore was outside the Secret Service's protective ring, and one of the shooters had a Russian accent."

"How many other guys you know that could take that long of a shot, Kolt?" Webber said with a slight bit of sarcasm.

"Only Unit snipers, sir," Kolt said.

Kolt and Webber locked eyes, almost as if they were at a standstill, not sure who should make the next move.

"Sir, you told me to prove that Shiner was still alive," Raynor said.

"I did at that." Webber let out a sigh. "You do realize that you just skated through a minefield. You've used up all your luck. Any more rogue ops will get you another ride on the Black Chinook."

"That bird has to land somewhere, sir."

"This isn't a joke, Raynor. You upstaged the Secret Service on this one. If you keep pushing, they're going to remember that you broke the law, and that will come back to bite us all in the ass. Stand down from this."

Raynor knew that Webber was giving him an out, but there was too much at stake for him to simply let it go.

"Sir, that is absolutely the wrong move. Shiner lost this round, but he's not done. He will try again, and this time he'll be twice as careful. We're already pre-positioned to go after him. We just need the attorney general to waive posse comitatus so we can make it official."

"That isn't going to happen, Raynor."

"Sir, we can't just stand by and let this happen." Raynor realized he was shouting and paused long enough to dial it down a notch. "There is a clear and present danger to POTUS. At least let us keep doing what we're doing. I'll make nice with the Secret Service, give them the credit. The training exercise story gives us cover from posse comitatus. Let's keep using it."

"You're a JAG lawyer now?" Webber drummed his fingers on the desktop.

Kolt's eyes turned toward Major Taylor as Webber addressed him.

"Judge, what do you think?" Webber asked.

"Handled delicately, sir, it's within your authority," Taylor said.

"If I say yes to this, you have to lock up the weapons. That's one line you don't get to cross."

"Actually, sir, our standard workaround should suffice. As long as all operators are using their official federal credentials, we are covered," Taylor said, "from a legal perspective."

"From a legal perspective, huh," Webber said, obviously still on the fence. He pondered it all for a few more moments, then gave a heavy sigh. "I don't want to think about all the ways this could blow up in my face. But it is the president of the United States. JSOC is too busy downrange in two dozen hot spots to add this to the plate."

He raised his eyes to meet Raynor's gaze. "I meant what I said about rogue ops. If you're going to do this, even as some kind of bullshit pseudo-FTX, at a minimum you need to bring the Secret Service on board. It's a joint exercise or none at all. If they don't want your help, this doesn't happen."

Raynor was pretty sure he could convince Jess Simmons to at least tolerate their continued presence in an unofficial status. "Understood."

"As for carrying weapons, I would prefer to avoid subjecting your questionable legal interpretations to a test in a court of law. Standard creds, appropriately backstopped.

"Do not dick this up. You are out of favors. And I don't need to remind you that Noble goes on alert status in four weeks. I'll indulge you that long, but not a day longer." Webber shook his head. "Honestly, Racer, I don't know if I'm supposed to hope that you're right about all this or not."

"Frankly, sir, I wish to God I was wrong. Because if we can't stop Shiner, getting fired will be the least of my worries."

The minor success in Baltimore, combined with tacit approval from higher for the ongoing shadow operation and open cooperation with the presidential protection detail, supplied a much-needed boost to morale. It also gave Kolt the opportunity to recall the rest of Noble Squadron and read them in.

Despite Webber's assertion that they had made the Secret Service look bad, SAIC Simmons seemed, if not contrite, then at least grateful for the unofficial assist in Baltimore. It probably helped that Raynor resisted the urge to remind Simmons that his earlier attitude had nearly cost the president his life. Special Agent Todd Kearney was assigned to act as a training liaison, and because Raynor was now able to coordinate directly with the protective service instead of sneaking around behind their backs, he was able to implement a five-on, four-off troop rotation, which was fortunate since there was little actual work for any of them to do.

It was another week before POTUS left the safety of the White House, this time for a jaunt to the West Coast to visit San Francisco, Portland, and Seattle. The outing gave the squadron a chance to satisfy the notional conditions of the training exercise and conduct a search of every rooftop and balcony within two thousand meters using fresh satellite imagery, Predator overhead coverage, and cell phone intercepts, all courtesy of Brian Kelly from the SCIF. This yielded nothing interesting. Likewise, a recce of each and every location where POTUS would be in the open yielded nothing actionable. An unplanned visit to Houston, New Orleans, and Biloxi, prompted by heavy flooding in the wake of a category three hurricane, was likewise uneventful.

Raynor was acutely aware of the ticking clock. He had nothing to show for his efforts, and Simmons was becoming increasingly territorial, even antagonistic. Worse, the nationwide manhunt for the sniper and his still unidentified accomplice was going nowhere. None of the leads generated in Baltimore had panned out. They had no video imagery of the would-be assassins, but the pair likely would have been careful to avoid looking at the cameras, keeping their heads tilted down at all times so that the visors of the caps they wore hid their faces. The DNA and fingerprints recovered from the shooting blind on the rooftop had yielded no matches.

Raynor wasn't sure what to make of Shiner's accomplice. Everything Raynor had heard about Shiner over the years, which admittedly was mostly rumor and hearsay, indicated that he was a loner. Raynor had assumed that he had been acting alone in Greece, but now he wasn't so sure. Was the other man his spotter? His apprentice? His employer, perhaps?

Which raised the further question of motive. The working theory was that Revolutionary Struggle had hired Miric for the assassination of the Greek PM, but who was calling the shots now?

With less than two weeks to go, Raynor was facing the very real likelihood that he would never know the answer. There was zero chance that he would be able to pick up the hunt again after Noble stood down from alert status, and the longer Shiner stayed off the radar, the less of a threat he would seem to the Secret Service.

Yet, Raynor did not believe the sniper would wait months or even weeks to strike. The dust from the assassination in Greece was already beginning to settle, and while the fate of the EU and NATO remained uncertain, it looked as if cooler heads would prevail. Despite the nationalistic rhetoric of the new PM, Greece simply couldn't afford to leave the EU, and POTUS and the State Department were doing everything they could to keep NATO together. If Shiner's plan was to deliver a one-two punch to utterly destabilize the West, he would have to strike before the figurative glue dried.

Then, with just a few days left before the switch to alert status, the White House press office announced that POTUS was heading to New York to commemorate the anniversary of 9/11. He would give a rousing speech about America's ongoing commitment to fight extremism everywhere, after which he and the first lady would place a wreath at the National 9/11 Memorial.

Raynor was certain that Shiner wouldn't pass up an opportunity like that, but whether he did or did not, it would be Kolt's last opportunity to stop him.

Standing at the edge of the pool that occupied the space that had once been the foundation of the South Tower of the World Trade Center, it was impossible for Raynor not to think about that moment, sixteen years ago to the day, when nearly three thousand lives had been lost in what remained the deadliest terrorist incident in history.

He had been on the other side of the world, racked out with the rest of his squadron in a large yellow-and-white festival tent, preparing for a still-classified joint readiness exercise, when an operations officer had burst in and delivered the news. News that would put the entire Joint Special Operations community on a permanent war footing. A war that he was still fighting.

Raynor had not come to the 9/11 Memorial to reminisce, nor was he here to sightsee. He knew better than to expend any brain cells on the ghosts of the place, and concentrated on the security briefing. SAIC Simmons was putting out the final itinerary for POTUS's visit, information that would not be made public, but that was essential for those assigned to protect the president and first lady. That included not only the agents of the presidential detail, but also several hundred NYPD officers, as well as two troops from Noble Squadron who were there strictly "for training purposes."

The visit to the memorial was only one of several stops that POTUS would be making in New York City, which meant that there would be several opportunities for Shiner to strike, but Raynor's gut told him it would happen here. Not only were there the symbolic considerations, but the openness of the site and the length of time POTUS would be exposed made it the obvious location from a tactical point of view. This fact was not lost on Simmons. There was a secure cordon of several blocks in every direction, with police patrols on every street, checking every building that faced the plaza. Raynor was hard-pressed to find any holes in the security plan, but he knew that if there was even one, Shiner would exploit it.

After dismissing the bulk of the gathering, Simmons moved over to where the Delta operators were clustered. "So," he said, making no effort to keep his voice down, "where are the Hardy Boys"—he glanced at Hawk—"and Nancy Drew going to be while the rest of us are working?"

Raynor felt a flush of anger. "The Hardy Boys" was a well-known nickname for Delta Force, mostly used by other Special Forces operators. If just one of the NYPD officers in earshot was a former Ranger, or even a reader of military literature, their cover was blown. As Kolt fought the urge to take a swing at the Secret Service agent, Slapshot stepped out to meet Simmons. "Well, I'm going for coffee," he said. "How 'bout I pick you up a nice big cup of shut-the-fuck-up."

The SAIC froze. Special Agent Kearney, who had been standing next to Digger during the briefing, stiffened as if preparing for a fight, one he knew he would lose. After a few tense seconds, Simmons managed a nervous chuckle. "Jeez. Lighten up."

"OPSEC isn't a 'lighten up' kind of thing," Raynor shot back. "You of all people should get that."

Simmons grunted. "Look, we took your advice seriously. You see that, right? Your guy would have to be a special kind of stupid to even show his one-eyed face in Lower Manhattan, much less try and take a shot at Champ."

"I hope there's more to your plan than 'be on the lookout for a guy that looks like a pirate,'" Hawk remarked.

"As a matter of fact—"

Raynor cut him off. "Jess, your precautions are fine. You're right. Shiner isn't stupid and he's not going to make the same mistake twice. But he's got the easy job. He only has to be in that one perfect spot at just the right moment, while you have to be everywhere all the time. So let us help you."

"I'm telling you, he's not getting inside our perimeter."

"Unless he's already here," Hawk said. "Hiding out like he was in Baltimore."

Simmons shook his head. "He's not. We've canvassed the area, checked every surveillance camera for a thousand yards out, kicked every box and every Dumpster in every alley. Maybe we aren't going to find him, but we're sure as hell not going to let him get the chance to take a shot. Protection is about denial of opportunity. That's what we've done here, and it's what we're going to keep doing."

"I guess you've got it covered, then," Raynor said.

"We do. So, I ask again, where are you going to be?"

"Don't worry, Jess. We'll stay out of your way."

Simmons held his stare for a moment, then shook his head and walked away. Kearney looked like he might follow his boss for a moment, but then he relaxed. "Sorry. He can be a jackass sometimes."

"Sometimes?" Digger said with a grin.

"His question stands," Barnes said. "What are we even doing here?"

Raynor stared out across the memorial grounds for several seconds, trying to see the area as Shiner did. "The same thing we've been doing. Figure out what they missed."

There was a long silence, which Slapshot finally broke. "I don't think they missed anything, boss. It's not completely airtight, but this place is locked down."

Raynor turned back, gazed at each of his operators in turn. "Hawk, you almost had him in Baltimore. Do you agree?"

"We were aiming high in Baltimore," she answered.

"Giving him the benefit of the doubt that he could make that shot. I'm not sure he could have done it. Maybe that's the real reason he bolted."

"We've pushed the perimeter out a lot further," Kearney said. "Put a lot of resources into watching the far-away threat. But we are concerned that maybe that's what he wants."

"Misdirection?" Kolt murmured. It didn't feel like the right answer. Everything he knew about the man told him that Shiner was an artist, specializing in long-distance murder and pathologically driven to sign his work with a bullet through the eye of his target. Yet he knew he couldn't afford to dismiss the possibility that he was wrong. And there was the matter of the second man, Shiner's accomplice. Maybe Baltimore had been a ruse. A feint designed to draw attention away from the close-in threat.

"Anyone else?"

"I think Kearney might be on to something, boss," Digger said.

"It's classic psy-ops," Slapshot added. "Like you said. He's been fucking with us."

Raynor nodded slowly. "Okay. We'll go with that. Assault teams go foxtrot, take the memorial plaza. Blend in with the crowd. If you see something, you say something. Then you do something."

"Like make a citizen's arrest?" Barnes asked with more than a trace of sarcasm.

Raynor ignored him. "Digger, keep Todd in your pocket and stay as close to POTUS as you can. Head on a swivel. Recce teams stay mobile . . ."

He turned, looking away from the memorial site, down the streets—Liberty Street ran east to west across the south end of the plaza. West Street and Greenwich Street framed it on either side running north and south. To the north, there was a clear line of sight running up Greenwich Street, but the area where the motorcade would be unloading was blocked by the newest addition to the New York skyline, the latest building with the address One World Trade Center, also called Freedom Tower. There were other possible vectors to the south, east, and west.

"Start walking," he finished. "Check balconies and rooftops. I don't care if you bump into NYPD on their way out. Check them again and keep checking until POTUS gets back in Stagecoach and drives away."

"How far out?" asked one of the recce operators.

"Until you get wet," Slapshot said with a laugh. "There's water about a klick in every direction."

Raynor knew that from his earlier map reconnaissance, but for some reason, the comment struck him.

One kilometer.

In Athens, Shiner had made a shot from that distance. In Baltimore, if they had read the scene correctly, he had been preparing to take a 1,200-plus-meter shot.

He took out his phone and opened the Google Earth app. As Slapshot had indicated, it was almost exactly one kilometer to Battery Park, at the southern tip of Manhattan Island. Past that point, the next solid ground was Governors Island, another kilometer beyond.

He wouldn't have put it past Shiner to attempt a shot at that distance. The seven longest confirmed sniper kills were all in excess of 2,000 meters. But he would also need elevation just to be able to see his target, and there were no structures on Governors Island high enough to give Shiner a view of the 9/11 Memorial.

Brooklyn was closer, just 1,800 meters away, on the far side of the East River, but when Raynor turned in that direction, looking east down Liberty Street, he saw the much closer high-rise buildings of the financial district.

To the west, down Liberty Street, there was open sky as far as his eye could see. According to Google Earth, the Hudson River was only five hundred meters away, but another kilometer and a half past that, barely visible on the horizon, was Jersey City and the forty-two-story-tall steel-and-glass structure at 30 Hudson Street, informally known as the Goldman Sachs Tower.

Two kilometers.

If Shiner was there, if he planned to take that shot, it would be one for the record books. But it was more than just a literal long shot. It was far more likely that Kearney was right, and that the real threat would come from somewhere a lot closer.

Sending a team across the river to check it out would almost certainly be an exercise in futility, and, worse, a dangerous misallocation of manpower.

He put his phone away and addressed the group. "We've got two hours. Get to it."

Slapshot waited for the operators to disperse before speaking his mind. "Okay, boss. I know that look. What are you thinking?"

"Let's take a walk."

SIXTEEN

It took less than ten minutes for Raynor and Slapshot to walk to the World Financial Center ferry terminal in Battery Park City. From the pier, they had an unobstructed view of 30 Hudson Street. The tower, the tallest building in New Jersey, was perched on the water's edge, making it appear even taller in contrast with the other buildings on the skyline.

After boarding the ferry, Raynor moved to the bow and discreetly brought out a Leupold M151 spotting scope and zoomed in on the slightly tapered upper floors of the tower.

He scanned along the edge of the rooftop, noting the positions of the raised suspension structures that held the window-cleaning scaffolds. There was no movement on the roof, no sign of any windows removed, no sign that anyone was there at all, but if Shiner was there, he would be in the prone, camouflaged. All but invisible. There was only one way to really know if he was there.

The ferry ride took just eight minutes, and delivered

them to the Paulus Hook terminal in Jersey City, practically on the doorstep of the Goldman Sachs Tower. The building was a destination for several of the passengers debarking, and the two operators moved along with the flow. Once inside the spacious glassed-in reception area, Slapshot approached the closest receptionist and held open his wallet to reveal his cover creds. "Federal agents, ma'am. We need to speak to your head of maintenance."

He continued displaying the card for another second or two, just long enough for the receptionist to see it without really seeing it. Raynor wished that he'd brought Hawk along. She had a gift for getting strangers to go along with whatever it was she needed them to do. Slapshot's approach was equal parts intimidation, charisma, and bullshit.

"Uh, sure," the woman said, reaching for her telephone. "I'll give him a call."

"Thanks." Slapshot flashed a Cheshire cat grin. "Say . . . I don't suppose you've seen anyone come through here wearing an eye patch."

The woman blinked at him. "Seriously?"

Slapshot turned to Raynor and raised one eyebrow in a "told you so" expression.

They rode up to the top floor in an express elevator, then moved to the fire stairs for the final ascent to the rooftop. Reaching the roof wasn't as easy as it looked.

"How often do you get on the roof?" Kolt asked.

"Every day, buddy," the building engineer said with pride.

"C'mon, really, level with me," Kolt said. "Every day?"

"Well, okay, two, three times a week max," the engineer sheepishly said, "but the job doesn't require more than that, honestly."

As the engineer opened the last door, both operators readied themselves for the possibility of an immediate hostile confrontation, but the space beyond was deserted.

The rooftop itself was sheltered on all sides by a high wall, part of the tower's ecofriendly design, but a steep metal staircase afforded access to the catwalk that ran along the outer perimeter. Raynor let Slapshot take the lead, advancing up the steps, cautiously, ready to duck back down at the first sign of trouble, but the catwalk, like the rest of the roof, was empty. The only thing moving was the air, rushing past in a stiff ten-mile-an-hour breeze. He stared out across the Hudson at the distant spire of Freedom Tower.

After clearing the corners, Slapshot came over to stand beside him. "Well, now we know one more place he isn't," he said, almost shouting to be heard over the wind. "What now? Ready to head back?"

Raynor checked his watch. It had taken them about forty minutes to get this far. POTUS would be arriving in just over an hour. Plenty of time for them to make it back to Ground Zero.

Plenty of time for a lot of things to happen.

"What if he's waiting till the last minute?" Raynor said, thinking aloud. "This is key terrain."

"What if we're just chasing our tail?" Slapshot retorted.

"You're giving this guy too much credit. It's not just the distance. A shot like that . . . It would be like threading a needle one-handed. Blindfolded."

Slapshot wasn't wrong. Trying to isolate a single human-sized target from a distance of nearly a mile and a half would be just the first impossible task Shiner would have to accomplish.

"I'm not saying he can make the shot," Raynor said. "But I think he's just arrogant enough to try it."

Slapshot's reply was a noncommittal grunt.

After the curious question from the federal agents, the receptionist kept a lookout for anyone sporting an eye patch, but she did not give even a second look to the man with dark glasses and white guide cane, holding the arm of the young man who walked beside him, mostly because she recognized them both from their visits earlier in the week. Even the enormous artist's portfolio dangling from a strap slung over the young man's shoulder failed to catch her attention. Most business executives favored electronic media for their presentations, but there were still a few who liked to go old school with butcher paper and printed charts on poster board. Had she been paying attention, she might have noticed that the young man seemed especially agitated, but even this she might have dismissed as the consequence of too much caffeine or Adderall.

The pair moved toward the elevators, out of sight and out of mind. Later, she would not even remember having seen them at all.

* * *

Lyle "Lizard" Dooley *was* jittery. Miric could feel the nervous energy radiating off the young man as they rode up in the elevator. As they exited from the car, Miric squeezed Dooley's elbow hard and steered him away from the other departing passengers.

"Get control of yourself," he hissed.

"I know," Dooley replied, his tone harsh and loud enough to draw attention their way.

Behind his dark glasses, Miric was obliged to ignore the stares. He was supposed to be blind, after all. Nevertheless, he held the young man there for several more seconds until the hallway was empty.

He had spent the last three weeks pretending to be blind. There was no telling how much information the authorities had been able to glean from the Baltimore rooftop, but the one thing he was certain of was that they would still be looking for a one-eyed man, so he had become a man with no eyes at all. He and Dooley had returned to Michigan, but only long enough to establish an alibi that would explain the young man's sudden departure and then his subsequent absence. From there, they had gone to a safe house in Rockville, Maryland, set up by Miric's partners in the Turkish intelligence agency, and waited for another opportunity to present itself.

The New York visit was far from ideal, but with each passing day, the risk to the endgame increased. There were many other pieces in place that were already in jeopardy. If he waited much longer, the entire strategy would collapse.

So it had to be New York.

"I got it," Dooley said. His voice was lower, but he was still shaking in nervous anticipation of what they were about to do.

Miric shared some of the other man's apprehension. Although the plan was his, it was a considerable deviation from his normal method of operation. There were too many variables that he could not control, too many things that could go wrong.

And it had been a while since he had killed someone up close.

"Good," he said, letting go of the young man's arm. "Just as we practiced."

They continued down the corridor, then turned and headed down an adjacent hallway, following the well-rehearsed route to an east-facing suite that was presently occupied by the marketing department of an investment bank.

As they approached, Miric abandoned the pretense of groping his way forward like a blind man. He even folded up his white cane and stuffed it into a pocket. He reached the double glass Herculite doors a few steps ahead of Dooley, threw them open, and strode inside.

The female receptionist looked up, smiling as she recognized him from his earlier visits. Miric took the Taurus semiauto from his jacket pocket and shot her through the eye.

Mehmet had once asked him why he always targeted the eyes of his victims. It had nothing to do with his own disability and everything to do with the fact that the eye was a reference point that he could easily find, even from long distances. But he also remembered the stories his grandmother had told him as a child, stories about the power of the evil eye. When he looked through his scope or down the iron sights of a rifle, he invariably found himself staring into the target's left eye.

Some childish, deeply superstitious part of him believed that if that person died while looking back at him, even from several hundred meters away, their death would forever haunt him.

The report was shockingly loud in the close confines.

With his left hand, Miric removed his dark glasses. His right continued to hold the pistol out before him, aimed at the doorway behind the reception counter. The woman was still seated but was now slumped over her desk, facedown.

He knew that every move he and Lizard had made since entering the building had been recorded and would be reviewed extensively in the hours and days to come. In fact, he was counting on it. His only concession to preserving his identity was a pair of thin black gloves to avoid leaving fingerprint evidence.

A man in shirtsleeves appeared behind the dead woman. "Delores, was that a—"

Miric pulled the trigger a second time. The man collapsed in a disjointed heap behind Delores in her chair.

Dooley was still at the entrance, trying to thread a heavy chain through decorative pull handles on the glass doors. Although the doors opened out, the chain would hold them together, preventing anyone from entering, especially once Dooley secured the links with a padlock. The young man had correctly pointed out that the chain would also make it harder for them to leave when they were finished, but Miric assured him they would not be leaving by that door.

The young man was fumbling with the links, his nervousness evidently robbing him of dexterity.

"Hurry!" Miric hissed, and then returned his attention forward to the door leading deeper into the office suite. He stepped over the body in the doorway and saw three more people—two women and a man, standing in the hallway beyond, paralyzed with fear or perhaps disbelief.

It took him just two seconds to kill them all. The last one to die, the woman farthest from him, managed to turn away in a futile attempt to flee, and his first shot at her missed completely. His second hit her squarely between the shoulder blades.

A door at the end of the hall burst open and an overweight man in an expensive suit charged out, brandishing a small J-frame revolver. With shaking hands, he stabbed the pistol in Miric's direction, but before he could pull the trigger, a .40-caliber round from the Taurus put him down.

Miric had always heard that everyone in America carried a gun and so was not surprised by the appearance of the man with the revolver. He waited a few seconds to see if anyone else would rush out to meet him. The hallway remained still. The only movement was from the whorls of smoke drifting in the air around him.

"Got it!" Dooley shouted from behind him.

"Wait!" Miric said. He advanced cautiously down the hallway to the first door, which was on his left. The dead woman lay in a heap in the doorway. The office beyond appeared to be empty. Miric watched and listened for a moment, then moved on.

In the next office, he found a man hiding under a desk, sobbing, praying perhaps. Miric killed him and kept going, moving relentlessly toward the office at the end of the hallway. There was no one else in the suite, which came as a relief to Miric. From their earlier scouting missions, he had estimated that the number of people in the suite at any given time might be as high as twenty.

As he pushed into the large office, he stooped over and retrieved the unfired revolver that lay beside the dead executive. If all went according to plan, he would have no need of an additional weapon, and it might even complicate the situation, but if experience had taught him anything, it was that sometimes the best-laid plans went awry.

The room beyond was enormous, easily three times as large as the other offices, but its most commanding feature was the view. The entire back wall was made of glass, and looked out across the Hudson River toward Lower Manhattan.

"Lizard!" he shouted. "Come."

He did not wait for the young man to catch up, but immediately went to work clearing an area in front of the large window. When Dooley finally arrived, his face betrayed his horror at the carnage Miric had left in his wake. Miric struggled to conceal his disgust at the other man's weakness. "Quickly. Set up the rifle."

Dooley knelt and opened the portfolio, revealing the partially disassembled Remington 700, and another of his firearms, a Mossberg 500 12-gauge pump-action shotgun, modified with a tactical pistol grip and a fourteen-inch barrel. He handed the latter to Miric, then began putting the rifle together.

With the shotgun held at a low ready position, Miric moved closer to the windows, close enough to reach out and touch them. He pointed the barrel of the shotgun at the windowpane, aiming low, slightly above floor level, then looked away and pulled the trigger.

The noise of the blast made the pistol's report seem like a toy by comparison. If the earlier shooting had not already gotten the attention of the tenants in neighboring suites, the shotgun definitely would, but that could not be helped. The police would respond quickly to 911 calls, but because they were in New Jersey, separated from the New York financial district by the Hudson River, the Secret Service would not be alerted to the active shooter situation. Not right away, at least. Miric would only need a few minutes. The chain around the door pulls would buy them the time they needed to complete their mission.

He looked down to see the effect of the first load of double-aught buckshot. There was a ragged hole, almost as big as his fist, in the three-eighths-inch safety glass. He pumped the action on the shotgun, shifted his aim a little to the left, and fired again, repeating the process, macerating the glass until half the pane was gone. He used the smoking barrel to clear away the last few hanging fragments then turned back to Dooley.

The rifle was still in pieces.

"We don't have time for this," Miric hissed, thrusting the shotgun at him. "Take it. And get out of the way."

Dooley's cheeks flushed red but he took the weapon and moved aside. Miric knelt and, with practiced efficiency, reassembled the rifle. He unfolded the bipod legs and set the weapon up on the floor directly in front of the smashed-out window.

He got down behind the rifle and peered through the scope, shifting and tilting the weapon until he located his reference points. He worked his way down by degrees until he found the target area.

Two kilometers away, flashing lights heralded the impending arrival of the target.

He let out a sigh of relief. The motorcade was just arriving. The timing was perfect.

He fed three rounds into the rifle's internal magazine and then began adjusting the scope to his zero.

"What am I supposed to be doing?" Dooley asked.

Miric rolled onto his side, looked up at him. Dooley had set the shotgun aside and was resting on his knees, looking completely lost.

In their rehearsals, it had always been Dooley behind the gun—the patriotic warrior striking the first blow in the war against tyranny, launching the second American Revolution. But even if he had possessed the skill, to say nothing of the nerve, to actually make the shot, allowing him to do so had never been part of Miric's plan. Dooley had a very different part to play in the endgame.

"Just one thing," Miric told him. He got up to his knees facing the young man and proffered the semiauto. "Take this."

Dooley accepted the weapon, reversing it so that he

was holding the pistol grip in his right hand, but his uncertain expression remained. "What should I do with it?"

Miric reached out with both hands, covering both the pistol and Dooley's hand as if preparing to offer a benediction. "Just this one thing."

He slipped his thumb into the trigger guard, and then in a single swift motion, thrust the weapon up under the young man's chin and pulled the trigger.

Blood and gray matter erupted from the top of Dooley's head, splattering the ceiling and the wall behind him. Miric let go, allowing both the weapon and the young man's body to fall away, and then lowered himself once more behind the rifle.

Although the area in the immediate vicinity of the 9/11 Memorial had been closed off to both vehicle and pedestrian traffic, the crowds gathered on the other side of the barricades were large and boisterous. When the first of nearly twenty police motorcycles traveling ahead of the motorcade rolled into view with lights flashing, the noise spiked toward a crescendo. A high school marching band, which had been playing their familiar game-night repertoire for nearly an hour, went silent, except for the drum line, who began pounding out a martial rhythm in anticipation of the impending appearance of the most important man in the world.

Twenty yards away from the band, "Digger" Chambliss had to press one hand to the side of his head in order to hear the comms traffic coming over the earwig in his right ear. He could feel every beat of the large bass drum reverberating through his body like some kind of sonic weapon. The band seemed like a particularly bad idea, not only because it was completely at odds with the solemn nature of the occasion and the intent of the memorial's designer to create a place for quiet contemplation and reflection, but also tactically. With the volume cranked up to "11" it would be almost impossible to hear shouts of warning or even gunshots.

But it was POTUS, so by God somebody was going to play "Hail to the Chief."

The motorcycles were followed by several police cars, marked and unmarked, and then the six imposing vehicles that looked like Cadillac Escalades straight off the showroom floor. They were, in fact, custom-built armored machines constructed on truck chassis. Digger didn't know which one held the president, designated Stagecoach, or sometimes "the Beast," but he guessed it probably wasn't the fourth in line, the one equipped with the Warlock electronic countermeasures system.

The ECM vehicle was readily identifiable because of the distinctive cylindrical antenna protruding from the roof. That antenna effectively blanketed the area with intense RF interference, disrupting wireless communications and making it impossible for a bomber to use a cell phone or some other remote device. The Warlock, and a similar system called Shortstop, could even be configured to trigger radio-controlled devices prematurely, but while that was a partially effective deterrent against IED attacks on convoys in war zones like Iraq and Afghanistan, it wasn't feasible for use in America's largest city, and not just because intentionally detonating

IEDs on city streets might put the civilian population in danger. Americans were in love with their smartphones, and disrupting the local cellular network was not something to be done lightly. The Secret Service had the ability to shut down all mobile devices in a two-kilometer radius, but rarely did so because of the shitstorm it inevitably caused.

The Secret Service operated on a restricted radio frequency that wasn't jammed by the Warlock, which was the only way for Digger to keep track of what was going on, and, if absolutely necessary, communicate with his mates. As far as the Secret Service was concerned, there was no ambiguity about Delta's role. They were observers only. Guests doing a ride-along. And guests, like fish, had a shelf life.

There had been no real friction between the two groups, but the general attitude of the PPD was that Raynor was chasing shadows. Baltimore *had* been a failed attempt, but it would have failed regardless of Delta's illicit interference. Of course there was a threat. There were dozens of threats, and managing them was what the Secret Service did. Every day.

Digger hoped that Racer was wrong—hell, Raynor probably hoped that, too—but wishful thinking was a recipe for disaster, so until the boss called it quits, he was going to keep doing his job.

But he really hoped Racer was wrong.

The motorcycles and police cars cruised past but the armored vehicles stopped right in front of the memorial. A dozen more vehicles pulled up behind Stagecoach and the decoys: vans carrying journalists; police cars; a blue shuttle van carrying the president's emergency medical team; ambulances; and a black truck that contained a mobile arsenal for use by the Secret Service in the event of a large-scale attack.

The drums abruptly went silent, the drum major holding his baton high, poised to give the signal that would begin the customary ruffles and flourishes.

The moment seemed to drag on forever, but then doors began opening and Secret Service agents began getting out, forming the protective bubble that would envelope POTUS as he moved from Stagecoach to the more sheltered dais between the two pools where he would be delivering his prepared comments.

The drum major dropped his baton and the horns and drums sounded.

Digger's head was on a swivel, scanning the crowd then coming back to the motorcade, back and forth, looking for any hint of a threat.

A message came over the comms, letting everyone know that Champ was about to make his move. Right on cue, the band began playing "Hail to the Chief." Digger glanced over and saw President Noonan, standing just outside the second armored SUV, smiling and waving, presumably for the cameras since very few in the crowd could actually see him with the vehicles blocking their view. After a moment of this, POTUS ducked down and extended an arm into the car, and then Mrs. Noonan emerged.

There was another radio update. "Challenger is out."

"Challenger" was the Secret Service code name for the first lady of the United States, who was now standing beside her husband, smiling and waving as well. Then, walking arm in arm, the first couple began moving toward the memorial plaza.

Digger was just starting to turn away again when, out of the corner of his eye, he saw a faint haze of red in the air, but it wasn't until he heard the screams that he knew something terrible had happened.

SEVENTEEN

Raynor's heart sank as he heard the eruption of chatter in his earpiece. The frantic voices were almost incoherent, but he didn't need to understand what was being said to know what had happened. Someone had hit POTUS while he and Slapshot had been wasting time hanging out on the roof of a high-rise tower a mile and a half away. Maybe it had been Shiner, or maybe someone else, but regardless, the worst had happened, and he was in absolutely the wrong place.

He turned to Slapshot, noted the grimace of helpless frustration that mirrored his own expression. He didn't need to say anything.

They bolted down the steps, back into the tower, and sprinted to the elevator foyer. Raynor had to fight the urge to step on the Secret Service transmission, asking for details. If this had been Greece, he would have done so already, but now that the situation had gone beyond merely a potential threat, the only thing for him and his operators to do was stay out of the way.

But he had to know.

Slapshot hit the button to call the elevator, punching it repeatedly as if doing so might bring the car even faster. It wouldn't, Raynor knew, but saw no point in disabusing his friend of that belief. Just then, he felt his phone vibrate in his pocket.

The caller ID showed New York City as the point of origin and a 212 area code, but Raynor didn't recognize the number. He accepted the call anyway. "Yeah?"

"Boss!" He recognized the voice immediately. It was Digger, and he sounded like he had just run the four-hundred-meter dash. "Shit's happening down here."

Raynor instantly grasped that Digger had sprinted to the nearest landline in order to call him. With cell phones jammed and no freedom to use the Secret Service radio freq, it was the only way to make contact.

A chime sounded, announcing the arrival of the elevator. As the door opened, Raynor put out a hand to stall Slapshot. He couldn't risk losing the call.

"Challenger got hit," Digger went on. "Don't know how bad yet. They're medevacking her now."

"Challenger," Raynor repeated, mostly for Slapshot's benefit. If POTUS had been the primary target, then the assassin had missed, striking the first lady instead. It was small comfort. "Did they get the shooter?"

"Negative. Still looking, but . . . Boss, it was a sniper."

"You're sure?"

"Pretty sure. High-velocity round. If I had to guess, I'd say it came in from high up and out of the west. Boss, that's where you are, right?"

"He's not here. We were on the roof when it—"

Just then, an ear-splitting klaxon sounded. Emergency strobe lights began flashing all along the corridor.

"Shit!" The suddenness of the alarm had startled Raynor, but he just as quickly realized that it could not be a coincidence. "Digger, stay right there. We gotta bolt."

After the first iteration of alarms, a voice came over the PA system, instructing everyone to remain where they were, secure their doors, and wait for the police to arrive. Since it was not only impractical, but damn near impossible to evacuate high-rise buildings in the event of a fire or some other disaster, the safer alternative was to only evacuate the people occupying the floors closest to the incident and send them up or down as far as needed to escape immediate danger. The fact that the occupants of the top-most floor were being told to stay put and lock their doors meant two things: whatever was happening wasn't on this floor but it was close—probably just two or three floors down—and it wasn't a fire.

"Active shooter protocol." Slapshot yelled to be heard over the alarms. Raynor saw that he had his old M1911 out. "He's in the building."

"Stairs!" Raynor drew his own weapon—a Glock 23—and sprinted down the corridor, following the path marked by the flashing arrows on the exit signs as the klaxons sounded again. He hit the heavy fire door at a run, and started down the austere concrete steps.

"Which floor?" Slapshot called out.

Raynor didn't know the answer to that question, but figured eventually they would run into someone who could tell them. Sure enough, over the din of the alarms, he could hear voices coming up the stairwell from just a couple floors down. As they rounded the corner onto the fortieth floor, they almost collided with a group of people headed up. One of the women in the gaggle saw their guns and started shrieking.

"Ma'am, it's okay," Raynor said, flashing his cover creds and trying for his best soothing voice, which was a challenge since he had to shout to be heard. "We're the good guys."

"Yeah," Slapshot added. "Where are the bad guys?"

"On our floor," said one of the men indignantly, as if they ought to have already known that. "I knew this would happen. It was only a matter of time."

"Which floor?" Raynor pressed.

"Thirty-nine," supplied the first woman. She had stopped screaming but seemed on the verge of a relapse. "Oh my God. It was right next door. I heard everything but no one believed me."

Raynor pushed through the cluster and kept going, bounding down the steps two at a time. When he reached the thirty-ninth-floor landing, he dashed to the fire door, grasped the handle, and was about to throw it open when a heavy hand came down on his shoulder and pulled him back.

"Slow down, hero," Slapshot growled in his ear. "You forget how we do this?"

"Damn it, Slap, we don't have time for 'slow is smooth' bullshit."

Slapshot's hand did not move.

Raynor knew his mate was right. There was no telling what they were going to find on the other side of that door, so they had to treat it and every other door, blind corner, and intersection like it was an ambush waiting to happen. With just two of them, clearing the floor was going to take a while, but it was the right call.

He backed away from the door, his Glock raised to avoid flagging Slapshot. "You get the door, I'll go through first."

"The hell you say, boss," Slapshot said, gesturing toward the door with his pistol. "I lead, you follow me."

Kolt nodded. Slap was more than just an operator, he was a seasoned assaulter, and no self-respecting Unit non-com would ever let the officer lead into the breach. Yeah, Kolt got it.

He got in position, and after a three-count, yanked the door open. Slapshot moved, leading with the pistol, covering the left side of the corridor beyond. Kolt was right behind him, covering the right side.

The hall was empty.

They got oriented and headed toward the east side of the building, bypassing dark and deserted office suites as they went. There wasn't time to clear them all, but Slapshot kept checking their six o'clock as they moved to make sure that no one was coming up from behind them. They rounded the corner to the side of the building that faced the Hudson, but stopped before crossing in front of a pair of glass doors leading into a suite with the lights still on.

Raynor pressed himself against the wall. "This is the one."

"See anyone?"

"Not yet." Still leading with the pistol, he pied the

corner. The reception area appeared to be empty, but he saw something else that confirmed his earlier appraisal. "The door is chained shut. From the inside."

"Some employee's good idea. Keep the shooter out?"

"Possibly, but I'm not buying it," Raynor said. "Slap, Shiner's in that office. Has to be."

"Lock himself in to buy time?"

"Only way to make sure no one could stop him."

"Yeah, but now he's trapped in there. You think he knew this would be a one-way trip?"

Raynor didn't answer. He had never bought into the idea that Miric would martyr himself. In fact, Kolt's entire rationale for hunting the sniper in spite of his apparent death in the explosion in Athens had been predicated on the idea that Miric was not suicidal. "Maybe he's got another way out."

"What, like a ladder? A rope?"

"Parachute, maybe. We're high enough for that." Raynor eyed the chain holding the doors shut. There weren't any wires or explosives attached to it. "We need to get in there."

Slapshot sighed. "Yeah, I suppose we do. You got a brick we can throw through that glass?"

Raynor reached behind his back and slid out the SureFire can. "Just this. Ready?"

"Do it."

Kolt finished tightening the suppressor on the threaded barrel, aimed the weapon at the top corner of the door on the left side, and pulled the trigger. The entire pane of half-inch-thick tempered glass instantly went opaque and then collapsed in a shower of fragments that looked like giant diamonds on the carpeted floor. Slapshot raked the remnant glass left in the door's bottom corners and moved in, pistol held out before him in a modified-isosceles shooting stance, ready to engage any target that presented itself on the left-hand side of the room. Raynor took the right.

They did not stop to check the bodies in the reception area or the hallway. Their job was to neutralize any threats that presented before attending to casualties.

The air stank of burned gunpowder, more than Raynor's single shot to break the glass door would account for. Another body lay in the doorway of the office at the end of the hallway. Beyond, Raynor could see daylight and feel the rush of wind flowing in through an open window.

But skyscraper windows didn't open.

He paused outside, waiting for Slapshot to catch up. When they were both set, he gave a three-count and moved in, clearing left as he had done before.

He saw the whole room in that instant, but did not allow his conscious brain to process any of it until he was certain that there was no threat. There was only one person in the room, lying awkwardly on the floor with his legs folded up under him like Freddie Mercury doing a knee slide, but while he did have a pistol in one outflung hand, along with a Remington 700 SPS and a short-barreled Mossberg 500 pump-action shotgun within easy reach, he wasn't a threat. The top of his head was missing.

"Clear," Raynor muttered.

"Clear," Slapshot echoed. "Is that your guy?"

Raynor glanced down at the body. "Nope. Must be the accomplice. Likely the guy that was with him in Baltimore." He moved to the window and looked out, searching for Shiner's escape route. He half expected to see a parachute canopy floating out in the river, or maybe one of the window-washing scaffolds lowering down the side of the building, but nothing looked out of the ordinary. "Maybe there's another exit."

"Maybe there's another explanation," Slapshot retorted. "Like the obvious one. This guy was the shooter. He came up here, locked himself in, killed everyone, took the shot at POTUS, and then popped himself."

Raynor turned back, fully prepared to challenge the scenario, but then Slapshot added, "Oh, and he missed, which according to you, Shiner never does."

That stopped Kolt. Shiner *didn't* miss. He wouldn't have even taken the shot unless he was certain of success, both of the hit and the exfil.

"You say Shiner's a hired gun," Slap continued. "Maybe they fired him. Hired this loser instead."

"Maybe—"

"Hello?"

The voice was faint, barely audible over the rush of wind coming in through the broken window, but both men were instantly on alert.

"Is it safe? Are you police? Can I come out?" The voice was male with an unusual cadence, possibly a foreign accent, and seemed to be coming from the hall behind them.

Slapshot looked over at Raynor and mouthed the word "Survivor?"

Kolt shrugged. Anything was possible. He nodded in the direction of the voice and they started moving. "We're federal agents," Kolt shouted. "Stay where you are."

"I hide under desk when shooting starts."

The voice was definitely coming from the nearest side office, the one just past the woman who had been shot in the back. "Move out into the open," Raynor called out. "Lie on the floor with your hands out in front of you."

"Yes, I am moving now."

Kolt pied the corner, peeked into the room, saw movement. A figure was crawling across the floor between the desk and the doorway, just a couple steps away. There was something in the man's right hand.

"Empty your hands!" Raynor barked. "Drop it!"

The man immediately let the object fall. It didn't appear to be a weapon, at least not a conventional one. It looked more than anything else like a folded-up collapsible nylon tent pole.

"You're blind?" Slapshot asked from behind Kolt.

"Yes." The man's voice rose at the end, almost like it was a question.

"Guess we can't ask him if he saw anything," Slapshot muttered.

"Just stay where you are," Kolt said. "We'll let you know when it's safe to move."

"Yes," the man said again. "Thank you."

He raised his head, smiling, his eyes hidden behind dark glasses.

But Raynor recognized him anyway.

EIGHTEEN

Raynor brought his pistol around, aiming it at the unarmed man.

Unarmed. The realization gave him pause.

It was Shiner. The man who had killed countless American soldiers, assassinated the Greek prime minister, attempted to kill POTUS, and possibly just murdered the first lady. But he wasn't armed, wasn't threatening anyone, and Raynor had absolutely no legal standing to take his life on American soil.

That moment of hesitation was all Shiner needed. Like some kind of spring-loaded toy, he launched off the floor and hurled himself straight at Raynor, slipping inside Kolt's guard, and slammed a shoulder into Raynor's chest. Miric wasn't a big man and the blow wasn't hard enough to hurt or even stun Raynor, but it did cause him to take a reflexive step back, right into Slapshot. In that instant, Shiner scrambled around the two men like a monkey scurrying up a tree, and leapt into the hallway beyond.

"Shit!" Raynor swore as he struggled to disentangle himself from Slapshot. Bunching up in the doorway had been an absolute rookie mistake on both their parts, as was letting a potential hostile get close enough to make a move like that.

They had both been snookered by a pair of dark glasses and a white cane.

Raynor twisted around, half crawling over Slapshot, and threw himself out into the hallway, aiming the pistol at the retreating form, but before he could pull the trigger, Shiner ducked around the corner and vanished.

Still half crawling, half flailing, Raynor got his feet under him and took off in pursuit, reaching the reception area just as Miric disappeared down the outside hallway. Kolt sprinted after him, feeling the crunch of broken glass underfoot. He could hear Slapshot shouting something, probably telling him to wait.

There wasn't time to wait. Shiner would never be more vulnerable.

It wasn't hard to piece together Miric's escape plan: kill his accomplice and stage the scene to make it look like a one-man suicide mission, then pretend to be a survivor of a shooting rampage that conveniently killed every other witness to the crime, and because he appeared to be blind, the police probably wouldn't even question his story. If anyone else but Raynor had been the first on the scene, it might even have worked. Now he was alone, unarmed, and effectively trapped in the high-rise. The only chance he had to escape was to outrun Raynor, which meant Kolt could not afford to wait for backup. Slapshot would just have to get the lead out and run faster.

Miric disappeared around another corner. The tower was a damned maze and Raynor knew he wasn't going to get a clear shot, so he holstered his pistol on the run, and then poured on a burst of speed to close the gap. The effort was already taking a toll. He had not earned his Unit code name because of his prowess as a runner. Still, there was only one place Shiner could go: the stairs.

Raynor almost caught him there. The heavy door slowed Miric down just enough that Raynor was able to reach the door before it closed. He blasted through it like a linebacker hitting the scrimmage line. Shiner hadn't yet rounded the landing at the midway point. For a split second, Kolt contemplated leaping off the top step, diving out into empty space in order to tackle the other from above, but his instinct for self-preservation was stronger than his urge to sacrifice everything to take the killer down. He wasn't that desperate. Not yet.

But Shiner evidently was. He was bounding down the steps four at a time with the surefootedness of a mountain goat, and leaving Raynor in the dust.

Screw this, Raynor thought. At the next landing, he skidded to a stop and hauled out the suppressed Glock that was tucked into his appendix area, then leaned over the railing and aimed down at the fleeing figure. Shiner was a moving target, but only about twenty feet away. Kolt led him for a second, but just as he was about to pull the trigger, a second form came into view right beside Miric—a security guard on his way up the stairs.

Raynor lifted the weapon, finger coming off the trigger automatically. "Stop him!"

Miric was already several steps past, and the guard was staring stupidly up at Racer.

"Shoot him!"

That seemed to get the guard's attention. He turned and drew something from his belt holster, aiming it down the steps. A stream of partially aerosolized liquid shot through the air, forming a hazy fog in the air above the steps. Raynor didn't dare slow down, but charged past the guard and headlong into the vapor cloud.

"Fucking pepper spray?" Kolt rasped as his eyes began to sting. "Shit!" He didn't know if he was angrier about missing his best opportunity to put Shiner down, or about very nearly shooting down a stairwell with no idea who else might be on it. Now he had to factor in other civilians on the stairs who might be hit by a stray shot or a ricochet. At least he wouldn't have to worry about the guard shooting *him*.

But Shiner's lead was growing by the second.

Kolt blinked away the pepper spray and drove on, taking the stairs one at a time in short quick steps to reduce the chances of stumbling. Maybe he would get lucky and Shiner would take a spill.

The nightmare spiral seemed to go on forever. He kept his left hand on the inside rail, letting it slide on the flights and gripping it on the landings in order to pivot around the turns. It wasn't long before he encountered more civilians. Some of them were hugging the outside wall, others were picking themselves up after being shoved out of the way by Miric. Raynor almost tripped over one of the latter, avoiding that fate only by vaulting the rail and launching himself over the stunned victim. His momentum carried him all the way to the landing, and as soon as his feet touched down, he slammed face-first into the wall.

The impact left him seeing stars and tasting blood, but he stayed on his feet. As he pushed away from the wall, he tapped the bottom of the mag, and brass-checked his Glock to ensure it was still hot. There were large painted numbers beside the door—"12"—the twelfth floor. Kolt turned, almost lost his balance, and resumed the pursuit; only now he had no idea how far ahead Shiner was.

There were even more civilians below, a veritable migrating herd. Racer surmised the order had been given to evacuate the entire building, or maybe just the lower floors. He wasn't sure if that would complicate things on the ground floor or not. If the police were locking the place down, they would hold everyone in the lobby until they had the situation under control.

They might not even notice a blind man slipping through their cordon, but they would definitely notice a guy running with a suppressed pistol. Kolt slipped the Glock back into his appendix and tugged his shirt down over the grip.

"Coming through!" he shouted, and when that garnered only dumbfounded stares and grudging compliance, he tried again. "Out of the way. Federal agents!"

The numbers on the wall ticked down and the gaggle on the stairs got thicker, slowing him almost to a walking pace.

He passed the landing on the second floor, wondering if Shiner was already outside the building, and if so, which direction he would go to make his escape. Then the steps ended and the only way forward was through the doorway beneath the exit sign. The door was open, with each person passing through holding it for the next in line.

"Out of the way," he shouted again, shouldering through the crowd until he was past the doorway and once more in the open lobby at the base of the tower. He scanned the crowd, looking for Shiner. There was no sign of the sniper, but he did see about two dozen men and women in identical blue uniforms with badges and peaked caps trying to corral the herd of evacuees.

Thank God, Kolt thought. He sprinted toward the nearest officer. "Did you see a blind guy come through here?"

Even before he got the question out, he heard screams of panic. All around him, people were hitting the ground. The officer he had been approaching was shouting, "Gun! Gun!" even as he dragged his service weapon from his holster.

"No!" Raynor shouted. He immediately realized that with all the jostling with the crowd his weapon either printed under his shirt, or his shirt had pulled up, exposing the pistol grip. Kolt looked down at the Glock while trying to raise his hands above his head but the officer already had his own pistol out, pointed right at him. Then something slammed into him and everything went black.

* * *

Thirty feet above the lobby, Rasim Miric was making his way through the deserted halls of the third floor at a dead run.

Although his original plan had been to remain in hiding, pretending to be a survivor of the shooting massacre awaiting rescue, he had anticipated the possibility that things might not go according to plan. He had known that the police would respond to reports of shooting by locking down the building and systematically evacuating everyone, checking IDs as they went. He wasn't certain that his cover story would pass muster, and so he had developed a contingency. The one thing he had not anticipated, that he never could have anticipated, was that the first responder on the scene would be the same man that he had encountered on the slopes of Mount Lycabettus, but then that was the very reason for a contingency—a plan anticipating the unanticipated.

He knew that man, recognized the face, and not only as the man who had almost caught him in Athens.

It was Racer, the American who had taken his eye all those years ago.

He didn't know Racer's real name. The American commandos had not ever used names or ranks or any other identifiers. Over the years, as he had watched American soldiers through the scope of his rifle and taken their eyes, he had often fantasized that one of them might be Racer. A foolish delusion, but one that had brought him a measure of satisfaction.

Racer looked different, older, without the beard he

had once worn to blend in or disguise his identity. But the eyes, his voice . . . those had not changed.

Miric had not dared to hope that he would get a chance to look into Racer's eyes again.

He came to a halt before a set of Herculite doors, locked, of course. A glance back revealed no sign of his pursuer. He drew the revolver from his pocket, aiming it down the corridor behind him, just in case, but no one else appeared. The ruse had worked. Racer had continued down to the ground floor.

Miric turned back to the glass doors and fired a single shot from the pistol into them. The glass frosted over, and then fell in a shower of glittering fragments. He started forward, running again. The layout was different, with a larger open area partitioned by low walls to form dozens of cubicle workstations, but he could see over them to the large framed windows, all that stood between him and escape.

When he got within twenty feet of the windows, he aimed the pistol straight ahead and started firing.

The window glass was thicker than the glass used for the doors, coated with a thin laminate layer to make it nearly unbreakable. The .38-caliber rounds had considerably less effect than the close-range blasts from the shotgun he had employed to smash a hole in the thirty-ninth-floor window. Spider web patterns appeared in the glass, radiating from small pock marks, but the window did not shatter.

Miric never slowed. An instant before contact, he turned his face away, taking the blow on his left side.

The glass gave way, crumpling around him like a heavy blanket, and then he was falling.

The drop was short, only about twenty feet, but the impact at the end was softer even than the collision with the window. He did not hit the ground, but instead landed on his side on the heavy-duty mesh screen that topped the protective scaffolding ringing the building above the sidewalk. The canopy, he had learned while scouting the building with Dooley, had been erected prior to a safety inspection several years earlier and never removed. Its function was to shield pedestrians from falling construction debris, but it worked equally well as a safety net.

Pieces of broken glass shifted beneath him, digging into him like coarse gravel, but he ignored the discomfort and crawled to the edge of the canopy, then rolled over the side, dropping down to land on his feet on the sidewalk below.

While the thick glass had somewhat muffled the sound of his shots, his exit did not go completely unnoticed by scattered onlookers loitering outside the building. Before any of them could react, or identify him as a possible perpetrator, he shouted, "They have guns!" and then took off running again.

He slowed to a determined walk as he rounded the corner. He realized that he had lost his sunglasses, probably in the fall from the third story, so he kept his head down and his hands in his pockets as he folded himself into the crowd of pedestrians making their way up the river walk from the ferry terminal. Evidently, word of the shooting incident had not reached these commuters, but they would soon learn what had happened, and they would remember him.

He took the next left onto Sussex Street, then a right onto Hudson Street, and another right a block later onto York Street, heading back toward the waterfront. Once there, he joined the flow of foot traffic heading back in the direction of the tower. As he moved, he risked a quick check for pursuit. There was none. He doubled back to his rental car, which was parked in a garage across the street from the tower, but he did not leave.

Not right away.

NINETEEN

The bruises to Raynor's ego hurt a lot more than the actual ones on his body, though the latter could have been a lot worse. He had literally dodged a bullet, with an assist from Slapshot, who had tackled him from behind an instant before the twitchy Jersey City cop could get a shot off.

Not dying had turned out to be the high point of his day.

In the hours that followed, Raynor was able to piece together a blurry image of the big picture.

From Digger, he learned that a bullet had struck the first lady in the right thigh. She was alive and in an undisclosed area hospital, but that was all Digger had been able to determine. Special Agent Kearney wasn't talking to him anymore.

The news channels were all reporting the identity of the would-be assassin, twenty-year-old Lyle Dooley, a resident of Pontiac, Michigan, who, according to his Facebook page, was a member of an organization called the New American Revolution Lightfoot Militia. The pundits were running with that ball, spinning a narrative of domestic terrorism spawned by anger over the outcome of the election. They were also reporting that Dooley had taken his own life to avoid capture. There was no mention in the media of Miric, or of any ongoing manhunt to find him.

Raynor hoped that the search was continuing in secret, but when he called Webber, hoping to get official or even tacit permission for Delta to join the hunt, he received a very different answer. "Get back here now. Do not talk to anyone."

The Delta commander had hung up without waiting for a response. Webber rarely wasted words when communicating with his subordinates, but the brevity of the message and the extreme degree of dispassion in the colonel's tone told him that things were a lot worse than he suspected.

He passed the message on to Slapshot. "Get everyone back to the compound, ASAP."

"Where are you going?"

"Probably to fall on my sword," he replied, hoping that the quip would not prove to be prophetic.

"For what? You were right."

"Everyone has a perspective. We'll see what Colonel Webber's is."

He caught a flight from Newark to Raleigh, and rented a car to drive the rest of the way. Three and a half hours after almost getting shot in the lobby of a Jersey City high-rise, he arrived back at the Delta compound and headed straight for Webber's office. This time, he didn't stop to change.

Webber was on the phone when Raynor went in. He had expected the Delta commander to be irate, but Webber did not look angry. He looked beaten.

The telephone conversation was mostly one-sided, with Webber listening and only occasionally replying with "Yes, sir" every thirty seconds or so. He met Raynor's gaze but offered no other acknowledgment until the call ended with one final "Yes, sir. Understood."

As he settled the phone back into its cradle, he let out a sigh, and after a long pause, said simply, "You're relieved."

The words hit like a gut punch. Before Raynor could say a word in his own defense, Webber went on. "Save it. This wasn't my call. I warned you what would happen."

Kolt finally found his voice. "Sir, respectfully, what the hell? We played by your rules. Maybe if we hadn't, we would have stopped this from happening. How in the hell is this our fuckup?"

"You didn't stop it," Webber snapped. "If you had, you'd be a hero right now. But you didn't. You didn't communicate the threat to Secret Service—"

"Bullshit. Simmons ignored—"

Webber raised a hand. "No, Kolt, it's not bullshit. You did what you always do. You tried to handle it yourself instead of following the playbook. You saw your opening and instead of calling for execute authority, you ran with it. So it is your fuckup. And now it's my fuckup too, because I didn't sideline your ass when I found out about this."

Raynor took a deep breath, biting down hard on his

protest. Almost anything he said now would probably only make things worse. "Who's taking the squadron?"

Webber raised an eyebrow. "Right now, that's the last thing I'm worried about."

"Sir, Noble goes to alert status in three days. At least let me bring my replacement up to speed."

"Racer, you're not getting it. We're shut down."

"The squadron?"

"The Unit."

Raynor suddenly felt light-headed. He understood now why Webber looked so utterly defeated. "That's . . . I . . ." He realized he had no idea what he was even trying to say. "Permanently?"

"Possibly. You'll recall that the CG signed off on the former SECDEF's plan to create a single unified JSOC counterterror unit. Now he's got the justification he needs to stand us down. I think it's safe to say we're not going to get any support from the new administration. I guess it's up to ST6 to save the world now."

Kolt remained silent. A million second-guesses ran through his head.

Webber let out another heavy sigh. "Or maybe not. It's tough to say how this is going to shake out. Someone did almost kill FLOTUS. Her husband may just be grateful enough for you trying your damnedest to save her that he'll overlook your maverick ops. Hell, he might even give you my job."

"I'm sure he can think of a better punishment than that," Raynor said halfheartedly.

Webber managed a tight grin. "Go home, Racer. Park

your ass in a chair. Don't talk to anyone until you talk to me first. You've survived worse."

"Yes, sir." Raynor started to turn away, then paused. "Sir, what about Shiner? They are looking for him, aren't they?"

Webber gave him a hard stare. "Forget about Shiner. He's not your problem anymore."

There was a light burning in the window of the Rockville safe house. After the confrontation with Racer in the Jersey City tower, Miric's first thought was that somehow his old enemy had gotten there ahead of him and laid a trap, but after the initial moment of dread, he dismissed this possibility. He had followed Racer to the airport, watched him disappear into the boarding area. There was no way that Racer could have tracked him down so quickly, or known about the safe house. Besides, enemies did not announce their presence by turning the lights on. A more likely explanation was that he or Dooley had left a light on by accident when they had left days earlier, but when he entered the dwelling, he realized that was also not the case.

Mehmet was sitting in a chair in the living room.

Miric's dread returned with vengeance. The Turk had been very clear about the fact that there would be no contact between them while he was in the United States. If Mehmet was breaking his own protocol now, it did not bode well for Miric. Mehmet appeared to be alone and unarmed, but Miric doubted either was the case.

Miric took a seat opposite the MIT officer. "I had not expected to see you here."

"Why New York?" Mehmet snapped.

"This is how you greet me? No 'well done, old friend'?"

"It was not well done," Mehmet said, his voice rising toward a shout. "You understood what was to happen, did you not? What we needed you to do?"

"I did," Miric replied.

"New York was too far away. Why strike there?"

Mehmet had left the particulars of choosing the time and place of the hit to Miric, albeit within a specified range for both. The failure in Baltimore had made it impossible to meet the original deadline, and the subsequent lack of opportunities had forced him to ignore the geographical constraints.

But he could not explain all that to Mehmet; not if he wanted to go on breathing. "It was necessary," he said. "And it does not matter. I heard on the news, the president's wife will be moved as soon as the doctors say she is safe to travel."

"It was reckless. What if you had killed her?"

"You chose me because you know that no one else can do what I can do. And that is what I did. Your plan is safe." He stopped, realizing that the Turk had probably already decided his fate. But perhaps there was a way to sway him. "There is a complication."

Mehmet's eyes narrowed. "Complication?"

Miric chose his words carefully. "I recognized one of the men protecting the American president. He is somebody I . . ." He faltered, his throat tightening with unexpected emotion. "I knew him once. An American commando." Miric recounted what little he knew about

the man called Racer, including the incident that had
cost him his eye.

"If he was with the president's security detail, then
he may still be with the same organization," Mehmet
mused. "Did he recognize you?"

"No." He did not know for a certainty that Racer had
recognized him as anything but the man he had pursued
in Athens. If Mehmet believed otherwise, he would almost certainly kill him on the spot. Even revealing this
much was taking a grave risk, but if he could convince
Mehmet that an American commando called Racer was
the real enemy, it would not only buy Miric a reprieve,
but give him a chance to settle an old score.

"But that may change," he continued. "The police
will eventually find CCTV of Konstantin Khavin with
the assassin, just as you intended. If this man sees my
picture—" He let the thought hang. "He needs to die.
Let me hunt him. Who better to kill him than the Russian Spetsnaz who helped Lyle Dooley shoot the American president's wife?"

Mehmet considered this for a moment, then nodded
slowly. "This is personal for you. Very well, I will give
you your chance to hunt this man. But you will do this
my way."

PART THREE
FINAL MANEUVER

TWENTY

The place Lieutenant Colonel Kolt Raynor bunked at
night was a beat-up old single-wide trailer, parked in the
middle of a grove of mature pecan trees at the end of a
rural chicken farm road a few miles northwest of Fort
Bragg. The exterior screamed for a pressure wash. The
interior, while clean and orderly, had a weary feel to it.
The furniture, what little of it there was, was mis-
matched, thrift-store chic. The austerity of the place
had never bothered Raynor. He certainly could have afforded better, but simply didn't see the point.

He had moved into the trailer not long after earning
his spot in the Unit, sharing the space with his friend
Josh "TJ" Timble, but he didn't really think of it as
home. "Home" was a place he had left behind all those
years ago when he'd joined the army. It was an ideal,
not a fixed location. A place for memories, something
to fight for, die for. The trailer wasn't any of those things.

It had been, once. Back when he and TJ had shared
the place, it had felt a lot more like a real home, a refuge

from the craziness of the constant high operational tempo, but that had ended with the disastrous mission in Pakistan in which Raynor had lost an entire assault team and TJ while attempting to rescue his old friend, who had been captured by the Taliban. During the three years that followed, the trailer had become a sort of self-imposed prison for Raynor. He withdrew from the world, drank himself to oblivion, and generally let everything go to shit for a while. Although he had redeemed himself, made it back into Delta, the trailer had become just a place to crash when he wasn't away on Unit business, or simply at the Unit, which was most of the time.

Now, it felt like a prison again.

He had not interpreted Webber's admonition to stay put as a literal order of house arrest, but there really wasn't anywhere for him to go. So, after a trip to the grocery store to replenish his bare cupboards, he did exactly as Webber had instructed. He parked his ass in one of his cracked red leatherette chairs, and turned on the television.

The twenty-four-hour news cycle was dominated by two stories: the recuperation of the first lady, and the ongoing investigation of the deceased would-be assassin.

FLOTUS was in stable condition in a New York City hospital, but would soon be transported to the VIP surgical suite at the Walter Reed National Military Medical Center in Bethesda, Maryland, where she would undergo surgery to repair the damage done by the would-be assassin's bullet.

The talking heads were quick to point out the distinction between the facility named for Major Walter Reed,

army physician and pioneer of the science of epidemi-
ology, and the previous hospital in Washington, D.C.,
the Walter Reed Army Medical Center, which had closed
in 2011 after scandalous reports of patient neglect. The
name had been carried over to the new joint-service military medical complex, which had expanded the facilities
of the Bethesda National Naval Medical Center.

This level of digression was typical, as the pundits
dissected every minute detail of the story and specu-
lated about everything from the method of transport—it
was thought that she would be flown to Joint Base Andrews aboard a VC-25A from the presidential fleet; if
the president did not accompany her, the plane would be
designated Air Force 1F—to the matter of what medical procedures she would undergo upon arrival, and
whether or not she would be able to make a complete
recovery. The empty chatter was aggravating to Raynor,
but far more troubling to him was the amount of attention
given to details of how FLOTUS would be moved.

The other story in the news, the investigation into the
dead shooter's background, was once again drawing attention to the problem of domestic terrorism and empha-
sizing the intense dissatisfaction of the American people
with their government. Although the media seized on
the opportunity to stage on-air battles between hard-left-
leaning gun-control crusaders and staunch, unasham-
edly racist defenders of the patriot movement, there
had been some actual developments in the case. The
founder of the militia with which Lyle Dooley had been
affiliated had reportedly turned himself in to the FBI, and
was, according to a Bureau representative, "cooperating

fully." Other members of the group had moved quickly to distance themselves from Dooley, presenting him as an unstable loner and an outsider. Raynor guessed their disavowal of Dooley had more to do with the fact that the sniper's bullet had struck the first lady instead of her husband than because they disapproved of his extreme action.

There were also unconfirmed reports that Dooley had not been acting alone. Although investigators were not commenting, there were rumors that police detectives, or possibly federal agents, had chased someone through the Goldman Sachs Tower following the assassination attempt.

Raynor breathed a little easier at that news. If the media were reporting it, then the FBI was probably taking it a lot more seriously than they were willing to let on, which meant that eventually someone would get around to asking him what had happened, and maybe then they would realize that he belonged in the game, not on the bench.

Twenty-four hours after leaving Webber's office, he was still waiting for that call.

He was just about to pop a frozen dinner in the microwave when he heard the crunch of tires on gravel outside. He glanced out the window above the kitchen sink and saw a familiar white BMW X7 pulling up alongside his own black Chevy Silverado. It was Brett Barnes's rig.

The doors opened and two men got out, Barnes from behind the wheel, and Slapshot from the shotgun seat. The latter carried an overstuffed plastic grocery bag in each hand.

Raynor went to meet them at the front door.

"Chimichangas y cervezas," Slapshot said, holding up the bags. "Figured you're probably getting sick of ramen noodles already."

The sergeant major seemed like his usual gregarious self, but Barnes looked around anxiously.

"Thanks," Raynor replied. "But are you sure you want to be seen around me?"

The big man pushed past Raynor and went inside, setting the bags on the counter. "Fuck, what are they gonna do, fire us?"

Barnes's frown deepened, but he didn't say anything. It clearly wasn't a laughing matter to him, but he had come anyway; Raynor had to give him that.

He took a cold Corona from Slapshot and grabbed the bottle opener from the top drawer. "Anything new?"

"Not a lot," Barnes said, breaking his silence. "Webber has me reporting directly to him, but all he really had to say was 'look busy.' We burned through some frangible and blew a shitload of doors in the shoothouse, which we all probably needed after the last few weeks."

"Are you the acting Noble Zero-One?"

"What?" The young major looked shocked by the suggestion. "No, sir."

"This is gonna blow over, boss," Slapshot added. He cracked the top off another bottle and handed it to Barnes.

"You guys staying awhile or just stopping by?"

"Do we need a reason?" Slapshot retorted. "Come on, boss, admit it. You're happy to see us. But yeah, there is something else. We stopped by the SCIF."

Raynor stood a little straighter. "Have a seat," Kolt

said as he moved toward the big chair. "Just kick those clothes off the couch."

"Your new BFF, hipster boy, is getting RFI'd to death about a certain one-eyed foreign national you had him tracking."

"Yes." Raynor had to fight the urge to pump his fist, knowing that if higher was pushing intel analyst Kelly requests for information then the calculus had just changed. "Finally."

"One thing, though. They think he's Russian."

"Russian?" Raynor shook his head and set the beer on the coffee table. "No, that's just a bullshit alias."

"Hey, preaching to the choir," Slap said.

"Their logic train is all jacked up. I need to get the fuck over there."

Slapshot put a hand on his shoulder. "Kolt." The sergeant major almost never used his given name. "Give it some time. Let them come to you."

"And if they don't?"

"They will."

After finishing off the six-pack, Barnes and Slapshot headed out, leaving Raynor to continue his electronic vigil.

"Racer will be back in the saddle in a matter of days, if not sooner," Slap said.

"I don't know, sergeant major," Barnes said, keeping his eyes on the road ahead. "Maybe this was that proverbial last straw?"

"No, man, he's been through tougher crap than this," Slap said.

They drove a few more miles in silence before Slap spoke again. "You're not really a fan of Racer, I know."

"It's not that, necessarily," Barnes said quickly, making eye contact with Slapshot. "It's just his style."

"You mean the kind of style where you lead from the front, risk your ass just as much as your men, don't take any shit, and trust your NCOs?"

Barnes sensed Slapshot was getting a little pissed about the topic, and knew he needed to reel it back in before the conversation became the talk of the squadron lounge in the morning. He knew enough from his short time in Noble to know that his own days would be numbered if that happened.

"It's just his maverick style of leadership," Barnes said, trying for a conciliatory tone. "It's not exactly the kind of leadership we were taught at West Point. Or anywhere else in the modern army that I've seen."

"How long have you been here?" Slap asked in a clearly irritated and rhetorical manner. "What, less than a year?"

Barnes didn't answer. He realized now that the less he said, the better. He knew he couldn't argue the fact that Raynor had been right about everything so far. And he had been fully aware of Raynor's throw-caution-to-the-wind reputation, which was practically an unofficial class in OTC prior to joining the squadron.

"I hear ya, sergeant major," Barnes said. He wanted to say that maybe if Lieutenant Colonel Kolt Raynor had been a little easier to deal with and played by the book once in a while, things might be coordinated and supported a little better, but he kept these thoughts to himself as he turned onto the main highway and headed back toward Fayetteville. Slapshot was solidly in Raynor's corner and not likely to tolerate even well-intentioned constructive criticism. He dropped Slapshot off at home, and then rolled the windows down to vent out the lingering odor of cheap Mexican food, attempting to preserve the new-car smell as long as he could.

Home was a three-bedroom, two-bath rambler on Lindsay Road, west of Fayetteville and south of Fort Bragg. It was a lot more house than he needed at present, but he had high hopes, both for his career and his personal life. He was single by choice—special operations was hell on relationships—but he wasn't going to spend the rest of his life kicking in doors. He wasn't a warrior monk like Raynor.

He hit the button on the garage door remote as he pulled the BMW into his driveway, timing it perfectly so that he didn't have to tap the brakes to wait for the door to roll up. He drove the vehicle inside, stopping with the front bumper a precise eighteen inches from the back wall. He made it as far as the door leading into the kitchen before remembering that he had left the windows down. As he turned back, debating whether or not it really mattered, out of the corner of his eye he glimpsed a car parked on the street at the edge of his driveway.

Barnes was instantly on his guard. He didn't recognize the vehicle, a midsized sedan, but he knew it had not been there when he'd pulled up.

After a moment's hesitation, he headed back to the BMW. He slid into the driver's seat, reached across the center console to the glove compartment, and took out his personal weapon, a Glock G21 Gen 4. As soon as the weapon was in his hand, he twisted, keeping the pistol aimed directly ahead as he got out again. He eased away from the vehicle, putting his back to the garage wall in order to keep an unobstructed view in every direction, and then started moving toward the still-open roll-up door. He quick-checked the rear of the Bimmer as he passed it, then turned to look outside.

Aside from the parked sedan, there was nothing out of the ordinary, but he wasn't going to make the mistake of going into denial mode, dismissing the vehicle's sudden appearance as coincidence and his own reaction as paranoia.

In order for the car to have pulled up so quickly, it had to have been following him. He kicked himself for not paying attention on the road; personal security was never something to take for granted, even on home turf.

He was fully alert now.

He didn't allow himself to speculate on the nature of the threat; there would be time for that later.

With the pistol still pointed forward, he backed away from the opening. He nudged the door of the BMW closed with his hip, and was reaching for the button to close the garage door when he spied movement across the hood of the vehicle. He swung the Glock toward it.

He saw the gun, pointed right at him, before he saw anything else, and that was all the PID he needed to break the five-pound trigger. But before he could, he saw a flash, and then he saw nothing at all.

TWENTY-ONE

Raynor was still wide awake, eyes glued to the fifty-inch high-def, when he again heard the sound of a vehicle coming up the drive. He checked the time—almost 2230—before grabbing his shotgun. He didn't believe for a second that it was Slapshot and Barnes, back with another six-pack, and he was pretty sure it was too late for a visit from the Jehovah's Witnesses.

He edged closer to the large window in the front room, careful not to silhouette himself, and looked outside. The porch light revealed another familiar vehicle: not Barnes's flashy POV, but a more conservative black Jeep Wrangler. Colonel Webber's ride.

Raynor set the shotgun down on the coffee table before heading to the front door, but he remained uneasy. An unannounced late-night visit from the Delta commander was either a very good sign, or a very bad one. He opened the door just as Webber started up the steps. "Sir?"

"Sorry if I woke you, Racer." Webber still looked

weary, but appeared to have recovered some of his hard edge. "We need to talk."

Raynor stepped back to let him in, and then hit the Mute button on the television remote. He was burning with curiosity, but knew better than to barrage his commander with questions that would probably be answered in short order.

"Keeping up on current affairs, I see," Webber said, nodding his head toward the silent TV. "Have you talked to anyone?"

"Slap and Major Barnes came by for a beer. We didn't talk shop." *Much,* he added silently.

Webber gave an indifferent grunt. He gestured to Raynor's chair, and then sank wearily onto the sofa. He stared at the shotgun for a moment, then met Raynor's gaze again. "You know they've identified the suicide you found in Jersey City. Lyle Dooley. I'm sure you've heard that the leader of the Michigan militia group Dooley belonged to turned himself in to the FBI. What you probably haven't heard is that he's identified the man the shooter was working with. A Russian calling himself Khavin. Described as medium height and build, and missing his left eye."

Raynor shook his head emphatically. "It's Shiner. He's Bosnian, not Russian."

Webber frowned at the interruption. "I've been paying attention, Racer. The only thing the FBI has to go on right now is what those redneck weekend warriors are telling them, and I doubt any of them know the difference between a Russian accent and a Bosnian one.

The only thing that mattered to them was the fact that he was Spetsnaz."

"Spetsnaz? Bullshit."

"Of course it's bullshit," Webber growled. "Now let me finish. The militia hired this Khavin to provide a block of instruction in rifle marksmanship a few weeks back. I guess these patriots like the idea of getting trained by our enemies. That's when Khavin apparently recruited this kid, Dooley. After that, they both dropped off the radar. "

"Shiner recruited him all right, but only because he needed a patsy. I'll bet you money that Dooley did not pull the trigger. On FLOTUS or on himself."

"You're missing the point, Racer."

"How's that, sir?"

"This Khavin was able to convince the militia of his bona fides as a former Russian special forces sniper. Of course it was an alias, and you and I both know that he wasn't really Russian, but any connection to Russia is something our government takes very seriously."

"What connection? He conned the militia. Talked smack. No different than those jerk-offs you find in sleazy bars all over the world that claim to be SEALs or snake-eaters. "

"There's a lot more to it than that. The Bureau and Langley are pursuing multiple lines of evidence, but long story short, Khavin . . . or Shiner, if you prefer . . . has been getting a level of operational support consistent with an outside party. Possibly a foreign government."

"Russia?"

"They would have a lot to gain by creating instability. To them the Cold War never really ended. We've been facing a sustained propaganda attack for the last decade. Putin has teams of GRU hackers targeting our agencies and personnel, looking for anything that they can use to diminish America's presence in Europe, destabilize NATO. The hit on the Greek PM could represent an escalation of that effort. Our best guess is that the plan was to break the alliance overseas first, then hit POTUS and capitalize on the political chaos that follows."

Raynor did not fail to note that Webber had connected the Athens assassination with the attempt on the president in New York. "Capitalize, how?"

Webber shrugged. "Probably by reclaiming some or all of the real estate lost after the fall of the Soviet Union."

"Your professional opinion, sir?" Kolt asked.

"Not mine," Webber said, "Langley's."

Raynor pondered this for a moment, but then shook his head. "I don't buy it. Shiner wouldn't work for Putin. He hates the Russians almost as much as he hates us."

"Racer, I'm not here because of your obsession with Rasim Miric."

"Then, respectfully, sir, why the hell are you here?"

"You're not that thick. An enemy government just tried to assassinate POTUS. I don't know what his reaction to that is going to be, but I have a feeling things are about to get very hot."

Raynor blinked as the message finally got through. "You think we're going to war with Russia."

"War with a little *w*. Our kind of war." He said it without even a trace of satisfaction.

Raynor knew what that meant. In the short term, the response would be a proportionate reprisal, to include targeting specific members of the conspiracy for capture or even assassination. Wetwork. Delta's bread and butter.

That probably wouldn't be the end of it though.

"If you made a house call at this hour then I assume I'm not grounded anymore?"

"Partly because we are still strung out across the globe," Webber said, "mostly because the Unit needs you right now. I'll make it official in the morning, but I wanted to tell you myself. I doubt anyone is going to make a fuss. I think the CG will back me. You were way ahead of the curve on this, and I intend to make sure everyone above my pay grade that matters understands that."

"Sir, I don't want recognition, I want Shiner. Something about this stinks. Maybe he is working with someone else, but it's not Russia."

"What's your bet?"

"Anyone that benefits from a shooting war between us and Putin. Take your pick." A buzzing from his belt holder momentarily broke his train of thought before he could start down the list of enemies. He dug out his phone and checked the caller ID—it was Barnes—then looked back up to meet Webber's gaze. "We need to focus on finding Shiner. That's the only way to figure out who's really behind this."

"Forget about fucking Shiner. As long as he's on

U.S. soil, he's the FBI's problem." Webber's tone was as unyielding as it had been the day before, but then he softened a little. "Look, I'll pass along your thoughts on this, but until it becomes an international man-hunt, there's nothing we can do about it." He pointed to the still-vibrating phone in Raynor's hand. "You going to answer that?"

Raynor hit the button to accept the call. "Yeah."

There was only silence on the line. After a few seconds, he checked to see if the call had dropped—it had not. "Hello? Brett, what's up?"

There was an odd noise, like a sigh, and then he heard, "Racer. I have waited so long to speak with you."

It was not Barnes.

TWENTY-TWO

For a long time, there was only silence on the line. Then Miric heard the voice again, that familiar voice that he heard sometimes in his dreams.

"How in the hell did you get this number? Or the fucking phone you are calling from?" Racer's voice was taut, as if each word was a trigger wire that might snap, unleashing a detonation of rage.

"You know how," Miric replied.

Racer was silent, motionless for several long seconds. Then he lowered the phone and turned to the man sitting across from him. Miric could see them moving, gesturing as they conversed, but no voices were audible over the phone connection and he realized that Racer had activated the mute function. In the display of the sophisticated M-wave receiver, which augmented the paired PSO-1M2 optical scope and SVD-63 sniper rifle, the two men were little more than vaguely human-shaped blobs, a lighter shade of blue than their surrounding environment. The M-wave device, which utilized the same technology found in airport security scanners and some video game controllers, didn't amplify visible light or even infrared, but microwave backscatter, interpreted by a computer to give him a rough approximation of what was going on inside Racer's home. The fact that Miric could distinguish that much was nothing short of astonishing since he was literally seeing them through the walls of the trailer, but he didn't need a clear view to imagine Racer in the grip of impotent rage.

Miric thought about commenting on this observation, but decided against it. They did not know that he could see them, and he was not yet ready to reveal that fact to them.

"Your friend is dead, Racer. I found him. I killed him. Soon, I will find you as well."

Racer's reaction was not quite what he expected. "You motherfucker. I'll rip your fucking head off. "

Miric smiled behind his rifle. The weapon, along with its hi-tech imaging system, had been an unexpected gift from Mehmet, who had assured him that he would need every advantage when going up against the commandos of the army's Delta Force. Miric would not have even believed a device like the M-wave receiver was possible, but as amazing as it was, the equipment was of less worth to him than the information that had put him here. Mehmet had given him something he could never have found on his own—the identity and location of the man who had taken his eye.

Lieutenant Colonel Kolt Raynor.

Mehmet had explained that the special operations

forces from NATO countries were a close-knit community, often conducting joint training exercises and working together in highly secret operations abroad. Mehmet himself had once been a soldier in the OKK—Turkish special forces—and still had contacts within the organization, some of whom had access to the uncovered identities and service records of their counterparts in allied nations.

Of course, that was something Miric could not ever reveal to Kolt Raynor.

Miric had traveled to North Carolina and easily located Racer's home—the man would always be "Racer" to him—and begun stalking him. He could have killed him at any time, but Mehmet's cooperation had a price. He could not kill Racer. Not yet. But he could hurt him.

"I do this for myself alone," he replied. "You took something from me, Racer. Now, I take something from you."

There was another silence as the men in the trailer discussed this. Then, "You didn't shoot the first lady for yourself. Or the Greek prime minister. Who called those shots?"

The question, and the dispassion with which it was asked, surprised Miric. "You are wrong, Racer. Everything I have done, every blow I have struck against America and her puppet kingdoms, was for me. Only me."

"You're the puppet, Rasim. They're using you like a dog, and when you've done what they want, they'll throw you down."

Racer's words made no impression on Miric. He

knew that Mehmet was using him, that he was just a game piece to be sacrificed when the time came, but he did not care.

"When you came to my country, I thought you were heroes. That you would help us avenge ourselves against the Serb butchers, but you did not." The words spilled out of him. He didn't know if Racer would understand him, if he was speaking Serbo-Croatian or English, and he did not care. He had held it in for so long. "You only pretended to care, but when you had the chance, you let them go, over and over again. Your peace"—he spat the word out like a curse—"brought no justice, no end to suffering. Instead of avenging us, you protected them! You ignored what they did to us, excused it because we were Muslims."

He realized he was on the verge of shouting and caught himself. The woods around him had gone still. The walls of the trailer were thin, and his voice would carry.

"Bullshit," Racer snapped. "You were there with us. You know how bad we wanted to take them down. It didn't matter to us one bit if you were Muslim or Christian or a fucking Hare Krishna. And yeah, I get that you were frustrated and that the politics were fucked up, but you can't put that on me or any of the guys that were there.

"I think this is personal," Racer went on. "Between you and me. Fine. Let's deal with it. Stop hiding behind a rifle like a coward and come face me."

Miric felt his cheeks go hot at the accusation of cowardice. He knew that Racer was trying to bait him, goad him into saying or doing something foolish, but he nevertheless had to fight the urge to simply pull the trigger. He took a deep breath, aiming the weapon. There was no need to calculate holdover and windage. The trailer was less than two hundred meters away. Still, there was a good chance his first shot would miss. There had been neither the time nor the opportunity to zero the rifle, although he had boresighted it before leaving the safe house in Maryland. That would suffice. The rifle had a ten-round magazine, and he would be able to make the necessary adjustments with each shot. He kept the reticle on the part of the light blue blob where he thought the left eye must surely be, and let his finger curl around the trigger.

The exercise calmed him. He was not a coward. He had the power of life and death in his hands, and he was going to demonstrate that to Racer.

Raynor fought to stay focused on the conversation. A few feet away, Webber was speaking quietly into his own mobile phone, calling for someone to head to Barnes's house. Raynor didn't know if the colonel was talking to the police or someone else from the Unit. He hoped it was the latter. The cops weren't equipped to deal with someone like Shiner.

Evidently, Brett Barnes had not been either.

Just thinking about it made Raynor feel ill. He had lost men in battle. TJ had died in his arms. But this? Losing a subordinate officer, a mate he'd just shared a beer with a couple hours earlier, on home turf?

Personal? Fucking-A it was personal. He wasn't just going to hunt Shiner; he was going to fucking kill him.

He muted the phone again. "How the hell did he find Barnes?"

Webber shook his head, raising a hand to ask for silence, but Raynor could tell his commander was just as worried about the question as he was. The Department of Defense went to extraordinary lengths to protect the identities of Unit members. Miric could have surmised that Raynor was at least American Special Forces sixteen years ago but it was a giant stretch that he would have learned that he was from a Tier One Special Missions Unit. Identifying and locating the men in Raynor's command was not as simple as doing a Google search.

Miric was definitely getting heavy-duty operational support from someone, and Raynor didn't believe for a second that it was the Russians. No, it had to be someone with solid intel on Unit operations.

"Fuck!" he whispered again, recalling the last time he had been compromised, just a few months before. Bill Mason, the traitorous VPOTUS, had sold Noble Squadron out to a Syrian fighter who blamed Raynor—incorrectly, as it turned out—for the death of his son. Raynor didn't have any proof, of course, which was why Mason was still alive.

Did Mason want to be president so badly that he was willing to hire an international serial killer to assassinate POTUS? Was that why Miric was now going after Raynor and his men?

Part of him wanted to believe it was true, but there

were a lot of holes in the theory. The Greek hit, as Webber had pointed out, looked suspiciously like an attack on NATO. No matter how cynical Mason was, Raynor couldn't believe he was willing to burn everything down just to get into the Oval Office.

So if not Mason, then who?

Miric was talking again. "You once called me a natural. I kill with rifle. It is what I am best at. Why would I reject my gift?"

Raynor unmuted the phone. "I was wrong. You're just average. You missed the president in New York. I think you just got lucky in Athens."

"I did not miss." Miric sounded calm again.

"So . . . what, you meant to hit the first lady? Really? Your fight is against unarmed women now? You're more of a coward than I thought."

"The age of America is at its end. Your empire is crumbling. I have hurt your leader, just as I have hurt you. Now, I will finish him."

"What do you mean?" Raynor repeated, his voice edging up. "Who are you working for, Rasim? Who?"

"It is day of reckoning, Racer. For America and you. An eye for an eye."

There was an ear-splitting roar of static from the phone's speaker, and then a second later, a loud crack as something punched through the thin aluminum walls of the trailer.

TWENTY-THREE

As he threw himself flat on the floor, Raynor swiped the shotgun off the coffee table. It wouldn't be much help as a defensive weapon, especially not while he was still inside the trailer, but he had no intention of staying there, or remaining in a defensive posture, one second longer than necessary.

From the corner of his eye, he saw Webber hitting the floor.

"You hit?" he shouted to the colonel.

Another round slammed into the trailer, masking Webber's answer if he gave one. It sounded and felt like someone was taking a hammer to the exterior. This time, he heard the report of the weapon as well, echoing in the darkness outside.

Raynor looked up and saw the splintered paneling and tufts of insulation where the two bullets had perforated the west wall about six inches below the ceiling. Without knowing where the rounds had ended up, it was impossible to judge the exact angle of the shots, but he knew the surrounding property well enough to make an educated guess about where the shots were coming from.

"He's gotta be up in the trees!" Raynor shouted. "Best guess about two hundred meters west. If we can get outside—"

There was another loud crack, and a third hole appeared in the wall, eighteen inches from the last.

"What the fuck's he doing?" The sniper's attack made no sense. Shiner was shooting at nothing. Wasting rounds, risking exposure, and why? To taunt them?

The answer came to Raynor even as another bullet slammed into the trailer. This time, it was accompanied by the noise of shattering glass as the round struck the window on the opposite wall, behind the sofa.

"He's trying to keep us pinned down here," Kolt shouted. He didn't think he needed to elaborate on all the possible reasons why. Maybe Shiner had wired the trailer with explosives on a timed detonator, or maybe this was suppressive fire to cover the approach of an assault team. Either way . . . "We need to move!"

Webber did not reply, and Raynor realized he had not heard a single word of acknowledgment from the man.

"Colonel Webber! We need to move."

No answer.

He high-crawled backward until he could see his commander on the floor in the narrow gap between the sofa and the coffee table. Webber wasn't moving.

"No. No!" Raynor started toward the fallen man, but another round punched through the wall, lower this time, and slammed into the coffee table. The impact jostled the small table into Raynor. "Shit!"

The blow was not enough to hurt, but it was tangible proof that Shiner wasn't just firing blind. Somehow, the sniper could see them.

"Sir!"

Nothing. Not even a twitch.

"Damn it."

Webber was either dead or dying, but as long as they were under fire, there was only one thing Raynor could do for him.

React to contact. Return fire. Destroy the enemy.

He backed away on his ass until he was clear of the coffee table, then sprang to his feet and bolted in the opposite direction, heading for the kitchen. He had to get outside, but trying to exit through the front door would put him right in Shiner's sights. His best option was the back door.

There was a strident shriek as a bullet blasted through the kitchen wall and struck something metallic. The microwave oven, Raynor guessed. Shiner knew he was moving, probably knew where he was going, but it didn't matter. There wasn't anything in the trailer that would stop a high-velocity rifle round, and even if there was, it wouldn't solve the problem or help Webber.

He kept running, weaving around the table and into the hall that led to the bedroom at the north end of the trailer. The back door was on his right, but he bypassed it and headed straight for the bedroom.

The room where he slept was no less Spartan than

the rest of Raynor's home. He didn't even own a bed, just a mattress on the floor. The room also contained a chest of drawers that doubled as a table or desk as needed. Lying atop the dresser was his holstered Glock 23 and a spare mag. He had more guns in the safe in the closet, but time was a more critical variable than firepower. He grabbed the pistol and was just turning for the back door when another bullet punched through the bedroom wall, sizzling through the air above his mattress before burrowing into the far wall. He was out the door and on his way down the wooden steps before the report reached his ears.

Although he still had not worked out how the sniper was tracking him through the house, the continuous shooting told him that Shiner wasn't moving.

He ducked down at the corner of the trailer, stopping only long enough to stuff the holster into his belt, then was up and moving again. He didn't hug the end of the trailer, but headed out away from it a few steps before cutting back toward it, angling toward the more substantial cover afforded by his pickup and Webber's Jeep. He reached it, dropped flat behind the right front wheel, but he didn't stay there long either. He rolled back toward the front bumper and bounded up again, sprinting for the woods.

I'm up. He sees me. I'm down.

He hit the dirt, keeping the shotgun out in front of him so he didn't clobber himself with it, and rolled to the right. He was nearly out of the cone of illumination cast by the porch light, and almost at the tree line. It occurred to him that he had not heard a report since leaving the trailer. If he was right about where Shiner was positioned, he was probably already out of the sniper's line of sight, but he wasn't going to bet his life on it. The most likely explanation was that Shiner was trying to break contact.

Raynor bolted up again, bringing the shotgun to a ready position, and headed for the nearest pecan tree. The narrow bough wasn't perfect cover, but it allowed him to remain standing. Then he was moving again.

The trees were evenly spaced and easy to find even as he plunged deeper into the darkness of the grove, but as he put more distance between himself and his home, he slowed to a deliberate walk, stopping frequently to listen for any sounds that might indicate where Shiner was; if he was moving or waiting to spring an ambush. He knew he was close to the spot where the shots must have come from—he had a clear line of sight between the tree rows all the way back to his trailer.

There was a faint glow in the darkness. With the shotgun at the high ready, he started toward it, finger ready to pull the trigger at the first hint of movement. The light was coming from something lying on the ground. Another step and he could see that it was a mobile phone, the screen illuminated and displaying the phone number of a call in progress.

Barnes's phone. Raynor's number.

Somewhere off to his left, an engine turned over and then eased into a low idle. Red and white lights suddenly became visible through the trees, and then began moving.

Raynor started forward, running at a full sprint. He

threw the shotgun aside and unholstered his semiauto on the run, even as the lights moved farther away. It took him only a few seconds to reach the road, but the red taillights—all that he could see of the retreating vehicle—were at least fifty meters away.

He fired anyway.

One of the taillights winked out, but the other one continued to recede into the distance until the car rounded a bend and it vanished as well.

Raynor didn't waste breath cursing Shiner's escape. He wheeled and took off in the opposite direction, heading back to the trailer. With the sniper threat neutralized, the next immediate task was assessing and treating the casualties.

There's still time, he told himself.

He refused to second-guess his decision to go after Miric. If he had stayed where he was or attempted to help Webber, one of those rounds would have eventually found him too. React to contact—infantry battle drill two—was army doctrine for the same reason that the airlines told parents to put their own oxygen masks on before attending to their children.

You couldn't help anyone if you were dead.

He passed his pickup, wondering if he should wait for the paramedics or just drive Webber to the hospital himself, then bounded up the steps and blasted through his own front door.

"Colonel Webber!"

Webber lay exactly where Kolt had left him, and Raynor knew, even from across the room, that it was too late for him to do anything for the other man.

He dropped to his knees alongside the Delta commander, checking for a pulse even though he knew he would not find one, and then gently, reverently, rolled him over onto his back.

If Shiner had been aiming for Webber's eye, he had missed, but only by an inch. The bullet had entered through Webber's forehead, just above the brow. The entry wound wasn't a neat, precise little hole; the supersonic round had far too much energy for that. The exit wound was a lot worse.

Jeremy Webber had been dead before hitting the floor.

Raynor just knelt there for several long seconds, staring in disbelief as the blood puddled on the tan rug. He knew that he had to do something, call someone. The police . . . CID.

He would have to call Lilian. Webber's wife.

Widow.

He shook his head, still unable to process any of it.

Shiner had come after him. At his home. He'd taken out Barnes as well.

How had he found either of them in the first place?

Who would he go after next?

He swallowed and then reached over to pick his phone up off the floor. The screen still showed the connection to Barnes's phone. He thumbed the button to end the call, and then dialed Slapshot's number.

The call connected almost immediately, and then Slapshot's voice poured from the speaker. "Kolt! What in the hell is going on? Webber called me a few minutes ago. Is he with you? We got cut off. He told me to

go over to Brett's place. He's dead, Kolt. Brett is fucking dead. Gunshot!"

"I know. Jason, just listen. We've been compromised.
I don't know how, but Shiner is targeting us . . . the Unit,
the squadron maybe. He hit my trailer. Call the staff
duty and alert the entire Unit. Families too. Get them
to the compound."

Slapshot processed this for a moment, then said simply, "Got it. You okay, brother?"

"No," Raynor admitted. "I'm really not."

TWENTY-FOUR

Hawk felt a profound sense of guilt as she plopped down on the couch next to Troy. She set a stainless steel bowl filled with just-popped popcorn in his lap like an offering, but the gesture did not ease her mind one bit. Troy put his arm around her, a casual, almost thoughtless action that was more possessive than affectionate. She dreaded the moment when he would inevitably attempt to stake his claim on other territories.

Guilt was the reason he was here, on her couch, eating her popcorn with his arm around her.

After everything that had happened—the assassination attempt, the uncertainty about Raynor's future, and maybe even the future of the Unit itself—Cindy Bird had felt an overwhelming need for some normalcy. Not Delta normal—the kind that came from emptying magazines in the shoothouse—but ordinary everyday normal. So, in a moment of weakness, when she heard Troy's ringtone coming from her phone, she had decided to answer the call instead of simply letting it go to voice mail.

It wasn't until they were together that she remembered why she had been avoiding him. She didn't love him. She didn't even really like him that much anymore. And the thought of actually sleeping with him made her feel faintly nauseous.

It had been her idea to stay in and marathon the *Expendables* movies. Wanton violence and mayhem would keep Troy distracted for a while, but eventually she was going to have to deal with the problem.

She needed to just tell him it was over. End it. She dreaded doing that even more than she dreaded the inevitable fight that would follow, but for both their sakes, it had to be done.

She picked up the remote and was about to hit the Pause button when her cell alerted.

Saved by the bell, she thought, but as she glanced at the message displayed on the device, her heart began to pound in her chest.

Just three numbers.

911.

"N, B, or C?" Troy asked.

Hawk did not look at him. "What?"

"What kind of emergency? N, B, or C?"

The military had stopped using that method of classifying weapons of mass destruction years ago, replacing it with the more comprehensive CRBN, which differentiated nuclear and radiological threats. Troy knew that. It was just a none-too-subtle putdown of the work she ostensibly did for the army.

"I guess I'll find out," she said, rising from the couch. *911?*

Whatever that meant, it could not be good. "I'm going to head in to work. I guess you can hang here or whatever." She cringed as soon as she said it. She didn't want him loitering at her place; she wanted him out of her life.

To her astonishment, he stood up. "I'll drive you."

"What? No. It's okay. I mean, I appreciate the thought, but I don't know how long this is going to take."

"It's probably just some bullshit," he said dismissively. "I'll drive. That way we can at least spend some time together for a change. And you can show me off to all your pogue buddies. Make 'em jealous."

"Troy, that's really not a good idea. I have to go. You should go, too. I'll call you when—"

"Shit, Cindy. What the hell? You embarrassed to be seen with me?" His eyes narrowed suspiciously. "Or is there someone you don't want me to see?"

A couple years earlier, back when she was in the augment pilot program and working with Raynor's AFO team to track down Libyan SAMs, Troy had happened upon her and Raynor having a conversation in public. It had been completely innocent—they were just talking shop—but Troy, in typical chest-thumping fashion, had tried to make a scene, and while Kolt had both talked him down and put him in his place, Troy had never forgotten the incident. He knew that Kolt and Cindy worked together, even though he was unaware of what they actually did, and whenever things got tense between the two of them, Troy's memory of the incident and his lingering resentment for Raynor bubbled to the surface like swamp gas, and he threw the accusation in her face.

"Troy, I really don't need this right now." She raised her cell and was about to finger Shaft's number when Troy's hand wrapped around her wrist like manacles. She instinctively tried to pull away, but he held on tight, squeezing. "Damn it. Let go."

"I said, I'll drive you."

With adrenaline already flooding through her as a result of the ominous page, Hawk was in no mood to tolerate Troy's display of alpha dominance. Through clenched teeth, she said, "Let. Go."

"Or what?"

A dozen possible takedown scenarios went through her head, but she resisted the impulse to act on any of them. Troy was a Green Beret. He had received some of the same grappling training as her, and probably a lot more of it. And he was stronger and bigger than her. The only advantage she would have in a physical alter- cation would be the fact that he didn't really know what she was capable of, but if the situation escalated—if she escalated it—there was no telling how it would end.

"Or I will scream my fucking lungs out until the neighbors call the police," she said, still speaking in a low voice. "So if you care about me, or give a shit about your career, you will let go of me now."

To her astonishment, he did let go. She wondered which argument had been most persuasive. Probably the latter. Police involvement would jeopardize Troy's se- curity clearance, and a domestic violence charge would invoke the Lautenberg Amendment to the Gun Control Act, making it a felony for him to possess a weapon, even for use in the course of his military duty. Not that she believed Troy was that smart about the law. Either would end his career in Special Operations.

"Fine," he said. "But I'm still driving you."

Hawk did not respond right away. She really did not know what to say to him, so instead she went back to what she had been doing before. She found Shaft's number in her contact list and initiated a call.

Her assault team leader answered right away, skipping the customary greetings. "Hawk. Get to the compound. ASAP."

"What's going on?"

"We got hit."

She could hear the urgency in his voice and sensed that he was not in a position to give further explanation, or perhaps did not have any information to give, but she needed some idea of what was happening, if only to come up with a plausible reason for ditching Troy.

"How bad?"

"Bad. I don't know the whole story yet, but we've been compromised. We're circling the wagons, bringing in the wives and kids . . ." He hesitated a second. "Or whatever. Just get here. And be careful." He hung up without waiting for an acknowledgment.

"Cin?" Troy asked. She realized that he was still staring at her. The suspicion was still there, but there was also something else. Concern.

She thought about what Shaft had just said: *We got hit.* He had not been talking about an attack against

America, another 9/11 or something like it. No, whatever had happened, it was a lot closer to home.

We're circling the wagons.

The Unit was under siege, the threat evidently dire enough to warrant bringing immediate family members to the top-secret Delta compound in order to guarantee their safety.

Every Unit wife knew what her husband did, if only in very general terms, but that degree of trust was extended in committed relationships, and those wives knew the potentially deadly consequences of even the most innocuous indiscreet comments outside the family circle. It wasn't a secret to be shared when the relationship was casual, or in Hawk's case, circling the drain. She wasn't concerned about OPSEC but she did know that revealing her secret life to Troy would mean committing to him in a way that she knew now she absolutely did not want to do.

But if Shaft was not exaggerating the gravity of the situation, and she knew he was not, then Troy was potentially at risk because of her.

Maybe she didn't love him, or even like him, but she was not going to have his death on her conscience.

"Okay, Troy. You win. But after this, you and I are going to have a talk."

"You're damn right, we are."

She shook her head. "You really don't get it, do you? You know what, you can come, but I'm driving. I don't feel like giving you directions."

"I know where you work."

"No, Troy. You don't."

* * *

At first, he was incredulous, even going as far as to accuse her of lying. Then, he was dismissive.

"So you're like an advisor for them on the NBC stuff?"

She decided to let him go on believing that, but almost as soon as he said it, something seemed to click inside him and he shut down completely. He stopped talking and simply stared straight ahead as she drove his truck down the back roads of Fort Bragg. At first, she thought this reaction was the result of his insecurity about Delta and the fact that he had washed out of selection, but then she realized it was something else.

Troy had finally figured out that Kolt Raynor, the guy Cindy Bird worked with day in and day out, wasn't just some burned-out pogue officer keeping track of gas masks, but a Delta Force operator.

How was he supposed to compete with that?

The silence was fine with Hawk. She really didn't want to talk to him anyway.

She pulled up to the gate leading into the secure area that Delta Force called home and stopped, rolling down the window to present her badge to the guard. The security team had probably been briefed on the emergency plan and knew to expect some unfamiliar faces, but just to avoid any problems, she turned to Troy and suggested he present his military ID as well.

She had explained to him, in the most general way possible, that there was a potential danger to the family and friends of Unit personnel, but by that point in the conversation, very little that she said seemed to reach him.

He refused to look at her, but in a tight voice said, "I'm not staying. You should get out here."

That was all he said. There was no halfhearted attempt to soften the blow, no meaningless empty reassurances, no "I'll call you." He did not even inquire about how she would get back.

That was fine with her. In fact, it was better than fine.

"Yeah, all right." She got out, leaving the door to the pickup wide open.

"He's turning around, guys," she said to the security officers, and headed into the compound, not once looking back.

She felt an amazing lightness as she trekked toward the cluster of large buildings and nearest security-controlled door, but the feeling evaporated when she headed into the Spine and remembered why she had come here.

Delta was not a typical military unit by any means, but one structure that was constant in all the armed services of the United States, no matter how elite or unconventional, was the chain of command. The death of Colonel Jeremy Webber was an unprecedented blow to the Unit, but just as in any other combat unit, there were protocols for ensuring that the chain of command remained intact.

After the call to Slapshot, the next thing Raynor did was contact Webber's second in command and long-standing heir apparent, Lieutenant Colonel (promotable) Richard Penske, informing him that he was now the acting commander of Delta Force.

Penske was intimately familiar with the job and the personnel under his authority, so in that regard at least, Raynor had no doubt that the transition would go smoothly. But just because Webber had been grooming Penske for eventual command, it did not mean the two men were in full agreement. One particular area of friction between them had been Colonel Webber's ongoing pet project: the redemption and rehabilitation of Kolt Raynor.

Penske's position was that persona non grata was a life sentence, and that rescinding it set a bad example. The only reason he had given conditional support to Webber's plan to bring Raynor back into the fold was that he expected Raynor to fail, and that inevitable failure would prove him right.

For five years, Raynor hadn't given a shit if Penske had been impressed with his work ethic or not, and he knew it was a long shot that he'd be able to substantively change the other man's opinion of him. Nonetheless, Raynor didn't believe Penske would be anything but professional in the execution of his duties, but if he wanted Kolt out, he would find a way.

Raynor had given a condensed version of events over the phone, just enough to get things moving. The conversation had been short and focused, and without recriminations, but Raynor knew those would follow in short order. Once he knew that everyone in the squadron was present or accounted for, he headed to Penske's office to make his report in person.

"Racer." Penske acknowledged him with a grim nod and gestured for him to sit. "Rough night."

"Yes, sir."

"Bringing everyone in like you did; that was the right move. Quick thinking."

Raynor was wary of compliments, especially from Penske. "Thank you, sir."

"For Pete's sake, Racer, call me Dick." Penske paused a beat. "Your removal was never actually formalized. I think Jeremy was waiting to see which way the wind would blow. Consider yourself reinstated for now."

This was even more suspicious to Raynor. The only possible reason for the show of conciliation was that Penske intended to keep him on a very short leash.

Penske went on. "He was also keeping me in the loop on your search for this Russian sniper. I thought he was making a mistake letting you skirt posse comitatus to look for the guy, but I guess you were right about the threat. What I don't get is how he found you. How were you compromised?"

Raynor let the mistake about Miric's ethnicity slide. "I don't know. But I do know that this isn't over. Shiner flat out told me he's going to take another shot at POTUS, and I think it's going to happen soon. Maybe in the next day or two."

Penske was interested despite himself. "Why do you say that? Your famous sixth sense?"

"He told me he didn't miss in New York."

"So he actually meant to kill the first lady? Why would he do that?"

"To create fear. Make the president look weak. Maybe

to establish this bogus connection to the militia and the Russians. He said, 'I did not miss.' I don't think he even wanted to kill her. Just wound her . . ." He trailed off for a moment. "Bethesda. That's where it's going to happen."

"I'm sorry, Racer. I'm not following you."

"A sniper doesn't stalk his target. He waits for the target to come to him, but it takes time to set up a good position and recce the battlefield. Presidential security relies on unpredictability. Denial of opportunity. POTUS has to schedule some of his public appearances in advance, but the times and routes of travel are kept secret until the last possible second. Shiner's original plan was to make the hit in Baltimore, but we stopped him. New York was rushed. Maybe he wasn't confident that he could make a killing shot at that range, so he settled for the next best thing. Wounding POTUS or FLOTUS ensures that they will eventually be transported to the VIP suite at Walter Reed. FLOTUS is being moved there today. I'm going to go out on a limb and guess that POTUS will put in an appearance at some point. That's when Shiner will take the shot."

"So, he wounded the first lady, just so he could maneuver his real target into a more favorable location." Penske shook his head. "That's byzantine, Kolt. The more complicated a plan, the more likely it is to fail. If he wanted POTUS dead, he wouldn't have passed up the chance when he had it. And he sure as hell wouldn't further complicate it by coming after you."

"You're wrong. This is a game to him. Setting up the pieces, executing the plan. He's getting off on it. He's a psychopath. The fact that I showed up just makes it even more of a challenge. That's why he came after me. He wants to make it personal. He thinks he has to beat me. That's his weakness. We can use that against him, draw him out. Maybe find out who's pulling his strings. And plug the leak."

"Why the hell would it be personal against you?" Penske asked. "If it was, why did he shoot Webber tonight instead of you?"

"Sir, the guy holds me responsible for losing his eye."

"Why you?"

"Long story. Bosnia PIFWIC hit that went wrong years ago. Shiner blames me to this day."

Penske appeared to consider all this for a moment. "I'll run it up the flagpole but I don't know if anyone is going to salute. Posse comitatus aside, our collective ass is in a sling over what you did in New York."

"Colonel Webber told me he was going to talk to the CG. Get him to put us back in the fight."

"That's not what he told me. In any case, General Allen would have just told him what I'm going to tell you. Stay in your lane. The manhunt for this assassin is not on JSOC's target deck."

"Talk to him," Raynor urged. "Convince him. Get him to talk to SECDEF. Hell, have him ask POTUS. Nobody else has even gotten close to Shiner. That's got to count for something."

Penske snorted. "Look where that got us."

"That's why we need to be a part of this, Dick. For the colonel and Brett. Shiner just made this personal."

"Racer. If I'm going to have any chance of saving the Unit, the only thing I need to convince him of is that we can get our house in order. That's all that matters right now."

"We were just attacked. Two of our brothers are dead and the guy that killed them is going after POTUS. That's the only thing that matters to me." Kolt's voice was rising, almost to a shout. He knew it, and he didn't care. "Does it matter to you, Dick?"

Penske placed his hands palms down on the desk and leaned forward. "Like it or not, this happened on American soil. There's nothing we can do about it except cooperate fully with CID and the other agencies who are already looking for Miric."

Raynor did not back down. "Then I'd like to take some leave."

"Do not even think about going off the reservation, Racer. You are a squadron commander, not some lone-wolf superhero. That Tier One wild bullshit you pulled a few years ago will not be tolerated." He continued to hold Raynor's gaze, but leaned back in his chair. "Jeremy believed in you. I told him it was a mistake to bring you back. That you were incapable of following orders. You've got a choice right now. Prove me wrong, or spit on his memory?"

He dropped his stare, not waiting for Raynor's answer. "Tell your squadron to sit tight until we get the all clear. That will be all."

As he made his way back down the Spine, Raynor realized what he was going to have to do. The writing was on the wall, at least as far as his career in Delta was concerned. The only reason he had been put back in charge of Noble Squadron was so that Penske would have the satisfaction of calling in the Black Chinook himself, and showing the top brass how he was putting the house in order.

Yet Raynor felt no sense of outrage or loss at the thought of ending his career with Delta. The only thing that mattered to him now was stopping Shiner.

Slapshot was watching CNN on the television in Raynor's office. The killings in Fayetteville had not made the news, and probably would not rate more than a passing mention at the level of the local network affiliates, but there had been a new development in one of the stories dominating the news cycle.

"Somebody leaked the Russian connection," Slapshot said. "Ivan's denying it, of course, but it just makes them look even guiltier. I think the shit might actually be hitting the fan this time."

"There is no Russian connection," Raynor said. He crossed the room to a free-standing shelf unit in the corner, opened it, and removed a plastic clamshell package that contained a ZTE Z223 flip-phone-style mobile device. "They're denying it because they had nothing to do with it."

"Tell that to Wolf Blitzer."

"Believe me. I'm tempted." As he headed back to his desk, Raynor pried the package open. He took out the phone and removed the plastic tab from the battery, then powered up the device. "Why aren't you with your family?"

"They're fine," Slapshot said, waving a hand. "The

best way to keep them safe right now is to take that fucker down."

The news coverage switched to an update on the first lady's condition. The graphic crawl at the bottom of the screen indicated that she would be moving to Bethesda as early as the following afternoon. Slapshot switched the set off. "So, did you get execute authority?"

"Penske's actual words were 'stay in your lane.'"

The big man clenched his fists. "You're shitting me. Shiner killed the colonel. He killed Brett, Kolt. How can he ignore that?"

"There's not a lot he can do. The law is the law."

"Fucking law." Slapshot's face twisted into a sneer. "So what are we doing, another extended urban training exercise, hoping to get lucky a second time?"

"No."

"But you've got some kind of plan."

"I do." Raynor finished activating the phone, then took a business card from his top desk drawer. He put both the business card and the burner phone in his pocket, then put his own mobile phone inside the drawer.

"Do we need to have another talk about sharing?"

Raynor looked his friend in the eye. "You've got things under control here. There's something I have to take care of."

"Boss, I've got your six, but you need to talk to me."

He started for the door. "Not this time, Slap."

"Kolt, wait."

Raynor didn't look back.

TWENTY-FIVE

Before becoming the owner-operator of Radiance Security and Surveillance Systems, a Virginia-based private military contractor, Colonel Pete Grauer had commanded an Army Ranger battalion. In that capacity, he had recommended a young officer named Kolt Raynor for Delta selection. Raynor had survived the grueling process and gone "behind the fence"—army slang for disappearing into the secretive ranks of Special Operations—and shortly thereafter, Grauer retired from active duty to serve his country as a private citizen. That should have been the end of their association, but subsequent events had brought them together again.

When Raynor had been cashiered from the Unit after the disastrous mission in Pakistan, Grauer had taken pity on his former subordinate, hiring Kolt for overseas security work, and ultimately providing operational support for the unsanctioned mission to rescue Delta personnel being held captive in the tribal area of Pakistan. That assignment had paved the way for

Raynor's return to the Unit, so Kolt was twice indebted to Pete Grauer.

Now, he was about to ask Grauer to grant a third wish.

Raynor drove all night to reach the Virginia suburb where Radiance was headquartered, arriving a little after 0630, but waited until 0800 to call the number printed on the business card. Grauer's number. The call went to voice mail, so Raynor left a brief message with a request to meet for coffee. Grauer called back within the minute, and a time and place for the meeting were agreed upon.

Fifteen minutes later, Kolt pulled his truck into the parking lot of an IHOP located in a shopping center off the Jefferson Davis Highway. Grauer was waiting for him in a corner booth.

"Racer. You're looking good. Helluva lot better than last time I saw you." He stood and shook Kolt's hand. He gestured for Raynor to sit but waited until the server had poured coffee for both of them to make his inquiry. "So, out with it. What's wrong?"

Kolt's former CO listened without comment as Raynor laid out the situation, beginning with the assassination of the Greek prime minister and culminating with the attack at Raynor's home the previous evening. He had stopped short of telling Grauer that he was probably finished at Delta and technically AWOL, but if the other man had not already figured that out, he soon would.

Grauer was silent for a long time after Kolt stopped speaking. Finally he said, "My condolences for your loss, Kolt. Webber and I went way back, and I know how much Jeremy meant to you. But . . . and forgive me for being frank . . . why are you here?"

"Shiner is an immediate threat to POTUS. And if we don't stop him and figure out who he's working for, we could be looking at a new Cold War with Russia. Or worse."

"I understand what you're saying," Grauer replied patiently, "but it doesn't answer my question. The FBI is hunting him. The Secret Service is protecting the president. Delta doesn't have the authority to do either of those jobs. Now I get that this is personal for you, but that doesn't change the way things are. So, I say again, why are you here?"

"I'm going after him, Pete."

"You as in . . . just you?"

"Obviously I can't use Unit resources or personnel."

"So you want to hire Radiance to do your legwork, is that it?" There was no mistaking the skepticism in Grauer's tone. "Not only is this crazy by the fact you are an active-duty army officer, but besides that you do realize that even if you did contract with us, we'd be bound by the same laws that prevent your Unit from operating on U.S. soil."

"I was thinking of something less official," Raynor replied. "Something more along the lines of what you did for Colonel Webber when you sent me to Pakistan."

"Unofficial doesn't mean pro bono. That operation was fully funded from the black budget. That's not me being stingy or unpatriotic. These operations cost money. A lot of money. I'm guessing you aren't bringing anything like that to the table."

"Not exactly."

Grauer was silent for a while, then said, "What is it you specifically need from me?"

"I know that Radiance is flying UAVs for Homeland Security. You've already got the eyes in the sky. All I'm asking is that for the next couple days you pay particular attention to the area around the Walter Reed National Military Medical Center. And that you let me have a look at your feeds. I could probably use some logistical support, too."

"We do border security flights for DHS, not domestic urban surveillance. They rely on local police for that. Bethesda is inside the D.C. flight restricted zone, so even if we made up some excuse to divert one of our birds, we would only be allowed to fly where they tell us to. Working for DHS doesn't give me a pass on that."

Grauer tapped his fingers on the table thoughtfully. "There may be a workaround. I'll look into it. But understand this, Kolt. If we find your guy, I'll be obligated to report it to the authorities immediately. Radiance isn't a vigilante organization. I'm not going to put POTUS, our company, or anyone else at risk to facilitate your revenge."

"This isn't about revenge, Pete. Shiner has to be stopped."

There was another long silence from Grauer. Finally, he spoke again. "Son, I get where you're coming from. You've always had good instincts, and judging by what you've told me, you are probably the one that should be hunting this guy. But you're out there flappin' on this one.

"Five years ago, we sent you into the FATA because Jeremy couldn't send anyone from the Unit. Any one of his operators would have taken your place in a heartbeat, but he knew he couldn't send them. He recognized his limitations, Kolt. That's a part of leadership that I don't think you've ever really grasped. You need to, or you're going to crash and burn again, and this time, you won't come back from it."

Grauer was right about everything, including Raynor's shortcomings as a senior leader. Following one-size-fits-all regs and bullshit orders had always chafed him, especially when it meant passing over the most obvious and effective solution. The harsh truth was that he was fundamentally incapable of being the kind of soldier Grauer and Webber and everyone else had always told him he needed to be. How he had made it as far as he had was as much a mystery to him as it was to everyone else.

"Just help me find him. I'll take care of the rest."

Grauer studied him across the table for a few seconds, then glanced at something behind Raynor. "I think those folks are here for you."

Raynor felt a cold surge of adrenaline slam through him. He'd known that eventually someone would take note of his absence from the compound, at which point Penske would notify the law and have an APB put out on him. But he had not expected it to happen so quickly. He turned slowly to see six familiar faces—Slapshot, Digger, Shaft, Hawk, and the rest of the alpha team—settling in around a pair of tables in the center of the dining area. They wore civilian clothes, but the former Ranger colonel was too canny not to know a group of Delta operators when he saw them.

Raynor looked back at Grauer. "It's nothing. I'll take care of it. Can I count on you, Pete?"

"All right, son. I'll do what I can, which won't be much." He downed the dregs of his coffee and then rose. "I'll let you pick up the tab. It's not like I'll be able to write it off as a business expense. I'll call you at the number you gave me earlier when I have it set up."

"Thanks, Pete." Raynor stood and shook the other man's hand, then picked up his coffee mug and headed over to join his mates. He grabbed an empty chair and sat down next to Slapshot. "How the hell did you all find me?"

"You think I didn't see that card you took from your desk?" Slapshot said. "The one with the Radiance logo. Did the math. I'm good at story problems. Gave the opportunity first to A team, and they jumped at it. I called shotgun. When we got into town, Hawk there called Pete Grauer's secretary and she told us where to find him. And you."

"She just volunteered the information? Pete's not gonna like that."

"I can be very persuasive," Hawk chimed in.

"I've noticed," Raynor replied. He also did not fail to notice that the female assaulter was smiling confidently, which was a stark contrast to the dour expressions of the others at the table. "So, I guess you're here to talk some sense into me. You wasted the gas."

Slapshot looked away from Raynor for a moment, glancing at the others as if looking for a vote of confidence. "Here's how it is, boss. We've got you covered back home. At least for a little while. The guys will give Penske the runaround for a while, cover a few command and staff meetings for you, but that won't hold muster long. So, if you've got this out of your system and you're ready to head back now, no harm, no foul. That's what's behind door number one."

"And behind door number two?"

There was another shared silent communication, and then Digger spoke up. "We're with you, boss. All the way."

Shaft added, "When he killed Brett and Webber, he made it personal for us, too. We've got as much right to take that fucker down as you."

Raynor shook his head. "Door number three. You guys forget you saw me, and head back now before Penske declares you AWOL. I'm not letting any of you throw your careers away over this. I'm at the end of mine."

"There's a problem with that," Slapshot said. "If you're cashing out, you really aren't in a position to give orders anymore."

Raynor frowned, then looked past his friend to the others seated around the table. "I appreciate that. I really do. But I won't let you follow me down."

His plea was met with stone-faced silence. Except for Hawk, who looked . . . different. It took him a moment to realize why.

She wasn't his subordinate anymore.

He shook his head, trying to clear the thought away before it took root. He didn't need a distraction like that. Not now.

"So I guess it's not going to be door number one," Slapshot said. "Well, I was afraid of that. So, where do we start looking?"

Rasim Miric had also driven all night to reach the Washington, D.C., metro area, arriving at the Rockville safe house about the same time that Kolt Raynor was sitting down with Pete Grauer some thirty miles away.

He had been forced to abandon the rental car as soon as he was a few miles down the road from Raynor's home. Raynor might have gotten a look at the license plate, but even if he had not, the shot-out taillight and bullet scars would surely attract the attention of the local sheriff's patrol cars. He had dumped the car on a dirt road just out of view of the hardball road, then begun the long hike back toward Fayetteville. It had taken him an hour and a half, mostly because he had kept to the woods alongside the highway, out of view of passing motorists. After another hour of waiting in the parking lot of a roadside hotel in Spring Lake near Fort Bragg, a target of opportunity presented itself in the form of a lone traveler in a car with out-of-state plates. Miric intercepted the man before he could reach his hotel room, killed him without either of them making a sound, and then dumped the body in the trunk of the car before driving away.

It would probably be several hours before anyone realized the man was missing, and even longer before a search led authorities to both car and body hundreds of miles away in a Maryland neighborhood several blocks from the safe house.

Mehmet was waiting for him inside. He was not alone. Four men that Miric had never seen before were with him, eating as they watched the news on television. The men were Caucasians with no discernible traits to hint at their ethnicity. Miric assumed they were also MIT officers, there to assist with the final phase of the plan, but they might have been hired guns, just like him.

They might even have been there to kill him.

Mehmet did not introduce the other men. "Is it done?"

"Yes. I spoke with him, said exactly what you told me to. And I killed two of his friends. He will come after me. I am certain of it."

The other man nodded in satisfaction. "Well done, old friend. Don't worry. The next time you see him, you have my leave to extinguish the light in his eyes."

So I am his old friend again? Miric thought. He was not fooled by the change in Mehmet's demeanor, but it did at least indicate that he was still useful to the other man. Mehmet would not kill him. Not yet. Maybe not at all. If the plan succeeded, and why wouldn't it, there would be no need.

Many weeks earlier, Mehmet had told him how the endgame would proceed. It was not enough to simply kill the American president, he explained. They could have done that at any time.

The knight—Miric—would attack first, weakening the NATO alliance by killing the pro-American leader of Greece.

Then, a second attack, one that would appear to be a failed assassination attempt, but was in reality a feint, designed to throw suspicion on America's most formidable rival, Russia. That suspicion would further weaken America politically.

The American people would know, or at least believe, that the Russians had tried to assassinate their leader, and yet there was little that could be done about it. Open war was extremely unlikely, especially with little hard evidence of a conspiracy. Even if the president ordered his espionage agencies and military to engage in a secret campaign of retribution—a new Cold War—the public would never know. The global perception that America was weak in the face of attack would become the reality.

The delay resulting from Miric's abortive attempt in Baltimore had nearly derailed the plan. President Noonan's foreign policy team was poised to undo the damage done by the loss of the Greek prime minister.

Of course the real reason Baltimore had been chosen was because it would ensure that the first lady would be taken immediately to Walter Reed hospital, per presidential medical emergency protocol, which was the real intent of that second attack: to maneuver the president into position for the final blow.

Checkmate.

President Noonan had to die. Although the preceding moves would make him appear weak, there was uncertainty about how he would respond to the unfolding events in the near term. It was not inconceivable that, in response to the assassination attempt and the injury to his wife and goaded on by the increasingly reactionary rhetoric of the media, he might do the unthinkable, initiate a full-scale military response or even play the game of nuclear brinksmanship with the Russian Bear, and in so doing, demonstrate the very strength that Mehmet and his government hoped to eradicate.

But Noonan's designated successor, Vice President Bill Mason, had proven himself weak and ineffectual, as well as conflict averse, both as a military leader and as secretary of state in the previous administration. He would choose the course of appeasement, and America's allies abroad would abandon her in droves.

Into that void of international leadership would step a new superpower: the Ottoman Empire reimagined, backed by the military might of the North Atlantic Treaty Organization, the economic power of the European Union, and the spiritual support of more than a billion Muslims all around the world.

The greatest risk to the plan, of course, was that the American authorities might see through the deception linking the attacks to Russia, and by recognizing Miric, Racer might have exposed that weakness. But rather than have him simply kill Racer, Mehmet had used Miric to draw attention away from the real attack.

He would have to risk exposure—and capture or even death—one last time, but if it meant that he would have a chance to repay the insult done to him by Racer all those years ago, it was worth it. Until he had come face-to-face with Racer, Miric would have believed it was enough to see America brought down. Now, he had something else to live for.

He ate and rested while Mehmet and the others continued to watch television until they heard the news they had been waiting for. The plane carrying the first lady of the United States had arrived at Joint Base Andrews, where a marine helicopter was waiting to transport her to the military medical hospital in Bethesda, Maryland.

"It is time," Mehmet said.

TWENTY-SIX

Even from a distance of nine hundred miles, Pamela Archer could smell the bullshit. The former U.S. Air Force officer had been at Radiance Security and Surveillance Systems for over six years, the last three of those as head of the UAV operations division and working closely with the company's president, Pete Grauer. She knew how things were supposed to work, and knew when Pete wasn't telling her the whole story.

Grauer had just ordered her to pull one of the three Predator B aircraft presently operating out of Key West, Florida—monitoring the Florida Strait for the Department of Homeland Security—and fly it almost a thousand miles north to fly circles around the D.C. restricted flight area. His stated intention was to provide a demonstration to lawmakers who were questioning the usefulness of Predator drones in combating the trafficking of narcotics and humans.

She excused herself from the flight operations center where the three-person crews operated the aircraft remotely—one pilot and two sensor technicians per bird—and ducked into her office to continue the phone call in private.

"Okay, Pete. That's what we'll tell the shareholders. What's the real story?"

Grauer made a sound that might have been a grunt of disapproval.

She headed off the denial she knew was coming. "Pete, I don't mind if you want to joyride one of my birds, but just be straight about what it is you really want."

Radiance did not actually own the aircraft—each of which cost in the neighborhood of seventeen million dollars—but operated them for DHS under an arrangement that allowed some latitude in how the aircraft were used. Archer was, nonetheless, very protective of her babies.

"It's a favor for an old friend. A mutual friend."

"Mutual?"

"It's Racer, Pam."

Pamela Archer sat down quickly.

Eight years earlier, as a UAV pilot for the 17th Reconnaissance Squadron operating out of Creech Air Force Base in Nevada, Captain Pamela Archer had been tasked with providing aerial surveillance and support for a special operations team—designated Hunter 29—searching the remote border region between Afghanistan and Pakistan for Taliban fighters. A malfunctioning sensor had forced her to pull her Predator drone off station, leaving Hunter 29 without overwatch deep in enemy territory, and in the hours that followed, Hunter 29 was all but wiped out. A subsequent mission to rescue the embattled team led to further casualties and the capture of a second team of American commandos. Four years later, she had learned the name of the sole survivor of Hunter 29, a Delta Force officer named Major Kolt Raynor, code named Racer.

Although she had done nothing wrong—indeed, as far as the Air Force was concerned, she had done everything exactly according to SOP—Archer blamed herself for the deaths of Racer's men and the failed rescue attempt. If she had trusted her instincts about the sensor malfunction and kept her Predator over Hunter 29's position just a little while longer, the Delta operators would have seen the enemy coming, and the tragedy would have been prevented.

She had been able to at least partially atone by helping Racer rescue his MIA comrades and thwart an al Qaeda attack on a CIA black site. While the debt Archer owed the men of Hunter 29 would never be fully settled, helping Kolt Raynor was one way to at least pay down the interest.

"What does he need?" she asked. "Be specific, Pete."

"Racer needs overhead surveillance of the area surrounding Walter Reed hospital in Bethesda."

Archer did not need to inquire about the significance of that destination. The joint military medical center in Bethesda had been in the news ever since the wounding of the first lady during the failed assassination attempt in New York City. If Racer wanted surveillance of the area around the hospital, it could only mean that he believed the threat to the first family was ongoing. "He's working for the Secret Service now?"

"No, Pam. That's why this is a favor to him. And something we're not going to talk about."

"Understood. I'll take care of this personally."

Grauer laughed—a gruff, humorless utterance. "I was afraid you'd say that. Promise me that this time you'll keep the bird in the sky where it belongs."

Pamela Archer just grinned.

After breakfast, Raynor and the others crossed the parking lot to the Best Buy in the main shopping center. They had to wait twenty minutes for the store to open, but were in and out in half that time. Their purchases— three LTE-capable tablet computers with prepaid unlimited data plans, six additional burner phones with Bluetooth headsets for each plus one more for Raynor's new phone, and battery backups to ensure that they could stay mobile almost indefinitely—were redistributed, and then they headed for Bethesda. Raynor let Slapshot drive while he called Grauer for an update.

Grauer informed him that a Predator B—formally known as the General Atomics MQ-9 Reaper—was presently winging north from Florida, but was still more than two hours out. He supplied Raynor with the dedicated secure IP address of the raw video feed and the phone number where he could reach the flight operations crew. Raynor plugged the IP address into his tablet and was rewarded with live video of a scrolling green mosaic, farms and forests seen from an altitude of fourteen thousand feet. According to the embedded GPS tracker, the UAV was now over eastern North Carolina, cruising at 170 knots. He watched for a few minutes, then switched to a live-stream broadcast of CNN.

Like many in the military, and especially in JSOC, Raynor was of the opinion that cable news outlets were de facto intelligence services for foreign governments and terrorist organizations, reporting sensitive, if not necessarily classified information for the free use of America's enemies. Now, they would be *his* primary source of intel, providing up-to-the-minute information on the location of Shiner's target.

FLOTUS had already arrived at Joint Base Andrews, and would finish the journey to the hospital by helicopter. She was reportedly in stable condition, awake and alert. Raynor also learned that POTUS was not accompanying her, but was expected to visit her in the hospital later in the day, probably before she went into surgery.

The Delta operators drove up Rockville Pike, passing through downtown Bethesda and then past the main gates of the Walter Reed National Military Medical Center. WRNMMC wasn't just a hospital, it was a military installation, and as such was a secure environment. But, because it *was* a hospital, providing medical treatment at all levels to thousands of patients daily—military personnel, dependents, veterans, and others—there were gaps in that security. The sprawling complex built around the distinctive tower—legend had it that the architect based his plans off a sketch made by President Franklin D. Roosevelt—was visible from the highway, and separated only by a wrought-iron fence. Through the fence, Raynor could see row after row of news vans parked on the front lawn, their telescoping satellite antennas poking skyward like naked tent poles.

Raynor gave the hospital itself only a cursory inspection. He was more interested in determining lines of sight and possible locations from which Shiner might be able to make his next attempt. As they rolled by, he snapped several photos of the horizon in every direction.

They stopped in a mall parking lot a couple miles up the road to coordinate their coverage strategy. Raynor brought up Google Earth on one of the tablets, and displayed his recon photos on the other.

"The clearest shot is from the south," he said. "From one of these buildings in Bethesda."

The screen showed the divided highway, but in the distance, several tall structures were visible.

Hawk checked the range on the satellite image. "The closest is about a thousand meters. That's within his range."

"It's also close enough that the Secret Service will probably check it out," Digger countered. "Especially after what happened in New York."

"We're not going to duplicate their work," Raynor said. "We'll push out farther if we have to. I wouldn't put it past Shiner to attempt to break his old record." He switched to another picture. "The National Institutes of Health campus is due west. There are some good vantages here, but they're close in. Maybe too close. And easy for the Secret Service to keep tabs on. They'll probably have teams on every rooftop there.

"Then there's the north." He switched to the last

image, which showed another road gently rising to disappear in the tree line.

"Lot of good places to hide there," Slapshot said.

"Yeah," Raynor agreed. "Too many. That's about a klick and a half from the main entrance."

"You're assuming POTUS is going in through the front door. Do we know for sure how he'll be arriving?"

"No." Raynor shook his head. "But my money is on helo transport. Marine One. The helipad is here." He tapped the satellite map, indicating a perfectly square paved area on the hospital lawn, just inside the south entrance, then shifted his finger to the nearest structure. "Med services are here. They might drive him, but foxtrot is also a possibility with all those cameras around."

"Visiting the old lady in the hospital," Slapshot put in. "Great photo op."

"I can call Todd and verify the method of travel if you want," Digger said.

Raynor looked up in surprise. "He's still talking to you? You're not on the Secret Service shit list with the rest of us?"

Digger grinned. "The bonds of brohood are strong. And he's still young and eager to impress."

"You mean naïve," Hawk added with a snort.

"Let's hold off on that as long as we can. If Simmons finds out we're in his AO, he might try to shut us down." Raynor turned back to the satellite map. "POTUS will be most vulnerable during movement from the helo to the hospital."

"Or when he leaves," Slapshot added. "What goes in has to come out."

"We're going to find Shiner long before either happens. Okay, specific tasks. Shaft, Venti, Joker . . . you have the south. Recce the area, try to narrow the list of possibilities. Mostly, you're just pre-positioning, waiting for the UAV to show us where he is. Stay entirely loviz." He emphasized the last part.

"Got it, boss," Shaft said quickly. "Basically, do what we've been doing for the last two months."

"Slap and I will hit the woods to the north. If he's there, FLIR will show us where he is."

"Hot today. Gonna be hard to differentiate body heat. Maybe we can call POTUS and get him to wait until after dark, when it's cooler."

Raynor shrugged. "I didn't say it would be easy." He turned to Digger and Hawk. "I want you guys on the inside."

"Secret Service knows us, boss," Digger said. "Probably better than any of you guys."

"Why do you think I picked you two for this detail? Try to stay off their radar if you can, but if . . . make that *when* we find Shiner, I want you guys coordinating with them, both to keep POTUS out of the line of fire, and to direct their assets to deal with Shiner."

The others stared at him in shocked silence. Finally Slapshot said, "Boss, I thought *we* came here to kill this fucker."

"That's why I came here. Then you guys showed up and I realized we have to at least make the effort to do this within the regs. We're just concerned citizens reporting a threat. The idea is to pull this off without going to jail."

"Right. So we call the Secret Service, then we kill him. In self-defense, of course."

Raynor didn't answer. He didn't have to.

Slapshot drove the Silverado around the wooded neighborhood half a mile north of the WRNMMC, while Raynor, in the passenger seat, looked for anything suspicious in the trees, and alternately monitored the livestream newsfeed.

The helicopter carrying FLOTUS arrived about an hour after the group dispersed to their respective assignments, and the news cameras captured every moment. The patient, strapped to a collapsible stretcher, was lifted out of the helicopter and then placed immediately into a waiting ambulance for the short ride to the back entrance, where the reporters were not allowed to follow. The coverage finished with an unconfirmed report that the president would be arriving within the hour.

That was how much time they had left to find Shiner.

"He could be set up in the attic of one of these places," Slapshot observed.

Raynor looked up as they passed between a pair of three-story brick manor houses.

"I hope not. If we have to, we'll check each one."

"You think folks'll just let us into their attics to poke around? We gonna pretend to be termite inspectors?"

"We'll tell them the truth. That we're part of the protection detail."

"That's the truth?"

Raynor shrugged. "We should be able to narrow it down once the UAV gets here. Speaking of which . . ."

He switched the tablet to the page with the UAV feed. The video image looked about the same as it had the first time he'd checked it, but the GPS indicated that the drone was now over Northern Virginia, still about eighty miles away.

At its present speed, the aircraft was about half an hour out—another thirty minutes before they would be able to start looking in earnest.

He called the contact number Pete Grauer had given him. A female voice answered, "Flight operations."

"This is . . ." He paused, wondering how to identify himself. *The client?*

"Racer? Is that you?" The voice did sound familiar. "It's Pam Archer."

He laughed despite himself. "Pete didn't tell me that you would be running the show today. Honestly, I didn't think he'd ever let you behind the stick again after you crashed Baby Boy in Pakistan."

Slapshot looked over, one eyebrow raised. Raynor mouthed, "Long story."

"He reminds me of the fact every time I ask for a raise," Archer said.

"In case I forgot to say it then, thanks. And thanks for doing this."

"I just do what Pete tells me. What do you need?"

"We're up against the clock here, Pam. Can you squeeze a little more out of her?"

"Done." On the embedded HUD, the flight speed indicator began ticking upward as the landscape below flashed by even faster. The numbers leveled off at about 240 knots. "Revised ETA, eighteen minutes."

Raynor grimaced. It wasn't as much as he'd hoped for, but beggars couldn't be choosers. "Thanks, Pam. Pete told you what we're looking for?"

"He told me where to point the cameras. I assume he told you that the area you want to look at is in restricted airspace."

"He mentioned a workaround."

"The airspace around Washington, D.C., is a special flight rules area. What it basically means is that all aircraft have to file a flight plan and stick to it, and be in radio contact with air traffic control. Within that airspace is a smaller flight restricted zone, where only government planes and scheduled commercial flights can go. Bethesda is within the FRZ, and we don't have a waiver to enter it or deviate from our flight plan. We'll only get one pass. That's the bad news. The good news is that the flight plan will take us along the outer edge of the FRZ. The bird is equipped with the ARGUS 1.8 megapixel dual-mode camera. Natural light and infrared. The resolution is good enough that you should be able to zoom in close enough to identify a person if they happen to be looking up. From fourteen thousand feet, which is as high as we can go without a flight plan, we can observe an area of about one hundred square miles. We'll also be recording FLIR data and you can review that after the pass. I can skirt the edge of the FRZ and give you an oblique view of the objective."

"Oblique," Raynor muttered. That news was even more disheartening, but he wasn't going to complain. "We'll work with it. Thanks, Pam. Let me know when you're set."

* * *

From the comfort of the air-conditioned flight operations center, a small modular building perched on the edge of the Key West International Airport, Pamela Archer teased the limits of the no-fly zone surrounding the nation's capital. Private aircraft—everything from small planes to remote-controlled quad-copter drones—were not permitted inside the FRZ, but inadvertent violations were commonplace, mostly the result of amateur pilots making minor navigational mistakes. The consequences of entering that space ranged from mild—a visual laser-warning system—to severe, which included the possibility of being engaged and destroyed by interceptor aircraft. While there was no physical risk to Archer or her crew, on the ground almost a thousand miles away, the penalties of anything beyond that first gentle warning were severe enough to ensure that she kept the Predator B well away from the virtual fence.

And now Kolt Raynor was pressuring her to get closer.

As promised, she had put the aircraft over the designated area—technically, about eight miles west of it—less than twenty minutes after Racer's first call. One of her techs oriented the gimbal-mounted camera in the direction of Bethesda and began transmitting high-def live video directly to Racer's tablet—the same images that now appeared on the big wall-mounted plasma screen in the op center. A smaller monitor showed the same landscape in grayscale, but it was too hot for infrared feed to be of much use to Raynor. The trees and landscape were still well defined, but everything appeared white, as if blanketed in snow.

Archer glanced at the other screens from time to time, but kept her attention mostly focused on the GPS, flying by instruments. The camera's resolution was startlingly crisp, allowing for a slow panoramic view of the target area. Racer and his Delta boys would be able to freeze and zoom any part of the image at will, or rewind and start over again if necessary. Unfortunately, the part of the image that Raynor was most interested in was at the effective limit of the camera's range, and partially obscured by the oblique angle.

She wore two headsets, one to monitor the air traffic control frequency assigned by the ZDC—the Washington Air Route Traffic Control Center—which played in her left ear, and one that connected her to the open conference call with Raynor and his mates. They were calling out areas of interest, but also complaining about the limitations of the technology and the ticking clock they were up against. As she finished her pass, Raynor addressed her directly.

"Pam, this isn't going to cut it. You've got to make another pass, closer this time."

"That's not going to happen, Racer. I told you, one pass is all you get."

"Bend the rules," he pleaded. "It's easier to ask forgiveness than permission. Tell the FAA it's a nav error. They're not going to shoot you down. Not over a populated area. You'll be out before they can even scramble the interceptors."

"Kolt, ground control has our transponder code. They know who this aircraft belongs to and who's operating it. If I violate the FRZ, they won't just shrug it off. At a minimum, I will lose my flight status and my job. Radiance will lose its government contracts and get fined out of existence. I am not going to do that to Pete."

"Pam, there is a sniper down there, the same guy who hit FLOTUS from a mile and a half away. In about ten minutes, he's going to take a shot at the president. He doesn't miss, Pam. If we can find him and stop him, nobody is even going to ask you to apologize for trespassing, but if we don't, this country is going to explode. That's what's at stake, Pam."

Archer felt her throat tighten. The passionate urgency in Raynor's voice seemed to vibrate through her entire body. Raynor was asking her to risk a lot on the basis of what really amounted to nothing more than a gut instinct.

Eight years ago, she had ignored her own instincts—followed the rules, played it safe—and men had died.

If she played it safe this time, how many would die?

"Five minutes," she said, her voice barely a whisper.

Racer, wisely, refrained from expressing his gratitude.

She realized that the sensor techs were looking at her, eyes wide. "Might be a good time for a smoke break," she said.

The two men exchanged a glance. One of them muttered, "Been meaning to quit." The other just shrugged and turned back to his monitor.

"Okay, then." Archer worked the joystick control, banking the UAV into a wide left turn. The landscape on the screen, an emerald tapestry dotted with houses and other buildings, and crisscrossed with a seemingly random pattern of roads and streets, began to shift and rotate. The GPS indicator showed the aircraft's position and the edge of the FRZ drawing closer, and then the line was crossed.

For a few seconds, nothing happened, but then a bright green light flashed at the top of the big screen. It was followed an instant later by a red light, then green again, strobing like a light show at a concert.

"That's the laser warning system," Archer said. "We're in the no-fly zone."

"Understood," Raynor said. "Stay on this heading as long as you can."

Archer nodded absently without replying. Five minutes was pushing it. She would be lucky to give him two.

After about thirty seconds, she heard Raynor's voice again. "We're over the north limit. All eyes on."

The Delta operators began talking amongst themselves, pointing out irregularities and suspicious areas in the field of view, dismissing them as shadows and artifacts. Archer ignored most of the chatter, staying focused on the task before her, but she paid attention when a female voice said, "Racer, we're hearing Marine One is ten minutes out."

"Roger, Hawk," Raynor replied. "Keep looking."

At almost the same instant, her left earpiece squawked. "Radiance Zero-Two, this is Leesburg Ground. You are off course and entering restricted airspace. Maintain your present altitude. Come right to three-three-zero and await further instructions. Acknowledge, over."

Archer considered ignoring the transmission. Radio silence and the nav error would both fit the narrative of a signal interruption. Things like that did happen, but if there was any kind of follow-up investigation, the story would fall apart. She tried a different tack.

"Leesburg Ground, this is Radiance Zero-Two. We have authorization to enter the FRZ, over."

There was a momentary pause as the air traffic control officer went looking for verification.

Just bought you an extra thirty seconds, Racer, Archer thought.

"Radiance Zero-Two, negative. You do not have authorization. Break off immediately."

"Time to double down," Archer said before hitting the push-to-talk. "Leesburg Ground, check again. The Secret Service requested us to provide aerial surveillance for the president's visit. They should have submitted the authorization waiver."

"Radiance Zero-Two, until we can confirm, you must leave the restricted area. If you do not immediately signal compliance, intercept aircraft will be alerted."

Archer looked up at the big screen. The UAV was almost directly above the Walter Reed medical center. "Sorry, Racer. I did my best."

She put her thumb on the push-to-talk, but heard Raynor's voice in her other ear. "Thirty more seconds, Pam."

"Acknowledge, Radiance Zero-Two."

Archer clenched her teeth and hit the transmit button. "Acknowledge. Turning right to three-three-zero. Radiance, out."

She squeezed the joystick handle, but did not move it. Not right away. For Racer's benefit, she started counting down. "Turning in five . . . four . . . three . . ."

A voice, so loud she couldn't tell who it was, blasted in her ear. "That's him!"

Archer hauled the joystick hard to the right, and let out the rest of her breath in a relieved sigh.

TWENTY-SEVEN

Raynor zoomed in on the frozen image. The angle of approach was perfect, giving him a head-on view of the man. The resolution wasn't quite good enough to make out recognizable facial features, but there was no mistaking the black patch covering the man's left eye. It didn't hurt that Miric was facing north, looking almost directly into the camera lens, as if he knew Raynor was looking right at him.

He heard Pam Archer's voice again, communicating with air traffic control, still trying to bluff them into believing she had permission to be there even as she talked her way through the course corrections that would take her out of unrestricted airspace. He ignored her, focusing instead on the fruit her bold action had produced.

"Get a location on him," he said.

"Got it, boss," Shaft came back. "Chevy Chase Trust Building. West tower. Address is 7501 Wisconsin Ave."

Raynor zoomed the image back out, noting the

location of the tall, sturdy-looking white commercial structure, smack in the middle of town.

"We're coming to back you up. Secure the area but do not engage." He turned to Slapshot, but the other man had read his mind and was already starting the truck. "Digger, get to Kearney now. Tell him we've located the sniper threat."

"On it, boss."

Slapshot put the truck in gear and took off, navigating the narrow side streets of the neighborhood, reaching the junction with the main highway in less than a minute. Rockville Pike, also known as Maryland Route 355 and, within the limits of Bethesda proper, Wisconsin Avenue, would take them directly to Shiner's doorstep.

Slapshot ran the stop sign, laying on the horn as he turned right, drifting the truck across all three lanes of traffic. Raynor heard agitated honking and the shriek of tires skidding on the road as panicked drivers unnecessarily slammed on their brakes. There was little chance of a collision. The pickup was already at highway speed and Slap had more hours of tactical driving under his belt than almost anyone else in the Unit, but the other drivers didn't know that. Kolt felt a mild bump as the truck's tires hit the low median—little more than a curb dividing north- and southbound lanes—but Slapshot maintained control and never slowed. When he had the pickup straightened out, he put the pedal to the floor.

Digger's voice sounded in Raynor's ear. "Message delivered, boss."

"Tell them they need to wave Marine One off until the threat is neutralized."

"Already did that, but I don't think they're going to deviate from the plan. Simmons thinks they can cover Champ better on the ground. Oh, BTW, he's not too happy about us being in the neighborhood."

"Fuck him," Slapshot muttered.

Kolt was in complete agreement, but he had promised Pete Grauer that they were going to play by the rules, and as much as he wanted to send Rasim Miric to hell, he wasn't going to let his friends throw their military careers away if he could help it. "How far out is the helo?" he asked.

Digger repeated the question, presumably asking Special Agent Kearney, then echoed the answer. "Five mikes, give or take."

"Figure another five to lock down the bird and unload. Is Simmons going to send agents to Miric's location?"

"Don't know. He's not telling me anything."

"Sounds like 'no' to me," Slapshot put in.

"We'll go with that," Raynor said.

The pickup crested the hill and started down. A line of trees on the roadside blocked Raynor's view of the medical complex, but jutting up above them was the distinctive tower at the hospital's front entrance.

"Shit," Slapshot shouted, suddenly braking hard. "Damn big-city traffic."

Raynor brought his eyes back to the road and saw the line of brake lights ahead. The three southbound lanes looked like a parking lot, and as he looked farther along, he saw why. Four black Maryland state police cars, their light bars flashing, were parked in a herringbone formation across the highway, blocking all access to the military base. Traffic was still moving, but at a crawl as drivers made the hard right turn onto West Cedar Lane.

Raynor checked Google Earth, plotting the most expedient course back to their destination. "Take the right," he told Slapshot. "We'll hit Old Georgetown Road in about a quarter of a mile. From there, it's a straight shot south."

"Great. What's an extra fifteen minutes?"

Raynor shared the big man's frustration. Although the detour would add only about a mile to the trip, the distance wasn't as much the problem as traffic congestion. They had moved exactly three car lengths since braking. At their present rate of movement, it would be at least a minute or two before they could even make the turn.

Raynor checked his watch, then did a visual sweep of the sky to the east until he saw what he was looking for—half a dozen black specks that looked like a small formation of migrating birds. The shapes weren't birds, but helicopters from the USMC presidential transportation fleet.

"Fuck this," Slapshot roared, and cranked the wheel hard to the left and hit the gas again. The pickup bounced onto the divider and shot forward along the median, passing the unmoving vehicles in the inside lane.

Raynor bit back a protest. They were committed now, and under the circumstances there probably wasn't a

better option. The move did not go unnoticed by the
state police officers manning the roadblock ahead. As
the truck drew close, the cops drew their weapons and
took defensive positions behind their vehicles, which
would have been a fatal mistake if Slapshot crashed the
barricades and kept going.

Fortunately for them, that was not his intent. As soon
as he reached the front of the line, Slap made the hard
right turn onto Cedar Lane. The side road was similarly
clogged with traffic coming and going, and for a few
frantic seconds, Kolt was certain that a collision was
unavoidable, but somehow Slapshot managed to thread
the needle, reaching the empty turn lane running down
the middle of the road.

Kolt let out the breath he had been holding. "Shit,
Slap."

"Fortune favors the bold," the other man said, not
taking his eyes off the road. "It's a rental. You got in-
surance, right?"

Before Raynor could reply, Digger broke in. "Helo
touched down."

"What happened to five mikes?"

"Sorry, boss. Plus or minus thirty seconds, right?"

Raynor shook his head in disgust. "Fortune just
fucked us, Slap. We're not going to make it. Shaft, you
have execute authority. Now."

"No shit?" Shaft replied. "From who?"

Raynor picked up Slapshot's questioning tilt of his
head, took a deep breath. "From me, Shaft, Noble Zero-
One."

"Dang, boss, okay," Shaft said. "I have control."

* * *

Although it was technically a single building, there were actually two structures at 7501 Wisconsin Avenue—two identical fifteen-story towers joined together at the base by a long two-story interior gallery.

Shaft had easily recognized it in the feed from the UAV. It was one of the most distinctive buildings in downtown Bethesda, and the tallest—just fourteen feet shorter than the tower at the medical center. The building had topped his initial list of likely locations for Shiner to operate from. It was almost exactly a mile from the hospital, which he now knew was within the sniper's comfort zone. If anything, it had seemed a little too obvious, which was why, after scouting the building's entrance and egress points, he had kept going, heading north to investigate other possibilities, eventually rendezvousing with Joker and Venti at a small park a few blocks to the north, at what he believed would be a central location.

Now he was regretting having second-guessed himself.

As soon as Shaft sent the location, and even before Raynor told them to get in position, he and the other two operators were up and moving, but even at a near run, it took them a couple minutes to reach their goal. They charged up to the southwest entrance at almost exactly the same moment that Marine One settled onto the helipad a mile away.

There was no point in updating Raynor on the fact that he and his team weren't even in the building, much less in position to execute the hit. It wasn't like they had the option of handing the ball to someone else.

"We're in the building," he said, acknowledging the go order as he headed inside and went directly to the elevator lobby.

The indicator above one of the doors displayed a downward-pointing arrow and was counting down from five, changing every few seconds.

"Come on." Shaft tapped his foot as he watched the number anxiously. "Four. Three. Two."

He tensed, ready to charge into the car as soon as the door opened, but realized that the indicator had frozen on the number "2."

"Who takes the elevator one floor?" Joker muttered.

Venti glanced around the lobby for a moment, then pointed. "Stairs?"

Shaft would have preferred taking the stairs for tactical reasons; there was no telling who or what might be waiting on the other side of an elevator door. But despite the seeming delay, he knew the elevator would still get them to the top a lot faster and with considerably less physical effort. The last thing they needed was to be sucking wind as they charged into a possible firefight.

The number finally changed and a bell tone sounded, announcing the arrival of the car. The three Delta assaulters stood aside waiting for the elevator's lone occupant—a middle-aged man whose attention was thoroughly consumed with whatever was happening on the screen of his mobile phone—to saunter off. As soon as he was clear, they moved inside like it was an objective they were intent on clearing. Shaft hit the button for the topmost floor and Venti stood ready to discourage anyone else from getting on with them.

As soon as the doors were closed, Shaft drew his Glock 23 from its concealed crotch holster, then took out the SureFire suppressor that had been rolling around in the pocket of his BulletBlocker duck jacket. Despite the heat outside, all of the assaulters wore some kind of overcoat to either hide lightweight body armor or, as in Shaft's case, actually provide ballistic protection. The jacket's inner liner was made of Kevlar, NIJ type III-A, rated to stop most pistol rounds, including .44 Magnum— or so the manufacturer claimed. It was standard kit, but whether to wear it or not was an operator's personal choice.

"Cans secure?" he asked, looking up.

"Roger," Venti said, holding up his own similarly equipped weapon and giving the suppressor a final tug for good measure.

Joker did the same, and added, "Stealth mode engaged."

"Digger, how we doing out there?"

Digger's normally laconic surfer cool was gone, replaced by almost frantic urgency. "Champ is in the open. He's making the walk."

"You're kidding." He knew the assaulter was not. "What part of 'sniper threat' don't they understand?"

"Whatever you're gonna do, brother, it has to be now!"

"No shit."

The elevator made it to the top floor without interruption, and as the doors slid open, the three operators exited the car tactically, weapons at the ready. Even so, Shaft was startled when he rounded a corner and almost crashed into a uniformed security guard coming from the opposite direction.

The guard's eyes went wide as they locked onto the suppressed pistol in Shaft's right hand. He made a grab for his own holstered sidearm.

"Stop!" Shaft said, aiming his Glock at the man to get his attention. He had absolutely no intention of pulling the trigger on a civilian. If a display of force didn't get the rent-a-cop's attention, there were other nonlethal options available. Just to be on the safe side, he added, "Secret Service, undercover. Move your hand away from your weapon."

That did the trick. The guard immediately raised his hands in a show of compliance.

Racer's voice crackled from the Bluetooth earpiece. "Shaft. What's going on?"

"Security guard, boss," Venti muttered over the open line.

Shaft lowered his own weapon but held the man's stare. "We need to get to the roof. It's urgent."

The guard, still evidently dumbfounded by the near-death encounter, nodded and gestured for them to follow.

The roof access stairs were only a few steps away, and after opening the door for them, the guard stepped aside to let them proceed. Shaft started up the stairs, leading with his pistol. The door at the top opened inward and was slightly ajar. He paused there, waiting for his mates to catch up. Venti was right behind him and

Joker was bringing up the rear, but Shaft was dismayed to see the security guard starting up the stairs.

He called down to the man in a stage whisper. "Stay there. Secure that door until our backup arrives."

The guard nodded and took a backward step. There was no time to wait for him to get clear. Shaft grasped the door with his left hand, easing it open, ready to engage whatever threat lay beyond.

The noise filled the close confines of the stairwell, hitting him like a physical blow. The sound was unmistakable: an unsuppressed pistol. His ears ringing, Shaft whirled, surprise already giving way to dread. Venti, close behind him, was also turning toward the source of the noise, blocking Shaft's view of what was happening below. Before he could complete the turn, there was a second report and something wet and warm splattered across Shaft's face.

Venti lurched to the side then collapsed and went tumbling down the steps, removing the last obstacle between Shaft and the killer below.

"Fucking guard," Shaft rasped, hoping that Racer would understand the warning. He brought his own pistol around, lining it up for a center-mass shot, even as the shooter corrected his aim.

Shaft broke the four-pound trigger at the same instant he saw the flash from the muzzle of the guard's weapon.

TWENTY-EIGHT

"Shaft!" Raynor shouted. There was no reply. "Shit!"

He hammered his fist against the dashboard in impotent rage. Beside him, Slapshot just kept staring straight ahead, intently focused on the road in front of them. Kolt fought the impulse to urge Slapshot to go faster; the big man was already pushing as hard as he dared.

They had picked up the pace a little after making the turn onto Old Georgetown Road; not because traffic was any lighter, but because the six-lane divided highway gave Slapshot a lot more room to maneuver around the slower-moving cars that impeded their forward progress. He slalomed the truck back and forth across the median, laying on the horn and flashing his headlights to clear a path, and blasting through intersections without slowing. Unfortunately, his aggressive driving had not gone unnoticed. One of the state police cruisers from the roadblock on Rockville Pike had nearly caught up to them, and Raynor knew the call for backup had almost certainly gone out.

The road took a sharp bend to the left. Directly ahead, Raynor could see the high-rise buildings of the downtown commercial area. Traffic in the southbound lane was snarled almost to a standstill, but the northbound lanes were almost completely empty.

He checked Google Earth again. Less than a mile to go.

"Shaft!" he called out again. "Venti? Joker? Anyone?"

Still no answer. He refused to dwell on what that almost certainly meant.

"Digger, what's the situation there?"

Hawk fielded the inquiry. "Digger is with Todd. Champ is still out in the open."

"Tell him they have to keep POTUS moving," Raynor said.

"I'll try."

"Don't just try, Hawk. Make it happen. Have a raving lunatic panic attack or something, but get POTUS under cover."

"Boss!" Slapshot yelled. "Twelve o'clock!"

Raynor looked up and saw more flashing blue and red lights—a line of police cruisers blocking both lanes, about a hundred yards away.

"Next left!" Raynor shouted.

Slapshot cranked the wheel in that direction, skidding and fishtailing across the vacant northbound lanes. He steered out of the slide and slotted the truck down the narrow side street. The way ahead was clogged with slow traffic and pedestrians, but Raynor had expected that. "Bumper it. Foxtrot from here."

Slapshot didn't question the decision, but managed to get halfway up the street before he had to slam on the brakes. Raynor took one last look at the satellite map, plotting the shortest route to the Chevy Chase Trust Building that wouldn't take them straight to the police roadblock, then threw his door open and took off running.

The street angled to the northeast before hitting a T-junction that led them back toward Wisconsin Avenue, where Kolt could finally see their destination just a couple hundred yards away. Instead of trying to dodge pedestrians, he veered out into the street, crossing the lanes of traffic as he ran, and sprinted the last hundred yards.

As he reached the northwest corner of the building, he heard Digger's voice again in the Bluetooth. "Champ is under cover. I say again, Champ is under cover."

Raynor kept going. The announcement took some of the pressure off, but only some. He slowed to a jog and for the first time since leaving the truck, looked over his shoulder. Slapshot was right behind him, easily keeping pace, barely even breathing heavily.

"He's gonna run, Slap. He missed his chance; he won't hang around. I'm not losing him. Not again."

"We can't cover all the egress points, Kolt," the big man said. "And we might have wounded eagles up there. But maybe Shaft and the guys are the reason he didn't get to take the shot."

"Fuck." But Slapshot was right on all counts. "Digger,

Hawk, you have to get Simmons to lock this place down. The building. The whole fucking city if he has to."

"I'll do what I can, boss. Right now, I think he'd rather arrest you," Digger said.

Raynor ignored the comment and headed inside the building with Slapshot in tow. They bypassed the elevator foyer and headed for the fire stairs, prepping their weapons on the move, keeping them trained up the stairwell. Kolt's legs and lungs were burning, but he pushed through the pain, stopping only when they reached the door to the top floor. They cleared the doorway and the hall beyond, then located the roof-access stairs from an emergency evacuation floor plan posted on the wall. Still moving tactically, they entered the stairwell to the roof, and found the bodies.

Raynor stepped over the first unmoving form—a man in a security guard's uniform—and covered the stairs with his weapon while Slapshot checked the body. Two more lay at the base of the steps; Raynor recognized both of them.

Venti lay atop Joker, eyes fixed and staring into the void. A pool of blood spread out around both men.

"This guy's dead," Slapshot whispered, rising again.

"He shot them. Back of the head, as they were going up the steps." Raynor was livid. Angry at the dead man for killing his mates, angry at the two assaulters for turning their back on someone they didn't know, but angriest at himself for putting them in the situation in the first place.

"Wonder who he was," Slapshot said.

Raynor had no idea other than that the man was

working with Shiner. Maybe when the body was ID'd, it would give some clue as to whom the sniper was really working for.

He stepped over the fallen Delta operators and started up the stairs.

Shaft lay sprawled out on his back just below the open door that led out onto the roof. Blood from a scalp wound was streaming down his face and staining the front of his jacket, but he was still breathing.

Raynor continued past the wounded operator, easing the door open wide to make sure there was no one waiting to ambush them on the other side, but did not go through.

Slapshot spoke from behind him. "Grazed him. Probably has a concussion. He'll make it, but he needs a doc, ASAP."

"As soon as we clear the roof." Raynor knew he would get no argument from the sergeant major. Security had to be the first priority. He looked down at Shaft, placed his nonfiring hand on the man's upper arm. "Hang in there, brother."

"Ready when you are, boss."

Raynor counted to three and then moved through the door, turning left just as if he was clearing a room. His sector of fire was empty, and he saw no movement in his peripheral vision, but the door was facing east, and he knew that Shiner had been facing north, toward WRNMMC.

"Left side clear," he whispered, moving close to the southeast corner of the raised superstructure.

"Right clear," Slapshot answered.

"Stay tight." He sliced the pie on the corner, expecting to see Shiner hunched over a rifle at the building's edge.

Miric was there, all right, kneeling with his weapon raised and ready, but it wasn't aimed at the distant military base. He was pointing it right at Raynor.

Kolt drew back and went to the prone position, even as the rifle barked. Concrete exploded from the corner, spraying him with grit. Raynor immediately alligator-rolled out into the open, firing at the spot where Shiner had been the moment before, but the other man was already gone. Kolt caught a glimpse of movement, but the other man ducked around the far side of the super-structure before he could adjust his aim.

"I have been waiting for you, Racer," Miric called out. "Now we end this."

Raynor rolled back behind cover and got to his feet. He looked at Slapshot, then pointed up. Slapshot nodded, stowed his pistol. He flexed his legs, then jumped, reaching up to grasp the edge of the roof of the superstructure. Straining silently, he pulled himself up, and with a final dynamic exertion, heaved himself over the lip, disappearing from view.

Miric shouted again. "Tell me, Racer. Do you play chess?"

"Not really. I'm more of a Call of Duty guy."

"Pity. You will die without understanding how you were beaten."

Raynor listened intently, trying to determine if the other man was moving, perhaps trying to come around from behind. "Slap, you there?" he whispered.

"Moving," came the whispered reply.

Raynor was not particularly interested in bantering with the sniper, but as long as the other man was talking, he was distracted, and that would give Slapshot a chance to get close enough to take him out from above. "I'm beaten?" Kolt shouted. "Even if you get past me, you aren't getting off this roof alive."

"You and I, we are just pieces in the game. Sometimes the lesser pieces must be sacrificed to ensure victory."

The sniper's confidence was more than a little unnerving to Raynor. "What victory is that? You missed your chance. The president is safe."

"Do you think so?"

"Got eyes on," Slapshot whispered over the open phone line. "He's hugging the wall. North side, right below me. I can take him, but—"

"But something stinks," Raynor finished. He thought about Athens and the explosive deception at Miric's apartment, and Jersey City, where the sniper had tried to shift attention to the militia movement and the Russians.

And chess.

"Shit. It's another fucking psy-op. He's playing us." He took a breath and called out again. "Let me guess. You're just here to create a diversion. Distract us while your buddies attack from somewhere else."

"Very good, Racer. I always knew you were not that stupid."

Raynor felt stupid. All his assumptions about Shiner had been wrong. Miric wasn't simply a revenge-crazed lone-wolf killer. He was playing for bigger stakes. And he was getting big-league assistance.

"Won't happen," Raynor retorted. "You don't think we thought of that? That's basic military tactics."

When Miric did not immediately reply, Raynor wondered if the bluff had worked. He pushed harder. "We've already got them in custody. They'll talk. It's over."

"I do not believe you," Miric said, but sounded more defiant than certain. "In a few minutes, we will see whether you are telling the truth."

We will see . . .

Raynor suddenly felt numb all over. "Digger, you there?" he barked, not caring if Shiner overheard.

"Go, boss."

"Tell Simmons to initiate ECMs. Now. There's a bomb."

"No!" Miric shouted.

"He's moving!" Slapshot shouted. "Front!"

Raynor heard the distinctive report of a suppressed pistol firing several times in rapid succession. He got his own weapon up just as Shiner rounded the corner at a dead run. Raynor broke the trigger, but was too slow by a millisecond. Miric overshot the corner, and then as Kolt corrected his aim, the other man pivoted toward him and charged.

TWENTY-NINE

Digger did not question Raynor's shouted warning. He had been following Racer's conversation with Miric, heard the sniper as much as admit that the real attack would come from somewhere else. It had to be a bomb, and a remotely activated trigger made the most sense.

He turned immediately to Kearney. "Todd, you need to activate RF jammers. Now."

The young Secret Service agent gaped at him in disbelief. "You said there was a sniper."

"Fuck," Digger snarled. "Do you want me to start shouting 'bomb'?"

His volume was already loud enough to qualify as a shout, as was evidenced by the fact that more than a few heads turned their way. They were outside the south entrance to the medical center—Building 10, also called the Eagle Zone—a stone's throw from the army of reporters who were camped out on the lawn. Behind it was Building 9, the Arrowhead Zone, where the actual hospital facilities were located.

"Okay," Kearney said quickly. "Keep it down. Are you sure? Where's it at?"

"Todd, if you don't turn on the ECMs right fucking now, you're going to find out the hard way."

Kearney did not look at all convinced, but without further protest, tilted his head to the side, bringing his mouth closer to his mic. "This is Kearney. We've got a possible RC device on premises. Initiate electronic countermeasures."

The noise of Raynor's battle with Rasim Miric was suddenly gone from Digger's Bluetooth earpiece. Hawk glanced over at him, nodding to indicate that she had lost comms as well, and within seconds, a hum of discontent arose from the assembled media as they began to realize that their electronic connection to the outside world had been severed.

Kearney was holding one hand over his earpiece, his expression grave. He looked like he was about to be sick. After listening for a few more seconds, he raised his eyes to Digger again. "Okay, Pete. It's done. SAIC Simmons is on his way. He's not happy."

"He should be," Hawk remarked. "We probably just saved POTUS, not to mention everyone standing here."

Simmons arrived just a few seconds later, visibly fuming. He ignored his junior agent and instead advanced until he was almost standing nose-to-nose with Digger. "What the hell do you think you're doing?"

He kept his voice low, perhaps to avoid attracting any more attention from the reporters nearby, but there was no mistaking the menace in his tone.

Digger resisted the urge to remove the other man

from his personal space. "There's a bomb here somewhere. They won't be able to remote detonate now, but
there might be some kind of backup trigger. You need
to evacuate POTUS, immediately."

Simmons shook his head emphatically. "There is. No.
Bomb. We swept for explosives."

"Well, you missed something," Digger shot back.

"And just how do you know that?" Simmons shot a
glance at Hawk, then returned his stare to Digger. "Kolt
fucking Raynor says it, so it must be true?"

"He's been right about everything else. Maybe you
should try listening to him."

"Agent Simmons," Hawk put in. "We heard Rasim
Miric make the threat."

Simmons made a cutting gesture. "That's all it was.
An empty threat. There's no way anyone could get a
bomb into that hospital."

He paused for a second, and then put his hands on
his hips in a display of authority. "You two have caused
enough damage. Tell Raynor that if I see or hear from
him or any of you again, I will file formal charges." He
turned to Todd. "Special Agent Kearney, escort them
off the base. Make sure they leave. If I see them again,
by this time tomorrow you'll be on a plane to Korea to
work counterfeiting." With that, he turned and started
for the entrance.

"At least keep the ECMs on," Hawk called out. "And
do another sweep."

Simmons did not look back.

Kearney turned to them, shrugging his shoulders
helplessly. "Sorry, guys. I gotta walk you out."

"We're not going anywhere, Todd." Digger turned to Hawk. "We've got to find that bomb."

"Simmons was right about one thing," Hawk said, as if thinking aloud. "There's no way the bomb could be inside the hospital. Secret Service has had that locked down since FLOTUS got here yesterday."

"Longer than that, actually," Kearney said, but then shook his head. "No. We aren't having this conversation. I'm sorry. You have to go."

"If it's not close to the VIP section," Digger said, ignoring the young Secret Service agent, "then it would have to be big. Big enough to take the whole building down. A truck bomb maybe, like Oklahoma City."

"They'd never get past the gate . . ." Hawk trailed off, then her eyes went wide. "What if it's been here the whole time? That's why Shiner shot the first lady. Why he only wounded her. They knew she would come here. They've been planning this for a while."

"Who?" Kearney asked, curious despite himself. "Who are they?"

"Focus, Todd. The priority is the bomb." Digger turned back to Hawk. "All right, where do you hide a couple tons of explosives in a hospital?"

"Basement?" Hawk suggested. "Packaged as . . . I don't know, a pallet of bedpans?"

"There's no long-term storage in the building," Kearney said. "There's a warehouse just for that."

Digger shook his head. "Underground wouldn't work anyway. It would contain the blast. No guarantee of bringing the whole place down."

"Well, you're the demo guy," Hawk said. "Where would you put it?"

"I'm usually trying to avoid causing maximum damage." He took a few steps back to get a better look at the building, trying to see it through the eyes of a terrorist intent on destroying it. Rising up behind the six-story structure was the nineteen-story tower, once the centerpiece of the old Bethesda naval hospital, and currently hosting, among other things, the naval postgraduate dental school and the graduate medical education program.

Digger pointed to the tower. "I'd put a fuel-air explosive up there. Two-stage thermobaric device. The initial blast would release a vapor cloud that would saturate the air around the tower with fuel. The secondary would ignite it. The blast energy would propagate down and out. Level the whole place. Even if it didn't, the shock wave and thermal effects would kill everyone within a hundred-yard radius."

"You sure they aren't just gonna lob Acme explosive tennis balls at the helipad?" Kearney said, clearly not buying Digger's detailed analysis.

"Did you look there?" Hawk asked. "At the tower?"

Kearney ignored the question. "And no one noticed this bomb that's been sitting there for weeks. Building maintenance was just struck blind."

"Disguised to look like an HVAC unit or a generator," Hawk suggested. "They could have had someone working on the inside. Brought it in one piece at a time."

"'They' again. Who are they?"

"Only one way to know for sure," Digger said.

"Simmons will have my ass if he sees you."

"Then we'll make sure he doesn't see us." Digger grabbed the Secret Service agent, propelled him down the walk. "If it's not there, we'll leave. Swear to God. But if it is, we need to know before Simmons shuts off the ECMs."

Kearney grimaced. "I am so fired." He sighed. "Come on."

Raynor got off another shot, a center-mass hit, or at least he thought it was, but Miric did not go down. He just twisted sideways a little as the round struck home and kept charging. Before Raynor could fire again, Miric slammed into him, and they both crashed to the rooftop.

Raynor felt something hot and damp against his skin. Blood. Shiner's blood. He had been hit, probably multiple times by both Raynor and Slapshot, but the wounds had not taken any of the fight out of him. The diminutive Bosnian wrapped his legs around Raynor's torso and threw his arms around Kolt's head as if he intended to rip it off his shoulders.

The sheer ferocity of the attack left Raynor momentarily stunned. This wasn't a grappling bout with his mates; Miric was trying to kill him. Fire blossomed on Kolt's cheeks as the other man's fingernails tore at his face, sinking deep into his flesh. Shiner was going for his eyes.

That shook Raynor out of his stupor.

He let go of the Glock and brought his right hand up, jamming it into the gap between himself and his opponent, to cover his eyes. As he did this, he brought one knee up, planted his foot solidly on the rooftop, and then thrust up with his hips, launching Miric forward.

The move broke Shiner's attack, but in no way reduced his rabid fury. Even as Raynor managed to roll Miric over onto his back, coming up inside his guard, Shiner began clawing at him again.

Raynor lowered his head, pressed into Miric's abdomen to protect his eyes. He could feel the other man's blood, hot and slick against his face. Miric was bleeding out. He would probably be dead in a matter of minutes, but adrenaline and pure hatred had given him some kind of berserker strength.

Kolt flung his right arm up, caught Shiner's left biceps, and slammed his shoulder down, pinning it. In the same motion, he hooked his left arm under Miric's right knee, capturing the leg. He leaned back, rising into a squat and holding his opponent almost upside down. Only the back of Miric's head was still making contact with the rooftop. Then in a move Raynor had practiced so thoroughly that it was all muscle memory, he folded Miric over, stacked him up, and drove down with all his weight.

He did not stop until he heard Shiner's cervical vertebrae snapping.

Half a mile away, in the parking lot of the base outdoor recreational area, Mehmet and three members of his operations cell had been watching the live-stream newsfeed of the president's arrival at the nearby medical facility on the tiny screen of a smartphone. They all wore coveralls and carried badges that identified them as civilian contractors. The names on the badges were aliases, but the jobs were real. Two of the four men had been working in the facilities maintenance department for nearly four months.

They had smuggled the components in and assembled the weapon during the first two months of their employ, but in order to maintain cover and ensure that the device was not accidentally discovered, it had been necessary to continue working at the military hospital, maintaining environmental systems and performing various other tasks, while they waited for Miric to carry out his part of the plan. The delay following the failed assassination attempt in Baltimore had been unnerving. The longer the weapon stayed in place, the greater the risk of discovery. But now, finally, Mehmet would be able to execute his masterstroke.

The reporter stationed outside the Eagle Zone administration building had wrapped up his coverage of the president's arrival and now the anchor in the studio was interviewing a medical expert, who was going to speculate on the exact nature of the surgical procedures the first lady would be undergoing. Also present were a pair of opposing political commentators, who were going to explain how the president's showing up to be with his wife was either an indication of presidential courage or a sign of weakness.

"I think it has been long enough," he told the men. "Prepare yourself, my brothers."

They rolled the windows down and opened the doors to reduce the effects of the anticipated shock wave.

The men—all Russian émigrés with military experience, recruited into what they believed was a sanctioned FSB operation to destabilize America—were willing to give their lives to achieve victory, but they also hoped it would not be necessary to make that ultimate sacrifice. That was why they were here, on base, partially concealed behind the Uniformed Services University building, almost a kilometer away from what would be ground zero for the detonation. There was still some risk, but it was a risk worth taking to preserve their cover to the very end.

When the authorities began investigating the cause of the blast, they would immediately assume that the bomb had been placed by someone working on the inside. That was why Mehmet could not risk triggering the device from outside the base. Suspicion would immediately fall upon anyone who had not reported for work that day, and there was a chance—if only a slim one—that the ensuing scrutiny would lead investigators back to the Turkish government, undoing everything he hoped to accomplish. No, they would detonate it from a minimum safe distance and then rush to the blast site to begin helping with the rescue effort, pulling victims from the rubble. Doing so would also give them a chance to make doubly sure that the president did not survive.

Mehmet was just about to switch to the phone dialer when the news feed abruptly went blank, displaying an error message.

Connection lost.

He thought nothing of it at first, but then noticed that the signal strength bars had all been replaced by the "no" symbol—a circle crossed with a backslash—indicating no reception whatsoever.

He frowned, staring at the display for a moment, then attempted to dial the number anyway. Intermittent signal disruptions weren't unheard of, and might clear up at any moment, but as soon as the phone displayed the message "No Connection," he knew it was not a transient interruption.

The significance of this filled him with apprehension. "The Secret Service is jamming radio signals."

"You said they would not do that," protested one of the Russians.

"I did not believe they would. It is standard procedure to use electronic countermeasures when traveling through unsecured areas, but this is a military base and a hospital. Signal jamming is very disruptive. They must have found Rasim and decided to take precautionary measures. We will have to arm the device manually." He put the phone in his pocket and turned the key to start the van.

The men exchanged anxious glances. Miric was not one of them and they did not care if he lived or died, but if the sniper had been killed, then it meant there was a chance the other member of their group, who had accompanied the sniper to the high-rise building in Bethesda, was dead as well. Mehmet, however, suspected there was another reason for their alarm.

"Do not worry. I will set it for a delayed detonation. We will have plenty of time to get clear."

This was technically correct, but it was also a lie. He could not take the chance of something else going wrong. If the Secret Service was on an alert footing, they would probably be moving the president soon, which meant there could be no further delay at all.

As soon as he reached the bomb, Mehmet would detonate it and they would all die together.

THIRTY

Raynor and Miric remained on the deck, bent and entangled, one living, one dead.

He felt a hand on his shoulder. "Boss, you okay?"

Kolt didn't respond. He heard the familiar voice but wouldn't let it break his grip on the man. Too many of his brothers were dead because of Rasim Miric and the man working with him. Stitch. Jeremy Webber. Barnes. And now Venti and Joker.

Raynor arched his back again and squeezed, putting everything he had into breaking whatever bones of Shiner's that were still holding together.

"Kolt, relax, man," Slapshot said, now shaking his partner's shoulder to snap him out of it. "He's dead. Can't get any deader."

Raynor shoved the lifeless body away and rolled up to his knees. His face stung where Miric's nails had raked him, but he felt dissociated from the pain, dissociated from everything. He didn't even look up when Slapshot dropped to the rooftop beside him.

Raynor stared dully for a moment, but then shook his head to clear it. "Digger . . ." He reached for the Bluetooth device, but it was gone, knocked loose during the struggle.

"Offline," Slapshot said. "Just a guess, but I'd say he got your message. You really think there's a bomb down there?"

"Yeah, I do."

Raynor rose to his feet and headed for the edge of the roof, facing north. He could see the medical complex in the distance, the distinctive tower jutting up above the other buildings like a monolith.

Now that Shiner was dead, he felt useless. The threat, the real threat, was a mile away. "I blew it, Slap. Tunnel vision."

"That's not how it looks to me," Slapshot said. "And since we didn't just hear a great big boom, I'd say you got that one right, too."

Raynor just gripped the top of the waist-high parapet. "I wish I knew what was going on down there."

"Digger's got it. He'll find a hard line soon enough."

Raynor looked past his friend and saw a black hockey bag nearby—presumably Shiner's. He also saw the discarded rifle lying near the corner of the superstructure. He went over to the latter, picked it up, and gave it a quick once-over.

The weapon was an SVD-63 Dragunov sniper rifle with attached PSO-1M2 optical scope, nearly identical to the system Shiner had used in Athens, but with one unusual modification. There was an additional scope attached to the upper receiver. Raynor placed the rifle's stock in his shoulder and peered into the eyepiece, but all he saw was an electronic haze.

"What the hell is that?" Slapshot asked. "Thermal?"

Raynor changed position, turning slowly to change his aimpoint and watching how it altered the display. "It's an M-wave receiver. You can see through walls with it. Slap, this is some next-gen shit. Shiner didn't get this from the Russians."

"Who, then?"

Raynor had no idea. In any case, the M-wave receiver was just in the way. He loosened the set screw holding the device in place and shoved it aside. Then, he pointed the rifle downrange and looked through the scope again.

The tower, also known as Building 1 and the President Zone, was not tall by comparison to most high-rise structures. At 264 feet, it was less than one-tenth the height of the Burj Khalifa—the tallest building in the world. It was shorter even than the brick condominium building in Baltimore where Hawk and the rest of A-team had missed Shiner by mere minutes. But because it stood more or less by itself, surrounded by structures that were less than a third of its height, the sense of being at high elevation was even more pronounced. No doubt the narrow profile of the tower added to this effect. The rooftop was a rectangle, about forty feet wide—the length of the average school bus—and twice that long.

At least it wouldn't take long to search, Hawk thought as they moved out into the open. There were just a handful of structures—some as large as garden sheds, others no bigger than a washing machine.

Digger pointed to a large metal structure—a cube, roughly ten feet on a side—and headed toward it. "I'll start with that. Check everything. We don't know what it's going to look like."

"This is crazy," Kearney said, not hiding his nerves. "We have EOD teams and dogs for this crap."

"No time."

Hawk headed for a smaller structure to Digger's right. It looked to her like a rooftop air-conditioning unit, but looks, she knew, could be deceiving.

Kearney followed her. "If we don't know what it looks like, how are we supposed to recognize it?"

Digger fielded the question. "If it's a thermobaric device, there will be a large drum containing fuel material. Powdered aluminum or something like that. Look for large containers. Fuel drums. Propane tanks."

"But generators and air-conditioning units will have tanks too, right?"

"Just start looking," Hawk said, exasperated. Kearney's can't-do attitude was starting to wear thin. She walked around the small structure, looking for some way to get inside. There were hinges on one side, but no visible latches or locks. The metal panel was smooth, except for a pair of recessed machine screws in the corners opposite the hinges. She took out her Gerber multiplier, unfolded the large screwdriver blade, and twisted each of the screws in turn until the panel popped open.

A sudden movement in the corner of her eye caused

her to look up. It was Kearney, dragging his weapon from its holster.

"Stop there," he shouted.

Hawk went to full alert, drawing her own weapon. Before she could identify a target, however, she heard the softened report of a suppressed pistol, and saw the Secret Service agent go down.

Raynor swept the scope back and forth, scanning the southernmost areas of the distant military facility. Beside him, Slapshot was rat-fucking Shiner's gear bag.

"Killer," the sergeant major exclaimed, holding up a spotter scope. "This'll do the trick." He moved to stand beside Raynor and held the optical device to his eye. "What am I looking for?"

"Miric went nuts when I told Digger to crank up the ECMs, so I'm guessing that a remote detonation was plan A. Secret Service protocol is to evacuate the president immediately. Maybe plan B is to hit POTUS when they're moving him out."

"Maybe Shiner was plan B."

"Maybe. But I—"

"Got something on the tower!"

Raynor jerked the scoped weapon up, trying to find the structure.

"Rooftop. Looks like a damn gunfight."

"Got it."

The PSO-1 scope paired to the sniper rifle did not have adjustable focus, so there was no way to zoom in any closer, but he could see enough to confirm Slapshot's assessment that a battle was taking place on the distant rooftop. He even recognized two of the combatants by their familiar clothes and hair color. A man that had to be Digger, recognizable by his blond locks, was standing behind a large structure, emerging every few seconds to squeeze off a few shots before returning to cover. The smaller form, with long black hair tied back in a ponytail, could only be Hawk. She was crouched behind a smaller object, but as Raynor watched she rose up, firing her pistol—he assumed she was firing, though her suppressor eliminated any telltale muzzle flash—as she made a dash for Digger's position.

She only got a few steps before stumbling and going down in a heap.

Raynor sucked in a breath. "Get up," he whispered through clenched teeth. "Come on, Hawk. Move your ass."

But Hawk didn't move.

Raynor shifted the scope away from the embattled operators, moving left across the rooftop until he spotted the enemy force. There were three men—or four if the unmoving form sprawled out near the access door was included. They wore what looked like light blue or gray coveralls. Any identification beyond that was impossible. Two of them were firing handguns, evidently outfitted with suppressors, but the third was making his way toward something—a large HVAC unit or emergency generator—located to the east of the access door, behind the superstructure that topped the elevator shaft.

Raynor instantly recognized what the man was attempting to do. "That's the bomb. He's going to attempt manual detonation. That's plan B."

"So fucking shoot him." Raynor wondered if he had misheard, but then Slapshot added, "That's a sniper rifle, isn't it? Take the shot."

"That tower's more than a mile away, Slap. I'm not a sniper."

"Oh, okay. I'll just give Stitch a call. See if he can pop over from Section Sixty."

Slapshot's voice was thick with sarcasm, but Raynor found himself wishing his mate, Sergeant Major Clay Vickery, was still around. Stitch would have welcomed the challenge of shooting an unfamiliar weapon at a target that was probably a record-breaking distance away.

"You've got the gun," Slap continued. "So you're the sniper. I'll spot. End of discussion. Now shoot that fucker."

Raynor put the aiming chevrons on the man in coveralls, who appeared to be trying to unscrew or pry open one of the panels on the suspected bomb. At the edge of the scope, Digger was exchanging fire with the two crows. One of them went down, but his partner grabbed the fallen man's pistol and began firing both weapons at Digger, unleashing a storm of fire that forced Digger behind cover again.

Slapshot was right, as usual. Maybe Digger would be able to take down the last two crows by himself, but if he couldn't, POTUS and a lot of other innocent people would die.

Kolt knelt down, resting the rifle on the half-wall. It was a far from ideal firing position, but everything about this was far from ideal. He reacquired the target, took a deep breath, and began methodically going through the steps like a wet-behind-the-ears kid in boot camp following the drill sergeant's shouted commands.

This wasn't going to be anything like zeroing on the hundred-meter range, or even busting plates at eight hundred meters from the sniper condo. This was a fucking mile, with an unzeroed weapon.

How much would the bullet drop over that distance? Ten feet? Twenty?

If he miscalculated the drop, the round would either sail over the target and drop somewhere on the far side of the tower—God only knew where—or it would strike the building, punch through a window or a wall, and maybe kill some poor motherfucker on the other side.

"No," he said. "I can't do this, Slap. Eagles too close and I'm not zeroed."

"I'll talk you in."

"I can't shoot up the tower just to get my range."

Slapshot was silent for a moment. "Okay, you're right. We'll have to zero dirty. By eye, go left about one-five-zero meters, and down about ten degrees."

Raynor did as instructed, opening his nonshooting eye. He kept looking straight ahead, not moving his eye or turning his head, but instead shifting his whole body behind the rifle, laterally at first and then rising up slightly for the tilt-drop. Once off the tower, all he could see was the green and gray background of the distant North Bethesda neighborhood where he and Slapshot had been only a few short minutes before. When he looked down, he saw the spacious green lawn in front of the medical center.

"Do you see the pond?"

"Yeah . . . Wait, you're not serious."

"As a fucking heart attack," the other man said. "Go to glass."

Raynor opened the eye that was behind the scope, adjusting slightly until the chevrons were on the small pond that was almost exactly halfway between the parking lot and the highway outside the base.

"Contact." He choked a little as he said it.

In a typical shooting situation, Slap would have talked him through holdover and wind conditions, but without a baseline zero, none of that mattered. "When ready."

Raynor leaned into the weapon, doing his best to brace it with his shoulder, then drew in a breath and let it out slowly, tightening his finger on the trigger. With the last of his breath, he said, "Sniper ready."

"Fire."

Kolt maintained steady pressure until the trigger finally broke. Despite his precautions, the weapon bucked against his shoulder, and his sight picture jumped. His ears were instantly ringing. He rarely fired unsuppressed weapons without ear protection and had forgotten just how shockingly loud the report was. He brought the scope back to where it had been a moment before, and started looking for the splash.

"Up three clicks," Slapshot said. His voice sounded distant, funereal, through the ringing in Raynor's ears, but what he said was even more ominous. Raynor's shot had gone high, missing the pond by a country mile.

He felt for the elevation knob on the scope and made the adjustment. Took another breath. "Contact."

"When ready."

The breathing cycle came a little more naturally this time. "Ready."

"Left point eight."

Raynor compensated for the wind and broke the trigger. He was better prepared for the kick, and the damage to his eardrums was already done so the report didn't seem as loud. And this time he saw an eruption of water from the edge of the pond. It wasn't quite exactly where he'd put the aimpoint, but evidently it was close enough for Slapshot.

"By eye, go to the tower."

Raynor shifted his aiming point back to the tower. How much time had passed? Thirty seconds? Not even?

For Digger, it was probably an eternity.

He found the blond assaulter in the scope, still crouched behind the large superstructure. The crow he had been trading fire with was still there too, hiding behind the elevator shaft, but as Raynor looked on, the man leaned out into the open and fired again. Digger moved at the same instant, and the crow dropped.

And then Digger went down, too.

"Shit!" Raynor snarled, not only because another one of his friends was down, possibly dead, but because he was now the only person on earth with a chance of stopping the last remaining crow from detonating the bomb.

"Freeze! Move away from the weapons."

Because of his lingering tinnitus, the shout from behind was faint, and for a moment, Raynor thought it was his imagination. Then he heard Slapshot yelling a reply.

"We're federal agents. Don't interfere."

Fucking cops, Raynor thought. *Perfect.*

He found the last crow, still working furiously to open the panel and get access to the guts of his bomb, and centered the chevron, center mass. "Contact."

"Drop the fucking weapons, or I will shoot you."

The cop's voice seemed louder. Maybe he was moving in closer. Raynor wasn't about to look, and he definitely was not going to comply.

"We're federal agents," Slapshot repeated forcefully. "We're trying to save the fucking president."

"Drop the weapons and show me your creds. Slowly."

Raynor knew he couldn't wait for Slapshot to talk the policeman down. He also recalled that his second zeroing shot at the pond had been a little low and to the right, and corrected his aim slightly, then took another breath, let it out, and squeezed the trigger.

"Stop!" The cop was almost screaming now, and Raynor expected at any moment to feel the sledgehammer punch of a nine mil hitting his body armor . . . unless the guy went for the point-blank headshot.

Raynor counted silently, trying to gauge the bullet's time to target.

One . . . two . . . three . . .

The crow jumped back in alarm.

"Careful. You just shot the bomb." Slapshot sounded unnaturally calm.

In the scope, Raynor saw the man looking around, clearly trying to figure out where the shot had come from, but after only a moment of this, the crow attacked the cover to the enclosure with renewed ferocity.

"Right, just a hair," Slapshot said, and then in a louder voice, "I'm reaching for my credentials. Don't shoot."

"Drop the—"

Raynor adjusted his aim and without any further hesitation, squeezed the trigger. The rest of the police officer's shout was drowned out by the report.

Raynor lifted his hands away from the rifle, but kept the stock against his shoulder, and his eye to the scope.

One . . . two . . . thr—

There was a flash of red mist.

EPILOGUE

Although the door to the room was open, Raynor knocked anyway before poking his head inside. "Hawk? You decent?"

Cindy Bird looked up from her hospital bed. She did not smile. "Come on in, boss."

Her voice was strained and she winced a little as she spoke. The lightweight body armor she had been wearing under her jacket had stopped the crow's bullet and saved her life, but she had not escaped completely uninjured.

Raynor entered. A helium-filled Mylar balloon trailed behind him, attached by a ribbon to a chocolate bouquet. The balloon was decorated with a camouflage pattern and a cartoon of a shouting drill sergeant and the message "Get Well, NOW!" in comic typeface. He had found it at the Base Exchange.

The television set in Hawk's room was on, tuned to CNN. The graphic crawl at the bottom of the screen read: PRESIDENT TO ADDRESS NATION—LIVE.

As far as Raynor knew, POTUS was still on the base, and intended to stay there over the objections of his protection detail. The first lady's surgery was going ahead as scheduled, and the president had made it clear that he was going to be there when she woke up. The unscheduled speech would probably touch on that topic, but it was far more likely that he would be speaking about the events of the past few hours. Raynor didn't think news about the bomb had leaked, but the media was already buzzing about the shootouts in Bethesda and on the roof of the naval hospital tower. The president would have to tell the country some version of the truth.

Hawk hit the Mute button, silencing the broadcast.

"Did Digger and Shaft get one of those?" she asked.

"Of course," Raynor lied. He set the bouquet on the table, then pulled a chair close to the bed. "How are you doing?"

"Couple cracked ribs. I'll live." She winced almost as soon as she said it. Raynor suspected her reaction had little to do with physical discomfort. "How're the others?"

"Digger picked up a new scar. Already got his stitches. Shaft is going to be here a few more days. They want to make sure there's no cranial bleeding. Digger and Slap are in with him right now." He didn't mention Joker and Venti. She already knew. "I drew the short straw and had to come keep you company."

"What about Todd Kearney?"

"Still in surgery." The Secret Service agent had been hit in the neck and had nearly bled out before the medics found him. His prognosis was guarded. Raynor felt like he needed to change the subject. "At least it's over now. Shiner's dead. So are the guys he was working with."

"Yeah. It's all over but the crying. The Secret Service will get all the credit, and we'll probably all go to jail."

"If you wanted glory, you should have joined SEAL Team Six," Raynor said, only half joking.

Delta operators were used to letting other agencies have the spotlight. Hawk knew that, and Raynor knew she didn't really care about who got the credit. She was just drained, physically and emotionally. They had won—stopped Miric; prevented a bomb attack that would have killed hundreds, perhaps thousands of innocent people, along with the president; and averted a geopolitical crisis—but they had paid a heavy price for victory.

"And nobody's going to jail," he added. "The president is going to know who really saved him, even if no one else ever does."

"So . . . we just drive on? Bury our dead and go back to work?"

"That's the job you signed up for."

She cocked her head to the side. "I signed up for? Don't you mean 'we'?"

Raynor managed a smile. "I think . . . I'm done with the job."

The declaration seemed to snap Hawk out of her funk. She sat up straighter in the bed, wincing a little. "What the hell, Kolt?"

Raynor had not anticipated having this conversation with her. He looked away, trying to figure out how to put what he was feeling into words. "When Colonel Webber let me back in, he told me I would have to work twice as hard, and that even that wouldn't be enough for some people. He was right. I did. And it wasn't. Now that he's gone, there's no future for me in the Unit."

"You know that's not true."

"It is true, Hawk. Penske, or the CG . . . they might not get rid of me right away. They might wait a few weeks, but eventually, they'll find a reason to push me out. And you know what? I don't mind.

"When I was PNG, I . . . well, it was bad. Everything just went completely to shit, but I think the worst part was that it was all completely out of my control. I didn't get to leave on my own terms. I was just out.

"What Colonel Webber did, sending me back to Pakistan, letting me come back to the Unit . . . It was like I got to come back from the dead, fix my mistakes. Atone. I've done that, and a lot more." Raynor brought his gaze back to her, saw that she was blinking furiously, trying to hide tears. He smiled. "But it was never going to be a permanent thing. At least this time, I get to leave on my own terms."

"You're gonna hate it." She made a sound that was somewhere between a laugh and a sob. "So what are you gonna do?"

"I thought I might ask Pete Grauer if he's got anything for me. If he's still talking to me after today, that is."

She nodded. "Well, I'm going to miss you."

"Hey, I'm just quitting my job. Resigning my commission. It's not like I'm going to the moon." He gave her shoulder a gentle, playful slug, and then in what was almost a passable Bogart impression said, "We'll always have Cairo."

She laughed, a real laugh this time. "That was a hell of a honeymoon."

There was a hopeful look in her eyes, and for a moment, he thought she was going to say something more, but then the look was gone, replaced by something almost like horror. She was looking past him, looking at the television. "Oh, my God."

Kolt turned and saw President Noonan speaking from behind a lectern adorned with the presidential seal. The graphic crawl at the bottom of the screen had changed. It now read: PRESIDENT TO RESIGN.

"I have to go." Raynor jumped to his feet and headed out of the room with just one thought. He had to speak to the president while he still was the president, because if he did not—if he could not convince Noonan to use his executive authority to legitimize the actions of Noble Squadron—then everything they had fought for, bled for, died for would be turned against them.

Mason—President Mason—would not pass up a chance to utterly destroy Kolt Raynor or the Delta Force.

As he started down the corridor, he dug out his phone and dialed the only person he knew who might be able to get him close to Noonan: SAIC Jess Simmons.

The electronic countermeasures had been turned off. The phone had a signal, but the call went to voice mail.

Raynor hung up and called again, but as the voice mail message began to play, somebody stepped directly into his path. He shifted right, trying to get around the human obstacle, but the man moved as well, intentionally blocking his escape.

"Colonel Raynor?"

Kolt looked up and saw not one but four men wearing dark suits. He thought they had to be Secret Service, but he did not recognize any of them.

"No, sorry. That's not me."

The man in front of him opened his jacket to reveal his creds—Secret Service all right—but not from the presidential protective detail. "Colonel Raynor, you're going to need to come with us."

"Are you arresting me?"

"Not yet, sir."

Seeing no alternative, Raynor gestured for them to lead the way.

They surrounded him in a diamond formation and escorted him down to the first floor and out the rear of the hospital, to one of the garden spaces in the courtyard between the buildings. The park was unoccupied but for one person sitting on a bench—a woman, tall and slender, with long straight dark hair, full lips, and high, sharp cheekbones.

"Hello again, Racer."

Raynor recognized her right away and felt his blood start to boil. It was Lauren Gellar.

Gellar was a spook—an intelligence operative—though her specific affiliation was unknown to Raynor. She might have even been a freelancer. All Raynor really knew about her was that she had been the person working behind the scenes to deliver Raynor and his squadron to a Syrian terrorist as part of a treasonous backroom deal to bring down ISIS, a deal that had almost certainly been brokered by then Secretary of State Bill Mason.

Hawk had given Gellar the nickname "Maleficent." Kolt was content to simply call her "the bitch."

"We need to talk."

"You don't want to hear what I've got to say," he said through clenched teeth. He started to turn away, but the Secret Service agents were blocking his egress route.

"Sit down, Raynor." Gellar's voice was sharp, like someone scolding a child. "Hear me out, then if you want, you can walk away and take your chances."

He stopped but did not turn. "Take my chances?"

"Sit. Please."

He relented, sinking onto the bench beside her. "Fine. Talk."

Gellar regarded him with a cool smile. "I hear you've been a busy boy today."

He didn't respond.

"I don't know if you've heard the news," she went on, "but our dear commander in chief has announced his intention to resign from office."

"I heard," Raynor growled.

"It was a very moving speech, courageous." She lowered her voice to approximate Noonan. "'America needs a leader who can put country ahead of everything else, and I can no longer be that leader. My family needs me more.'" She shook her head. "Just between you and me, he's scared shitless. People trying to kill him left and right. That definitely was not what he bargained for."

She paused a beat. "So you know what's going to happen next, right? Tomorrow at ten A.M. eastern daylight time, William Mason will take the oath of office and become the forty-sixth president of the United States."

"Your point?"

Gellar leaned forward, lowering her voice to a conspiratorial whisper. "You broke the law today, Racer."

"We saved the president's life," he shot back. "And a lot of other lives, too."

Gellar shrugged. "That's one possible narrative. Here's another. Two of your men were killed today. Their deaths are directly related to your illegal activity, which means you are guilty of second-degree murder."

Raynor was breathing hard in an effort to contain his anger. "I guess that will be something for a jury to decide. I look forward to testifying."

Gellar smiled again, but this time it was forced. Impatient. "Do you really want to take that chance? It's not just your career; your life is at stake here. You'll drag everyone else who followed you down as well. But President Mason doesn't—"

"Vice president."

"For another eighteen hours . . . Very well, Vice President Mason doesn't want to see you in prison, Racer. I know you and he have . . . history . . . but he respects you. That's why I'm here."

"He respects me." Raynor shook his head. "That's why he tried to have me and my squadron killed in Syria last year."

"You don't have any evidence of that. And we've already had that conversation." She let that sink in for a moment. "You asked me to get to the point, so here it is.

"You are a weapon, Kolt. An attack dog. You get the

job done no matter what. Any obstacle in your way—
rules, regulations, laws—you blow through them. You
don't quit. President Mason doesn't want to lock you up.
He wants to set you free so that you can do the job you
were born to do."

She raised a hand to silence any protest and kept talking. "This isn't ever going to be common knowledge,
but we've identified the man you killed today. The man
trying to detonate the bomb. He's an officer of the Turkish Intelligence Service."

"Turkey?" Despite his rage, Raynor was curious.
"Turkey's our ally."

It made a lot of sense, though, and explained how
Shiner had learned Raynor's identity and location.

"An ally is just a patient enemy," Gellar said. "We
have a lot of enemies, Kolt. The Turkish government is
denying involvement, of course, calling the man a rogue
agent. Maybe he is, maybe he isn't. That particular fire
is out for now, but the burns are going to sting for a
while. We're more vulnerable now than we've ever been,
which is why we need men like you."

Raynor leaned forward as if preparing to leave. "In
case you haven't noticed, that's the job I've been doing."

"And now it's time for you to move to the next level,
where you won't have to deal with bureaucratic bullshit
and red tape. No more chains of command. I want you
to work for me."

"For you?"

"After he takes the oath of office tomorrow, President
Mason will appoint me the next ambassador to Tungsten. I believe you're familiar with that agency."

Raynor was. A couple years earlier, he had been temporarily seconded to the ultrasecret counterterror shop headquartered in Atlanta. "You want me as an embed again?"

"No, Kolt. I want you to run operations."

Raynor blinked in disbelief, then shook his head slowly. "You just want to keep me on a short leash. You're afraid I'll tell the world Bill Mason is a traitor. I don't even have to prove it. Just that accusation will be enough."

"You're right. Unfortunately. I wasn't exaggerating when I said that we're vulnerable. Like it or not, Mason is going to be the president, and if you decide to take him down, there's a chance you could take the rest of the country down in the bargain." She shrugged. "It doesn't have to be like that. The choice is yours.

"Come work for me at Tungsten. Keep serving your country and killing America's enemies. Or . . ." She shrugged. "Do it your way. Take your chances."

She rose and stood over him, one hand extended, holding out a crisp white business card. "Take some time to think about it. Just not too much time."

Raynor didn't take the card. "I don't need to think about it," he said. "I won't serve under Bill Mason in any capacity. Period. I'm out. And before you say something you're going to regret, let me tell you how this is going to go down. You're not going to prosecute me or any of my people for anything. They're all heroes, and you're going to treat them that way."

Gellar opened her mouth to respond, but Raynor raised a hand to cut her off. "You're right. Things are pretty fucking unstable right now, and whether I like it or not, Mason is going to be president. At least until he fucks up again. I'm betting he won't be able to help himself, but that's on him, not me. I'm not going to be the one to pull the pin on this shit grenade."

"And I'm supposed to believe that you're just going to drop your vendetta?"

"Vendetta," Raynor snorted. "Grudges are for people like you and your boss. Stay out of my way, and I'll stay out of yours. I've put in my twenty and then some. Just give me my letter and give my people the respect they deserve." He turned and started back down the path to the hospital building.

"You're making a mistake," Gellar called after him. "That's not a threat. Just an observation. You live for this. The action. The rush. You're going to miss it."

Raynor kept walking, but Gellar's parting shot hung over him like a cloud. Hawk had said almost the same thing. He hoped they were both wrong, that he was more than just an adrenaline junkie or a mad-dog killer.

There had to be other reasons to get out of bed in the morning, right?

He looked forward to finding out.

"Cindy," he muttered as he pushed through the door. He was going to have to get used to calling her that.

He looked forward to that, too.